SF Boo

MW00442179

## DOOM STAR SERIES
*Star Soldier*
*Bio Weapon*
*Battle Pod*
*Cyborg Assault*
*Planet Wrecker*
*Star Fortress*

## EXTINCTION WARS SERIES
*Assault Troopers*
*Planet Strike*

## INVASION AMERICA SERIES
*Invasion: Alaska*
*Invasion: California*
*Invasion: Colorado*
*Invasion: New York*

## OTHER SF NOVELS
*Alien Honor*
*Accelerated*
*Strotium-90*
*I, Weapon*

Visit www.Vaughnheppner.com for more
information.

# Cyborg Assault

## (Doom Star 4)

by
Vaughn Heppner

ISBN-13: 978-1496145772
ISBN-10: 1496145771
BISAC:  Fiction / Science Fiction / Military

# Prologue

The cramped chamber reeked of disinfectants and other, more sinister chemicals. The walls were white, and they shivered from the ongoing pulse of the ship's fusion engine.

The chamber contained three people: an arbiter, a technician and a wretched prisoner. The last was a naked woman strapped to an articulated frame. A dozen cables adhered to her bruised skin, some providing nutrients, other stimulants and the rest compelling obedience.

"She's too stubborn," the arbiter said. His name was Octagon. He wore a white uniform with red tabs on the shoulders and a double row of crimson buttons on the front of the jacket. He had narrow features and suspicious eyes, and like most Jovian men, he was bald.

"I suspect she's undergone sphinx therapy," the technician said. He was a small man in a blue gown and with a deferential manner.

Octagon scowled. "You know I detest technical jargon."

The technician grew pale, and he spoke quickly. "They must have tampered with her brain, Your Guidance. It's likely impossible for her to tell us what she knows."

Octagon studied the woman. She was young and pretty, even with her shaved head, contorted muscles and sweaty skin. It had been a pleasure watching the foul Secessionist squirm. Octagon pursed his lips, giving a small headshake. No. Pleasure had nothing to do with this. He must maintain decorum and remember the tenth article of the Dictates. He had a ship to purge, and this was the first lead he gotten that might allow him to crack into the higher circles.

"It's time for a braintap," Octagon murmured.

The technician looked up in alarm. "Your Guidance, Yakov will not approve of—"

"I am the Arbiter," Octagon snapped.

The technician nervously rubbed his hands, and he spoke with caution. "A braintap is a delicate operation."

Octagon swiveled his head to gaze at the technician. "Tell me now if it is beyond your capabilities."

"Rehabilitation is not always possible afterward, Your Guidance. Our... subject is pilot-rated, second-class, meaning—"

"I know what it means," Octagon hissed.

The technician began to blink rapidly.

Octagon's eyes narrowed. How deep was the Secessionist hold on ship personnel? Had they broken the technician's loyalty?

Deftly, Octagon unclipped a spy-monitor from his belt. He adjusted the settings and swept it here and there. Then he aimed it at the medical equipment, searching for bugs.

"If I've angered you—"

"Silence," Octagon said.

The technician wilted, backing up a step.

Octagon changed settings, carefully watching the monitor. Finally, he eyed the technician. "Your index is in the ninety-fourth percentile."

"I am loyal to the Dictates," the technician whispered.

"What is your moon of origin?"

"Ganymede, Your Guidance."

"The same as Yakov's," Octagon said.

"I received my training on Callisto and had a first-class induction rating."

"Your rapid speech indicates nervousness, which in turn implies guilt. What do you have to be guilty about, hm?"

"I serve the Dictates, Your Guidance."

Octagon clipped the monitor back onto his belt beside his palm-pistol. "You will begin the braintap."

2

"At once," the technician said. He hurried to a trolley and pushed it beside the prisoner's shaved head. In moments, a buzz emanated from a cranial saw. Like a barber, the technician ran it over her head, cutting away a portion of skull. Prying it free with core-pliers, he plopped the skull-bone into a green solution.

"We save the cut in case rehabilitation is required."

"I'm more interested in unlocking her secrets," Octagon said.

The technician nodded, and he began to work in earnest. Soon, a blue gel lay on the exposed part of the prisoner's brain. There were yellow streaks in the gel, connected to a glassy black ball with tiny barbs dotted around it. The technician rolled a second trolley near the prisoner's head. It held a bulky device with a screen. He turned it on so it hummed. That caused a tiny glimmer to begin emanating from the various barbs on the ball.

The prisoner twitched.

Octagon avidly watched the proceedings, although his gaze kept slipping down to the prisoner's breasts, which were perfectly shaped. It was a pity to ruin such a prime specimen of womanhood. But then, she shouldn't have joined the Secessionists. It was her own fault, and pity was a useless emotion.

"I've bypassed the first layer of conditioning," the technician said, who closely watched the screen. He tapped keys, seemed to hesitate and then he tapped faster.

Shimmers played upon the glassy ball's barbs.

Octagon moved closer, examining the prisoner's brain. Lines of light moved through the yellow streaks in the gel. They sank into the gray matter underneath.

"I've reordered her synaptic connections," the technician said. "As expected, this rerouting will expunge certain memories."

"No! I must know her secrets."

"This is understood," the technician said, his deference no longer in evidence. "What we attempt, well, we attempt to foil sphinx therapy through new connectives. Naturally, this entails neuron loss. However, the core memories are stored in multiple

3

areas and thus withstand the brainpurge to a greater degree than the sphinx-tampered connectives."

"When can I question her?"

The technician glanced up and quickly returned his attention to the device. "If rehabilitation is required, we must proceed with delicacy."

Octagon pursed his lips. "My primary need is knowledge."

"If you would allow me to add a cautionary note?"

"Yes, yes, speak," said Octagon.

The technician frowned. "The deeper the braintap, the more difficult it is to reconnect her synapses in the old order. Sometimes there is a brain-burn, bringing imbecility."

"I'm willing to risk that," Octagon said.

The technician hesitated before tapping keys. The prisoner groaned as her eyelids flickered.

"What's happening?"

"This is strange," the technician said.

"What?"

The prisoner's eyes snapped open. They were blank. Then confusion filled her eyes. Her mouth hung slackly and drool dribbled down her chin.

"What did you do?" Octagon demanded.

A beep began to emit from the bulky device. The technician grew pale.

"You," the prisoner whispered in a hoarse voice. She stared at Octagon.

He scowled and then leaned nearer. He had nothing to fear, as restraints held her. "You have deviated from the Dictates," Octagon said. "You are a Secessionist."

The prisoner groaned, and pain contorted her features.

Octagon looked up.

The technician wiped a sleeve across a suddenly moist forehead. He typed quickly on the keypad, and he kept biting his lower lip. "This shouldn't be happening," he whispered.

"Fix it!" Octagon said.

"I'm trying."

Octagon put a hand on the articulated frame. Heat radiated from the prisoner's skin. He asked, "Do you belong to a triad?"

4

She was staring at him again. Her lips moved, and words bubbled from her throat. "Yes," she admitted.

Octagon's eyes glittered. "Are you the liaison to a higher circle?"

Her lips twisted as if she tried to keep from speaking. But she said, "I am the liaison."

Yes, it was as he suspected. Finally, he was going to break into a higher circle. "Who is your operative?" Octagon asked.

There was a loud buzz from the technician's device. Several motes glimmered from the glassy barbs. The prisoner made a horribly deep groan as every muscle went rigid.

"What occurs?" Octagon demanded.

"No, no," the technician said, his fingers flying across the keypad.

The prisoner sighed, and the rigidity left her muscles. She relaxed and then went limp.

"Talk!" shouted Octagon. "Tell me the operative's name." He grabbed her shoulders and shook, which caused cables to jiggle.

The prisoner's mouth sagged and more drool slid down her chin.

With his thumb, Octagon peeled back an eyelid. It was like peering into an animal's eye, a brute beast.

"How long will she remain in this state?" Octagon asked.

The technician had grown paler. His small fingers moved listlessly over the keypad.

"I asked you a question," Octagon said, releasing the prisoner, straightening and then adjusting his uniform.

"Something odd occurred," the technician whispered. "I must perform an autopsy. Maybe they implanted a mote into her cortex."

Octagon frowned. "Explain yourself," he said.

"Arbiter, I can't explain it. I attempted a braintap. I followed the standard procedures. But by what I'm seeing, a brain-burn has occurred."

"She's become an imbecile?"

The technician shook his head. "The memories are there, but the connectives were irretrievable burned. We should eliminate her body as a last mercy."

5

Octagon walked stiffly backward. His gaze kept flickering from the prisoner to the technician.

"I did my best, Your Guidance. But her memories are beyond us now. Perhaps—"

Octagon pressed a stud on his belt. The door to the operating chamber swished open. A squat man with long, dangling arms, heavily-muscular arms entered. He was a myrmidon, a gene-warped creature.

"Take him to my quarters," Octagon said.

"Arbiter!" the technician cried. "I tried my best. You must believe me."

The myrmidon moved fast, and his large hands proved irresistible. The technician cried out a second time, his arms twisted behind his back. Shoved by the myrmidon, the technician stumbled for the door.

"Please!" the small technician sobbed. "I tried."

"Hm," said Octagon. "We shall see. We shall see."

The technician and myrmidon exited the operating chamber. The door slid shut.

Octagon regarded the inert prisoner. This was infuriating. He'd had a lead into a Secessionist triad, one aboard a military vessel. The prisoner could have opened up everything for him. Octagon snarled in frustration, and he drew his palm-pistol. He should remain calm. He was an Arbiter after all. He lived by the Dictates and with decorum.

He aimed, squeezed the trigger and shot the drooling prisoner. Sight of the smoking hole in her forehead helped compose his features. He clipped the pistol back onto his belt. He must display serenity for the good of the crew. First, however, he was going to have a small chat with the technician. They would chat after he attached a shock collar to the bungler's neck. The thought brought a tingle of pleasure to Octagon's lower abdomen.

As the fusion engine pulsed, as the bulkheads around him shivered, Octagon headed for the door. Nothing must stand in the way of the continued implementation of the Dictates, the most perfected life-system devised by men. Certainly, this crew wasn't going to defeat him. By Plato's Bones, he was going to crack this nest of intriguers if he had to brain-burn the lot of

6

them. Even Yakov might end up on the obedience frame. The thought brought a grin to Octagon's lips. Then he exited the operating chamber, hurrying through a narrow corridor to his quarters.

# The Engagement

## -1-

In 2351, the Jupiter System thrived as one of the richest in resources. The population there swelled and their wealth grew, despite the intense radiation belts and the heavy gravity-well. The reason was the gas giant itself. Like Saturn, Uranus and Neptune, Jupiter's upper atmosphere contained massive quantities of deuterium and helium-3. These plentiful fuels drove the system's fusion economy.

Automated factories floating in Jupiter's upper atmosphere collected the deuterium and the more important helium-3, an isotope of helium. At scheduled intervals, heavy boosters lifted the fuels to the nearest moons, the Inner group, where vast storage facilities stood. In historical terms, the gas giants were like the Solar System's Persian Gulf, in the days when oil ran the Earth's economy.

Plentiful fusion power had allowed the first Deuterium Barons to turn the otherwise inhospitable moons into vast industrial basins. That in turn had enticed more colonists seeking escape from the nascent Social Unity Party. The vast exodus of wealthy, intellectual and daring people had been the driving force behind the increasingly harsh Anti-Emigration Laws of Inner Planets.

The growing wealthy class of the Jupiter System had turned toward intellectual pursuits. This held truest for the rich on

Callisto, the fourth Galilean Moon. Many there had become absorbed with philosophy, and became particularly concerned with the examined life. This had inspired the Dictates, a codex of axioms that governed a neo-Socratic lifestyle.

Backed by fusion-powered heavy industry, the lords of Callisto had created the Guardian Fleet. For over one hundred years, the Fleet grew in political power until it ruled the system. Serving as a velvet-covered platinum fist, the Fleet had ensured Callisto's dominance over the rest of Jupiter's sixty-two moons.

If Social Unity propaganda was the measure, the Guardian Fleet was one of the strongest in the Solar System. Many claimed it was the reason for building the Doom Stars. Others said the lust to gain access to the deuterium and helium-3 rich gas giants was the real reason. Whatever the case, in 2351, the Jupiter System was awash in wealth, ships and inhabited moons.

\*\*\*

"I'm not receiving any video, *Rousseau*," Marten said.

Marten sat at the controls of his shuttle, the *Mayflower*. He glanced at a note taped to the board: *Double-check everything*. The shuttle had originally been designed to transport eighty Highborn in comfort. With its modifications, the shuttle had proven roomy enough for Marten, Omi and Osadar.

As Marten waited for an answer, he leaned back and stared out of the polarized window. Visible through it was the vast gas giant, the largest planet in the Solar System. Its mass was two point five times as great as the rest of the planets combined. Presently, the Great Red Spot on Jupiter seethed with movement.

The *Mayflower* was in a medium orbit and outside of the worst of Jupiter's radioactive magnetosphere.

The gas giant's magnetic field was ten times as strong as Earth's field. The sun-side of the magnetosphere acted as a buffer that deflected the solar wind around Jupiter. The magnetic tail reached almost as far as Saturn's orbital path.

Marten pressed more buttons, running a diagnostic, seeing if any high-intensity radio bursts might be interfering with the video-feed. The gas giant often gave off radio bursts at ten-meter wavelengths. Jupiter's violent upper atmosphere also created super-bolts of lighting. Those bolts gave off a million times more energy than a lightning bolt on Earth and often interfered with ship-to-ship transmissions. Marten detected only minimal interference. What was causing the video blackout then?

His frowning highlighted Marten's angular cheeks and his intense blue eyes as he watched the blank vidscreen. His blond buzz-cut matched his lean build. Because of the long trip, his worn silver suit was badly faded at the elbows and knees.

"Come on," Marten muttered, moving toggles. He expected the screen to waver, flicker and then he would see his first Jovian.

The warship *Rousseau* was a dark blot, several kilometers away. According to the specs Marten had been studying, it was an *Aristotle*-class dreadnaught. That made it the largest class of ship produced in the Jovian System. It was roughly spherical, a giant ball bearing with asteroid-like particle shields. It dwarfed the *Mayflower* and contained hundreds of crewmembers. Marten had read somewhere that *Aristotle*-class dreadnaughts had been built to operate and fight on their own, not just as part of a fleet.

"*Rousseau*—" Marten began to say.

"Prepare for a boarding inspection, *Mayflower*."

Marten opened a channel to Omi's room. "You'd better get up here," he said.

"I'm coming," Omi said.

Marten tapped the console. The free Martians had been beaming endless shots of the cyborgs that had died in the Mars System nearly a year ago. The Jovians must understand the cyborg danger. Marten grimaced. How was he supposed to explain Osadar to them?

"Is your communications equipment faulty?" Marten asked. "I'm not picking up any video images."

"There is a malfunction, yes," the *Rousseau's* com-officer said.

*Oh.* "How many people are you sending?"

"One officer." A clanging noise occurred over the radio-link. "We have launched the pod, *Mayflower*. Prepare for boarding in twenty minutes. *Rousseau* out."

Marten cut the link, and he stared out of the window at the dark blot of the warship. Yes, he could visually make out a flare, the pod's exhaust.

His heart rate quickened. Maybe he could hide Osadar and keep that little surprise for later. He knew he should have radioed ahead about her. He'd asked Osadar about it, since she'd grown up in the Jupiter System. She'd rejected the idea. When he'd asked her why, she had said that events would squash all their hopes. But why accelerate the day of doom?

The cyborg had reason for her pessimism, but Marten didn't share it. However, a long life of bitter surprises had taught him caution concerning authorities—any authorities.

Marten opened a channel to Osadar's room.

"The time has come," Osadar said in her strange voice, speaking before he could.

"You've been monitoring the conversation?"

"I have already armed myself," she said.

Marten unbuckled his straps, wondering if he should order Omi to hurry. They'd been avoiding each other for weeks. Cramped quarters for these endless months had put a strain between them. It was probably inevitable. It was human.

Marten glanced at the flaring engine again, signaling the approach of *Rousseau's* pod. His gut twisted with nervousness. They'd reached a new system, a free system and a rich one. Would the people here accept Osadar's strange story?

Marten pushed for the hatch, floating in the weightlessness. It was time to meet his first Jovian.

***

Marten and Omi floated near the *Mayflower's* airlock. Omi seemed much like before with his muscled shoulders and bullet-shaped head. Each of them wore a Gauss needler. The metallic, sliver ammunition was ejected through magnetic impulse. The needlers were set on low so that the slivers would not puncture the shuttle's skin. Each of them had donned a vacc-suit, minus the helmet, as the suits were their cleanest garments.

"What do the Jovians look like?" Omi asked.

Marten unhooked a handscanner, which was keyed to the ship's computer. The computer controlled the video cameras outside the shuttle.

As Marten watched, the pod braked with hot exhaust. It was tear-dropped-shaped, and its polarized window was black, hiding the Jovian pilot. Slowly, the pod eased beside the *Mayflower*, which was many times larger than the pod.

"I don't see anyone yet," Marten said.

"I mean when they first hailed us," Omi said.

"Their com-equipment was faulty. It didn't show any vid-shots."

"That sounds suspicious," Omi said.

Marten shrugged as he studied his handscanner. Trust an ex-gang enforcer to be distrusting.

Omi leaned near and glanced at the tiny screen. That annoyed Marten, but he still moved the scanner, allowing Omi a better look.

"Their boarding tube's snaking out," Omi said.

Marten tilted the scanner back to him. Sure enough, a docking tube stretched between the pod and the *Mayflower's* outer hatch. That was quick work, seeing as how the pod had barely matched velocity with them. On the scanner, the pod seemed motionless, but both space vehicles moved in an orbit around Jupiter. Both ships thus had an appreciable speed. Usually, it took time for pilots to adjust velocities just right between two spaceships. The stretching tube was flexible, but it could only flex so much. That the pod's pilot already sent the docking tube... it spoke of extreme self-confidence.

"These Jovians are good," Omi said.

Marten nodded. The magnetized flex-tube made noise against the *Mayflower's* hull. He heard faint hissing sounds as the tube pressurized.

"See anyone moving?" Omi asked.

"The tube is dark."

Omi glanced at Marten.

Marten kept his eyes on the scanner. He'd gotten tired of looking at Omi several months ago.

12

"Seems like they're going to a lot of trouble to keep themselves from being seen," Omi said.

"I suppose," Marten said.

"Are Jovians usually this paranoid?"

By the movement in it, someone was already in the flex-tube, maybe more than one. Marten recalled that the *Rousseau's* com-officer had said one boarding-officer would inspect them. The first worm of doubt now seeped into his gut.

"How many sets of feet do you see?" Marten asked. He meant feet pressing against the flex-tube.

Omi studied the scanner. "Three," he said.

A *clang* outside the *Mayflower's* hull startled Marten. The outer hatch was opening. Why would the com-officer have lied about the number of people boarding the shuttle?

"—Move!" Marten shouted.

Both ex-shock troopers propelled themselves away from the airlock. Omi jammed on his helmet, sealing it. Marten was only seconds slower. Each squeezed through the nearest hatch. Omi turned and began to close it.

"Wait," Marten said. Clamped onto the wall was a heavy plasma cannon. In Earth-like gravity, the cannon would need a tripod mount for a soldier to use. Because of weightlessness, it was possible for one man to wield it here.

The airlock began to open.

Marten chinned his visor shut and moved away from the hatch. Omi eased the hatch so it was almost closed. Both men stared at Marten's upheld handscanner.

Instead of one, three tall beings stepped aboard the *Mayflower*. Their helmet visors were black. Each figure looked quickly around. One reached up and undid his helmet's clamps.

Marten moistened his mouth as he activated the plasma cannon. He felt it vibrate and heard it hum. It was a wicked weapon, obviously not meant for such confined quarters. The cannon shot a superheated charge of plasma. Such a charge would destroy the airlock and open the *Mayflower* to space.

Omi cursed softly.

On the small screen of the handscanner, a cyborg swiveled its plasti-flesh features back and forth in tiny, machine-like jerks.

Marten and Omi traded startled glances. Marten nodded curtly. Omi only hesitated a moment, then he swung open the hatch. Marten dropped into position and aimed the plasma cannon at the cyborgs.

It was a frozen moment.

Then the cyborgs began to draw stubby tanglers. As fast as they were, Marten had time to think, *Tanglers. They meant to capture us.* Instead of curses, Marten pulled the trigger.

The heavy plasma cannon bucked as it spewed orange death. Marten had forgotten to set himself. The discharge applied Newton's third law of motion. For every action, there was a reaction. The discharging cannon shoved Marten backward.

Omi clanged the hatch shut. Three splats against it told of tangle-balls hitting. Then the *Mayflower* shuddered gently.

Marten lifted the handscanner, staring at a fuzzy screen.

"Now what?" asked Omi.

"Cyborgs!" Marten hissed. "The cyborgs are in the Jupiter System." His heart pounded with adrenalin. "All those months—"

"Cyborgs are in our ship," Omi said, in his maddeningly calm way. "They're beside us in a warship."

Marten blinked rapidly as he clutched the plasma cannon. Cyborgs captured normal people and put them into horrible machines. That's what Osadar had told them. They converted you into a cyborg. Death was preferable to capture.

"Marten?"

Marten kept blinking. Were the Jovians allied with the cyborgs?

"Marten?" Omi asked.

Marten quit blinking as he stared at Omi. "We have to kill the cyborgs in the pod," he said. He was surprised at how calm he sounded.

"Any idea how?" asked Omi.

"Close the hatch behind us and then open this one," Marten said, dipping the nozzle of the plasma cannon toward it.

"What if a cyborg survived?"

"Shut the hatch!" Marten hissed. "We don't have time to jabber."

14

Omi stared at Marten through his helmet's faceplate and then he floated toward the rear hatch.

Marten raised the handscanner, using his thumb to click a keypad. "Osadar?" he said. "You'd better be ready."

"I'm in the control room," she said. They were using tight-link communications. "The *Rousseau* is hailing us, asking what happened."

"You can't answer because our communications are out," Marten said. "Can you tell if the person hailing us is human or cyborg?"

"By the voice, human," Osadar said.

"Ready," Omi said beside Marten.

Marten took a deep breath. "Open it," he whispered, "and then brace yourself for decompression." Marten turned on his magnetic hooks, sealing his vacc-suit to the wall.

Omi opened the forward hatch. Escaping air smashed it open as the vacuum of space rushed in. In seconds, the air was gone from their chamber.

Marten shut off his hooks and drifted through the hatch. The wrecked airlock had a plasma hole in it straight through to space. Metal had melted and frozen in twisted globs. Three cyborgs drifted in the chamber. Two were missing part of their torsos and emitting blue sparks. The third lacked a head.

"The shuttle is secure," Omi whispered over the tight-link.

"See if you can open the airlock," Marten said.

"Are you sure that's wise?"

"Listen to me," Marten said. "Cyborgs do everything fast. We have no time to waste. Open the airlock now!"

Omi floated to the airlock as Marten checked the plasma cannon. This was bad. He only had two charges left. Then he'd have to hook it to a charging unit.

"The *Rousseau* has become insistent," Osadar said over the tight-link.

"Keep them talking," Marten said.

Omi cranked the damaged airlock wider, enough to allow a man to squeeze through.

Marten drifted nearer. They had to kill all the cyborgs in the pod. Their one stroke of good fortune was that the pod had maneuvered around the *Mayflower,* meaning that the airlock was aimed away from the *Rousseau.*

The long flex-tube detached from the *Mayflower's* hull and retracted into the pod.

*Cyborgs always move fast.*

Marten clutched the heavy plasma cannon and eased into the airlock. While staying as far back as he could from the outer opening, he studied the tear-dropped-shaped pod. It was smooth, dark and had huge lettering on the side he couldn't read. The black window by the front… was someone staring out of it and watching the airlock?

*What should I do? If they send more cyborgs—*

A hatch slid open on the pod. There was a flicker of movement. A humanoid shape jumped out of the hatch. Hydrogen spray trickled from its back. No, that was a thruster-pack. The cyborg might be cradling a weapon that Marten couldn't see from here.

Marten swore softly as he knelt in the airlock. He brought up the plasma cannon. He knew he should wait until the cyborg was closer. But time was against them. He had to kill all the cyborgs in the pod… and on the *Rousseau.* Clearly, that was impossible. But if he wanted to keep on living as Marten Kluge, he was going to have to achieve the impossible.

Marten braced himself against a wall, targeted the bastard, and squeezed off two shots of roiling orange plasma. The first glob missed. The second orange blob consumed the cyborg's midsection.

Marten made a strangled laugh. He hated cyborgs. He dreaded them. He watched the pod, waiting for some signal concerning its next move.

*What are they thinking over there in the* Rousseau?

"Marten," Osadar said over the tight-link.

*Here it comes,* he thought.

"A cyborg is on the com-link," she said. "It's demanding to know what has occurred. Do you have any idea what I should say?"

"Can you mimic a controlled cyborg?"

"Not efficiently," Osadar said. "There are too many variables that—"

16

"Open a channel and try to mimic a controlled cyborg the best you can. Tell them you have secured the ship. Then disconnect the com-unit. By then, I'll be there with you."

"They'll destroy us," Osadar said.

"We're dead anyway. This way... this way we might be able to hurt them before we die."

"I fail to—"

"Please, Osadar," Marten said. His mouth felt bone dry. It was hard to talk. "Just do it while they're still wondering what could have gone wrong."

"Understood," said Osadar. "I am complying."

***

On his way to the shuttle's control module, the answer came. Marten didn't like it, but it seemed like the only way to survive the cyborgs. Either the melded creatures possessed a Jovian warship with a skeleton number of humans left, or the cyborgs were allied to the Jovians who controlled it. Those Jovians would all have to die if he, Omi and Osadar were to survive. That was a grim thing, but he wasn't going to go soft now. He had clawed and fought his way out to Jupiter. He would claw and fight until he took his last breath, God willing.

Marten grimaced as he recalled his mother's most quoted saying. She'd died in the Ring-Works Factory around Mercury. That seemed like a long time ago now. Political Harmony Corps had come for her then. As much as Marten hated PHC, it had still been composed of humans. The cyborgs—he was doing the humans aboard the *Rousseau* a favor killing them. If he could pull this off, that is.

Marten told the others his plan and they moved fast throughout the *Mayflower*. In six minutes, they met back at the airlock. Each of them had a hand-case and wore a vacc-suit with a helmet.

Osadar had already shrugged on a thruster-pack. Omi hooked tether lines between them.

"This will never work," Osadar said over the tight-link. Her facial features were as much plastic as human, as much a mask as a face.

"I enjoy useless gestures," Marten said.

Osadar stared at him.

"It's a joke," Marten said.

"Useless, yes," Osadar said. She floated to the open airlock and pushed off toward the *Rousseau's* drifting pod.

Omi jumped next, and afterward Marten jumped. Using her former piloting skills, Osadar maneuvered toward the pod, keeping the *Mayflower* between them and the *Rousseau*.

As he floated behind Omi, Marten studied his handscanner. Using it, he initiated a specially coded program aboard the *Mayflower's* computer. The shuttle's engine thrust particles from the exhaust. Gently, the shuttle eased toward the *Rousseau* in the distance.

Soon, Marten floated through the open hatch of the cyborg pod. This vessel had one-fifth the space as the *Mayflower*. They would not be making any intersystem journeys in it. They might not make any journeys whatsoever. Shortly after boarding, the three of them crammed into the pod's control room. Voices spoke out of the com-unit. The voices spoke in a high-speed chatter.

"Can you understand them?" Marten asked.

From within her helmet, Osadar nodded solemnly.

"Well?" Marten asked.

"They are getting ready to fire on the *Mayflower*."

"You have to tell them that everything is fine," Marten said. "Tell them the other cyborgs are piloting the vessel to the warship."

"They will never believe me," Osadar said.

"Do it anyway."

Osadar sat at the single pilot's chair. Omi had already shut the hatch and pressurized the cabin. Opening her visor, Osadar opened a channel to the *Rousseau*.

Marten tore off his vacc-suit gloves and ran his fingers over the handscanner, using its keypad to pilot the shuttle.

Osadar was having a deliberate and unimaginative conversation with the cyborgs. The enemy queries were getting closer to deducing that the assault had failed.

"Engage the pod's engines," Marten whispered to Osadar. "Get us out of here."

Her fingers flew over the pod's controls.

Marten slid onto the floor and braced his back against a bulkhead. Omi did likewise.

Through the tiny screen of the handscanner, Marten studied the *Rousseau*. The scanner picked up the feed from the *Mayflower's* forward cameras. The Jovian dreadnaught was similar in configuration to a Social Unity battleship, but with a more compact design. It was like a giant ball bearing with asteroid-like particle shields. One of them was locked open, revealing a hanger bay inside. The pod had no doubt come from there. If the bay was still open….

Marten watched the screen. He saw the hanger door lurch and begin to close. The *Mayflower* could fit through it. The heavy particle shield also began rotating into a defensive posture.

"Give us full thrust!" Marten shouted. His fingers typed over the keypad.

Over three kilometers away on the *Mayflower,* the warfare pod they had installed back in the Mars System activated. The shuttle possessed five Wasp 2000 missiles. Those missiles entered the launch tubes.

Several things happened at once then on the *Mayflower*. The engine engaged at full thrust, pushing the shuttle faster toward the much larger *Rousseau*. The Wasp 2000s ignited from the launch tubes, leading the charge at the *Aristotle*-class dreadnaught. Almost immediately, the dreadnaught's point-defense cannons opened up. They targeted the missiles. A Wasp 2000 disintegrated. Another blew into a plume of light, while a third exploded in space, slightly damaging the *Mayflower* behind it. The fourth and fifth missiles slammed against the warship. One struck a particle shield, harmlessly blowing away asteroid-like rock. The last flew through the closing hanger door and exploded.

The hanger door froze.

The *Mayflower* closed with the *Rousseau*. The dreadnaught's point-defense cannons began to target the shuttle.

As growing G-forces pushed Marten against the pod's bulkhead, he pressed a button.

The accelerating *Mayflower* ignited its fusion engine, blowing the atomic pile in a nuclear explosion of obliterating power.

The Highborn Praetor commanded the *Thutmosis III*, and he was worried as his badly damaged missile-ship sped toward Jupiter.

The giant ship was a stealth vessel, painted with anti-sensor coating and colored as black as the void of space. Almost a year ago, they had circled the Sun gaining terrific velocity. Then they had broken Sun-orbit and shut off the ship's engines. Like a rock from a slingshot, they had sped silently toward Mars. At the right moment, the Praetor had launched a decisive salvo of missiles and drones. Unfortunately for the crew, they had one other mission to accomplish. Using teleoptic scopes and as they'd passed Mars, the Praetor had relayed precious combat information to the Doom Stars.

It was then that Corporal Bess O'Connor of the former Phobos moon-station had logged a blip of a lightguide message. With it, the SU commander of the former moon-station had launched hunter-killer missiles after the *Thutmosis III*. Phobos no longer existed. Highborn asteroid busters had destroyed the Martian moon during the battle. As a final quirk of fate, one of the deceased moon's hunter-killers had struck the *Thutmosis III* long after Phobos' destruction. The strike had killed eighty percent of the *Thutmosis III's* crew and crippled the missile-ship.

For many harrowing months afterward, the Praetor and the last survivors had labored intensely to effect repairs. Their problems had nearly been unsolvable, as the *Thutmosis III* had sped from Mars under terrific velocity. The hunter-killer had struck the ship before it had begun deceleration.

With the horribly damaged engines, the *Thutmosis III* had been unable to decelerate. For everyone aboard ship, it had looked hopeless. Unable to brake, the ship would leave the Solar System like a bullet fired from an inter-solar rifle. The crew would die hundreds maybe even a thousand AUs out of the Solar System of old age, starvation or asphyxiation.

The Praetor had taken their one chance, repairing the damaged engines enough to dare nudge the ship in a path toward distant Uranus. During the journey there, they had labored around the clock, taking stims to keep alert. Using the distant gas giant's gravity-well as a pivoting post and engaging the engines for a greater length of time, the Praetor had redirected the ship at an angle toward Jupiter. He had also managed to decelerate the vessel slightly.

The vast orbital paths of the Outer Planets gas giants and the extreme distances between them meant that a shallow curve could achieve this last hope.

Now the ship sped toward the largest planet in the Solar System. Unlike the *Mayflower* that had headed from the Inner Planets outward, the *Thutmosis III* headed from the Outer Planets inward. It was the reason why the much slower *Mayflower* had reached Jupiter before the much faster moving *Thutmosis III*.

The Praetor sat in his command chair on the bridge. It was one of the least damaged sections of the ship. The Praetor had become gaunt this last year. He had washed-out pink eyes, a wide face and a strange demeanor, which had been made stranger by a long and steady diet of stims. There was the tiniest tic now under his left eye.

The modules around him were empty and the bridge lights were dim. A constant whine sounded in the background. It came from deep inside the ship, from its tortured fusion engines. At times, the whine climbed an octave. Whenever that occurred, the tic under his left eye became more pronounced.

The Praetor pushed his big head against the rest of his command chair. Jupiter neared. Soon now, he would retire to the acceleration couches. He would strap in. They would engage the engines and hope the repairs held. If they didn't—

The Praetor shuddered and closed his eyes. That made the tic under his left eye more visible as it jerked the loose skin there. The Praetor had lost weight as concern had stolen his appetite. He would face anyone or anything man-to-man or chest-to-chest. Nothing in the universe frightened him physically. Give him a foe to battle—

His eyes snapped open. Anger filled his face. Grand Admiral Cassius had given him this command post.

The Praetor's nostrils flared. "I won the Third Battle for Mars," he whispered. "It was my missiles that opened up the enemy to the Doom Star lasers."

His upper lip curled, and he gazed into some unseen distance. "You shall not steal my victory from me, Cassius. I'm coming back. You can count on that."

A strange laugh bubbled from his throat. He shivered, and he was unaware that he did so. When the *Thutmosis III* had hurdled out of the Solar System—

The Praetor closed his eyes again. He had never understood loneliness until then. The idea of his ship rocketing outside of the Solar System and into the emptiness of space—the void was a *thing*, a beast that had spread in his soul. It had smothered courage, smothered daring and intellect alike. Shooting outside the Solar System, alone, with no hope of seeing Earth again, with—

"Enough," the Praetor whispered.

He moistened his mouth and forced himself to study the faint holoimage before him. His great enemy was velocity, speed. He had built up great speed while circling the Sun. Now he needed to shed that speed. A small part of him was tempted to aim directly at Jupiter and crash into it. That would end the agony. That would end the loneliness that he'd felt while hurtling toward Uranus, unsure whether the barely-repaired engines could slow them enough as they whipped past the gas giant.

If this didn't work—

"It will work," he rumbled. He lifted a fist and hit the arm of his command chair. In the past, he would have struck hard and forcefully. Now, it was a feeble gesture. The loneliness, the emptiness of deep space—

*Why did such loneliness exist?*

"Are you afraid?" he whispered at himself. "Are you a coward, Praetor? Or will you survive so you can spit in Grand Admiral Cassius's face?"

That was the antidote to his worries—anger, injustice and revenge. He must cling to them. No, he must gird himself with anger, with the sense of injustice committed against him and with thoughts of vengeance. He must buckle them like armor against the awfulness that lurked out there in the empty void of space.

Soon, he must engage the engines. He would have to time it right, letting Jupiter's vast gravity-well help slow them. The engines and gravity-well needed to slow the ship to less than Jupiter's escape velocity.

Could they do it? Could the badly damaged ship stand the strain? And if they did it, what awaited him in the Jupiter System?

That was the least of the Praetor's worries. He was Highborn. The pathetic Social Unity humans had joined with cyborgs. Those cyborgs had proven deadly. A Doom Star had died. But neither cyborgs nor Homo sapiens had proven tough enough to face the Highborn and survive.

The Praetor laughed as he pushed out of the command chair. If he could halt the *Thutmosis III*, he knew what he'd do in the Jupiter System. He would conquer it for the Highborn. He would show the ranking warriors of the Master Race that he was greater than Grand Admiral Cassius. With a crippled ship, he would conquer a planetary system. What Highborn had ever achieved that?

The facial tic quivered as the background engine whine rose an octave. First, he needed to shed the ship's velocity. Soon, the survivors would strap onto the acceleration couches as they made their last attempt to survive in the Solar System.

If the engines failed, or if it looked as if they might fail, then he would aim the *Thutmosis III* at Jupiter. Or he would crash the ship into a human vessel or into an orbiting habitat. If he was about to die, he would try to kill as much of the

24

universe as he could. Why he felt this way, he had no idea. He just knew it would make him feel better killing others if he himself wasn't going to be allowed to live.

## 3

When the *Mayflower* exploded, Marten, Omi and Osadar had already been moving away from it in the stolen pod.

With their head start and by accelerating at full thrust, they outran any appreciable heat damage. Heat from a nuclear explosion in space had the shortest kill-radius of the three dangers. It also helped that the pod's exhaust nozzle was aimed at the blast. A heat shield between the exhaust and the inhabitable quarters of the pod dampened what might have otherwise proven fatal.

The EMP blast washed over the pod's electronics and fused several key functions, including life-support. It also knocked out engine control, which didn't really matter as the most critical damage came from a piece of shrapnel. The size of an Old Earth penny, the jagged shrapnel sliced through the pod's exhaust. Then it sliced through the heat shield and the engine. Lastly, it ricocheted out of the pod, barely missing the command chamber.

The penny-sized piece of shrapnel damaged a heat coil, causing the engine overload. Luckily, although ship engine controls were fused, the emergency detachment sequence wasn't. It activated and began the procedure. With a shudder, the engine-half of the pod separated from the forward compartments, but both halves still possessed the same heading and velocity. Fortunately, the pod designers had considered that possibility.

A red strobe-light washed the command chamber as a klaxon wailed.

"Hang on!" shouted Osadar.

All three of them had already sealed their vacc-suits. Thus, they spoke via radio.

The command chamber shook as a non-lethal blast violently separated the pod. Emergency hydrogen-thrust now accelerated them away from the engine compartment. Fifty seconds later and through the polarized window, Marten caught a glimpse of a white flash.

They waited. The explosion had obviously created shrapnel, shrapnel that could possibly destroy their compartment.

After two minutes had elapsed, Marten said over their helmet radios, "It looks like we made it."

"Yes. Harmony has been achieved," Osadar said from the pilot's chair. "We are sealed in a speeding coffin, doomed to certain death."

Marten made a harsh sound. "I've been in worse situations. We're alive. We've escaped a wretched fate and now must rely on our wits to survive."

"Fate haunts you," Osadar said. "Whatever you do, you are doomed."

"You're wrong," Marten said. "Political Harmony Corps, Highborn, cyborgs, everyone has had their shot at me. I'm still alive and now we're in the Jupiter System, not lost between Mercury and Venus. We should be able to rig a distress beacon."

"To call more cyborgs onto us," Osadar said.

"Do cyborgs control the entire system?" Omi asked.

"You'd think we would have picked that up on our radio during the journey here," Marten said. "There would have been fighting. But we've heard nothing about that."

"Yet they are in the Jupiter System," said Osadar. "They possess Jovian warships."

"One less than before," Marten said, with a curl to his lip.

"Never fear. More will come. It is inevitable."

Marten squinted at Osadar. Listening to her, he hardened his resolve to do something. He began to examine the tiny command chamber. Soon, he'd torn off half the panels to see if he could fix something. They needed to recycle the air in their vacc-suits, to find a way to open the hatch—this crazy pod didn't have manual override. What ship designer had left that out? What did that say about the Jovians? Had some of them really allied with cyborgs?

A sea of stars glittered outside the speeding coffin, as Osadar had called it. Jupiter was behind them. Marten could no longer see the gas giant. Sixty-three different asteroids and large moons made up this system, all orbiting Jupiter.

There. Marten could make out a yellow moon. It had to be Io, the one that spewed sulfur dioxide into space.

During the trip here, he'd studied the *Mayflower's* computer files, reading what it had on the Jupiter System. He'd also questioned Osadar.

Jupiter had a Confederation made up of unequal members. Of the four Galilean moons—the biggest moons in the system—Io orbited the gas giant the closest. Io received massive doses of radiation. An unshielded person would receive 3,600 rems a day. Five hundred rems over a few days brought death.

Jupiter spewed radiation and heat, twice as much heat as it received from the Sun. Anyone living on Io needed constant protection. Jupiter's massive gravitation and proximity and the gravity from nearby Europa and Ganymede pulled and pushed at Io. The planetary body constantly stretched like a rubber band. That friction heated the insides of Io enough to create the most active volcanoes in the Solar System. It also created permanent lava lakes. Those lakes were Io's prized possession. Fissionable materials spewed up from the moon's core. Those fissionables helped feed the system's reactors. It meant that lava miners on floating platforms and under harsh radioactive conditions made up the majority of Io's population.

The second Galilean moon—Europa—also received massive amounts of radiation, five hundred and forty rems a day. Ice one-hundred kilometers thick covered the surface, with liquid water below. The ice mantle made Europa the smoothest planetary body in the Solar System.

While staring at Io, Marten wondered if the pod had enough radiation shielding. He shook his head. How did it help him worrying about that now? He had to fix the air-recycler first, attach water and waste tubes to their vacc-suits. If he failed, they would die in less than a day.

Marten went back to the panels and began to work.

*** 

Three days later, Marten sat back in despair. They had air, but no extra water and their suit's disposal systems were near their limit. His stomach growled. He was hungry and tired. According to his best estimate, they had traveled at least twenty-one thousand kilometers from the cyborg-infested dreadnaught.

Omi floated near the sealed hatch. Osadar sat in the pilot's chair, staring out of the window.

Marten picked up a calibrating wrench. He had to keep trying.

"What's that?" Osadar whispered.

It took Marten several seconds to respond. "What do you see?"

Osadar pointed at the window.

"Stars?" asked Marten.

Osadar swiveled in the pilot's chair. Behind her helmet's visor, she had an elongated face that suited her elongated body. Her arms and legs were titanium girders with hydraulic joints, presently hidden by her vacc-suit. Silver sockets cupped black plastic eyes, with tiny red dots for pupils.

Marten recalled that cyborgs had enhanced vision.

Osadar faced the window again. "There is a flare of light. A vessel is braking, likely matching velocities with us. That means the cyborgs have found us."

With his heart beating faster, Marten floated toward the window. He saw nothing but stars. Wait, far in the distance, one of the stars pulsed the slightest bit.

"Do you wish me to kill you?" Osadar asked.

"Listen to her," Omi said hoarsely.

"I entered the conversion machine," Osadar told him. "It peels off your skin, removes organs—"

"No!" Marten said. "We keep fighting."

"Once you're on the conveyer," said Osadar, "you will wish you had chosen otherwise."

"If it comes to that, Omi can shoot me."

29

"You are mere humans," said Osadar, "with pathetic human reflexes. Once you decide to shoot each other, you will already be tangled and on your way to conversion."

"You're depressed," Marten said. "You know what helps me get out of my depression?"

"Yes, your inability to correctly assess reality."

"I get angry. I get angry with people or cyborgs trying to use me. I've learned you have to bend sometimes. You do it, waiting for your one opportunity to strike back."

"Bravado is useless against the cyborgs," said Osadar.

"The cyborgs lost on Mars," Marten said.

"That was a minor setback," Osadar said. "Social Unity and the Highborn are even more doomed now than before the Battle for Mars."

"That's an odd way to look at it."

Osadar shook her head. "I believe the Highborn have frightened the Neptunian Web-Mind. That will make it even more ruthless than before."

"How could that be possible?" Marten asked.

Osadar stared into space.

Marten glanced back at Omi. Omi shrugged. Marten studied the dot. It seemed brighter than before, making his gut twist. More cyborgs—he had no idea how to defeat them this time.

Osadar spoke again. "I do not know how, Marten Kluge. But I know that whatever the cyborgs have decided to do, it will be to destroy the Highborn. A sense of fear will compel them."

"Can computers fear?"

"They are not computers, but symbiotic creatures of flesh and machine. Beings of any kind are always more dangerous when they fear their enemy, for then they fight with the ruthlessness of terror."

Fear bit into Marten as the bloom of starry brightness began to turn into a spaceship. How could he defeat the cyborgs a second time? He had no idea.

## 4

The ship was a small asteroid or a large meteor. To Marten, staring out of the pod's window, it seemed as if someone had magnetized the inter-solar rock. Then that someone had brushed it over a planetary junkyard. Pipes, tanks, tubes, missile-clusters, engine-exhausts, globes and other assorted junk stuck to it. He suspected that the life-supporting chambers were buried in the center of the meteor. Instead of adding particle shields to a regular ship, the builders had started with a tiny asteroid and added to it.

Using his handscanner, he studied the ship's dimensions. It was smaller than the *Rousseau* had been.

"A *Thales*-class vessel," Osadar said. "They were being phased out before the war with Social Unity thirteen years ago. The near total annihilation of the Jovian expeditionary fleet returned them to favor."

"That makes it a military vessel."

"And therefore the probability is ninety percent that it is under cyborg control," Osadar said.

Marten bit his lip as his gut curled. They had nothing to fight with but two Gauss needlers. He hated the helpless feeling. He should have recharged the portable plasma cannon.

"I'm picking up something on my headphones," Omi said. "They're asking if anyone is alive."

"Do not answer," Osadar said.

"Should we just sit here and die until our vacc-suits give out?" Marten asked. "Answer them."

"You will regret it," Osadar said.

Marten fiddled with his helmet radio, hearing nothing but static. The EMP blast from the *Mayflower* had damaged it. He was unable to pick up anything from the ship outside. It was hard enough understanding Omi and Osadar.

"They've acknowledged," said Omi.

In seeming despair, Osadar bent forward and rested her helmeted forehead on the control panel.

"We'll kill the first ones," Marten told her.

Osadar said nothing.

Marten watched the meteor-ship. A piece of the junkyard fired jets, detaching itself from the small asteroid. It was a black globe, probably the same size as their original pod.

*Here we go again.*

As Marten watched the globe ease toward them, a headache spiked a point between his eyes. Did cyborgs control the *Thales*-class warship? Or were Jovians allied with cyborgs? None of this made any sense.

* * *

Forty-six harrowing minutes later, Marten set his Gauss needler at high velocity. Then he waited with a tripping heart as the red flare of a slowly moving laser-torch cut open their tomb. Omi stood beside him, with his own needler out.

Marten clunked his helmet against Omi's as he chinned off his radio. They would speak through the metal of their helmets. "If it looks like they're going to capture us…" Marten said.

"Yeah," Omi said, his voice sounding tinny and faraway, "in the heart."

"In the heart," Marten agreed.

The laser-torch cut its last section of bulkhead. Someone with a clamp on the other side removed the section. The being poked its head in, and stopped short.

Marten's tongue felt raspy and his heart hammered as he knelt to the side. He aimed his needler at the enemy faceplate. He liked that his hand was steady and that his voice didn't crack.

"The last people were cyborgs," he said over the radio. "So let's get a look at you, friend, before I riddle you with needles."

For a moment, nothing happened.

*Goodbye, my friend*, Marten thought, on the verge of bellowing with rage and shooting Omi.

Then the staring visor went from black to clear. A pale, frightened man regarded him. The man had a round face, a small nose and a small mouth.

Marten's stomach relaxed a fraction, and he eased pressure from the trigger. "Are cyborgs on your ship?"

The man blinked rapidly almost as if trying to comprehend the question. Finally, he asked in a strange, clipped accent, "Cyborgs? Do you mean like the creatures they've been broadcasting about from Mars?"

"That's right," Marten said, trying to determine if the man was faking ignorance.

"What's wrong?" a woman asked over the crackling radio-link. "Is anyone hurt in there? If they are, we need to get them out fast."

A vacc-suited hand pushed the pale, blinking man deeper into the chamber. Then another helmet poked in. That person stopped suddenly.

"You have a weapon," she said.

"We're nervous," Marten said. His needler pointed rock-steady at her faceplate. "I'd like to see your features, if you don't mind."

"What does that have to do with—"

"Just do it," the pale-faced man pleaded, clutching her suited arm.

The woman hesitated and then her visor became clear. It showed a pretty female with small features and a round head.

"We ran into cyborgs earlier," Marten explained.

Her features changed into something like a person facing a crazed killer high on stimulants.

"Cyborgs... yes, I understand," she said, pasting on a tremulous smile. "We don't have any aboard the *Descartes*. Please, put away your weapon. And-and you can come with us."

Her look did it for Marten—that talk of cyborgs was crazy.

"It-it would be better if... if you gave me your weapon," she said.

Marten holstered the needler and shook his head.

33

"Ship protocol—"

"Will have to take a back seat today," he said, patting his holster.

She nodded quickly, and said, "If you'll follow me then. And just to let you know… the Force-Leader will want to know how you managed to become trapped in one of the *Rousseau's* pods. I do not wish to insult you, but you don't seem like a Jovian guardian."

"I'm not. I'm Marten Kluge. My friends and I just arrived from Mars."

## 5

The ride to the meteor-ship was short and uneventful. They docked with a hiss, a clang and a jolt that threw Marten against his restraints. Then he unbuckled himself and he and his friends floated after the two who had cut them out of the sealed pod.

They entered an airlock. There was more hissing and Marten felt the air-pressure grow around him. The inner lock rotated open and they entered a narrow corridor lit by a diffuse glow. A flexible membrane covered what had the bumpy outline of asteroid rock.

Marten realized they were inside the meteor, and this membrane likely helped seal in the atmosphere. Some rock was porous and would allow air to escape.

The two Jovians unsealed their helmets, cradling them in their arms. The woman had short, brown hair like fuzz, and the roundness of her head was even more pronounced than before. She looked back, waiting for them.

Marten unsealed his helmet, twisted it off and left it hanging from the back of his neck. He tasted the ship's air. It was recycled from renewers, no doubt. It had a hint of oil and burnt electrical gear. Were they having technical problems aboard ship? Or was it more ominous than that?

Behind him, Omi removed his helmet. Osadar made no move to take off hers, which seemed like a wise precaution.

"There's something you should know," Marten began.

The pretty woman frowned, maybe hearing trouble in Marten's voice.

"Ah...." Marten had been thinking about this the entire trip to the ship. "We came from the Mars System. I know I told you that, but—"

"I'm an artisan," the woman said, interrupting, "a mechanic. You should save your explanations for the Force-Leader or for the Arbiter and his myrmidons."

"Excuse me?"

Before the artisan-mechanic could explain, she gasped in horror, staring past Marten.

Marten turned. Osadar had removed her helmet. Her cyborg forehead gleamed, with the stamped letters and numerals OD12 on them. The plastic features and the strange eyes—Marten tried to visualize what the Jovians saw. Osadar had a space-zombie's features, like one of the living dead that someone had only half-resurrected from Suspend or from a battlefield corpse-pile.

"Quick," the artisan-mechanic gasped. "Go! Alert the ship-guardians."

The small man Marten had first aimed his needler at moaned in dread.

"If you'll just listen for a moment," Marten tried to say.

Marten's voice galvanized the small Jovian. He sprang from the chamber and scraped against the membrane of the narrow corridor. He curled his legs and shoved off again. Then he sailed out of sight down a bend in the corridor.

"There's no need for alarm," Marten said.

"Emergency!" the pale-faced woman shouted into a com-unit.

Omi shoved against Marten's shoulder and twisted past him.

The pale-faced woman squeaked. And she lowered the com-unit as she stared at Omi's needler. It was an inch from her forehead. A tinny voice squawked out of the com-unit.

"Tell them everything is fine," Omi whispered.

The woman stared at the needler, too terrified to move.

Omi tapped the muzzle against her forehead. He did it twice. She moaned each time. "Tell them now," he said, in his enforcer's voice, the one he'd used in the slums of Greater Sydney.

36

Trembling, the woman lifted the com-unit. "Ah... we're-we're fine, just fine."

"We should flee the ship," Osadar whispered to Marten.

"They'd just shoot us down," Marten said. "We have to talk our way out of this."

"We have a hostage," Omi said.

The woman's trembling increased.

"She is an artisan," Osadar said. "You have nothing with her."

"What's that mean?" Omi asked. "Artisan?"

"Put away your needler," Marten told Omi. "We can't shoot our way out of this."

Omi didn't even glance at Marten. The tough Korean kept his eyes on the woman.

"Please don't kill me," she whispered. She arched her body toward him, seemingly promising her flesh.

"Omi," Marten said, gripping the Korean's gun-arm. "We're in their warship. They must have space marines of some kind."

Omi glanced at him.

"We've come in peace from the Mars System," Marten told Omi, although he spoke for the woman's benefit. He wondered if she'd kept the com-line open. Even in her terror, there was something competent about her. He was also speaking for the benefit of whoever listened. "We're nervous because you became scared. Osadar is a cyborg from the Mars System. But she broke her programming. She's fighting against the Neptunian cyborgs now."

The woman bobbed her head in the manner of those willing to agree to anything.

"Put away your needler," Marten said.

Without a sigh and without saying he was sorry, Omi holstered his weapon.

"Go," Marten gently told the woman.

With wide eyes, she watched Omi. He nodded.

Woodenly, she turned around. With a tight sob, she began to float down the corridor.

\*\*\*

The woman floated through a hatch. Marten followed her into a narrow vacc-suit-rack chamber. It was packed with military personnel in blue uniforms, short-billed caps and stubby hammer-guns aimed at him.

Probably, he should have given the woman his needler in the damaged pod. But it was too late to change that now.

"There are three of you," a tight-faced woman said, likely the commander of the blue-uniformed people.

Through the hatch, Marten said, "Come in slowly."

Omi came in first. When Osadar followed, the line of military people stirred uneasily. Hammer-guns rose into firing position.

Marten expected them to discharge. It's what any Martian would have done—at least any Martian that had met cyborgs. With cyborgs in this system, Marten tensed, expecting a fusillade of shots.

"Who—" The tight-faced ship-guardian tried to form words. Shock stole the last color from her already pale features. "What are you?" she whispered.

"Cyborg," another ship-guardian said, a man.

"What?" the tight-faced woman asked him.

"That's a cyborg."

The tight-faced woman frowned with incomprehension.

"A true cyborg," the man said, almost in awe, "like the videos from Mars."

The tight-faced woman looked at Osadar again. The shock was beginning to wear off. Fear, repugnance and horror swept into its place. The woman swallowed uneasily.

Many of the hammer-gun bearers reacted the same way. Any one of them could start firing.

Marten realized that to these people cyborgs conjured up the memory of the horrible videos from Mars. They apparently had no idea they had lost one of their own ships to the cyborgs.

Marten raised his hands until they were over his head. "We've escaped from Mars, from the fighting there. Osadar— that's the name of our cyborg—she deprogrammed herself."

"What?" the tight-faced woman asked.

"Osadar is deprogrammed," Marten said.

"Osadar?" the woman asked. She obviously didn't comprehend.

"The cyborg is deprogrammed," Marten said.

"Speak clearly."

"The cyborg is no longer under Neptunian control. It means she has her mind back. She thinks and feels just like you and me."

"I don't understand that," the woman snapped. "She's melded with a machine."

"We should disarm them," the man said.

"Yes!" the tight-faced woman said. She thrust her arm out, the muzzle of her hammer-gun aimed at Osadar's head. "Drop your weapons!" she shouted.

"Why not let your artisan come to us," Marten suggested, with his hands in the air. "Let her draw out our needlers so you don't get nervous. We don't want you to accidentally shoot us."

The tight-faced woman chewed that over for a half-second. "Good idea." She gave the order. She had to give it a second time more harshly than the first.

Timidly, the artisan-mechanic floated to Marten and drew the needler from his holster. After all the needlers were in the hands of ship-guardians, the commander cocked her head. She had an implant in her right ear, a black mote.

"Which of you is the leader?"

"I am," said Marten.

"You're coming with me," the woman said. "You and—" Her eyes narrowed. "Cyborg, do you understand me?"

"I do," Osadar said, with a hint of weariness.

"If you resist, we will have to destroy you. Do you understand that?"

"Destroy equals death," Osadar said. "I understand."

"She's still human," Marten said.

The tight-faced woman gave no indication that she heard his words. She spoke louder at Osadar, as if that would help the cyborg understand better. "We're taking you to a holding cell. Both you and the man will enter it. We will lock you there for now. Any resistance—"

"I will not resist," Osadar said. "You are the authority and speak for the philosopher-governors."

The tight-faced woman blinked in surprise.

"I was born in the Jupiter System," Osadar said.

"Born?" asked the woman, as if Osadar spoke absurdities.

"She's human," Marten said. "The Web-Mind on Neptune tore down her former body and replaced it with a cyborg body. But in her heart, her brain, her soul, she's still just as human as you or I."

The tight-faced woman squinted, making it impossible to see her eyes. "No tricks, do you understand? We're ship-guardians and will do what we must to secure our vessel. To the holding cell with the cyborg. And you," she told Marten, "are going to the Arbiter. He'll know what to do."

## -6-

Two ship-guardians with drawn hammer-guns urged Marten through the narrow companionways.

A Velcro-like fiber had been laid on the deckplates, and both the ship-guardians and Marten wore Velcro-pads under their boots. A ripping-sound accompanied their progress through the meteor-ship. Marten figured it would have been easier just floating toward wherever they were going, but he adjusted to their procedures. He hoped Omi and Osadar were okay.

The ship was a maze of narrow halls, corridors and shafts. He passed cubbyhole quarters and heard the throb of a fusion engine down the corridor as they passed by. Grilles emitted recycled air. In a larger room, mechanics clanged metallic tools against what looked like twenty-foot drums placed side-by-side. Space was a premium in there, too. Some of the floating personnel squeezed between the drums, using hand-monitors to check on something.

Marten would hate to see their recreation room, if they had one. It was likely a closet with stationary cycles parked side-by-side. Twice, he and the ship-guardians squeezed past personnel in brown smocks, artisan-mechanics. The mechanics gave off an oily, machine odor. Marten was sure he gave off a rank, sweaty odor. He badly needed a shower.

It was difficult to tell, but Marten believed he moved into the depths of the meteor-ship, into the most protected portion. Until now, the halls had been painted blue and gray. Abruptly, the corridor ahead became red and white.

41

"Halt," a ship-guardian said. They were the man's first words.

Marten noticed a red light wink above. It was on the ceiling, marking the change in colors. It seemed to be part of a recorder or a camera.

A door opened in the red and white companionway. Two tough-looking men stood there. They were different from other Jovians. There was something elemental about them, something that spoke about gene labs and modified test-tube babies. Were these the myrmidons the woman had spoken about earlier?

The two squeezed out of the opening. They were nearly identical in appearance. Each was shorter than Marten, but immensely broad of shoulder and deep of chest, with knotted, muscular arms that almost dangled to the deckplates. They had low, hunched heads, black helmets and fierce, darting eyes. They wore white trousers and jackets, with epaulettes on their shoulders. They had various devices on their belts—rods, disks and restraints.

They vaguely reminded Marten of Major Orlov's red-suited killers from Sydney, Australian Sector. The fight in the deep-core mine—

"Go," the ship-guardian told him.

Marten glanced back at the man.

"The myrmidons will take you to the Arbiter. Go," the ship-guardian repeated, motioning with his hammer-gun.

Marten walked into the red and white corridor. One of the myrmidons grabbed his wrist. The man's fingers tightened like a spring-loaded clamp, and Marten had a sense of dynamic strength, likely much greater than his own.

"Come," grunted the myrmidon. It was hard to call it a word. The short, powerfully-built man jerked his arm.

Resistance seemed useless. The two myrmidons could likely wrestle him to the Velcroed deckplates in short order. Marten twisted his wrist anyway. He twisted and jerked hard, exerting force at the thumb. The thumb was the weakest spot of a gripping hand. The myrmidon's thumb was like iron, but Marten must have caught him by surprise. He ripped his wrist free.

The myrmidon whirled toward him. Marten felt the second myrmidon at his back, ready to apply whatever force was necessary to subdue him.

In the hallway, in the gray and white portion, a ship-guardian gasped.

"Just show me the way," Marten said. "I'll follow you."

The myrmidon in front of him bared his lips, revealing small teeth. The muscles in his arms bunched, and Marten was sure the man was about to attack. Then the myrmidon's head twitched as if an insect had bitten him or perhaps some implant in the black helmet had buzzed.

The myrmidon stepped back, making Velcro-ripping sounds. He twitched his head in a signal to go *that way*. Then he marched for the door.

Marten followed, with the second myrmidon breathing against his back.

They entered the first spacious room Marten had seen, although it was still confined compared to Highborn standards. A man in a white uniform with red buttons and shoulder-tabs sat behind a desk. There were screens behind him, various hanging vidshots of people and several pithy sayings.

Marten read one: *Temperance breeds happiness.*

It seemed innocuous enough, but it set Marten on edge. More than ever, the two myrmidons reminded him of Political Harmony Corps killers, but with the gene-warping of a Highborn. The white-uniformed man had the feel of a political officer or a hall leader like Quirn.

The desk was big. It had a screen and controls built into it. There was a bronze statuette of a man in a flowing robe who looked outward with a serene gaze. The statuette's arm was half-lifted and a finger pointed to nothing.

The white-uniformed man lacked that serenity. He was short like all the other Jovians, hairless, thin and had sharp features. The thrust of his narrow face was a stern, downward turn, as if he disapproved of everything.

"Sit," the man said. He had a surprisingly deep voice, and he was obviously used to giving commands that others obeyed.

There was one chair before the desk. Marten took it. He felt the two myrmidons settle into position behind him.

"I am Arbiter Octagon," the man said. "When speaking, you may refer to me as 'Arbiter' or as 'Your Guidance'. Do you understand?"

Marten nodded.

Arbiter Octagon folded his hands on the desk. "We intercepted some of your transmissions. You claim to have arrived from Mars."

"I am from Mars. Are you aware that cyborgs have invaded the Jupiter System?"

Octagon shook his head minutely as he spoke with quiet menace. "Do not query me. You are here for me to determine your status. I am the sole arbiter on the *Descartes*."

"I'm not trying to—"

Octagon raised a finger.

One of the myrmidons clapped a hand onto Marten's shoulder. The myrmidon applied pressure, grinding Marten's shoulder-bones together. He ceased abruptly, before Marten could cry out or try to squirm free.

"Consider that as a crude demonstration," Octagon said. "You are obviously an out-system barbarian, a creature given to direct stimuli. Therefore, failure to follow my directions will result in pain. Comply, and you will continue to sit here in relative comfort."

"I'm trying to help you," Marten said.

Octagon gave a sharp, humorous bark of laughter before he shook his head. "What do you call yourself?"

"I'm Marten Kluge."

"Wipe that angry look from your face or you will experience more pain."

"You think this is my angry look?" Marten asked.

Octagon sighed, throwing himself back against his chair. "Collar him," he said.

Marten began to twist around and tried to rise. Powerful hands gripped him. In seconds, one of the myrmidons snapped a metal collar around his neck. The click seemed ominous. As the myrmidons relaxed their grip, Marten grabbed the collar, intending to rip it off. A buzz sounded, and from the collar, volts sizzled through him.

Marten went limp in the chair, releasing the collar as if it were on fire. The buzzing stopped and volts no longer charged through his flesh.

"Yes, much better," said Octagon, who smiled for the first time. It was a cruel and predatory expression. He leaned forward, holding a small box. "This is a pain meter. If I dial it low like this. You feel this." Using a narrow thumb, Octagon pressed a red button.

A mild shock caused Marten to clench his teeth. The pain ceased the moment the Arbiter lifted his thumb off the button.

"However, if I dial it up to this—" Octagon twisted the switch and let his thumb hover over the button. He raised his eyebrows. "Shall I press the switch?"

Marten licked his lips. He knew what Octagon wanted. He should speak meek words. But rage pounded in his skull. Marten lunged, catching them by surprise. He made it across the desk and slapped the pain meter out of Octagon's hands. The Arbiter must have never expected that. Before Marten could strike the bastard, the two myrmidons grabbed him, wrenching his arms as they slammed him back against the chair.

Octagon was white with fury as he snatched the pain meter from where it floated. There was something wild in his black eyes, something feral and twisted. His mouth moved, but no sounds issued.

Marten would have tried to lunge again, but the myrmidons held him tight.

"Release him," Octagon whispered.

Gingerly, the powerful hands let go.

"That was a mistake, barbarian. It shows—" The thumb stabbed onto the red button.

Agony lanced through Marten. It was impossible to move. Numbing jolts flashed through him. He couldn't even croak in pain. Finally, it stopped.

Marten panted in his chair as sweat trickled down his back. His mouth tasted dry and it was difficult to focus. He wanted to kill Arbiter Octagon. But he couldn't attempt it now. He needed to hide as his parents had once hidden in the Ring-Works Factory. He couldn't hide physically. No. He would have to resort to the trickery of his Highborn days. He would have to eat dust until Octagon relaxed his guard.

"I am the sole arbiter aboard the *Descartes*," Octagon murmured. "I ensure obedience to the Dictates. I determine rank, grade and sometimes lower the undeserving in class. You are outside the stratum of the enlightened. You are a barbarian, living in the ignorance of an unexamined life. That is why I put a training collar on you."

Octagon adjusted the pain dial as he sat back in his chair. He examined Marten as if examining some untrustworthy piece of equipment.

"Barbarians are akin to animals even though they hold the guise of humans." Octagon pursed his lips. "Even humans trained in the Dictates at times fail to maintain their temperance. Hence, a need for arbiters arises. I am highly advanced in the Dictates. I have examined my life under the Dictates' fulfilling philosophies. I use reason instead of relying upon passion such as a brute as yourself practices. I am of the eleventh rank! I understand that is meaningless to an out-system barbarian. Therefore, let me say that eleventh rank meant years of toil, years of study and self-examination. I understand myself. And now, I understand the human condition. It is a squalid affair filled with a bewildering set of inner mandates of spurious use. 'Fill the belly.' 'Lay at ease.' 'Rut with a female.' It is chaotic, leading to debauchery and a disintegration of spirit."

Marten was finally breathing normally again. He sat straighter. He was highly aware of the two myrmidons behind him. He also noticed the position of Octagon's right thumb on the pain meter. Marten dipped his head.

"Might I say a word, Arbiter Octagon?" Marten asked.

Octagon gave another of his humorless barks of laughter. "How quickly the barbarian heels, eh? But I know that you think to trick me, to distract me from the truth. In reality, this shows me that you have a cunning mind. Therefore, you are dangerous." With his left hand, Octagon pressed a switch in his desk. He leaned forward, scanning a screen.

"Caught in a damaged pod of the *Rousseau*," Octagon said, as if reading information. "I wonder what fanciful tale you shall spin for me, hm?"

Marten touched the collar. "This device leads me to realize that lies are useless."

"Oh, you are a clever barbarian," Octagon said. "You think that I'm a fool. Fortunately for you, I follow the Dictates, I have learned to control my passions. Your attempted cleverness might anger a lesser man than me, one much lower than eleventh rank. I have harnessed my passions. Reason alone guides me. Thus, barbarian, you will feel pain now not because you've angered me but because my rationality tells me that you need further training."

The thumb stabbed down.

Marten squirmed as pain flooded. His mouth sagged. Then the thumb lifted and the pain ended.

Octagon leaned forward with a hungry look. "Yes, I'm beginning to detect fear in you, barbarian. I see it as a gleam in your eyes. You are trying hard to maintain your pose of toughness. Let me assure you that I shall root out every vestige of cleverness in you. The Dictates demand honesty. If nothing else, I will make you an honest brute."

A blue light blinked on the desk. Annoyance flickered across Octagon's features. "Hold him," he snapped.

Powerful hands gripped Marten's shoulders.

Octagon set down the pain meter. He composed his face so the cruel smile disappeared. He let serenity spread across his face until his features resembled those of the statuette.

Marten was reminded of Hall Leader Quirn, another philosophical fraud.

Octagon pressed a switch. "Yes, Strategist," he said in a quiet voice.

"Has the interloper explained his presence aboard the pod?" a female asked from a desk-speaker.

"We are exploring the matter," Octagon said gravely. "He is proving troublesome, however."

"I hope you have refrained from any harsh tactics."

47

Octagon gently cleared his throat. "The interloper's barbarian instincts are deeply imbedded, as I'm sure you already would know, Strategist Tan."

"Please, Arbiter, none of your didactic word-essays. This is a possible emergency."

Octagon leaned back from the screen and glanced at a wall. Gentleness and calm returned to his face. He bent over the screen.

"I will employ emergency—"

"You will not," Tan said. "You will question him another five minutes at the most. Then you will escort him to the command center. Force-Leader Yakov is eager to hear his explanation."

"I hear you, Strategist, but I feel that I must protest."

"I am the philosophic guidance aboard the *Descartes*, Arbiter. I have been elevated to the governors. I am sixty-ninth ranked. You do understand what that means, yes?"

"Your radiance suffuses us with enlightenment," Octagon said.

"Enough of that," Tan said. "Maintain decorum throughout your questioning. You have less than five minutes left. Do you desire further clarification?"

Octagon moistened his lips. "As always, you are succinct. I am bidden by the Dictates and your own flawless reasoning to comply with your wishes."

"I have given *orders*, Arbiter."

"Yes," he said. "I understand. Thank you for your precision."

The blue light flashed, perhaps signaling an end to the conversation.

Octagon leaned back in his chair. He picked up the pain meter. He scowled at it and then he glared at Marten.

By struggling with himself, Marten kept his features bland.

"I am the sole arbiter aboard the *Descartes*," Octagon said. "The Strategist—" His mouth tightened as he twisted the dial first in one direction and then in the other. He watched Marten as he did so.

"If you would like my story," Marten said, "I can tell you now."

48

"I detect smugness in your words," Octagon hissed. His thumb stabbed down.

Marten clenched his teeth as the jolts roared through him. It was one gigantic sensation. He felt himself twisting in the chair. Hatred filled him. He would have glared at Octagon, but his eyes were painfully screwed shut.

Abruptly, the pain ceased.

Marten sagged. His jaw muscles ached. But he stirred, and he whispered, "Did that little jolt come because of your emotions, Arbiter, or was there a reason for it?"

"Impertinence," Octagon whispered. "That implies future malice."

"Your system has been invaded."

"Bah! You cling to the absurd notion that cyborgs have entered the Jovian Confederation. It is another of your base lies."

"Look in your holding cell, at the cyborg there."

"A creature of your own devising," Octagon said.

"I've seen other cyborgs."

"Lunacy," said Octagon, "sheer fabrication of an unfettered, emotional mind. I wonder if you were sent here by Social Unity to spread discord among us. Believe me, you shall fail in the attempt."

"How did I come to be in the dreadnaught's pod?"

"I am querying you, barbarian, not you me."

"No. You've been telling me many things, but asking very little. Why is that, *Your Guidance?*"

The dark eyes seemed to shine as Octagon's features froze. Carefully, he slotted the pain meter on his belt. "You are a fool, filled with false illusions. Strategist Tan uses our ship as a taxi. Soon, she shall depart. Then all governance decisions revert to me. You and I shall have long discussions concerning questions, answers, emotional states and rational understanding of the Dictates. It is the human heart laid bare to our superior understanding. We have examined man's nature and we know it thoroughly. Here, we act with reason, without malice or subterfuge."

The blue light flashed on the desk. "Arbiter Octagon," said the Strategist, "we await the interloper in the command center. Report on the double."

Octagon bared his teeth as the blue light flashed again, cutting the connection. He rose, and he signaled the two myrmidons.

"Bring him," Octagon said. He stared at Marten as the predatory smile made a faint reappearance. Then Octagon Velcro-walked toward the door.

## 7

In his worn silver jumpsuit and old boots, Marten marched between the myrmidons. Octagon brought up the rear. They continued to use boot-pads because weightlessness reigned. That told Marten the meteor-ship was still near the hijacked pod.

With an effort of will, Marten focused on that instead of the shock collar and myrmidons. He needed to use his wits, as he had little else now. Were ship personnel inspecting the pod?

Octagon cleared his throat.

The myrmidons halted. The one in front whirled around to face Marten.

"Barbarian," Octagon said softly.

Marten scowled, and the myrmidon facing him made a low, growling sound. There was little intelligence in the myrmidon's eyes, but eager readiness for battle. There was also something akin to the hatred of the neutraloids in him. The squat, black-helmeted myrmidon was bestial, made to enforce Octagon's orders. And Octagon supposedly gave his orders through reason alone. The dichotomy between myrmidon and philosophic governance—what did that say about the Jovians?

Marten smoothed away the scowl as he turned toward Octagon.

"Remember, that you will remain with me long after Strategist Tan leaves the ship."

"Why do you care?" Marten asked.

Octagon's right hand dropped to the pain meter hooked to his belt. "I have certain theories regarding barbarians," he said softly. "You couldn't understand, however, even if I explained it to you."

"Try me."

"Enjoy your liberty of impertinence, barbarian, for it shall be your last. Now go, hurry."

They entered a narrow hall that led to a hatch. The first myrmidon darted through. Marten followed, walking past a man-sized statue. It was ivory-colored and showed a sparse intellectual in a toga. The statue had a serene smile, with an unfocused gaze. His hands were near his hips, the palms outward in an imploring gesture.

The statue startled Marten, and it took him a moment to realize he'd entered the roomiest place he'd seen. Large screens showed the stars. Spacers in zero-G worksuits floated around the pod or magnetically walked across its surface. From time to time, white particles of hydrogen-spray propelled a work-suited spacer elsewhere.

The room, or command center, had small modules along the walls, with black-uniformed personnel squeezed into each. The people in the modules wore ear-jacks and stared at vidscreens and other monitors. Marten recognized thermal scanners, broad-spectrum electromagnetic sensors and neutrino and mass detectors. Passive sensing systems allowed one to spot an enemy without giving oneself away. Active systems *pinged* a noticeable pulse off the enemy, who if alert would realize they were being scanned.

Marten noticed the ceiling then. A golden triangle was inlaid there, with a silver, lidless eye peering out from the center.

"Bring the barbarian here," a woman said.

Marten refocused as one of the myrmidons pushed him toward a tiny woman. She stood beside a seated man in the center of the command room.

The tiny woman, surely no more than four feet tall, wore a stylish red jacket and slacks. She had hairless eyebrows, and she seemed older than the others. She also had smooth, fine-boned features—bio-sculpted features, Marten suspected. She was beautiful in an elfin way, exotic. She wore a tight red cap that hid any hair and she wore a shield-like emblem where her jacket's front pocket should have been.

"You have the honor of standing in the presence of Strategist Tan," Octagon said. "If at any time she addresses you, you will respond in a mild tone and use the honorific of 'Your Visionary' or 'Exalted One'."

"Exalted One?" Marten asked, bemused.

Octagon stiffened, and his slender hand moved toward the pain meter.

"Hold," said Tan. She had a firm voice, full of assurance, adding to her strange beauty. "You applied a shock collar to him."

"Yes, Exalted One," Octagon said.

"The reason?" she asked.

"Unbridled emotionalism."

"I would know your proof?"

"The barbarian's drawing a weapon against his rescuers," Octagon said. "His attempt to take a mechanic hostage in our ship, thinking that would thwart us. His swift changes from rage, to pseudo-rationality and to actual aggression. His—"

"Perhaps it is true that emotionalism stirred those actions," Tan said. "However, they could have formulated from other sources."

Octagon's head twitched minutely. "Exalted One, you are far too highly ranked for anyone present to assault your logic. Still, I feel compelled to point out that my advanced studies were and continue to be in Barbarian Psychology. While I would laugh at anyone who suggested that intuitive... hm... *feelings* could help clarify a situation, nevertheless—"

"You *intuited* his emotionalism?" Tan asked, with a faint hint of amusement.

Octagon's mouth opened. He shut it with a click of his teeth.

"How interesting," she murmured.

"You are sixty-ninth and I am eleventh," Octagon said hurriedly. He was silent for a moment. "My word choices have failed me."

"It is of little matter," Tan said. "We shall proceed to my second query. And for the sake of argument, I will grant you his emotionalism. Even given that, why collar him?"

"Barbarians react within strict parameters to pain. I apply the stimuli and can easily interpret the reasoning behind his responses. That helps me gauge the truth."

"His reasoning?" asked Tan.

"Emotions stem from pseudo-reasoning."

"Hm," said Tan. "You are the ship's arbiter. I have no desire to step onto your prerogatives. However, I feel that events have crossed into abnormality. The cyborg in the ship's holding cell is the obvious proof. These fugitives arrived in the *Rousseau's* pod, a badly damaged pod, possibly indicating a battle. Yes... I am intruding into your area of expertise. But not lightly, Arbiter Octagon. I wish to assure you of that."

"I lack the philosophic height to judge your actions, Exalted One. But I must—"

"Well said. For the duration then, I insist that you keep your hand off the pain meter. I have a different methodology than yours, and will now apply it to the barbarian."

"If I could just—" Octagon tried to say.

"Please," said Tan, flicking one of her tiny hands at him, "desist."

Octagon bowed his head.

"In fact," said Tan. "Move back and make your myrmidons heel."

Octagon hesitated. It was barely perceptible. Then he snapped his fingers. The myrmidons left Marten, following the Arbiter. Octagon went to a raised monitor several feet behind the command chair. Octagon pressed several toggles there and began to scan the personnel in the modules. A few sat straighter or seemed more absorbed in their vidscreens.

"Did you understand our dialogue?" Tan asked Marten.

"Yes."

"You realize that we find your presence in the dreadnaught's pod... highly unusual?"

"I'm from Mars," Marten said. "We just arrived in your system—"

Tan held up her hand.

54

Marten ignored it as he kept on talking, "When the *Rousseau* hailed us—" Marten groaned, doubling over as the shock collar buzzed. Pain flooded through his body. He heard Tan speak sternly. The pain ceased and Marten heard Tan scold Octagon.

"In fact," Tan added, "remove the collar."

Exalted One—" Octagon tried to say.

"Silence," she said. "Now remove the collar as ordered."

There was a click from the collar. Marten tore it off, and he nearly hurled it at Octagon. He became aware of the others watching him. Most seemed fascinated, as if witnessing a strange beast. The myrmidons seemed ready to fly at him. Controlling his urge, Marten managed a harsh grin. He held out the collar for someone to take.

"There," Tan said. "My methodology is already proved correct."

"Please, Exalted One—"

"Arbiter," she said, "I detect strain in your voice. I begin to wonder if extended duty has worn down your... razor's edge of rationality. Now take the collar and observe."

Octagon whispered to a myrmidon. The gene-warped Jovian hurried to Marten, snatching the collar, clicking it to his belt and hurrying back to Octagon.

"We shall begin anew," Tan told Marten.

"Thank you," he said, rubbing his throat.

She gave an airy wave. "Your presence in the pod is strange, and you were in the company of a cyborg. That implies you belong to Social Unity."

Marten waited, deciding to follow their ways.

"Ah, you show decorum," Tan said. "I find that interesting. Do you belong to Social Unity?"

"No."

"Are you from Neptune?"

"I am not."

"I notice a barcode tattoo on your forearm. That indicates a Highborn soldier."

"They inducted me on Earth, yes."

"So you *are* Earthborn and originally belonged to Social Unity."

"I was born in the Sun-Works Factory. My parents were Unionists."

"Meaning what?" asked Tan.

"Political Harmony Corps hunted us," Marten said, "butchering many and torturing the rest. My parents escaped into the vast Sun-Works Factory. The majority of the habitat is automated, which means that hundreds of kilometers are devoid of humans."

"I'm familiar with the Mercury Factory. There is no need to elaborate."

Marten nodded. "I grew up longing to reach the Jupiter Confederation."

Tan made a soft sound, with a twitching smile.

Marten liked her smile, and he found her smallness stimulating. In fact, her beauty stirred him. "Maybe you think I'm making that up to try to please you," he said. "Back then, Social Unity controlled all four Inner Planets. The Jupiter Confederation was the first free system."

"Free?" Tan asked.

"Free of Social Unity."

"Ah. Yes, of course. Continue."

"We almost had fuel for a secret spaceship we'd constructed. It had taken us three years of hiding like rats to piece it together, to write the software—" Marten shrugged. "PHC found us. They killed my mother and father. I escaped to Earth."

"So you *have* lived under Social Unity?"

"Rather say that I survived in the stifling world of thought control," Marten said.

Tan's eyes narrowed. "Do you seek to teach me dialectics?"

Marten glanced around. Octagon watched him avidly. The personnel in the modules looked aghast. Only the black-uniformed man in the command chair seemed unfazed. Marten had made a blunder, but he wasn't sure what.

"I don't know your ways," he said. "If I've offended you, it wasn't intentional."

"He is a clever barbarian," Octagon said. "That much I've determined."

56

"A barbarian," Tan murmured. "Yes… thank you, Arbiter, for reminding me of his out-system status. He cannot know our ways, nor is he enlightened. He is an ignoramus, straining through life with half-knowledge at the very best. We should pity him, not collar him. Nor should I take quick offense at his unintentionally degrading comment."

"The *Rousseau* has gone off-line," the black-uniformed man in the command chair said.

Tan regarded the man coldly. "We have our orders concerning the dreadnaught."

The man made no response, nor did he betray any emotion or quirk.

"Still," said Tan, "events rush forward. You have a point." She studied Marten. "Do you have a name?"

Marten told her, and he said, "I've been a soldier. I've learned that sometimes events rush forward with blinding speed."

Tan seemed amused. "Continue."

"I was at Mars during the battle. I fought there. Surely you've received broadcasts concerning it."

Octagon made an angry sound.

Tan lofted her eyebrows, waiting. When nothing further occurred from Octagon, she told Marten, "We have received many broadcasts from Mars. But I'm now changing the topic. The Force-Leader just made an excellent point. Your history is quaint, and likely unusual for a barbarian. But none of that explains how you came to be trapped in a Guardian Fleet pod."

Here it was. Marten had been wondering the best way to tell them he attacked one of their warships. He recalled something Osadar had told him about Jovians—their attachment to form, to rank. Listening to them, observing them, Marten realized Osadar was right. He had something in his zipped pocket that might alter his status with them. As a barbarian—he was beginning to hate the title—he was almost an animal to them.

"He hesitates," Octagon said, as if making a telling point.

"You must tell us the truth," Tan told Marten. "Although I am loath to tell you this, we have methods for determining liars. It is unpleasant, as I'm sure you can understand after visiting the Arbiter."

"I've waited before revealing myself," Marten said.

Tan lifted an eyebrow.

Marten began to unzip a flap on his thigh.

Octagon spoke sharply. It alerted Marten as the myrmidons leapt, propelling themselves with fantastic speed. Weightless, they were able to fly at him in a single bound. But Marten had been waiting for something like that. He flattened onto the deckplates. The two myrmidons flew above him. One, reaching down, managed to grab Marten's arm. Marten struck the wrist, dislodging the hold.

By that time, Tan said, "Arbiter! End this outrage and restrain your myrmidons."

Octagon called out.

The two myrmidons had struck modules or bulkheads, halting themselves there. Smoothly, like weightless high-divers, they pushed off and sailed back to their position beside Octagon. The one Marten had struck glared at him, but they hunched their heads in obedience beside the Arbiter.

"If you are removing a weapon," Tan said, "it is ill-advised."

"I understand," Marten said. "I am withdrawing my credentials."

"Ah. By all means, continue."

Marten removed the credentials given him almost a year ago by Secretary-General Chavez. Marten held out the booklet.

"That is what exactly?" Tan asked.

"This is from the Mars Planetary Union. If you'll examine the signature, you'll see it's from Secretary-General Chavez himself."

"Regrettably," Tan said, "Chavez died in the aftermath of the Highborn Hellburner."

"All the more reason you should look at this," said Marten.

"Explain your statement."

"The Highborn are at war with the Solar System. The Mars Planetary Union and the Jupiter Confederation were allies once. Maybe it's time to ally again."

"Against the Highborn?" asked Tan.

"And against Social Unity and the cyborgs," Marten said.

"Mars lacks extra-planetary fighting capacity."

"But it has willing soldiers," Marten said. "I should know. I led some of them into successful battle."

"Hm," said Tan. "Let me see that."

The seated, black-uniformed man pushed off from his chair, taking Marten's credentials and bringing them to Tan.

She scanned the cover, opened the booklet and studied the contents. "The seals and documentation are in order, and I recognize the former Secretary-General's signature. Hm. This puts a new light on the matter." She snapped the booklet shut, returning it to the black-uniformed man.

He returned it to Marten, who put it away.

"I apologize for the Arbiter's harsh methods earlier," Tan said, with a new note in her voice.

Marten wasn't sure, but there seemed to be a hint of promise in it. She was small, but the longer he spoke with her, the more beautiful she seemed.

All that proved too much for Octagon. "I must protest, Exalted One. Like a rogue virus, the interloper was bottled in the *Rousseau's*—"

Tan lifted a small hand. Octagon's words stopped. Without turning to regard him, she said, "He is an accredited representative of the Mars Planetary Union. That makes him part of the governing class. Perhaps... he has been unable to avail himself of a proper Jovian education. Still, the art of governing teaches even the unexamined soul certain critical facets of higher thought. You above all others should accord him the correct honor, Arbiter."

"You teach me, Exalted One."

"It is my duty to do so," she said.

"As it is mine to learn from my superiors, Your Radiance," Octagon said.

Marten was amazed. A piece of paper, no, a *credentialed* piece of paper, seals and an inked signature had dramatically shifted his status with these strange people. Osadar had said before that Jovians had a high regard for form. The reality of the situation was much stronger than what Osadar had explained. He'd have to remember that.

"Could you enlighten us regarding your presence in the pod's pilot chamber?" Tan asked.

"Exalted One," Marten began.

"Please," Tan said, "let me… guide you concerning Jovian etiquette. In theory at least, you belong to Mars' governing class. That makes us equals. As equals, I'm sure I don't need to point out to you that I am not exalted compared to yourself. Despite the Arbiter's truth earlier of an unexamined life, for only Jovians truly attempt to decipher the inner workings of the human heart. Even governing inferior humans infuses the governors with unavoidable realities. Those realities teach universal laws or axioms."

The black-uniformed man gently cleared his throat.

Tan smiled indulgently. "Ah. I wax prolix at a time of crisis. It is an unfortunate habit of the enlightened to examine every angle. Sometimes, a sudden thrust of decisive nature is more suited to the situation."

"May I?" asked the black-uniformed man.

Tan gave the barest of nods.

"I am Force-Leader Yakov of Ganymede," the man told Marten. Yakov had a pelt of fine silver hair. And although small and round-headed like the others, he had lines around his mouth and bunched muscles at the hinges of his jaw. A feeling of deadliness emanated from him, the subtle hints of a trained soldier. "I lead the *Descartes* during hostilities. I wish to query you."

Marten nodded.

"I have your permission then?" Yakov asked.

"Oh," Marten said. "Sure."

"First," said Yakov, "who exactly is the cyborg that was trapped with you in the pod?"

"She is Osadar Di. In Neptune, the Prime Web-Mind converted her."

"If you would," Yakov said, "please explain what that means."

"They have a process in Neptune by which a person is torn down and rebuilt into a cyborg. They program the cyborg. Osadar, however, broke her programming."

60

Yakov's manner tightened. "That could have been a ploy, allowing the Web-Mind to insert a spy into your ranks."

"I'm sure that's possible," Marten said. "But Osadar saved our lives on Mars, killing other cyborgs. According to the Martian broadcasts, all the cyborgs were slain in the Mars System. Osadar did nothing to help save any of them. Finally, for nearly a year, she has traveled with Omi and me aboard the *Mayflower*."

"If you will pardon my interruption," Tan said. "Your statement lacks precision. You said all cyborgs died on Mars, but Osadar survived and she is a cyborg."

"All programmed cyborgs died on Mars," Marten said. "Look, I don't think you people understand just how much danger you're in. The cyborgs have come to Jupiter. They're here and they've likely been converting Jovians."

"Explain, please," Yakov said.

Marten glanced from Yakov, to Tan, to angry Octagon. Before he could say another word, one of the technicians spoke up.

"I'm getting a voice signal from the last known location of the *Rousseau*. They're requesting urgent evacuation."

Force-Leader Yakov swiveled in his command chair to look at Tan.

Tan frowned, moodily staring at the largest screen. "I must attend the War Council."

"I could give you a shuttle," Yakov said.

"No..." Tan said. "The Chief Strategist was explicit. All military vessels of the Guardian Fleet are to rendezvous at Athena Station."

"What are the coordinates of the voice signals?" Yakov asked the technician.

The technician read off a series of numbers that were meaningless to Marten. But they must have made sense to the Force-Leader.

"You could use the shuttle," Yakov told Tan. "Then I could delay my arrival by first examining the distress call. Then I would—"

"The *Rousseau* was controlled by cyborgs," Marten blurted out. "That means a Web-Mind is probably already operating in your system. You have an emergency. If I were you, I'd tell your War Council—" Marten closed his mouth as a new possibility slammed into his thoughts. The possibility sickened him, and he wondered if it was already too late to save the Jovian System.

"Again he hesitates," Octagon said. "The barbarian obviously hides pertinent information. We are reckless to take his credentials at face value. I suggest we hook him to the obedience frame."

Marten laughed harshly, which made Octagon scowl.

"This War Council," Marten asked, "where does it meet?"

"That is privileged information," Tan said.

"If it's near this Athena Station," Marten said, "I would think twice about going. Before you ask me why, let me tell you what happened to the *Rousseau*. The sooner you know what's going on, the better for everyone."

As Tan, Yakov and Octagon listened, Marten told them about the harrowing ordeal Omi, Osadar and he had recently undergone against the dreadnaught.

## 8

With a strangled sound, Octagon drew a palm-pistol and aimed it at Marten. It was a neat little gun and had been strapped to his belt. It was oval, with handgrips like brass knuckles, and fit into Octagon's slender palm.

The myrmidons crouched like beasts, ready to fling themselves at Marten.

"His entire fabrication of lies is a web meant to bewilder us into inactivity," Octagon snarled. "Social Unity must have sent him as a saboteur or as a fragmentation agent. His single mote of truth is that he attacked the *Rousseau*. I await your word, Exalted One. I will terminate this enemy saboteur."

"Put up your weapon," said Tan.

"Your Visionary, I must—"

Small Strategist Tan turned toward Octagon. Her words came out cold and clipped, cutting him off. "You have served too long in isolation, I see. Maybe you've forgotten that you regulate temperance, not *govern* this ship."

Octagon sputtered.

"Yes," said Tan. "I note your red shoulder tabs and red bars and crescents, but you are a probationary authority. I am a governor. I am a strategist on the War Council. You will seek to teach me nothing, unless you wish me to relieve you of your station."

Octagon's features blazed crimson. His pistol-hand quivered as tendons rose.

"Must I summon ship-guardians?" asked Tan.

With a hiss of expelled air, Octagon lowered his palm-pistol.

Tan held out a tiny hand toward him.

Octagon blinked at her. The flush left his cheeks, as he turned pale. He began to tremble.

Inflexibly, Tan held out her hand.

Octagon said hoarsely, "Exalted One, I crave your pardon. You...you speak truth that I have maintained my post too long. I have served here for two entire cycles. There is a reason for that, but I am reluctant to state it."

"Then don't," said Tan.

"Except for me," Octagon said, "none from Callisto serves aboard the ship."

Tan glanced at Yakov sitting in the command chair. "That has no bearing on your status," Tan told Octagon.

"That is understood," said Octagon. "The guardian-soldiers of the *Descartes*—soldiers of Ganymede and Europa—are shining examples of duty. They guard with no ulterior loyalties. During my two cycles here, I have only discovered three instances of class overstep."

"Three?" asked Tan, betraying surprise, and again glancing at the stoic Yakov.

"There might have been more oversteps," Octagon said, "but I acted decisively to quash them. During each guardian's off-duty period, I demanded a careful hour of study, periodic examination and my precise explanation of the Dictates."

"You have been zealous," admitted Tan.

"As you've implied, Exalted One, I have overworked myself. That is not sufficient reason for my... unwarranted display of moments ago. I dare not say more. Otherwise, I fear that my restraint will depart."

"Hm," said Tan, as her outstretched hand lowered. "I appreciate that you've shackled your... display. Restraint is the watchword."

"It is the watchword," echoed Octagon.

"Yes," said Tan, "this is an unusual situation. Although, it is in such situations that our philosophical approach must show itself superior to the untamed life."

"You expound truth," Octagon said.

Tan gave a nearly imperceptible nod. "Clip the weapon onto your belt. Then silently recite to yourself axiom twelve of the Dictates."

Out of the corner of his eye, Marten had been watching the command-room personnel. Through subtle glances, a raised eyebrow, the slight twist of a lip or hunched shoulders, he thought to detect hostility toward Octagon and his myrmidons.

"Representative Kluge," said Tan. "Your account is fantastic. Cyborgs controlling a Jovian warship, an *Aristotle*-class dreadnaught, it's inconceivable."

"I'm guessing there have been some strange happenings lately," Marten said.

Tan and Yakov exchanged a glance. It showed Marten he'd guessed correctly. Perhaps there had more than just a few odd occurrences.

"What I'm about to suggest is conjecture on my part," Marten said, trying to frame this in the Jovian manner. "But it seems the cyborgs want to gain control of all military vessels in this system. They likely have a limited capacity to alter humans into cyborgs. Gaining military control of space would be the most strategic use of their limited numbers."

"Given your premise," said Tan, "your reasoning is sound."

"Might the greatest strategic asset be control of the War Council?" Yakov asked softly. "And after that, control of the Grand Chamber?"

"I must protest your statement," Octagon said, sharply.

Tan waved him aside. "Not now, Arbiter. This is a crisis, one way or another. If you are a saboteur," she told Marten, "we need to know for whom. And if your fantastic story is true—"

"Please, Exalted One," Octagon said, "permit me to interject a comment."

"Refrain," said Tan.

Octagon clutched his monitor-board, obviously struggling to maintain silence. His myrmidons threw savage glances everywhere.

"May I ask you a command question?" Yakov asked Tan.

Tan gave the Force-Leader a cool glance. "Permission granted," she said slowly.

65

"Why do you suppose Athena Station ordered us to immediately report to Fleet Headquarters?" Yakov asked.

"I am to attend the emergency War Council meeting. You know that. If you would be so kind as to make your point, Force-Leader...."

"Why has Athena Station ordered a different ship to the *Rousseau's* last known location when we're much closer to the stricken vessel?"

"That is for Fleet Headquarters to decide," Tan said stiffly, "not for flag officers of guardian status to question."

"Under regular conditions, I agree," Yakov said. "My question has a subtler twist."

Octagon's head snapped up as he stared at the Force-Leader.

"Proceed," Tan said slowly.

"Suppose Representative Kluge has spoken accurately," Yakov said. "Cyborgs control the *Rousseau*. Suppose one takes it a step further, and cyborgs control Athena Station."

"That is a preposterous premise," Tan said.

"Exalted One," Yakov said, "I retreat before your superior virtue."

Tan studied the silver-haired Force-Leader.

The personnel in the modules busily studied their screens or monitors. Octagon wore a hungry expression, anticipatory. He clicked several toggles on his board.

Marten noticed a black bulb in the ceiling. Was that a camera? Did Octagon record the events here?

"You've aroused my curiosity," Tan said at last. "A guardian with a subtle point. Very well, proceed with your line of reasoning."

"As you wish, Exalted One," Yakov said.

Marten now noticed that Yakov's right hand had gently slid open a small panel on his chair's armrest. The Force-Leader's fingers hovered over a set of black buttons.

"If in some insidious manner Athena Station was controlled by cyborgs," Yakov said, "that would give them an advantage, allowing the infiltration of other warships."

"An obvious conclusion," Tan said.

"It would also explain why we weren't sent to help the stricken dreadnaught, but a ship many more days away was."

"Given this absurd premise," said Tan, "you're right."

Yakov's features tightened. To Marten, it seemed the Force-Leader's right hand stiffened, as if getting ready to press buttons.

Tan must have noticed something. She said, "You have an unorthodox comment to make. Please, grace us with your wisdom."

Yakov nodded as his right hand inched away from the armrest buttons. "If Athena Station is cyborg-controlled, that would mean the War Council has ceased to exist."

"Continue," said Tan.

"If that is true, you and any delayed strategists would constitute the new War Council. Possibly, you are the new Chief Strategist."

"Mutiny," Octagon whispered. His hand dropped to his belted palm-pistol.

Yakov swiveled around. "I have appealed to the highest authority aboard the *Descartes*, Arbiter. Mutiny occurs when the lower-ranked seeks to strip his or her superior of authority."

"Athena Station logged a direct order to the *Descartes*," Octagon said. "You seek to contravene that order. That is mutiny."

"Strategist Tan supercedes military command," Yakov said.

"She does not supercede the War Council. It has logged a direct order for her." Octagon dipped his head toward Tan. "You shine in authority, Exalted One. But the War Council—"

"Is not here," said Tan. "It might well be infested with cyborgs as the Force-Leader suggests."

"Surely you do not accept the barbarian's outlandish story," Octagon said.

"Have a care, Arbiter," Tan warned.

"Exalted One," Octagon said, straightening behind his monitor-board. "I fear I must protest. While I hold your authority in supreme—"

"No more," said Tan. She drew a shiny rod from her jacket, aiming it at Octagon. "You will leave your palm-pistol on the monitor and take your myrmidons to their chamber. There you shall await my word."

Octagon blinked. Then he scowled. "I wish to state article five of the governing—"

"If you continue flaunting my authority," Tan said, "I shall terminate you. Either obey me or die. The choice is yours."

With a jerky motion, Octagon unclipped his palm-pistol and hooked it to the monitor-board. Without glancing right or left and with his chin high, Octagon marched out of the command center, with the two myrmidons trailing him, growling to each other.

After the Arbiter had left, Tan glanced at Yakov. The Force-Leader dropped his gaze. Frowning, the elfin Strategist sheathed her shiny rod.

The seconds passed. Finally, she asked, "What do you propose?"

"I wish to test Representative Kluge's assertion," Yakov said.

"How so?"

"In the most direct manner possible. We will head to the damaged dreadnaught and see what sort of survivors we find."

"Which is dire mutiny," Tan said, "as it is in direct disobedience against logged Athena Station orders."

"Perhaps you could give me new orders," Yakov said softly.

"You heard the Arbiter. The War Council has given me its orders."

"Exalted One," Yakov said, "you've already pointed out that the War Council might no longer exist. Given such a possibility...."

"Speak your thoughts," Tan said.

"If cyborgs control the War Council, shouldn't we resist rather than meekly accept defeat?"

Tan studied the screen showing the drifting pod. Finally, she faced Marten.

The force of her eyes, Marten found himself drawn to them. Green eyes, exotic features, a tiny but feminine body. What would it be like to hold her?

"You are evidence of some unknown peculiarity," Tan said. "It is slim evidence for your outlandish statements. But the possibility of cyborgs, the consequent loss of Jupiter and our superior way of life—I have new orders for you, Force-Leader."

"I await them," said Yakov.

"Let us establish the fate of the *Rousseau.*"

## 9

Marten, Omi and Osadar endured the ship's acceleration in the closet-sized holding cell.

Marten had asked that his friends be released, but the distrust of Osadar ran high. Not wanting to leave them in a cell alone, he'd asked to share their confinement. He wished to assure his friends that events moved in their favor, or so he'd told Tan.

Thankfully, the pressing Gs were of short duration, and weightlessness returned. According to Yakov, they were several days from the dreadnaught. The *Rousseau's* velocity had taken the damaged vessel away from the location of the attack and the pod had traveled away in the opposite direction for many days.

While in the holding cell, both Marten and Osadar agreed that some cyborgs would have survived the *Mayflower's* detonation. The rugged dreadnaught design, the voice signals earlier and cyborg durability all suggested it.

In low tones, Marten told them what had occurred in the Arbiter's quarters and in the command room. Then he asked Osadar what point Octagon had been making by saying he was the only one from Callisto.

"Those of Callisto follow the Dictates closer than anyone else in the system," Osadar said. "Governors, arbiters and almost all force-leaders are from there. They distrust the others for good reason and code weapons on that basis."

"Meaning what?" Marten asked.

"Hammer-guns will not fire when aimed at myrmidons, arbiters or governors. The palm-pistol you spoke about would not fire against the Strategist. Also, the palm-pistol is likely imprinted to Octagon's pattern. Only he could shoot it. The Strategist's rod operates on similar principles."

"Knives would work against them," Omi said.

Osadar shook her head. "I could defeat the myrmidons barehanded. No one else aboard ship, including you two, would have a chance against them. They are incredibly strong, fast, well-trained and genetically superior to men."

"It seems such gene-warping would go against the Dictates," Marten said.

"The opposite is true."

"So what are these Dictates?"

"There are many gradations concerning them." Osadar shook her head. "None of that matters now. It would be more useful for you to learn the nature of the ranks. Highest are the philosophers: the rulers, governors and probationary agents such as arbiters. They have the greatest experience, the most virtue—"

"What does that mean?" Marten asked. "The most virtue? Does that mean someone like Tan never has sex?"

Osadar regarded him with her nearly expressionless gaze. "Ruling is politics. According to the Dictates, it is an art. Just as few have the skills or aptitude to become surgeons, so only a few can make good rulers. A surgeon is trained for many years. He must have a steady hand and the correct equipment. A ruler must have the right aptitude, a good education and then he must have virtue: honesty, integrity and a rational mind. A ruler by necessity must have been steeped in the tenets of the examined life."

"Does Yakov captain the ship?" Marten asked.

"He is a guardian, a soldier, a man of action or spirit."

"What's *that* mean? Spirit?"

"The Dictates divides humanity into three classes," Osadar said. "It divides them according to their primary motivation. The lowest class is the man of appetites or base desires. To fill his belly, to have sex and other basic wants drive him more than any other need. Artisans make up the large majority of humanity, and they belong to this stratum. Aboard ship, those are the mechanics, engineers and technicians.

"The second class is composed of men and women of spirit or courage. They are the fighters, the warriors. In the Jovian System, they join the Guardian Fleet and the various police agencies on the moons and asteroids. The smallest class is composed of those who are devoted to reason. They are the rulers, the governors and arbiters."

"So Yakov is a guardian, belonging to the second class?"

"Yes, although the classes are graded more finely than that," Osadar said.

Marten considered these ranks. "Are arbiters like political officers?"

"No. Arbiters ensure that people conform to the Dictates and that everyone lives a temperate life."

Marten couldn't help but think about Tan's eyes, her face and body, the way she moved. Was she temperate?

*I've been in space too long. I need a woman.*

There was a clang at the hatch then.

Osadar put a titanium-reinforced hand on Marten's wrist. It seemed much too skeletal. Hydraulics moved her knees, ankles, wrists and fingers. Many of her movements caused slight *whirring* noises.

Osadar lowered her plasti-flesh lips near Marten's ear. "The Arbiter and Strategist are both from Callisto. That is the key. Yakov and his crew are from Ganymede and Europa."

The hatch began to swing open.

"Those of Ganymede yearn for the leadership, which has been denied them from the beginning. The highest of Callisto suppresses—"

"You are to come with us, Representative Kluge." The hatch was open and the stern-faced ship-guardian of earlier looked down at them. She held a hammer-gun beside her leg, not aiming it at them, but clearly ready to do so. Others were behind her, equally armed and wearing blue uniforms.

"What about us?" Omi asked. "When do we get out?"

"You will be allowed to exercise later," the ship-guardian said. "For now, you must show restraint."

"Where are you taking me?" Marten asked. He floated upright in the cell.

"Force-Leader Yakov would like to query you again." Before Marten could answer, the ship-guardian grabbed his arm and yanked him out of the holding cell. The woman propelled him to the others. Then the ship-guardian slammed the hatch shut, spinning the wheel to lock it.

Clearly, they feared Osadar. It was a healthy emotion. But it wasn't going to help him get Osadar out of there.

\*\*\*

The ship-guardians marched Marten through a narrow passageway. Slender doors flanked each other on both sides.

"This is the officer's quarters," the ship-guardian said. She halted before the end cubbyhole and pressed a toggle. The door slid open.

"Enter," the ship-guardian said. She leaned near as Marten passed by. "Remember, we shall be outside, standing guard."

Marten entered a small room. Yakov sat behind a minuscule desk that nearly spanned the room's width. A muscled statuette sat on a miniature rock, with his chin resting on his fist as he thought deeply.

There was a stool before the desk. A few vidshots were on the walls showing a small woman and two children in various acts of play. The woman was pretty, the children a boy and girl with blond hair. One shot showed a young and intense Yakov with a hussade stick in his hands standing among a team of serious-eyed players. Those in front lofted a silver trophy.

"Your wardroom?" asked Marten.

Yakov sent down a computer stylus and examined Marten in his same stoic manner as earlier in the command center. "Time is our enemy, Representative. We will therefore forgo pleasantries and speak about realities."

Marten glanced at the hussade vidshot again. There was the essence of Yakov, he decided, before it had become hidden by age and responsibilities.

"How many times have you faced these cyborgs?"

Marten sketched his original meeting with Osadar and the raid later into Mons Olympus, the raid that had ended at the orbital fighter and his liftoff from the Red Planet.

73

Yakov listened intently, occasionally jotting notes onto his computer screen. After Marten had finished, the Force-Leader asked, "You are a soldier, isn't that what you said before?"

"Highborn-trained."

"You were in the Free Earth Corps?"

"You've heard of them?"

"We monitor Inner Planets news, yes."

"Have you ever heard of the *Bangladesh*?"

"I have priority one concerning space-combat intelligence," Yakov said.

"And that means what exactly?"

A faint smile touched the Force-Leader's lips. "The *Bangladesh* was an experimental beamship that attacked the Mercury Sun-Factory. The Highborn attempted to hijack it."

"I'm among the two sole survivors of the hijacking," Marten said. "The other is vegetating in one of your holding cells."

"You were in Free Earth Corps *and* space-combat trained?"

"The space-combat training was my reward for excellence in the Japan Campaign."

"The reference fails me," said Yakov.

"It doesn't matter other than this: I've fought in the hellholes, both on Earth and in space. I fought on Mars and helped the Planetary Union against Social Unity."

"Essentially then, you are of guardian class?"

"You're forgetting my Mars Union credentials."

"On the contrary, Representative, I have carefully listened to everything you've said." Yakov seemed to measure him as he would a hussade goal. "By your own admission, you betrayed the Highborn, your sponsors."

"I prefer to say that I got tired of being a slave."

The faint smile reappeared on Yakov's lips. There was something feral about it this time. "Why do you believe the cyborgs have infiltrated the War Council and Athena Station?"

"Why as in what is their reasoning for doing it or why as in how did I arrive at my conclusion?"

"The latter," said Yakov.

"Because you were ordered away from the damaged dreadnaught," Marten said. "And because cyborgs controlled

74

the *Rousseau*. Now that I think about it, Osadar said there was a ninety percent probability that your ship was cyborg-controlled."

"Her statement is obviously false."

"Not if Athena Station is cyborg-controlled and they sent you orders."

"Clever reasoning," said Yakov. He reached into his black uniform and withdrew two colored disks. He set the disks on his desk, sliding them back and forth with his fingers. Possibly, it was a nervous gesture. "Your deprogrammed cyborg strikes me as durable. What is your analysis concerning our common enemy?"

"If I understand your question right," Marten said, "I think that some of the cyborgs survived the *Mayflower's* detonation. You're heading into terrible danger."

"You believe that some of the dreadnaught's armaments are intact?"

"I wouldn't bet against it. And I'd be ready for vacc-suited cyborgs trying to storm their way aboard your ship."

"You suggest I shoot any survivors attempting to reach the *Descartes*?"

"You're a rational man," Marten said.

Yakov raised a slender hand. "I am a soldier-guardian. I do not attempt to rise above my class."

"Force-Leader, let's cut the crap."

Yakov waited, remaining stoic. Marten wasn't fooled anymore, not after seeing the picture of the intense young Yakov with the hussade stick and trophy.

"Why ask me all these questions?" Marten said. "You know what to do. Go in firing lasers, missiles or particle beams if you have them. Kill anything that moves. If you don't, you risk losing your ship and possibly your lives. Worse, you risk capture and conversion."

Yakov slid the colored disks back and forth. "Your credentials are from Mars. I must therefore assume you've been briefed about our Confederation."

"No. There was no time for that."

"That strikes me as illogical."

"War and emergencies seldom lend themselves to logic," Marten said.

Yakov put the colored disks back into a pocket. "Tell me, Representative. What do you think the cyborgs hope to gain in our system?"

"I have no idea."

Yakov studied Marten. "You might be interested to know that I have hailed the *Rousseau*. They refused to answer. Later I detected ship transmissions to Athena Station. As curious, a gel-cloud hides the vessel from our passive sensor arrays. Why would they deploy such gels if they were stricken?"

Marten shrugged.

"You claim ignorance concerning our Confederation. Therefore, you are likely unaware of the philosophic purity of our rulers." Yakov glanced at the statuette on his desk. "I am from Ganymede, meaning that I am a realist instead of a philosopher. I fear that our Strategist will make critical blunders once we reach the *Rousseau*."

"Who controls the ship-guardians?" Marten asked.

Yakov looked up sharply. "I've studied the Mars Campaign. The cyborgs are ruthless and deadly to an inhuman degree. This is no time for philosophers, but for a realist who sees what is and acts decisively in the critical moment. You heard the endless babble in the command chamber." Yakov shook his head. "I must lead the *Descartes* into battle, not Tan or Octagon."

"Your ship-guardians must understand that."

"How little you know," Yakov murmured. "If I move openly, it might unleash the Secessionist—" The Force-Leader scowled. "This is a time for unity, not division. However, I'm certain the philosophers will dither and argue until the cyborgs have captured everything. In my heart, I believe this is the moment to act. Yet too many of the crew will hesitate or even turn against me if I attempt what needs doing."

"That's why you need me, isn't it?"

"Explain," said Yakov.

"Where are my weapons?"

"Ah, I see. You realize that our hammer-guns will not fire on the myrmidons. Octagon also realizes such a thing. He has

76

already confiscated your hand weapons from the security locker. I suspect he has inspected them and wears one now in lieu of his lost palm-pistol. That was a propitious moment, a rare occurrence, when the Strategist disarmed him. I should have acted then."

"Osadar could defeat the myrmidons for you."

Yakov shook his head. "I distrust *all* cyborgs."

Marten hesitated. Then he blurted, "Let Omi and me do it."

Yakov studied him, before shaking his head again. "The myrmidons would slaughter you two."

"I don't think you understand. Omi and I survived the Japan Campaign and took advanced Highborn-training on the Sun-Works Factory. Give us vibroknives and you'll see what two ex-shock troopers can do."

"I'm afraid we have no vibroknives."

"Force blades?" asked Marten.

"I can give you knives, which mean nothing at all against myrmidons. Ordinary men cannot defeat them."

Marten frowned. He'd seen them, had felt their grip. The myrmidons were tough, but they hadn't seemed like supermen. Just how good were they? He said, "Lend us your most trustworthy ship-guardians as backup."

Yakov looked away. It was a subtle thing, but he seemed worried. After a time, he said, "In cadet school, I was captain of our hussade team. We won the Ganymede Star. Even after our victory, the stylists insisted that ours was the inferior team. And they were right."

Marten watched the Force-Leader. "How did you win?"

"By risking everything and rushing the pedestal. It was a mad gamble, but it gave us victory. And it gave me this command slot." Yakov swept his fingers through his silver hair. "I'll risk everything again, this time on a mad rush to kill the myrmidons and gain control of my ship. Otherwise, philosophic fools will kill us all."

Yakov picked up the stylus. "I'll show you the ship's layout. Then you must help me pick the ambush site."

Marten nodded, realizing he was in it now.

77

## 10

Gharlane of Neptune, the prime cyborg of the stealth-assault, stood in his favorite chamber on Athena Station. The station was on a medium-sized, asteroid-like moon. In orbital proximity, its closest companion was Callisto.

Gharlane dressed in Jovian styles, with a governor's red uniform. He was large and robotic: polished metal merged with plasti-flesh parts and a face capable of only minimal expression. His eyes were golden-metal orbs that moved smoothly in black plastic sockets.

Gharlane didn't smile, although a strange serenity filled him. His favorite chamber contained the newest in holographic imagery. It showed Jupiter in the center, with the important moons in their orbits and bright pinpoints representing the major warships in the system. Red pinpoints were dreadnaughts, yellow were meteor-ships and blue were clusters of patrol boats. There were fifteen capital ships in the system, fifteen dreadnaughts and meteor-ships.

Gharlane moved through the various holo-images, feeling majestic, akin to a god. His left shoulder passed through holographic Jupiter and he eyed Io, turned and passed a hand through icy Europa.

Gharlane understood that the Jupiter Web-Mind—his master—did not approve of these emotions or his present actions. The Web-Mind only allowed them for a precise reason. To eradicate the emotions that compelled these actions might well eradicate Gharlane's higher *genius* functions.

Gharlane was all too aware that after the successful conclusion of the stealth-assault he would have to go under the psycho-scanner. It was unavoidable, and he accepted the inevitably. However, that was a time far in the future. For now, he focused on a holographic image of Athena Station.

"Zoom in," he said.

Athena expanded before him. The surface was brightly lit, with hundreds of low domes, towers, antenna-clusters, sensor stations and interferometers. There were repair docks, supply depots, laser bunkers, and missile sites. It also had girders dug into rock, stretching into space and attached to various spacecraft.

Athena Station had been the heart of the Guardian Fleet and the second most heavily defended location in the Jovian System. The defense satellites around Callisto and the laser bunkers on the surface were considered three times as powerful as the weaponry on Athena.

In the last few months, a non-Jovian installation had been added. It was buried half a kilometer under the surface and it churned throughout the cycles. Horrified, naked, freshly-scrubbed humans entered the complex on a conveyer. After a thorough tearing down and intricate rebuilding, shiny new cyborgs exited the machine. These cyborgs then joined the ongoing campaign.

Unfortunately, the conversion process was too slow, and they had failed to achieve the timetable set for them by the Prime Web-Mind in the Neptune System. The problems had begun several months ago, as the stealth-capsules entered the system. A zealous Force-Leader had burnt two of the seven capsules and damaged three others. The Jovian Force-Leader had almost ended the Jupiter Assault before it had commenced. The same Force-Leader presently captained the *Rousseau*, but as a converted cyborg known as CR37.

"Resume normal imaging," Gharlane said.

The holographic of Athena Station became a small dot again in the greater Jupiter System.

Before Gharlane could give another command, a panel in the wall opened. He turned and regarded two basic-type cyborgs.

They were taller than he was, with elongated torsos. Each was a composite of flesh, steel, plastic and graphite bones. Each had been a Jovian less than four months ago. They had dead eyes now, incurious eyes, with immobile features.

"Yes?" Gharlane asked.

"The Web-Mind wishes an immediate link," the foremost cyborg said in a mechanical voice.

Gharlane was aghast. He had suppressed an impulse from the Web-Mind. Now he noticed a blinking red pinpoint. It represented the *Rousseau*. Obviously, the Web-Mind had sent these two to check on him.

Gharlane opened his internal link. Immediately, the two cyborgs departed and the panel closed.

"I will run a self-evaluation," Gharlane told the Web-Mind. They spoke via a tight-link radio-signal.

*You must not spend any more time in the holographic command room,* the Web-Mind told him.

"Noted," said Gharlane.

*The* Descartes *deviates from its heading. It moves toward the disabled dreadnaught.*

"I have already ordered the *Hobbes* to the disabled ship," Gharlane said.

*Our vessel will not arrive until much later. And one-to-one combat ratios are poor odds. Send... the two nearest patrol boats in conjunction with the* Hobbes.

"I wish to point out," said Gharlane, "that there is a high probability that members of the *Mayflower's* crew reached the *Descartes*."

*The bearing on combat ratios—*

"The files show that the *Mayflower* is from Mars, containing survivors from the latest conflict there. They have shown high survival capabilities."

*The combat ratios—*

"Battle is not all ratios and mathematical computations. There is a chaos factor involved."

*Metaphysical ramblings are further indication of anomalies, Cyborg Gharlane. That bodes ill for your continued use.*

"I use logic to deduce factors beyond my perception," Gharlane explained. "Metaphysics has no bearing on that. Continual success against the odds indicates high-level chaos factors. I will order the *Hobbes* to rendezvous with the *Kepler*. Together, they will engage and overcome the enemy meteor-ship."

*That will delay the engagement with the* Descartes. *You thereby risk losing the remnants of the dreadnaught. We need the crews and we need the vessels, particularly the engines.*

"Your objection is noted. And I have reevaluated the situation as we've talked. My conclusions have changed. Our presence has already likely been discovered. We must switch from stealth tactics to first-strike attacks. Let the crippled *Rousseau* do what it can against the approaching ship. I will use our two meteor-ships with others on a mass strike against Callisto. We must assault the heavily-guarded planetoid before their guardians are alerted."

*You are premature. We should continue to subvert the Guardian Fleet.*

"The meteor-ship heading for the *Rousseau* indicates the Jovians know about our presence. Thus, stealth no longer aids but hinders us. It is time for massive strikes."

*Negative.*

"If you will examine—"

*Further argumentation will push your anomalies to rogue-level status. You will undergo immediate and full systems overhaul.*

Gharlane hesitated for a fraction of a millisecond. Then he said, "The two meteor-ships will unite and defeat the *Descartes*. Any survivors there will face interrogation and conversion as we continue with the stealth assault."

*That is acceptable. On another matter, the cyborg converter needs....*

As the Web-Mind continued to communicate with him, Gharlane glanced around the darkened room. The red pinpoint of light indicating the *Rousseau* blinked wildly. He wanted to remain and walk through the holographic Jupiter System like a divine being. With something akin to a sigh, Gharlane headed for the panel. They should strike Callisto now. He knew it was the wiser course. But the controlling Web-Mind held the final decision. He would prefer to launch missiles at this meteor-ship, but the vessel's crew would detect the missiles and broadcast the attack throughout the system. No. A close approach by other warships was still the best way to capture the enemy vessel and crew.

Gharlane paused. Maybe there was a third way. Yes, he needed to consider this carefully.

## 11

Omi rolled his shoulders. "A gun would be better."

"If you'd rather go back and sit in the cell with Osadar…" Marten said.

"No," Omi said. "I started with knives." He gripped a stainless steel blade with a razor's edge on one side and a deadly point on the end.

They floated down a hall, moving toward the myrmidon chamber. Ten feet behind them were three Jovians. They were smaller men, but tough-looking and determined, if scared.

Ship personnel had received face-to-face orders to report to their station or remain locked in their sleep quarters. It meant the passageways were clear. According to Yakov, Octagon, his myrmidons and Tan had not received such orders.

"You remember Stick?" asked Omi.

"I'll never forget him."

Omi grunted. "Stick and Turbo, they were loony, but good in a bad spot. Stick loved his knives. He was an artist with a blade. I never viewed knives as he did. They're a tool. A gun is a better tool. But before I became a gunman, I used to cut people for Big Arni."

"Surely Highborn knife-tactics are superior to whatever you did in Sydney."

"Yeah," Omi said. "But you always remember your first kill. It's like laying your first girl. You never forget."

Marten's nostrils expanded. Omi was nervous, which was a bad sign. Osadar had been telling Omi about the myrmidons. Facing gene-improved killers didn't sound like a life-extending action. But they'd killed Highborn before. He'd killed a shuttle-full of them through sneaky tactics. That would be the best way to kill the myrmidons. The problem was the myrmidons always expected trouble.

Marten blew out his cheeks as his stomach fluttered. It was a bad feeling. He tried to make himself angry. The myrmidons had collared him, allowing Octagon to shock him many times.

"Yeah," Marten whispered, his grip tightening on the knife-handle.

"You say something?"

Marten shook his head.

They floated around a corner. Down the companionway, he could see the region of the ship with red and white hall colors. It made Marten's stomach churn.

"Two on one," he said. "They're fast—"

"I know what to do," Omi hissed. "Zero-G fighting, the crazy way." He hefted his knife. "A gun would be better, or our needlers."

"Octagon has them."

Omi wiped the back of knife-hand across his mouth. Then he took out a small device, holding it in his free hand.

Marten signaled the three Jovians. They curled against the wall and gave him a thumbs-up sign. Marten pushed down to the floor, curling up in a fetal ball, trying to wedge himself at the junction of the wall and floor padding. Omi did the same thing. The Jovians were in position.

"Now," Marten whispered.

Omi clicked the device.

Three seconds later, the meteor-ship's engines engaged. After five seconds of thrust, the engines cut out, returning weightlessness to the *Descartes*.

"Let's do it," Marten said, shooting for the red and white part of the hall.

A klaxon rang. Yakov's voice sounded over the ship's intercoms. "All hands, report damage and injuries to the proper authorities. Then tighten yourselves for further ship maneuvering."

Marten aimed an override unit at the door. It was one of Yakov's achievements to have gained the needed code.

Nothing happened.

Marten scowled and tried again, clicking the button.

The door swished open. Omi shot through. Marten followed and the Jovians hurried to catch up. The chamber was three times the size of Yakov's wardroom. It contained exercise pulleys and a sparing automaton. A myrmidon tore his arm out of a pulley's wires, with blood welling and floating around him. He must have smashed into the wires during the short acceleration. There was no sign of the second myrmidon.

The squat man snarled as his dark eyes gleamed with murder-lust. Omi leapt. The Korean had always been the best at zero-G combat. With his free hand, Omi grabbed the myrmidon. The trick was to lock onto an enemy, anchoring for the knife thrust. If one *just* thrust, he cut minimally and ended up shoving himself away because of the third law of motion.

Omi tried for a leg lock. The bleeding myrmidon struck a savage blow, sending Omi spinning against a wall. Fortunately, the Korean kept hold of his knife and he stayed conscious.

"Attack together!" Marten shouted.

The Jovians flew at the myrmidon, with their free hands outstretched. Their knives were tucked protectively near their chests.

Three seconds later, Marten understood why everyone said myrmidons were unbeatable. The squat man had freed himself and moved with sublime grace. He used his long arms to grabble the first Jovian as he wrapped his legs around the Jovian's torso. The myrmidon savagely twisted the man's head. Neck bones snapped. Then the myrmidon was letting go as a knife slashed his side. The myrmidon hissed as he put a hand behind a Jovian's head and punched with the other, crushing cartilage and breaking teeth.

Then Omi attacked from behind, thrusting his knife into the kidney zone. The myrmidon howled and hurled the broken Jovian from him. He spun and might have slain Omi.

But Marten had been waiting for something like that. As the myrmidon whirled, Marten pushed himself leg-first at the killer. He wrapped around the myrmidon's torso as the killer struck Omi a devastating blow. Marten forewent style and knife-fighting theory. With two hands, he plunged the heavy blade into the myrmidon's back. The myrmidon snarled, trying to twist around. Instead, he merely rotated Marten and himself as Marten yanked out the blade and plunged it in again. He did it a third time, hacking at the squat neck. It was like trying to cut gristle.

The myrmidon grabbed Marten's foot and twisted. Marten bellowed, and he stabbed into the killer's back. He rotated the blade, probing for a vital organ.

The myrmidon sagged as blood pumped from him. The door at the end of the room swung open then. The second myrmidon appeared, with only a cloth around his waist.

"Flee!" Marten gasped.

Omi's face was puffy, with one of his eyes swollen shut. All three Jovians floated in the room, either dead or unconscious.

The myrmidon snarled as his muscles bunched. Omi shot out of the first door. Marten followed. In less than a second, each braced himself against the junction of floor and wall.

"Now!" shouted Marten.

Omi clicked his device, the one linked to Yakov. As the myrmidon hurtled after them, the ship's engines engaged with terrific thrust. It brought pseudo-gravity to the ship. As before, it quit in three seconds.

Marten and Omi shot back into the chamber. The squat killer had hit his head against a bulkhead. He was dazed, but far from out.

Marten and Omi attacked. In a savage brawl lasting fifteen seconds, they took horrible buffets. In return, they killed the second myrmidon.

"We can't stop now," panted Marten, as he drew his knife out of the inert corpse.

Omi spit a globule of blood that wobbled in the weightlessness. His face was horribly bruised, and he could barely peer out of the least swollen eye. One of his arms dangled because the myrmidon had yanked it out of the socket.

"Wait," Omi whispered. He let go of the bloody knife so it floated. Then he grabbed his arm, clenched his teeth and shoved his shoulder into place. He groaned, but instead of complaining, he grabbed the knife and nodded to indicate he was ready.

Marten's ribs ached and he could hardly move his head because his neck hurt.

"Octagon has our needlers, right?" Omi asked.

Marten grunted a monosyllable answer.

They floated out of the chamber and toward Octagon's room.

Marten was surprised Octagon hadn't come charging to help his myrmidons. The Arbiter either believed they could handle the situation or he was too frightened by the ship's sudden acceleration and Yakov's warning that further maneuvering would take place.

"He can kill us both in seconds with that gun," Omi whispered.

Marten reversed his grip, holding the point. During shock trooper training, he'd gained some efficiency hurling knives.

Omi tensed as he used the override unit. The door swished open. Each stood to the side. They glanced at each other across the open door, showing their surprise. Octagon should have fired warning shots.

Marten steeled his nerves and glanced into the room. He would only throw after assessing the situation. He laughed.

Octagon floated unconscious. Either the first or the second surprise thrust had rendered him helpless.

Marten rushed in, keeping his knife ready, in case Octagon was trying to fake them. He tore a Gauss needler from a holster at Octagon's side—it was his own gun from the Mars System. Marten checked the charge. It was fully loaded. Too bad they hadn't hit Octagon's room first. Three Jovians would still be alive then.

The Arbiter groaned.

"Close the door," Marten said.

As Omi hurried to comply, Marten searched the Arbiter, extracting what could possibly be dangerous devices. Then a thought struck.

"Hurry to the myrmidons," he told Omi. "Search their uniforms for any hidden devices."

"What sort of devices?"

"Something keeps hammer-guns from firing. If we can find those and put them on ourselves—"

"Right," Omi said. He headed out.

Marten kept searching. He found a gray disk attached to the Arbiter's stomach. Marten peeled it off.

Omi returned shortly, holding two similar gray disks.

"Was it on their stomachs?" Marten asked.

Omi nodded.

Marten ripped open drawers. He found Omi's needler and a hammer-gun. "Take this," he said, giving Omi the hammer-gun. "Then put a disk on a dead myrmidon and see if the gun shoots or not."

"Does it shoot now?" Omi asked.

Marten aimed it at a bulkhead and pulled the trigger. The gun jerked in his hand as a heavy pellet dented the wall.

"It works," Marten said.

Omi took it and hurried out again.

Marten continued to search the Arbiter's desk. He discovered a monitor-board that showed areas of the ship. He moved toggles and heard voices from those areas. This was a spy-board.

Omi returned, with a grin on his puffy, bruised face. "I attached the disk to a corpse, aimed and pulled the trigger. Nothing happened. I backed up and tried it again. Again nothing. Then I aimed at the other corpse and put a hole in him. These work. Or they make it so the hammer-guns don't work."

"Put one on," Marten said, as he attached a disk to his stomach. "We'll give Osadar the last one."

"She's still in the cell."

"We're breaking her out."

"Your new friends aren't going to like that," Omi said.

"Yakov will stay happy," Marten said. "We'll remove Tan and give him control of his own ship."

"He might turn on us after we give him what he wants."

Marten pondered that. This desk, this room, might contain more surprises. "Okay. You have a point. This is going to be our headquarters. One of us must always be here, monitoring the crew." Marten explained what he'd discovered.

"Got it," Omi said. "What do we do with him?"

Marten studied the unconscious Arbiter. "Tie him tight like a hostage. Then figure out this desk better, particularly the audio-feeds throughout the ship. I'll get Osadar."

"You'd better hurry."

"I know. Surprise and speed are two of a soldier's best weapons. I was listening that day." Marten headed for the hall.

## -12-

Marten steeled his resolve as he floated ahead of Osadar. He would have liked to talk with Tan, get to know her better as he studied her exotic features. The woman stirred him. Was that because he had been cooped up with Osadar and Omi for nearly a year? Or was it because he genuinely found the Strategist exciting?

Tan made muffled, protesting sounds.

Marten scowled. Was he doing the right thing?

Osadar cradled Tan like a small child, with a titanium hand clamped over the woman's pretty mouth. Osadar had proven faster than the Strategist, who had tried to draw her shiny rod as they'd entered her quarters. Now cyborg strength proved overpowering against the small woman's muscles.

Marten floated ahead of them. He had out his Gauss needler, but he hoped to achieve this without killing any of Yakov's crew. He'd chosen to deal from strength, and by freeing Osadar he might have chosen wrongly. But an apropos Highborn maxim said to make your decisions decisively. Even if it was the wrong decision, it was better to be bold about it than to hesitate. It made no sense to let qualms guide him, not with the dreaded cyborgs loose in the Jupiter System. Gilded philosophies meant nothing against graphite bones and tanglers. He needed plasma cannons and fusion-driven lasers.

Fortunately, the narrow corridors were still empty.

Marten holstered his needler and unclipped a medkit. Soon, he hefted a pneumospray hypo. It held Suspend, a drug that

90

slowed biological functions. It was a perfect drug for the badly injured, organ-thieves and kidnappers.

They reached the holding cell. Marten typed in the code and turned the wheel. With a noisy *thump*, he opened the hatch and turned around.

Tan stared at him above Osadar's metal hand. She stared with a mixture of fear, rage and indignation. She looked small and helpless in Osadar's skeletal arms. She looked beautiful.

Marten scowled as he rolled up one of Tan's sleeves. "Your philosophies will get us all killed. I know, because I've fought the cyborgs before. This will knock you out for a time," he said, showing her the hypo. "Afterward, we will revive you. You will live, and hopefully the cyborgs will have been destroyed by that time."

Tan made muffled sounds against Osadar's hand, and she squirmed, or she tried. With a *whirr* of sound, Osadar tightened her grip. Tan cast an accusatory look at Osadar and another at Marten.

"This gives me no joy," Marten muttered. He pressed the hypo against the Strategist's pale skin. Air hissed.

Tan made a louder muffled sound.

Marten turned away as he shook his head. He'd rather be kissing the woman, holding her. But he had to act wisely, and he had to do it now.

"She's out," Osadar said.

"Put her in the cell."

Osadar laid her down, using restraints to secure the limp woman so she wouldn't injure herself during acceleration.

Marten shut the hatch, turned the wheel and reset the code to one only he knew. Now—

"We are making a mistake," Osadar said.

Marten cocked an eyebrow.

"I am a cyborg and Omi and you are shock troopers. We three could gain control of the ship for ourselves."

"That's a bit ambitious."

"We could achieve it nonetheless."

"Then what?" asked Marten.

"Then we have a capable military vessel under our control."

"We three would have to fix all damage, ensure the fusion engine remained—"

"We would keep a skeleton crew," Osadar said.

"We could never trust them."

"Trust would not be the issue, but effective control."

"Omi, you and me—"

"Highborn methods could achieve control," Osadar said.

"Maybe," Marten said. "Yakov is a sly man. I'd hate to have him plotting against me."

"We would have to drug him as you have Tan."

"Again," Marten asked, "to what end?"

"Escape to Saturn or Uranus."

Marten chuckled grimly. "I don't see why you think the planetary systems closer to Neptune would have escaped the cyborgs' notice."

"The Jovians have no chance against the cyborg infiltration. That is the issue."

"You keep forgetting Mars," Marten said.

"Doom Stars demolished the Mars Assault. The Jovians have these cramped vessels. We must flee while we can or face certain death."

"Aren't you getting tired of running away?" Marten asked.

"Flight is a primary survival tactic."

"So is fighting. It's time to fight, Osadar. It's time to kick the cyborgs in the teeth. Besides, we're running out of fleeing room. We have a military ship and the hope of others. That means a fleet."

"The cyborgs will have a bigger and better fleet."

"They're plasti-flesh, steel and enhanced bio-brains, but they're not magic. You escaped their programming. The Highborn killed an entire planetary attack force."

"The Highborn are many times superior to the Jovians," Osadar said. "For us, here, I foresee doom."

"When haven't you foreseen doom?"

"We should take possession of the ship and live free for as long as it is possible. Any other choice is unrealistic."

"We damaged the dreadnaught, remember?"

"Through incredible good fortune," Osadar said.

"Wrong!" Marten said. "We outthought and in the end we outfought them. What we've done once, we can repeat."

"You have false hope."

"Isn't that better than full-blown pessimism?"

"No. I am never disappointed by an outcome, because I expect the worst. When events prove beneficial, I am amazingly surprised."

"Wouldn't you agree that by following my plans you've been surprised more often than not?" Marten asked.

Osadar appeared uneasy. "It is tempting fate to answer your question in the positive."

"I need your wholehearted support," Marten said.

"It is still yours."

"I'm glad to hear it. Now let's hurry."

***

"There is a change in plans," Yakov said over the Arbiter's desk-screen.

Marten sat at the desk, with the others out of sight. He had turned the statuette. It now faced him with the upraised arm and the finger pointing nowhere. He'd done it to remind him the Jovians viewed things differently than he did.

By the vidshots on the wall behind Yakov, the man must be in his wardroom. The Force-Leader attempted to look calm, but strain showed on his face.

"A change?" asked Marten.

"I have hailed the *Rousseau* many times. The last time, a Jovian officer answered."

"You actually saw her?" Marten asked.

"I did."

Marten blinked in consternation. "Cyborgs boarded my shuttle. I killed them."

"I have no doubt concerning that."

"But the officer—"

Yakov made an abrupt gesture. "The gel-cloud confirms my suspicion. And that the officer said the ship had a fusion-core leak."

"A human officer aboard the dreadnaught," Marten said. "Are Jovians allied with the cyborgs?"

"I consider that a strong possibility," Yakov said. "One of the lesser moons yearning for freedom from the Dictates may have decided to trust the cyborgs. It complicates matter. Therefore, before walking into a trap, I will send probes." Yakov stared out of the screen. "You have captured the Arbiter?"

"And the Strategist," Marten said.

The skin seemed to stretch across Yakov's face. "I have altered a military pod. The Arbiter will enter it, fly to the *Rousseau* and report to us what lies behind the gel-cloud."

"That will take days."

"There are too many parameters that I do not understand," Yakov said. "Therefore, I will proceed with caution, using probes and fallbacks."

"Why will the Arbiter report anything to you?" Marten asked.

Yakov smiled grimly. "In reality, he will report nothing. The pod's cameras will report."

"So why send the Arbiter?"

"I wish to rid my ship of him, and his 'act of courage' will impress certain of the crew. His coming death will then inspire them, making my military decisions easier."

Marten wondered what the real reasons were, or if Yakov told him the truth. "What if the *Rousseau* frees the Arbiter?"

Yakov shook his head. "I have altered the pod. He will not survive the journey."

Marten glanced at Octagon, trussed from head to toe in black tape. Had the Arbiter heard all that? Or was the man still unconscious?

"You must take him to the pod," Yakov said.

Was the Force-Leader trying to draw him out of the Arbiter's chamber? Did Yakov know he'd freed Osadar?

"Time is critical," Yakov added.

"I'm on my way," said Marten. Then he cut the connection.

***

Marten pushed the mummified Octagon through the companionways. Twice, he passed ship-guardians with hammer-guns. They eyed him closely, although neither they nor he said a word.

94

Omi had trussed Octagon with black tape. It was an old hostage-taking trick. From heel to the crown of his head, Octagon was wrapped with black strands of tape. There was a slit for his mouth and nose so he could breathe. Otherwise, he looked like an ancient Egyptian mummy. Even wrapped tight, Octagon attempted speech.

"Save it," Marten said, pushing against the man's heel, propelling the weightless form toward the pod hanger.

Octagon made more noise.

"Quiet," Marten said, using the butt of his needler to strike Octagon's shin. That brought a groan. "If you insist on speech, I will have to use pain to modify your behavior."

Octagon remained quiet throughout the rest of the journey.

A nervous technician waited by an open hatch, one marked as the entranceway to a pod. The man had stringy hair, bulging eyes and a crumpled gray uniform with grease stains on the left sleeve. He didn't strike Marten as competent or efficient.

"Well?" Marten asked.

"What?" the technician asked.

"You're Yakov's man, aren't you?"

"Y-Yes."

"Did you reconfigure the controls?"

The technician bobbed his head.

"You're sure you know what you're doing?"

That brought the first spark of belligerence to the technician. "Commander, I am eighth ranked among the technical staff, a specialist Diamond Grade in communications and—"

"Good enough," Marten said. "Lead the way."

"Force-Leader Yakov ordered me to—"

"I'm giving you new orders," Marten said, as he waggled the needler. "Do I need to explain to you how shock troopers deal with disobedience?"

The technician's eyes widened with fright. "No, Commander. I obey."

Maybe Yakov was willing to lose a technician to trap a dubious ally in the pod with Octagon, but maybe not. Maybe Yakov meant everything he'd said. Marten hadn't dealt long enough with Jovians to know.

95

"Get shears or scissors and start cutting out the Arbiter," Marten said.

The technician moved as Marten stood guard by the hatch.

Soon, the technician cut busily, starting at the feet as Marten had instructed. The shears made *crunch-crunch* noises, and the technician peeled away tape.

Soon, Octagon's arms were free. He shoved the technician away and peeled the black tape from his face. The various pieces floated in the pod's control module.

"You will rue this, barbarian," Octagon hissed.

Using his needler, Marten waved for the technician to come float near him by the hatch.

The technician hurried to comply.

"I will beg the authorities to give you into my care," Octagon said. "Then you and I shall have long conversations concerning this barbaric display of ingratitude and indignity. The pain you shall receive—"

"Will be nothing compared to the exalted feeling I'm receiving now," Marten said.

"You dare to use such a word? Strategist Tan is *exalted*. Her philosophic heights soar above your wormy existence that you profane the word by uttering it."

"Look at my bare neck, Arbiter. There's no shock collar now. A free man dares whatever he wants."

"Your neck will wear a collar soon enough, rest assured."

"That's how you like it, isn't it? You're not man enough to fight your own battles. You need the myrmidons to terrorize others. Then you sit in safety and press a button to hurt people. You're a deranged sadist, Octagon. But I'll tell you what this barbarian offers. You have a bitter fate waiting for you. Come at me if you desire, and we'll fight."

"Fight like animals?" Octagon sneered.

"Fight however you want to fight," Marten said. "It doesn't matter to me. Trade blows with me and kill me with your bare hands if you're able. In turn, I'll try to kill you barehanded. You won't get a better bargain anywhere. It's more than you offered me."

"So speaks the barbarian elevated only a little higher than the wild beasts. I spit at your offer to tussle like artisans or to wrestle like a myrmidon. I am a refined man, a philosopher."

"You're a cowardly sadist and a hypocrite of the worst sort. But you're still a man. I'll give you that. This is your last offer."

"Bah!"

Marten holstered his needler. "You're headed for the damaged dreadnaught."

Shivering with hatred, Octagon glared at Marten. "You are a fool, barbarian."

"I've been called worse." Marten pursed his lips. "It grates against me offering you advice. You shocked me, and I remember that too well. But you are a man and they're cyborgs. If it looks like they're going to capture you, space yourself."

"Suicide is against the Dictates."

"Yeah, well, it's just advice. You follow your philosophical conscience if you want. I'm just saying, if you want to avoid Osadar's fate, you'll let vacuum kill you fast. Good-bye, Arbiter."

"We shall meet again, barbarian. This I vow by the Dictates."

Marten had an impulse to shoot. He disliked leaving a hated enemy alive who promised vengeance. Maybe it had become too easy these past years killing people. Whatever the case, Marten suppressed his instinct, and he nodded at the technician to leave. The man hastened to exit. Marten glanced once more at the glaring Octagon. Then he, too, took his leave, closing the hatch behind him.

Marten floated into a small chamber connected to the pod hatchways.

Yakov waited there together with five blue-uniformed guardians. Each had a drawn hammer-gun and wore hard expressions.

"You freed the cyborg," Yakov said. "You knew my wishes concerning that. Why did you do it anyway?"

"I needed her help to capture Tan," Marten said.

"What?" asked a ship-guardian, an angry man with flat features and a chin-beard. "What have you done to the Strategist?"

Yakov glanced at the angry man.

"Answer me, barbarian. Where is Strategist Tan?"

"Restrain yourself, Anshan," Yakov said.

"He harmed the Strategist," Anshan said.

"I'm sure she is well."

Anshan squinted suspiciously at Yakov. "Was that your doing, Force-Leader?"

"You will refrain from questioning me."

Anshan reddened, and he tightened the grip on his hammer-gun. "You're avoiding answering me."

"Enough of this," Yakov said. "You must tell me now. Where does your ultimate allegiance lie, with them or us?"

Anshan blinked three times. Lines appeared on his forehead the first time and deepened with each blink. "No!" he shouted. "The barbarian must possess mind-altering powers to have convinced you to harm a strategist, a philosophically pure governor."

"You swore on the Manumission Decree," Yakov told the man.

Anshan violently shook his head. "You're breaking Article Four of the Dictates."

"He is under a compulsion," another ship-guardian whispered. "They tampered with his mind."

Anshan raised his hammer-gun at Marten. "You have defied the Dictates, barbarian." As the others watched in amazement, Anshan pulled the trigger.

Nothing happened.

Anshan's eyes widened so the whites seemed to drown his pupils. He twisted around, aiming the gun at Yakov. "You are party to secession! That is mutiny, which I am sworn to forestall!"

Marten fast-drew. There were crackling sounds as heavy needles broke the sound barrier. Anshan sagged as shock crossed his flat features. Then he slumped down.

The other ship-guardians pushed away from Anshan. One was open-mouthed. Another trembled. A third whispered, "They had a deep plant among us. We're compromised."

The ship-guardians glanced uneasily at one another and then suspiciously eyed Marten.

"I just saved your life," Marten told Yakov.

By a visible effort, Yakov spoke. "Anshan was from Europa. The arbiters are known to use compulsions there. He must have slipped past our auditors, or his compulsion was coded to selected actions."

"We must log this death with Arbiter Station," a ship-guardian said, the tight-faced woman from earlier. She had thin nostrils and a line of a mouth covered with black lipstick. Marten had heard someone call her Pelias earlier. The ring of her gun-hand looked sharp, making it seem as if she enjoyed giving pain.

Yakov made a harsh sound, startling the others. "Each of you took an oath on the Manumission Decree. Does that mean nothing to you?"

"Has the call been broadcast?" Pelias asked. "Are we seceding?"

"You've seen the Mars videos," Yakov said. "The cyborgs are deadly creatures—murderous aliens of inhuman effectiveness. Those creatures have come to our system and likely infiltrated Guardian Fleet warships. Tell me, Pelias Will you trust your life to a philosopher or do you wish for a realist, a man of action like me, to handle the situation?"

Pelias squinted at Marten. "The barbarian released a cyborg."

"That one is deprogrammed," Yakov said. "But you're missing the point. You swore on the Decree."

The fingers of her gun-handed whitened. "Are we seceding?" Pelias asked stubbornly.

Yakov stared at her. "I am taking control of the *Descartes*."

Pelias studied Marten more closely. "Why didn't Anshan's gun work against the barbarian?"

Yakov turned to Marten. "The shock trooper has obviously purloined a nullifier."

"From Strategist Tan or the Arbiter?" Pelias asked.

"Those from Callisto have become our enemies," Yakov said slowly. "Therefore, you shouldn't sound dismayed at their loss of status. Taking a nullifier, it was a tactical move on his part. Notice, he has made no attempt to elevate his status."

"Is that true?" Pelias asked. "It was a tactical move?"

Marten nodded.

Pelias scowled even as she holstered her hammer-gun.

"Go back to your stations," Yakov said. "Await further orders and be ready to act in accord with the Manumission Decree."

Pelias hesitated.

"On this ship," Yakov said, staring at her, "we have seceded."

Pelias's scowl smoothed away. She motioned to the others. They took Anshan's corpse, floating out of the chamber.

After they left, Yakov put his forehead against a bulkhead, squeezing his eyes shut. When he opened his eyes and faced Marten, he said, "I owe you my life."

"You saved ours before by rescuing us from the pod."

Yakov moved away from floating blood globules. He seemed more composed again, more like the Force-Leader in the command room. "You have purloined a nullifier, a cagy move. You have thereby proven yourself even more mentally dexterous and dangerous than I'd expected. That compounds my anxiety regarding you."

"It should make you feel better," Marten said. "We're on the same side, and you need competent help. If more of your crew mutinies, you have soldiers willing to gun them down to bring the others back into line."

"That should ease my anxiety about you?"

"Who else can I turn to but you?" Marten asked. "That ensures my loyalty, which is what you're really worried about."

Yakov pondered that. "Where is the cyborg?"

"In Octagon's former chamber."

"Former?"

"I'm commandeering it," Marten said.

"And no doubt familiarizing yourself with his devices."

"Force-Leader, you strike me as the deadliest Jovian I've met, the one most likely to defeat the cyborgs. I kidnapped the Strategist for you, slew the myrmidons and put the Arbiter aboard the altered pod like you asked. What more can I do to make you trust me?"

"Return the cyborg to the holding cell."

Marten shook his head. "You're going to need Osadar before this is through, especially if cyborgs storm your ship."

Yakov studied the blood globules. "Will you come with me to the command room?"

"By all means," Marten said.

***

Upon entering the command room, Yakov signaled a woman at a module. She climbed out and left the room.

Marten floated to the empty module. It was built for a Jovian person's frame. Aboard the *Mayflower*, everything had been too big, here everything was too small. Marten squeezed into the module and familiarized himself with the vidscreen and controls.

And then, like everyone else, Marten was surprised. The ship gave a noticeable lurch as a large drone detached from it. Around the room, voices said.

"Force-Leader?" someone asked Yakov.

"We're taking precautionary measures, Primary Gunner."

"I must log an objection," the Primary Gunner said. Her name was Rhea.

Rhea spoke from a module across the room from Marten. She had short brunette curls, and her black uniform stretched tightly across her curvaceous figure. A blue medal dangling from a choker around her neck only heightened her loveliness. The choker reminded Marten of Molly and the day he'd gone to see Hall Leader Quirn. He wondered if Rhea kissed as well as Molly had. The Jovian exuded a similar sort of worry. He could hear it in her voice.

"Since the Arbiter has strangely decided to hurry to the *Rousseau*," Rhea said, "the Strategist should be here. We need her authorization to detach any active drones."

"I am logging your objection and your reasoning," Yakov said, who played with the controls on his chair. "Do you have any further clarifications?"

Rhea licked her lips, glanced around the room and dropped her gaze as she noticed Marten staring at her.

"No, Force-Leader," she said.

Yakov nodded in his calm way and went back to studying the main screen.

Marten tore his gaze from her and adjusted his vidscreen. He could now see from cameras on the meteor-ship.

A large Zeno drone had detached from the ship and floated away from them. The drone was long with a bulbous head. Cursive Jovian script decorated the sides. As Marten examined it, the drone fired its chemical engine. With a stabbing orange flame, the drone accelerated away from them and toward the last known location of the *Rousseau*. After a five-minute burn, the Zeno's engine shut-off. The drone had already been a tiny orange dot. Now it winked off and disappeared from the ship's teleoptic sights as it coasted.

There was a critical advantage in space combat with a chemical engine versus a fusion engine. In order to operate a fusion engine had to maintain a continuous reaction. Thus, fusion engines always gave off a faint heat signature and spewed neutrinos. The chemically-fuelled drone could remain cold until needed and thus aided its ability to remain hidden until it ignited again.

Despite its size, the drone was small in stellar scale, hidden by the immensity of space, even the space of the Jupiter System. Interferometer sweeps, a hunt for thermal signatures and electromagnetic pulses would now likely search in vain for it. Radiation from Jupiter and Io's ionized sulfur spewing from its volcanoes only made things more difficult.

In ancient Twentieth Century terms, space combat was often like a submarine captain and his detection crew, with radar, sonar and other technicians grouped together around their highly sensitive equipment. It was often a matter of endless listening and searching, seeking to find the enemy lurking under a cold layer of ocean current. For a variety of reasons, finding hidden drones often proved an order of magnitude more difficult in space than finding torpedoes or submarines in the old days.

There was another lurch to the warship. Yakov must have released another Zeno.

"I am ordering a practice drill," Yakov announced. "We will take this opportunity to engage the *Rousseau* in a war-game maneuver."

"Force-Leader," Rhea said. "I must object and point—"

"For the duration of the drill," Yakov said, "we will assume battle-status. You will therefore refrain from further outbursts, Primary Gunner."

Rhea shifted uneasily, highlighting her figure.

Marten realized he was staring at her again. He forced himself to glance at Yakov.

The Force-Leader studied the main screen. He looked up, and said, "Engine room, be ready to engage the fusion core."

Rhea stared out of her module at Yakov. Her lovely features showed that she was in an agony of spirit. Perhaps she had similar feelings as Anshan. As her shoulders slumped, she turned back to her control board.

Marten wondered if he should attempt to speak with her later. Whatever happened with Octagon and the drones would take days to occur. That was the reality of space combat and the distances such combat entailed.

-14-

Two days passed as Arbiter Octagon glided through the void, seething with indignation. Once again, he inspected his white uniform and the black marks all over it from the tape the barbarians had used on him. Rubbing the marks hadn't helped, but only spread the blackness deeper into the fabric.

Octagon glared at the starry void. How he longed to make Marten Kluge pay. How he longed to hear a shock collar click shut as a myrmidon placed it around the barbarian's neck. By Plato's Bones, he would shock him many times. He would make Marten writhe on the floor. He would ask questions, appear mollified, and then the shocks would begin anew. Marten would howl for mercy. Yes, yes, he would even appear to grant it. Then he would use special myrmidons to perform degrading acts on the barbarian. That would break the man's stubborn will. He would permanently remove the smirk from the Earthman's lips.

Octagon scowled as thrusters rotated his pod. That was new and unexpected. Now Jupiter appeared in the corner of his single polarized window. Once more, as he had for days, he clicked toggles and attempted to regain control of the craft. His efforts had no effect on the thrusters, which increased their power. The acceleration pushed him deeper into the cushioned chair.

Despite the Gs, Octagon reached out and struck the panel. He'd finally reached his breaking point. He swiveled around in the pilot's chair. Now his chest strained against the straps. While choking against the straps, adrenalin gripped him. His thoughts sped up. He wondered as he had before if the others monitored his actions. Were they observing him even now, mocking his display of anger? Were they recording it, to damn him later before the Philosopher's Board on Callisto? He must control himself. He must continue to mask his emotions.

He recited appropriate maxims and thought about the Dictates. Calm, calm, he needed serenity. He closed his eyes. He needed to think, to engage his reason.

Yakov was in on the conspiracy. That explained the *Descartes'* sudden acceleration, the acceleration that had hurled him at one of the walls. The blow had rendered him unconscious. Yes, Yakov had allied with the barbarians. The Secessionist Plot had finally erupted into action. Oh, for months now, he had tried to ferret out their secrets. He had known that Yakov was untrustworthy. No one else had believed him. Even Tan had been fooled. She had wronged him, disarming an arbiter of his palm-pistol in the presence of an enemy barbarian.

Could Tan be in on the plot?

Octagon shook his head. Tan had lived on Callisto most of her life. It was inconceivable the Strategist had thrown in her lot with those of Ganymede. No. It was impossible.

Octagon swiveled back to the control panel. The Gs pressed him into the cushions. His lips were a tight line. He would not let them see him emote. They would witness perfect control. Perhaps he had smote the panel a single time with his fist, but that's all he would give them.

With serenity, he moved toggles and observed their uselessness. Was there some secret way he could reroute the controls and regain use of the pod? A mechanic or a technician would know the answer. He had never sullied himself with such base endeavors before. Trust a barbarian to send him on a flight without any proper crew to accompany him. Why, the barbarian had wanted a display of fisticuffs between them. Marten Kluge had reveled in the degrading offer, as if it proved his manhood. What it had shown instead was the shocking lack of decorum among barbarians. But that wasn't the issue now.

Cyborgs—

Octagon frowned. The barbarian possessed a cyborg. Could the *Rousseau* have cyborgs among its crew? That was such a fantastic proposal that it was laughable.

Hm. Why would Marten Kluge continue in his bizarre deception? Once he reached the dreadnaught—

Octagon's jaw dropped. A bomb! The barbarian had surely planted a bomb in the pod. Or maybe Yakov had inserted one. They were using him as a pawn. They would blow up his pod when it reached the dreadnaught and declare Octagon a casualty of an enemy attack. That would unleash the last restraints on the meteor-ship's crew and possibly on other warships with crews from Ganymede and Europa.

In desperation, Octagon stared at the control panel. He tried the toggles again, and then once more, moving them faster. The cruelly cunning barbarian—Marten Kluge was an animal. Octagon wanted to weep with rage, with fear.

He hated this feeling of helplessness. Oh, if ever he escaped this fate, he would dedicate his life to capturing Marten Kluge and practicing a thousand degradations upon him.

*** 

CR37, the chief cyborg of the crippled *Rousseau,* watched the mass detector. He floated on the emergency bridge, wearing a vacc-suit and helmet. Red lights washed the circular chamber, and the green-glowing detector showed that a pod had broken through the gel-cloud and approached the ship.

An unconditioned human monitored the dreadnaught's board. She was the last of the deception crew, operators used to lure human-controlled warships into docking with ships infested with cyborgs. She had last spoken with a human calling itself Force-Leader Yakov.

The female wore a black uniform, and she had been chosen for her features, which Jovian males considered compelling. She had a pale face, with overlarge eyes and lips thicker than average. She lacked a vacc-suit. Thus, if this chamber were breached, she would die.

CR37 had once been the Force-Leader of the old *Rousseau.* Behind his darkened visor, his features were now like that of any other cyborg. He was inhuman in appearance and reminiscent of a zombie from the horror vids. Like others of his kind, he had been personality-scrubbed and given graphite-bones, motorized strength and cybernetic interfaces.

The ramming shuttle several days ago had been devastatingly effective. It had also alerted special AI routines in him. The AI had detected a spark of personality and run a deep diagnostic. The probe had uncovered a hidden truth. CR37 had unconsciously retained a hint of Jovian System sympathy. It had been a tiny thing, something he'd unconsciously implemented by rerouting certain warship safeguards.

One of those tiny but critical things had occurred with the lowered particle shield and the open bay door. There had been other things like improperly sealed bulkheads, downed firewalls and missing emergency routes. When the enemy shuttle had turned into a fireball, it had created more damage than its attack should have warranted. Within the dreadnaught, point-defense ammunition had ignited, multiplying the damage.

Now, the *Rousseau* was a shell of its former self. Despite the damage, the ship was still a dreadnaught, meaning it was more powerful than a meteor-ship. It possessed heavy particle shielding, unlike smaller vessels. Much of that shielding was still in place. Unfortunately, the hull behind the shielding had been ruptured in a hundred places. The missile tubes were worthless. The last, operational laser was under repairs, and the magnetic guns were hopelessly mangled. The dreadnaught had point-defense cannons, however, many of them. And it would soon have minimal motive power. Several complements of cyborgs had survived the devastating explosions, and they affected repairs.

CR37 studied the approaching pod. Incoming information from Athena Station confirmed that the pod originated from the *Descartes*. The meteor-ship had sent the pod in direct contradiction to the logged Guardian Fleet orders. Logic dictated that the crew of the meteor-ship was aware of the cyborg infiltration.

As CR37 studied the mass detector and the approaching pod, he calculated possible responses. If the meteor-ship had received the shuttle's survivors, they would know about the cyborg strike against Jupiter, or they would have been able to deduce it. Why otherwise had the meteor-ship's Force-Leader flaunted direct orders from Guardian Fleet headquarters?

With this conclusion reached, CR37 opened a com-link with point-defense control.

"You are receiving incoming target information," CR37 said.

"I have received the data."

"Query," said CR37. "At what range can you assure the pod's destruction with a ninety-five percent probability?"

"Computing. In eight point three-seven minutes."

CR37 considered the possibilities as he computed range. The pod might contain nuclear material with x-ray pumping. He reopened the com-link.

"Begin pod destruct in two point three minutes."

"I have received."

CR37 closed the com-link and continued to watch the passive mass detector. There might be other surprises. He needed to launch probes beyond the gel-cloud in order to cover a broader spectrum of space. The probability of other enemies was high, but at the moment, there was little he could do about it.

*** 

Tears of fear and frustration leaked from Octagon's eyes. Despite the pressing Gs, he'd crawled out of the main compartment and to the tiny hatch. Reason dictated a bomb aboard the pod. The barbarian and Yakov needed him dead. Preferably, in the most graphic manner possible.

He must frustrate them. Since he couldn't regain manual control, he must escape and warn others. He shuddered. Escaping the pod entailed frightful risk.

With the greatest difficulty, Octagon donned a vacc-suit. He'd only worn such a suit once during his space training. Sealing the helmet took several tries. At last, he heard the magnetic seals click together.

The air in his vacc-suit rapidly became stale. Before he faded into unconscious, he engaged his tanks. How could he have forgotten to do that? The rush of cool, breathable air—he inhaled deeply and splotches no longer interfered with his vision.

Octagon slapped a button and blew the hatch. As if hurled from a magnetic gun, he shot out of the pod. He flew past the thruster, almost burned by the exhaust. Then he began to tumble end over end. He was in space, alone, with many hours of air and utterly helpless. Terror gripped him. The hopelessness of his position caused him to howl in anguish.

Fortunately for his sanity, he wondered if the others could be recording his suit. They would mock him if they heard these howls. He fought for self-control, and nearly failed. Searing hatred came to his rescue.

"Marten Kluge," he whispered. All-encompassing hatred stilled his screams. He began to pray, even though beseeching nonexistent divine beings was against the Dictates. In this instance, primordial instinct overrode Jovian logic. He prayed for survival and a chance to exact fierce retribution. He prayed, broadening the scope of his whispers to include any entity, good or evil, who might grant him his desire. Whatever the cost could be to exact his revenge, he told any listening entity that he would gladly pay it.

## 15

Shocked silence reigned in the *Descartes'* command center. On the main screen, Marten, Yakov and others saw Octagon flee the pod and begin to tumble in space and quickly dwindle from view.

It brought a pang to Marten, as he remembered shock troopers tumbling away from the particle shields of the *Bangladesh.* He almost felt sorry for Octagon.

"Communications, can you raise any audio?" Yakov asked for the third time today.

The com-officer frantically worked her board. She had nimble fingers as various beeps and clicks emanated from the equipment. Finally, she glanced helplessly at Yakov.

"I still can't understand it, sir," she said. "Why has the Arbiter continued to maintain radio silence? And why now has he rushed out of the pod?"

"His actions seem deranged," Yakov said quietly, as if speaking to himself.

Marten thought Yakov a splendid actor, having maintained the ruse in front of his crew for two long days.

Yakov glanced at his command staff. Something about the way he eased forward seemed to suggest an insight had occurred. "Perhaps the Arbiter received signals we've been unable to hear or see?"

"From where?" asked Rhea, the Primary Gunner.

Marten had attempted a conversation with her yesterday in the nourishment chamber. She had taken her concentrates and

111

hurried away. He'd watched her leave, deciding that she moved with exquisite femininity.

"Representative Kluge," said Yakov. "You claimed several days ago that the dreadnaught possessed cyborgs. In your estimation, would these cyborgs try to communicate with the Arbiter and force him to surrender?"

Marten blinked several times before he realized the words had been addressed to him. "Yes," he said. "Something badly frightened your Arbiter."

"Force-Leader, look!" Rhea shouted, pointing at the main screen.

The screen was linked to Octagon's pod, to the cameras outside its hull. The pod had passed through the gel-cloud. Now the teleoptic sights zoomed onto the battered remains of the *Rousseau*. A fog of microdebris hung around the roughly spherical warship. Blue lights shined in areas. In other places, orange flares burned, subsided and then burned brighter. A discharging arc writhed in space, emanating from the engines. There might have been movement among the debris, possibly crewmembers in zero-G worksuits. There appeared among them the signature hydrogen-spray of thruster-packs.

"The dreadnaught has taken heavy damage," someone said.

"There's a sensor lock-on to the pod!" Rhea shouted. "It's a weapon's lock-on. Force-Leader, why would they want to fire at our pod?"

Bright stabs of light fired by the battered dreadnaught indicated defensive cannons.

"I have audio, Force-Leader."

There were garbled words for two seconds. Then, on the main screen, sight of the battered dreadnaught vanished.

Once more, shocked silence ruled in the *Descartes'* command center.

"They destroyed a Guardian Fleet pod," Rhea said in disbelief. "I don't understand it."

Yakov rubbed the top button of his uniform, a prearranged signal for Marten.

Marten cleared his throat, and he noticed Rhea staring at him. "I've told you that cyborgs have invaded your system. They took control of the dreadnaught. After I learned that, I

112

barely escaped with my life. Unless you destroy every infestation, the cyborgs will continue to grow in numbers until they overwhelm you. I know that's what they attempted at Mars."

"The Arbiter must have recognized the danger," Yakov said slowly. "It's why he fled his pod." Yakov sat straighter. "We are duty-bound to rescue Arbiter Octagon."

"That means nearing the *Rousseau*," Rhea said. "Will they fire on us?"

"We must assume that Representative Kluge's report is accurate," Yakov said. "We shall therefore act accordingly."

Rhea swept a curl from her eyes. "We can't fire on a Guardian Fleet warship."

"You are correct," Yakov said. "Unfortunately for us, the *Rousseau* no longer belongs to the Guardian Fleet."

Rhea turned pale. "Force-Leader, you cannot believe—"

"Rhea Merton," Yakov said. "We belong to the Guardian Fleet. We are guardians, each one of us, selected from tens of thousands of applicants and rigorously trained to do our duty. In this horrible moment, we find ourselves without an Arbiter and without a Strategist or any official of philosopher class. We must therefore apply what reason we can to the situation."

"I know we're practicing a war-drill," Rhea said. "But we can no longer continue radio silence. We must report this to Athena Station and ask for clarification."

"You have not considered the implications of the dreadnaught's unwarranted assault." Yakov solemnly glanced around the chamber. "It is my duty as Force-Leader to correlate all factors and make a logical deduction. Marten Kluge and his cyborg is item under one. The Arbiter's seemingly insane flight from a perfectly functioning pod is another item and the *Rousseau's* vicious attack is the third. Something strange has occurred aboard the dreadnaught. Given our information, the logical conclusion is that cyborgs have entered our system."

"But—" Rhea tried to say.

"The Inner Planets war has shown us cyborgs," Yakov said. "These cyborgs are said to originate from Neptune. Neptune is closer to Jupiter than it is to Mars. I say to you therefore that we are under attack."

113

Marten watched officers nod, while Rhea appeared thoughtful.

"Given the truth of my statement," Yakov said, "we must destroy the dreadnaught and gain cyborg samples to show and warn others."

"Go against a dreadnaught?" Rhea whispered.

"A badly damaged dreadnaught," Yakov said. "Communications, replay the image of the *Rousseau*. We must discover the best means of destroying it. Weapons, begin to warm the gun and missile tubes. Engine Control...."

Yakov continued to give orders as the *Descartes* assumed battle status, ready to engage the cyborg-infested dreadnaught.

## 16

On Athena Station, Cyborg Gharlane settled into a full-body interface. He grew rigid as electrical currents surged through him, connecting him with other cyborgs in the room. Occasionally, one of their eyelids flickered. Liquid computers gurgled nearly, and there was a faint odor of ozone among them and a nearly imperceptible hum.

It was a mass mind-link, adding to the Jupiter Web-Mind's computing and analysis power.

The secondary cyborgs lost the last vestiges of their identity as they merged into mind-link. As the prime cyborg, Gharlane was unique in that he retained self-awareness and could individually communicate with the Web-Mind while interfaced.

Using Athena Station's interferometers, mass detectors, thermal scanners, and broad-spectrum electromagnetic sensors, Gharlane studied the situation between the *Descartes* and the dreadnaught.

Soon, Gharlane told the Web-Mind his findings.

The Jupiter Web-Mind was a marvel of technology, the most advanced artificial intelligence in the Solar System except for the Prime Web-Mind itself.

The Web-Mind's capsule was parked in a deep hanger on Athena Station. The capsule contained a biomass computer merged with metric tons of neural processors. Hundreds of bio-forms had died to supply the Web-Mind with the needed brain mass. Each kilo of brain tissue had been personality-scrubbed and carefully rearranged on wafer-thin sheets surrounded by computing gel. Other machinery kept the core temperature at a perfect 98.7 degrees Fahrenheit. Tubes fed the tissues the needed nutrients. Sensors monitored bio-health. Sub-computers did a hundred other necessary chores to keep the Web-Mind functioning perfectly. The biomind could outthink any known entity and track many thousands of cyborgs. The Prime Web-Mind was supreme, but the Jupiter Web-Mind possessed override authority here. It could adjust the master plan to emergencies.

"Further—" Gharlane halted his summary of the situation. With the mass detector, he spotted an object hurtling much too fast toward Jupiter.

"Priority one scan," Gharlane said.

He had permission to override the mind-link. Every scope, every mass meter and thermal sensor now strained at the selected point.

In the dim room, plugged cyborgs twitched and eyelids flickered faster. The ozone odor increased, as did the humming.

Gharlane sensed the Web-Mind turning more of its brain-mass to the new situation.

"The vessel's specifications are similar to a Social Unity missile-ship," Gharlane said.

*Your analysis is false*, the Web-Mind said.

"I mean without a missile-ship's regular particle shielding."

*Explain your logic.*

"I deducted the mass of particle shielding and compared the under-vessel to the basic, SU missile-ship design."

*What prompted such action?*

"Firstly, the vessel appears to have stealth capabilities," Gharlane said, "which would logically imply that any particle shielding would have been subtracted from its mass."

*That was insufficient reason for your comparative values.*

"I recalled the analytical study of the Third Battle for Mars. The study indicated the presence of hidden missile-ships— Web-Mind, I request an immediate discontinuation of our stealth campaign."

*You are evading my question.*

"Not for any nefarious reasons," Gharlane said. Soothing chemicals injected into his brainpan then, helping to stem his

116

emotional excitement. "Web-Mind, the enemy vessel indicates reinforcements from Social Unity. Our stealth campaign has now been compromised on two levels."

*Notice the angle of the attack. The vessel comes from out-system, not from Inner Planets.*

Gharlane made fast computations. "There was sufficient time for a deep strike and turnaround—"

*Are you suggesting that the masters of Social Unity deduced our Jupiter Assault a year ago and sent vessels bound for here at the curtailment of the Third Battle for Mars? At that juncture, they lacked sufficient vessels to face a single Doom Star. The Highborn vessels were still within the Mars System. Your thought is gravely unbalanced.*

"The stealth vessel is here, implying strategic action. That it matches its approach with the meteor-ship's action proves my thesis. The probability that the two incidents are independent of each other is twenty-seven percent."

*Twenty-NINE point six-five percent.*

Gharlane studied the Web-Mind's data. "Ah. I failed to take into account the chaotic principle."

*Our stealth campaign has proven effective. Given another thirty-seven days, we will gain complete system-movement control.*

"Agreed," said Gharlane. "But now we must initiate a surprise strike against the remaining vessels and against the defensive establishments of the Galilean moons."

*You are stubborn, and still yearn for an immediate missile assault against Callisto.*

"It is the logical action."

In several seconds, the Web-Mind ran through a thousand scenarios. It computed odds, vectors and random factors.

*We are under-strength for an optimal strike.*

"Which means we must strike at once," Gharlane said. "For we are also under-strength against an alerted Callisto defense."

*Position the missiles for a surprise assault and begin the preliminary countdown. We shall observe the stealth vessel with Social Unity missile-ship design specifications.*

"A surprise strike should place all military vessels under my control."

*You are the hand, Cyborg Gharlane. I am the intellect. If you fail to remember that, I shall delete you.*

"I have received," Gharlane said.

*Patience is the great virtue. And cyborgs cannot panic. Thus, ultimate victory shall be ours. Await the next development as you begin preparations for a sustained strike.*

A discharging impulse sent sparks and blue arcs writhing over Gharlane's body. He sat upright in his mind-link bed. Then, with a clang, he slid his feet onto the floor.

They should immediately begin the strike, he knew, but the Web-Mind sought optimal conditions. He was unable to disobey a direct order, although on some deep level he desired to run the cyborg assault along his parameters. Gharlane wondered, for just a moment, if the biomind in the Web-Mind meant that it coordinated too many factors. Did the many kilos of brain tissue argue against itself in an ongoing roundtable? That might explain the Web-Mind's need for optimal percentage levels.

In the dim, humming chamber, Gharlane examined the plugged cyborgs. He might have shrugged, but such a response had long ago been scrubbed from him. He strode for the exit in order to implement his directives.

## -17-

The *Thutmosis III* sped for Jupiter at hyper-velocity, although it no longer hurtled through the void at its star-spanning speeds. Side-jets had rotated the squat vessel until its engines were aimed in the direction it traveled.

Within the crippled warship, the remaining crew readied for an intense period of deceleration. A single laser of medium strength functioned, and the ship retained four anti-missile pods.

The *Thutmosis III* had a triple-structured hull, with reactive armor on the outer surface. A nanosecond before a missile or shell hit the reactive armor, targeted sections of the hull would explode outward. The shape-charged shrapnel would theoretically obliterate the incoming mass, enough to steal its ship-killing power. The outward-blowing kinetic energy also acted as a shock absorber. It was a paltry defense, many factors less protective than six-hundred meters of asteroid rock, but it was better than a single, non-reactive hull.

The Praetor was on the bridge in his command chair, observing several concerned Highborn. He only possessed a skeleton crew, and everyone was stretched to the breaking point. They sat rigidly, with tight skin and the haunted eyes of deranged killers. Their big hands were on the boards and ready to begin their final battle for survival.

To Homo sapiens, the desperate Highborn would have seemed like starved lions ready to rend a training master into bloody shreds. Three times throughout the harrowing journey, fights had broken out. Because of them, five Highborn had died.

Twice, the Praetor had waded into battle, using his fists to enforce discipline. He was the dominant officer, Fourth-ranked among all Highborn by the old scale. Who knew his position now since the conclusion of the Third Battle for Mars.

The Praetor surveyed the others. They respected him just a little more than death from decompression. And they were concerned about catching Jupiter's heavy gravity-well and braking their out-of-control vessel.

"Is the system still peaceful?" the Praetor asked, with menace in his voice.

"I monitored an explosion earlier," a thick-necked officer said.

"Was the explosion directed at us?"

"I would have informed you if it had been."

The Praetor glared at the weapons officer.

The thick-necked officer returned the Praetor's stare. His name was Canus and he had a burn-scar on his left cheek. The burn-scar was composed of angry red flesh, raised flesh with little ridges. As the Praetor stared at him, the madness in Canus's eyes lessened and soon he dropped his fierce gaze.

"Lord," Canus added, although there was still truculence in his voice.

The Praetor knew they were all under tremendous pressure. He also knew that he must remain strong—stronger than the others. A Highborn could climb rank without harm to his life expectancy. Sinking in levels often entailed his violent death.

The Praetor rubbed his fingertips against the polished steel of his armrest. Then, with a sudden movement, he opened a ship-wide channel.

"Attention, *Thutmosis III* crewmen. This is the Praetor speaking. We have achieved the impossible and repaired our engines and ship-structure to withstand the coming deceleration. There is a possibility that the Jovian premen will attempt to attack us at our most vulnerable moment. If that occurs, I assure you we shall let them know they have been in battle with the Highborn. Our weapons are ready. If they prove insufficient, we shall ram our foes. We will not sink quietly into the dark night of oblivion. Rather we will blaze with glory against any who dare set themselves against us. The universe thought it could conquer us and defeat our fierce will. The universe is now discovering that we are the superior form of life. We shall do more than survive. We shall dominate the Jovian System and bring it into the Empire of our devising. You have made me proud. You are proud soldiers. Together, we shall attack our problem head-on in the truest style of the superior being."

The Praetor raised his massive hand and made a decisive gesture.

A pale officer licked his lips. Then the officer's big hands roved over his board. He engaged the fusion core, and the ship's engines fired with violent life. Every Highborn aboard the crippled *Thutmosis III* found himself slammed against his acceleration couch.

The Praetor, Canus and one other Highborn on the bridge, shouted wildly, roaring at the universe. Their emotions had overloaded and they bled their tension in the only way they knew, with a predator's roar of aggression.

Despite the massive Gs, the Praetor raised his fist, shaking it at the universe, hoping his derelict ship could survive the horrible forces pressing upon it.

## -18-

Alarms rang in the *Descartes*. On the ship's main screen blazed a bright dot, the brightest object in the region of banded Jupiter. The glowing dot was more luminous than the Sun or any of the nearby moons, and certainly brighter than the stars.

"Give me an analysis," Yakov said, who had lurched forward to stare at the teleoptically-enhanced sight.

The hunched officers worked furiously, while Marten frowned at the glowing dot.

"It approaches from out-system," Rhea said.

"Is it cyborg reinforcements?" asked Yakov.

"I have a match on the engine's heat-signature," Rhea said. She looked up, surprised. "Force-Leader, it's a SU missile-ship."

Yakov massaged his forehead. It was a rare indication that he was under stress.

"Their speed is excessive," Rhea said. She touched the blue medal dangling from her choker. Then she went to work. Soon, she said, "Given their deceleration rate, it will take them many orbits around Jupiter before they could conceivably come to a halt."

Yakov stared at the white dot.

So did Marten, as he thought about the Storm Assault Missile.

"The ship's energy output has increased," Rhea said. "And the ship's heading has veered. It will take them...." She madly typed keys. "Force-Leader, it will take them ten thousand kilometers from the *Rousseau*."

"How long will that take?" snapped Yakov.

"In approximately three point four hours."

Yakov swiveled toward Marten. "Do you think it's an actual SU missile-ship?"

"Not if it came from out-system," Marten said.

"Who drives it then?" Yakov asked.

Marten spoke to Rhea. "Given its flight path, can you calculate its point of origin?"

She stared at him. She had beautiful eyes. They were green, and larger than ordinary Jovian eyes.

Abruptly, she turned to her screen, typing quickly. "It must have come from Uranus."

"Are you sure it's a military vessel?" Yakov asked.

"The engine's heat-signature is a one hundred percent match to a SU missile-ship," Rhea said. "It must be a warship."

"Why would those from Uranus send a warship here now?" Yakov said.

"Their secret service must have stolen SU ship designs," Marten said. "Maybe they meant to slip such vessels into Inner Planets."

"Why?" asked Yakov.

"If cyborgs are here," Marten said, "maybe cyborgs also attacked the Uranus System."

"And?" asked Yakov.

Marten glanced at Rhea. She dropped her gaze, and after a moment, she turned back to her board.

"Are they fugitives from a successful cyborg invasion?" Marten asked.

"The assertion is preposterous," Rhea said. She brushed curls from her eyes. "The barbarian could as easily suggest cyborgs commandeered the ship. The truth is otherwise."

"How can you know any of that?" Marten asked.

She gestured angrily. "It has an SU heat-signature and it comes from Uranus. Why couldn't it be an SU warship returning from a diplomatic mission? That is the logical deduction."

Marten shook his head. "That it's here now at this juncture indicates something else. If it belongs to Social Unity, why

123

stop in the Jupiter System? The ship must contain more cyborgs."

As Yakov stared at the main screen, his eyes glittered. "No. That isn't a cyborg ship."

"It seems like the likeliest explanation," Marten said.

Yakov shook his head. "If you're right about the *Rousseau* and Athena Station, it shows that the cyborgs have been acting secretly. This new ship blazes its presence. Everyone in the system will note it. And that would be contrary to a hidden attack. Therefore, the new ship contains something other than cyborgs."

"It is mere supposition that cyborgs are in our system," Rhea pointed out.

Marten made a harsh sound. "Cyborgs attacked my shuttle."

"The Arbiter didn't believe you," Rhea said. "Why should anyone else?"

"The Arbiter fled his pod for a reason," Marten said. "The *Rousseau* sprayed a gel-cloud to hide itself for a reason. Its com-officer said there was fusion core damage, but you all saw it earlier. That was battle-damage. They lied to us. Athena Station ordered the *Descartes* away from the stricken ship. Give me a good reason for those actions."

"He is an out-system barbarian," Rhea told Yakov. "His motivations are hidden and likely antithetical to the Dictates."

"It might be time to active the Zenos," Yakov said softly.

Rhea clutched her slender throat. "No! You cannot attack a Guardian Fleet warship."

"If I use the drones," Yakov said, his eyes tight, "it might inadvertently begin the secession. And if cyborgs *are* here it's time for system unity, not discord."

"It's time to attack," Marten said. "If the new ship brings reinforcements, you must strike before the cyborgs become even stronger. If that ship doesn't contain reinforcements, the cyborgs on the *Rousseau* will likely be worrying about the new vessel."

"The barbarian is wrong," Rhea said.

"I'm not wrong," Marten said, "and I'm not a barbarian."

Rhea sneered at him. "The Earthman is likely a provocateur, sent to start a civil war among ourselves."

Marten stared at Rhea a moment longer. Then he turned to Yakov. "You must decide quickly, as the Zenos still have a long way to travel. You must accelerate them now to strike as the new ship approaches the *Rousseau*."

Yakov ran a hand through his silver hair. Indecision twisted his usually stoic features. He glanced at the main screen, at Marten and then at Rhea Merton, the Primary Gunner.

"We're loyal to the Confederation," Rhea said. "We each took a solemn oath with our three center fingers placed on the Dictates. We swore to uphold and enforce them. Now I must insist that you tell us where the Strategist went. We should have heard from her by now. Tell us what happened, Force-Leader."

Using his sleeve, Yakov wiped his forehead. Then he sat straighter and opened a slot on his armrest.

"No," Rhea said weakly. "We're Confederation officers. That is a Guardian Fleet vessel."

Without a word, Yakov decisively pressed two buttons.

Marten turned to his screen. In space where they coasted toward the *Rousseau*, the two drones engaged their chemical engines. The Zenos began to accelerate.

## -19-

The *Rousseau's* chief cyborg, CR37, studied the ship's sensors. If these readings were correct, the decelerating ship was under tremendous stress. Could the ship have launched from the Uranus System? Simply backtracking the trajectory indicated the humans there had sent it. Had the Helium-3 Barons of Uranus discovered the Cyborg Master Plan? Was this ship meant as reinforcement for the Jovians?

"You have a message, sir," whispered the unmodified woman, a crewmember. There were dark circles around her overlarge eyes and her paleness had increased. Her compelling nature had become haggard with worry.

CR37 stood beside her. For a moment, a chaotic impulse surged through him. He wanted to wrap his fingers around her delicate neck. He wanted her to squirm, to scream for him. His fingers would press into her soft flesh as he snapped her neck-bones. It seemed unjust that she should keep her humanity while he had lost his. He would adjust this wrong and delete the irritant from his sight.

Perhaps sensing his mood, the woman stared at him.

Suppressing the chaotic impulse, CR37 moved the toggle underneath a flashing orange light. A harsh voice immediately spoke through the intercom.

"This is the Praetor of the Highborn speaking. Any interference with our progress shall be met with annihilation. Our intentions are benevolent and beneficial to you premen— to the folk of the Jovian System. We have tracked you and we wish a confirmation that you understand our peaceful intention.

126

Respond to our message or we shall have to take forceful measures. The Praetor of the Highborn out."

"You have a second message," the woman whispered.

CR37 opened another channel. High-speed chatter occurred. He clicked the toggle, took a jack and inserted it into a slot in his chest. Gharlane sent him personal orders.

After a short time, CR37 detached the plug and swiveled his plasti-flesh head, studying a screen. The bright dot had grown. It was nearing fast. Highborn rode that dot. Highborn had come to the Jovian System.

"Engine control," CR37 said. "I need power to turn and face the incoming ship with our point-defense cannons."

There was static on the line, but the answer came through. "Power online."

\*\*\*

"They fail to respond," the Praetor said. All around him, the ship shook as high-pitched whines and clangs told of the fierce stress. The Gs pressing against his lips make speaking difficult, as if they were formed of lead.

"There is a rupture on level six!" an officer shouted.

"Tell damage control—"

"Coil three is overheating!" Canus shouted. "Lord, we must disengage the engines."

"Negative!" the Praetor snarled. He lay on an acceleration couch, enduring as he had once endured circling the Sun. His tough skin had flattened and moisture leaked from the corners of his eyes. He recalled the deep void of space, the emptiness that would await him if they failed here. It made his voice hoarse as he spoke. "We live or die today in the Jupiter System. We shall not bypass it. Continue deceleration."

"Lord, the enemy vessel has begun to rotate."

"Laser team," the Praetor snarled into his intercom, "do you have a lock on the warship?"

"Our laser won't affect them, Lord," a voice said over the intercom.

"Never mind that!" the Praetor shouted. "We fight. We attack. If that doesn't work—Canus, can you change our vector to an intercept course?"

"Lord, we don't know their intention. It may prove peaceful."

"Answer my question!" the Praetor snarled, wanting to crawl across the floor and throttle Canus's thick neck. He couldn't move, however. Only the damage control party in their battleoid-suits could move under these tremendous Gs. Even they would find it difficult now.

"Yes, Lord, we could manage."

More pressing Gs hit the ship and those within it. As he lay on the acceleration couch, the Praetor's lips peeled back to reveal his big teeth, white teeth meant for rending meat. Every ten minutes, the engines pulsed with greater power, decelerating at higher levels for one point five minutes. It slammed them to the limit of Highborn endurance. One by one, they passed out until the engine lessened its terrible output and the gross Gs throttled down to horrible pain levels. The Highborn, being resilient, regained consciousness quickly. It was three minutes until the next big thrust pulse.

The *Thutmosis III* shook worse than before. There were grim sounds throughout the ship, metallic groans, creaks, rattles, mini-explosions and the continuing high whine that nearly made thinking impossible.

"Weapons, where's that laser?" the Praetor roared.

"Lord, we're ready."

"Put it on visual," the Praetor said.

A holographic image appeared before him. It showed a port opening on the side of the *Thutmosis III*. It wasn't a *Zhukov*-class primary laser. Highborn Command had modified a captured Social Unity missile-ship, turning it into a gigantic stealth vessel. The modified ship had relied on missiles, carrying many detachable pods. Those missiles had all been fired during the Third Battle for Mars. Highborn Command had added several medium-range lasers for defensive use. Only one of those lasers had survived the hunter-killers from Phobos.

A focusing mirror poked out of the port. The front section was red with power.

"Target acquired and locked-on," Canus said.

"Should we give them one more chance for friendly discourse?" another Highborn asked.

"Kill them!" the Praetor shouted. "They had their chance."

From the holographic image there lanced a bright beam, streaking out into the void of space.

*\*\**

The range between the two warships was short in stellar distances, nearly sixty thousand kilometers and closing fast.

Light traveled at approximately 300,000 kilometers per second. The time lag between firing the laser, its journey across space and to the target was almost negligible in space combat terms. Normally, the *Rousseau* would have possessed motive power. Today it lacked that, but drifted instead. That made it a stationary target. That meant the Highborn calibrating system could snipe at the dreadnaught with comparative ease.

The dreadnaught did have particle shielding. And the laser's wattage was mid-level and it would take time to chew through the asteroid rock.

As the laser stabbed through the darkness, the dreadnaught lowered particle shielding just a fraction. Through that slit opening, its point-defense cannons began spewing depleted uranium pellets. Those pellets would take time to reach the *Thutmosis III*. And the enemy's position could change by the time the pellets reached the projected impact point.

Gharlane had ordered CR37 to lay the pellets in a large, predictive pattern. In effect, CR37 shot the pellets as mines, putting them in the enemy ship's projected path. Instead of using nuclear detonation, CR37 would rely on kinetic force. He would use the ship's velocity against it, and that it lacked particle shielding. It would take time to hurt the enemy vessel, but the cumulative effect might be enough to destroy it.

A klaxon began to wail. The unmodified human turned to him, with horror twisting her pale features. "A laser—" she whispered, before she choked up.

CR37 clicked a toggle. A tri-screen activated. From a hull camera, he saw the enemy laser. It chewed into particle shielding at the edge of a point-defense cannon.

"Raise the shield," the woman whispered. "Or the laser might breach the hull. Maybe it will slice into our chamber." She wilted as he stared at her.

CR37 turned back to the tri-screen. Gharlane had given the order. They must lay down the pellets, even at the cost of further ship-destruction.

## 20

On Athena Station, Gharlane stood in the former Guardian Fleet Command Center. It contained the latest in liquid computers and AI-enhancers. Cyborgs worked the modules. On the walls were various screens. One showed an interferometer enlargement of the beaming Highborn vessel. Another showed the *Descartes*. Another showed the Zenos burning for the *Rousseau*. The crippled warship was taking hits from the Highborn laser.

Audio bursts had increased throughout the system. Callisto Orbital Defense demanded clarification. Guardian Fleet warships still under Jovian control also wanted assessment of the situation.

It was clear to Gharlane that with the Highborn's declaration and attack, phase one of the cyborg stealth campaign was effectively over. It was time for open strikes. The first should occur against Callisto.

A ping in Gharlane's mind alerted him to the Web-Mind's radio linkage. He stood straighter and moved his head minutely to the left.

"Gharlane here," he said.

*I have assessed the probabilities,* the Web-Mind said. *With eighty-seven percent certainty, the current attack means that the Highborn are allied with the Jovians.*

"I am not convinced of that. The Praetor's messages indicate troubling rogue factors."

*The messages were coded sequences.*

"Do you say that because of the immediate ignition of the two Zenos?" Gharlane asked.

*Highborn and Jovians are attacking in concert. The conclusion is obvious. They have a working alliance.*

"If that is true, it is time for open strikes."

*First, it is time to implement the subversion campaign.*

Gharlane shifted his stance as he observed the number seven screen. The Highborn laser stabbed through space. It hit the *Rousseau* with uncanny accuracy.

"The random factors are too high to implement the subversion campaign," Gharlane said. "It could produce unknown backlashes."

*The Highborn have joined the battle for the Jupiter System. They have achieved a surprise attack. To maintain over eighty percent chance of system victory, we must immediately implement the subversion campaign.*

Gharlane had uncovered the Secessionist Plot through captured officers of Ganymede and Europan origin. The Secessionists awaited the opportunity for a system-wide rebellion against Callisto and the Guardian Fleet. Through mind-analyzers, truth serums and pain inducements, he had also discovered the code words that would initiate warship takeovers and planetary coups by the Secessionists.

*The Secessionists will divide the Jovians and sow discord at this critical juncture.*

"It will also alert Callisto Orbital Defense and all remaining Guardian Fleet warships."

*There is a high probability that the two factions will begin interspecies infighting.*

"Other than this single vessel, there is no evidence of further Highborn presence."

*This vessel surprised us. Therefore, the probability is high that the genetic soldiers have other stealth vessels in the region. We must strike hard now before the Jovians and Highborn can coordinate their respective ships. Also, the appearance of the vessel at this point indicates that our stealth assault has been compromised.*

"Shouldn't we wait until—"

*Begin an immediate implementation of the subversion campaign. Then increase the attack velocity of the two nearest meteor-ships against the* Descartes.

Although Gharlane had grave reservations, he said, "I have received."

The Web-Mind broke the radio-linkage and Gharlane gave the needed orders. Half the cyborgs in the Command Center switched tasks. They began to broadcast the latest Secessionist code sequences to different warships and to Ganymede, Europa, Io and other moons.

Gharlane strode to screen eleven. It was split in two, showing camera shots from two cyborg-controlled meteor-ships. Each focused on the other. They were the *Kepler* and the *Hobbes*, identical in size and function to the *Descartes*. Each now began to accelerate, increasing their velocity.

***

Marten joined a badly shaken Yakov at the Primary Gunner's module. Rhea was hunched over the controls, her slender fingers adjusting critical passive sensor arrays.

"They're meteor-ships," she said.

Marten wondered how she knew. On her screen, they were dots drowned by a sea of stars.

Rhea pressed a button. On the screen, the view shifted slightly. Brighter dots moved away from the first two. Rhea leaned closer to her various monitors.

"The ships have launched Zenos," she said.

"Their projected trajectory?" whispered Yakov.

Rhea twisted around to face him, causing her breasts to strain against her black uniform. "They're targeting us, Force-Leader. They think we're Secessionists."

"Maybe they're cyborg-controlled vessels," Marten said.

Rhea refused to look at him or respond to his words.

"Or they're Jovians allied with the cyborgs," Marten told Yakov.

Now Rhea gave him a cold glance. "No Jovian would make an alliance with a cyborg."

Stung, Marten asked, "Are you referring to Osadar?"

"You must self-destruct our Zenos," Rhea told Yakov. "You must show the Confederation that we are still loyal guardians."

"Make a run for Ganymede," Marten suggested.

Several minutes ago, turmoil had struck as a message from Athena Station arrived. It had shocked Yakov, who had informed Marten it was the Secessionist code. From incoming radio messages, it was clear that several warships with crewmembers from Ganymede, Europa and Io had received similar instructions.

Yakov studied Rhea's screen. "The two meteor-ships have fired Zenos at us. The Secessionist broadcast came from Athena Station. None of this makes sense."

"Yes it does," Rhea said. "Arbiters broke the Secessionist plot. They have now broadcast the *go* message to see which crews are loyal to the Confederation. Since Athena Station believes we're in rebellion, they have ordered our destruction."

"That's madness," Yakov said. "They wouldn't order our ship's destruction, but arrest us later in port."

"Forget about that," Marten said. "You must run for Ganymede as you alert everyone about the cyborgs."

Yakov was shaking his head. "Are those two ships Guardian Fleet vessels or do they contain cyborgs like the *Rousseau*?"

"Once they launch drones at you," Marten said, "what difference does it make?"

"You speak from barbarian emotionalism," Rhea murmured.

Yakov scowled. "Do you realize what the broadcast means? Secessionist crewmembers are likely even now slaughtering arbiters and ship-controllers as they take over several warships. The philosophers of Callisto will never forgive us for that."

"Launch Zenos at the two meteor-ships and run for Ganymede," Marten said. "Anything else is suicide."

"Do not listen to the barbarian," Rhea pleaded. "We must make peace. We must surrender."

Yakov rubbed bloodshot eyes before he floated to his command chair. From there, he began to issue orders.

134

In moments, the *Descartes* rotated toward Jupiter and applied thrust. It headed into the gas giant's gravity-well. It used the planet's pull to help build velocity. Ganymede was on the other side of Jupiter, making it many days away from their present location.

\*\*\*

On the *Rousseau's* emergency bridge, CR37 continued his attempts to foil the enemy.

The Highborn laser fired with uncanny accuracy, at times burning exposed point-defense cannons. Sometimes, it melted through the hull behind the cannons.

"Rotate the ship three degrees," CR37 said.

The laser from the hard-braking Highborn ship chewed into asteroid rock as the dreadnaught rotated just enough to throw off their aim. The laser melted rock then, creating gas, liquid and slagging off boulder pieces. It other words, the laser proved ineffective against too much mass and density, that of simple interstellar rock.

"Enemy Zenos have achieved lock-on," the unmodified woman whispered. Her hands trembled as tears ran down her soft cheeks. Some of the tears floated around her face.

CR37's fingers blurred across his controls. He attempted electronic countermeasures, spewed chaff and prismatic crystals. He used everything to try to deflect the huge drones from his warship. Lastly, he turned his ship, aligning the final point-defense cannons with the Zenos' approach path.

\*\*\*

The two Zenos increased speed as their chemical fuel burned fast.

Then one of the *Rousseau's* depleted uranium pellets struck the first drone's hull. It almost caused the drone to veer off-target, but internal guidance redirected it at the nearing dreadnaught.

Then another pellet struck.

Internal computing calculated the odds of hitting the target. The odds had dropped below the required number. The Zeno's primary function ceased and the secondary level attack commenced.

Rods sprouted into position, each aimed at vulnerable points on the dreadnaught. The Zeno warhead exploded with thermonuclear devastation. As the explosion obliterated the drone, x-rays and gamma rays used the aimed rods, traveling along them. Before the explosion destroyed the rods, they had concentrated the deadly radiation against the dreadnaught. That radiation stabbed like a spear instead of simply expanding and dissipating in a nuclear fireball.

Those x-rays and gamma rays hit the *Rousseau* with ugly power. The unmodified woman sitting beside CR37 died instantly. The cyborg's brainpan lacked enough shielding to protect him, and he died several seconds later. The x-rays also melted several critical fuses. At that point, all but one point-defense cannon fell silent. That cannon now lacked proper targeting data.

The second Zeno zoomed at the *Rousseau*. It closed to five hundred kilometers, four hundred, three hundred, two, one hundred kilometers and then sped into the ship. The thermonuclear device ignited with obliterating power.

While particle shielding protected much, it failed to protect enough. Every living thing in and around the *Rousseau* died. And vast quantities of mass hurtled outward from the terrific explosion.

## 21

The *Descartes* accelerated down the mighty gravity-well of Jupiter.

*Gravity-well* was a term, useful in any system with a planetary body. The Sun, Earth and Jupiter each had a gravity-well. The Galilean moons of Io, Europa, Ganymede and Callisto also had gravity-wells. Jupiter had the biggest gravity-well after the Sun. The meaning was simple. Jupiter pulled things toward it because of its massive size, because of the gravitational attractive force it had on other masses such as people, ships, moons and passing comets. To escape Jupiter, to leave it, one needed a certain velocity—the escape velocity. If a ship failed to reach the escape velocity, it would orbit Jupiter, unable to leave.

In this instance, Jupiter was at the bottom of the well. To fire a rocket out of the well took more power than it would to shoot a rocket down toward Jupiter.

This was simple, gravitational mechanics, and it had consequences in space combat. The common misconception was that space lacked terrain other than planets and asteroids, comets and moons. But that was false. There was gravity, among other factors such as radiation, solar wind, the ecliptic of the planets and such. A ship high in the gravity-well had high ground just as an archer on a hill shooting down had an advantage over an archer shooting up the hill.

In the Jupiter System, this was even more the case than in the Mars System.

This was one of the reasons why Athena Station had been chosen as the Guardian Fleet Headquarters. It had the high ground in comparison to the four Galilean moons, which were closer to Jupiter and thus deeper in the well.

Marten sat in his module, enduring the acceleration and observing the others. He would trade places with Omi soon and get some sleep.

"Yes," Yakov said. He watched the main screen and witnessed the *Rousseau's* death.

"You really did it," Rhea said, her eyes wide with shock. "You destroyed a Guardian Fleet warship."

Marten switched to the same visual. It was a long teleoptic shot of the obliterated *Rousseau*, visible now because it no longer hid behind a gel-cloud.

"You must engage your logic," Yakov told Rhea. "Athena Station broadcast the Secessionist code. No one there would do that if he or she were Guardian Fleet personnel. Either Secessionists gained control of Athena Station or cyborgs did. It is more logical to believe that cyborgs captured the station than Secessionists."

"No," said Rhea, "that is illogical. Why would cyborgs broadcast the code?"

"Obviously," said Yakov, "to create disunity among us."

Rhea gripped her choker. "None of that matters anymore. The tracking Zenos will destroy our ship. We must take to the lifeboats and escape with our lives."

Marten chewed the inside of his check. The *Descartes* used the technique of sledding down the gravity-well to build up velocity. Unfortunately, the following ships also went down into the gravity-well after them.

Marten studied his screen. The enemy ships were red dots. The *Descartes* was a yellow dot. The green dots were the speeding Zenos.

Marten spoke to Yakov. "There may be a way to discover if the ships chasing us are cyborgs or Guardian Fleet vessels."

"I'm listening," Yakov said. He sounded weary and looked older.

138

"Radio Callisto Orbital Defense," Marten said. "Tell them everything you know. Then ask them if they ordered those ships to attack us. If they didn't, they're cyborgs."

Yakov pondered the idea, soon nodding. Then he ordered the com-officer to open a channel with Callisto Orbital Defense.

\*\*\*

Aboard the hard-decelerating *Thutmosis III*, thick-necked Canus broke the Guardian Fleet's ship-to-ship code. He was thus able to intercept Yakov's message to Callisto.

"Well done," the Praetor said, after listening to the message.

"The premen maintain a primitive system," Canus replied hoarsely from his acceleration couch. "They use a simple 1-2-3 dynamic with an override code-sequence set at the second level."

As he endured the terrible Gs, the Praetor pondered the Jovian message, playing it over a second time, ingesting the innuendos. "Replay the warship's demise," he said, meaning the *Rousseau*, although he didn't know the dreadnaught's name.

The *Thutmosis III's* passive sensors had recorded the destruction. By studying a computer-list of Solar System warships, the Praetor knew it had been a Guardian Fleet dreadnaught, a durable warship, but inferior to those of Inner Planets.

"We've stumbled into a civil war," Canus said, after watching the video a second time.

The Praetor grinned viciously. "That's perfect. We shall join the weaker side, use our superior tactics, leading them to victory and thereby gaining their gratitude."

"Premen are notoriously fickle with their gratitude," Canus said.

"I controlled the Sun-Works Factory for many months," the Praetor said. "There I learned the full extent of their ingratitude. We gave the premen discipline and meaning, and they turned on us like sneaking curs, with their tails between their legs as they snapped at us. It is the condition of inferior stock. In this system, I will use their initial gratitude, which

139

sometimes gushes with irrationality. I will use it to begin my rule. Yes, even among premen there are killers. I will seek those out, break their will to mine and build a corps of enforcers."

"First we must defeat the cyborgs," Canus said, as he scratched the red burn-scar twisting across his cheek.

"No," said the Praetor. "First we must stop the *Thutmosis III*." He showed his teeth in an aggressive smile. "However, it is also time to begin winning premen gratitude. Show me the warship that destroyed the dreadnaught."

Through the ship's powerful sensors, the Praetor soon witnessed the situation between the *Descartes* and the following meteor-ships. The Praetor ran figures, studied the holographic display and listened a third time to Yakov's warning to Callisto Orbital Defense. By then, Canus had intercepted the ruling philosophers' answer.

"Give me the political situation report on the Jupiter System," the Praetor said.

It came online. Despite the harsh conditions, the Praetor read the report with incredible speed, skipping the non-essentials. During that time, the ship rapidly closed toward the actively hunting Zenos.

"It will take us many circuits around Jupiter to halt our velocity," the Praetor said thoughtfully. "Before that, we must have chosen sides and gained allies. Otherwise, we risk having both sides trying to destroy us."

The Praetor balled his mighty hands into fists. He squeezed, letting his nails dig into the flesh of his palm. He was the superior being in this system. The cyborgs, they were no longer human. They did not count, as they were mechanical aliens. As the dominant being here, control and rule would naturally fall to him—if he could reach the levers of power.

"Weapons: heat the laser," the Praetor said.

"The target?" asked Canus, trying to sound unconcerned as the continuing deceleration caused rattling and high-pitched whines.

"Target those drones," the Praetor said. "Let us show these premen our gratitude for destroying the dreadnaught for us."

"They only destroyed the dreadnaught to help themselves."

140

"Do not seek to teach me the basics," the Praetor warned. "I know more than you, more than everyone here combined. We shall give them life. They shall fawn on us because of it, and we shall insert ourselves into their struggle. Our superiority will then give us control of the system."

Canus nodded grudgingly. "Your plan is well-conceived," he muttered.

"On my word," said the Praetor, "target the first drone."

## -22-

Gharlane wore a vacc-suit as he inspected massive Voltaire Missiles on Athena Station's asteroid surface.

He was like a mote as the missiles towered three hundred meters over him. In effect, they were corvette-sized spaceships. But instead of living quarters and crew, each was double-packed with lethal weaponry to help fight its way to the target. Each also possessed a new and improved artificial intelligence to do the fighting. The payload was hundreds of megatons of thermonuclear power. A fusion core drove each at the highest acceleration of any craft in the Jovian System. A Voltaire seldom hid like the chemically-fuelled Zeno, but came on powerfully to subdue the target through mass, weaponry and superior ECM.

Coils were still attached to many of the gargantuan missiles, and cyborgs scurried everywhere, using the rail-system to make last minute adjustments. Some cyborgs climbed the outer rungs and entered the rockets, manually checking the more delicate systems.

Above the missiles was the blackness of space. Athena Station lacked an atmosphere, causing the stars to shine brilliantly like cold gems. Jupiter hung in the distance, its Red Spot barely visible as the gas giant rotated.

Gharlane turned around. On the asteroid there were squat buildings, laser ports, waiting anti-missile rockets, ready for immediate launching, sand-accelerating guns used to knock down incoming objects and a bewildering forest of antennae. They helped scan the void for anything that might harm the

142

station. The original gaining of Athena Station had been the greatest cyborg achievement to date.

Gharlane had wanted to strike at Callisto Orbital Defense then. The Web-Mind had overridden the desire, and Gharlane had come to see that the Web-Mind had been correct. The Guardian Fleet had been much too strong then and could have possibly converged in time to halt much of a first strike.

Gharlane raised his helmeted head, peering up at a giant missile. The Voltaire was unlike the Jovian dreadnaught, which was smaller than an Inner Planets vessel of a similar type. He read the big letters on the missile's side.

*Voltaire Missile, AE 1029, Article Seven-Ten.*

Once activated, the AI would take control of the craft. Gharlane had studied the specs on the AI. It was an advanced artificial intelligence, with breakthrough crystal technology. Presently, the crystal AI lived in a virtual reality world of careful Jovian devising. The AI didn't realize it lived in a make-believe world. Instead, it went on a hundred different expeditions in the virtual world, gaining experiences that would hopefully stand it in good stead the day it awakened to reality. The day that occurred would sentence it to a quick combat death, one way or another.

Gharlane had never expected such an abundance of military hardware. The Jupiter System was awash in combat vessels, missiles and armored satellites. By studying historical files, it was clear the Jovians had been rebuilding ever since 2339. The annihilating defeat of its expeditionary force to Mars many years ago had horrified them. Since then, they had added ships and hardware every year to insure victory in case Social Unity attacked the Jupiter System.

*Attention, Cyborg Gharlane!*

"I am ready to receive," Gharlane said over the radio embedded in his head.

*Immediately link to a secure channel.*

There was a priority one tone to the Web-Mind's command.

Gharlane glanced around. He was in a maze of the giant missiles, with crisscrossing rail-lines and busy cyborgs doing a hundred last-minute chores.

Gharlane magnetized his boots and began to run, building up speed. Then he snapped off his magnetic boots and leapt. He flew like a man in a dream, using his hands and feet to propel himself from missile to missile, turning, using his cyborg reflexes to keep him from harm.

In moments, he lightly magnetized his boots. Gharlane ran over metallic surfaces and slowed his speed before entering a single-storey building. He floated into a lift, pressed a red button and rode it down three levels. Hurrying through a dim corridor, he came to an electronic bed with a body depression. Medical monitors on top ran through sequencing numbers, the middle monitor rapidly changing from 1 to 99 in blue numerals. Gharlane shed his vacc-suit and lay down in the depression.

He stiffened as his entire self merged into a direct link with the Web-Mind.

Without any introduction or explanation, the Web-Mind shot a series of images into Gharlane.

First were interferometer shots of the Highborn vessel. Its laser stabbed with precision and destroyed a Zeno. Then a different image invaded Gharlane's thoughts. Two enemy Zenos activated at the last possible moment, suddenly appearing. The *Descartes* must have detached them. The first cyborg-controlled meteor-ship chasing the *Descartes* attempted an evasion tactic. A blinding flash of nuclear energy ended the attempt and effectively ended the much-needed meteor-ship. It was usually a risky maneuver to chase an enemy ship, as it could easily detach drones in one's path.

*The Highborn and Jovians continue to work together, although system-wide radio traffic proves that our subversion campaign has spread grave unrest among the Jovians.*

*You will gather our nearest vessels and form them into a taskforce, including the second meteor-ship following the* Descartes. *The taskforce will follow the missile strike against Callisto. They will constitute a second wave assault. Later, they will strike Ganymede. The enclaves on Europa and Io represent a four percent danger and therefore can await destruction. Once Ganymede receives its nuclear bath, the Jovians will cease to threaten us.*

144

"I await your instructions," Gharlane said.

The Web-Mind flooded Gharlane with the data that needed to go out to the cyborg vessels.

*We will launch the missiles in ninety-three hours,* the Web-Mind added.

"Calculations indicate a quicker timetable would achieve greater success."

*Negative. Callisto is presently on the other side of Jupiter as Athena Station. Soon it will begin to swing around the planet in relation to us. Calculating the speed of our missiles and Callisto's orbital path, the strike will hit at the most propitious moment to achieve surprise.*

Gharlane reevaluated. "I have received," he said. Then he arose to begin the preparations.

# The Strike

## -1-

In the lonely vastness of space, Arbiter Octagon continued to tumble end over end. In his ears, he heard the harshness of close breathing. It was a hoarse sound, a bitter one and it told about the futility of his existence.

His throat was raw from screaming. His eyes had bled a thousand tears. Now he stared like a dead man at the many stars shining in mockery around him.

Soon, he would choke to death on carbon dioxide. He would likely beg for an extension of life to whatever being could hear in the chilling vacuum of space. He realized that the Dictates were a bloody pack of lies. Man wasn't logical, but a seething bed of passions. Men yearned for existence and they desperately wanted things. Men did not rationally reason out each step as the Dictates implied. Perhaps for the first time, Octagon realized that man was not a rational animal, but a rationalizing beast, making excuses for whatever suited his yearnings.

All these cycles aboard the warships, and before that the grueling courses readying him for duty as an arbiter—everything was composed of lies. It was all the bloody, pathetic ravings of idiot-buffoons. It had led to this, to his tumbling in space, hopeless, helpless and defeated by a primitive barbarian. The Dictates....

Arbiter Octagon frowned as something entered his vision. Something out there—

His jaw dropped as his mouth hung slackly.

The something blazed brighter than anything else did, making it greater than a star, greater even than Jupiter, at least from his vantage.

Octagon's frown changed texture as a decided change came over him. The futility of life dribbled away. A dim thing, a chattering thing, an animal longing burst into life and quickly become hope. The hope thudded like his heartbeats and revived his spirits. It also rekindled his hatred for barbarians, for the supreme bastard of them all: the arrogant Marten Kluge.

The brightness was a flare of exhaust. It grew larger and larger as he stared at it. In time, Octagon realized it was the exhaust of a pod.

*It's a rescue pod. I'm being rescued.*

A weird smile twisted Octagon's face. It wasn't a sane smile, rather that of a madman whose prayers had been answered. The universe, maybe the Dictates or some divine being, realized that he had been unjustly abused. Now he was going to be allowed to exact his revenge against barbarians, against vile Marten Kluge.

Octagon laughed with glee, a wild, whooping noise.

As he tumbled end over end, as he twisted his head to get a better view, he read the pod's lettering. Ah, he was in luck. This wasn't a pod from his old ship. This one said, *Pod 3, Hobbes.*

A fierce grin stretched Octagon's lips. A new ship, a different Force-Leader and Arbiter would listen to his tale. In a matter of weeks, he was going to be before the Philosopher's Board on Callisto. They would hear his story. They would learn that he had been right and Strategist Tan had been wrong. This could well mean a leap in status.

Octagon rubbed his gloved hands.

The bright flare had died. Now smaller jets appeared as the pod slowed and moved toward him. An airlock opened and a vacc-suited rescue-worker jumped out. The worker was strong, for the leap quickly accelerated the worker. A tether line hooked to the worker's belt played out behind him.

Octagon's grin was beginning to hurt, he smiled so widely. The indignity of his kidnapping and the horror of being launched in a prefixed pod—he continued to whoop with laughter. Oh, his certain death had miraculously changed into life and coming revenge. He could almost feel the thrill of shocking a captured Marten Kluge for the first time.

"Hurry!" shouted Octagon. He waved his arms as his hysterical laughter increased. Oh, this was the most glorious moment in his existence. What had he ever done to deserve this? It was uncanny. It was—

The vacc-suited worker reached him. It was such a serene thing. The worker grabbed his boot and halted the slow tumbling. With a strong hand and a deft twist that shoved against his hip, the worker hooked the tether line to Octagon's belt.

"Oh, thank you, thank you, thank you," Octagon whispered.

Then something cold blossomed in Octagon's gut. It came from the sight of a silvery sheen, something... *metallic*. The worker's faceplate—Octagon craned his neck, trying to get another glimpse.

The worker drew him closer and Octagon had his first good look into his rescuer's faceplate. Behind the glassy visor was a mask-like face with black, plastic sockets and silver eyeballs. Each ball bearing-like eye contained a red dot for a pupil. His rescuer wasn't human, but a cyborg.

The cold in Octagon's gut mushroomed outward until his arms and legs felt numb. If a cyborg was rescuing him... that meant the melded creature would take him to a converter. Evil Marten Kluge had warned him about this. The barbarian had suggested that suicide would be preferable to cyborg conversion.

With a hoarse cry, Octagon grabbed the tether-line's hook, trying to tear it off his belt.

The cyborg moved with an insect's speed. It gripped his wrists, immobilizing his hands. Then the thing activated a thruster-pack. They lurched. Octagon whipped his head back and forth. He saw the hydrogen particles propelling them. He saw the open airlock in the pod. It was like the jaws of a beast.

148

It was hideous doom, and the airlock seemed to grin and hiss with Marten Kluge's voice.

"No," Octagon said. "You can't do this."

The cyborg paid no heed as it jetted for the pod. With a madman's bellow, Octagon attempted to fight, to flail against fate. Remorselessly and with steely strength, the cyborg tightened its hold, taking him to a sinister new future that promised a metallic world of enslaved electrons and motorized limbs.

## 2

The *Descartes* headed toward Jupiter, deeper into the heavy gravity-well. Behind it followed the last Zeno, rapidly closing in. At the present speeds, the ship had less than ninety minutes until the drone reached it. Unfortunately, the Highborn ship had already swept past in its comet-like rush and no longer fired its laser.

Marten sat in his module in the command center. He scowled at his screen, at the Praetor's wide face, at the pink, arrogant eyes and the predatory features chiseled in flat planes. Marten quietly replayed the Praetor's system-wide speech. He heard the harsh voice that had once told Training Master Lycon that the shock troopers needed to be gelded. What he couldn't understand is why the Highborn had sent a lone ship all the way out here.

Marten clicked off the Praetor's image. On the screen, he brought up Chief Controller Su-Shan. She'd spoken to Yakov, to the officers of the *Descartes*. Marten had learned that she was the ranking governor of the Guardian Fleet. She was presently in one of the laser-satellites of Callisto Orbital Defense.

Su-Shan had the same elfin quality as Tan. She wore a golden headband, had pale hair and strikingly green eyes. Surprisingly, she wore a sheer robe. Every time she'd moved, Marten had caught a glimpse of her perfect breasts or the slenderness of her waist.

Marten replayed her quiet voice. It was utterly devoid of emotion. She'd spoken with Yakov, demanding an audience with Strategist Tan. When Yakov had said that was impossible, Su-Shan had informed Yakov about armed uprisings on Ganymede and the detention of visiting dignitaries. She'd told him of his coming destruction and that of every terrorist. She said it in such inflectionless tones that Marten couldn't decide if it was comical or chilling.

Marten froze her image. He'd listened to Yakov's attempts to reason with her. She'd fallen silent then, as if waiting for Yakov to halt his flood of nonsense. When he'd stopped talking, she'd continued where she had left off, as if Yakov had never spoken.

Marten squeezed out of the module and moved to Yakov in his chair. The Force-Leader examined a holographic image. It hovered over a rectangular section of flooring before him. Yakov made adjustments with a control unit. The orbital paths of the four Galilean moons appeared as dotted lines around holographic Jupiter.

"Ours is a complicated system," Yakov said.

Marten nodded.

Jupiter dominated everything with its size and its horrendous gravitational pull. It meant that moving here took much greater fuel as compared to other planetary systems. It also meant that maintaining a high orbit, the high ground, was even more advantageous here than elsewhere.

It would take eleven Earths placed side-by-side to stretch across Jupiter's visible disk. More than one thousand Earths would be needed to fill Jupiter's volume. Because Earth was denser than Jupiter, the Jovian planet only had three hundred times the Earth's mass.

Yakov fiddled with the control unit. A sea of pale dots appeared. They were everywhere. Some circled the Galilean moons. Some traveled between them. Others boosted from Jupiter and headed to the Inner group moons. The majority of the dots were obviously civilian or corporation spaceships. Yakov adjusted the control, and orange dots appeared among them, a fraction of the number.

"Those are the known locations of Guardian Fleet warships," Yakov said. "By their maneuverings, we should now be able to tell if they're cyborg-controlled." He pressed a

151

button. Two of the orange dots turned green. "Those are under Secessionist control, those who have radioed us."

"It doesn't look as if any of those can help us against the Zeno," Marten said.

"They cannot," Yakov said.

After Jupiter, the biggest bodies were the four Galilean moons. The last two were larger than Mercury, while Io was larger than Luna of Earth. Io, the nearest to Jupiter, completed an orbital circuit every 1.77 days. According to Yakov, the mineral complexes on Io had light defensive equipment, enough to hurt orbital fighters, but negligible against even one meteor-ship.

"The cyborgs could easily cripple mining on Io," Yakov said.

"How does any of this help us against the Zeno?" Marten asked.

"Patience," Yakov said.

Europa was an ice-ball. The intense radiation from Jupiter and Io's volcanoes made it a harsh place on the surface. Its ice provided most of the system's water and protected the deep communities there.

A green dot orbited Europa.

Yakov indicated it. "We have a Secessionist dreadnaught and several patrol boats there. At the moment, it is our greatest concentration of strength."

"This orange dot," Marten said, pointing out a ship moving between Europa and Ganymede. "It's not traveling in a direct route. Is there a reason for that?"

"Yes. The reason is the Laplace resonance."

"Meaning what?"

Yakov began to explain.

The first three Galilean moons formed a pattern known as a Laplace resonance. For every four orbits Io made around Jupiter, Europa made a perfect two orbits and Ganymede made a perfect one. The resonance caused the gravitational effects that distorted the orbits into elliptical shapes. Each moon received an extra tug from its neighbors at the same point in every orbit. However, Jupiter's strong tidal force helped to circularize the orbits and negate some of the elliptical shape.

152

Those forces also affected ships traveling between the three moons.

Yakov clicked his control unit.

Three orange dots were highlighted as they moved into a low-Ganymede orbit. Those were clearly Guardian Fleet ships. Their commandant had threatened planetary bombardment if the surface fighting did not cease at once.

To try to stem the fighting between Secessionists and Guardians, Marten had recommended a doctored file. Too many Jovians still refused to believe that cyborgs had infiltrated the system. Therefore, Yakov recorded mock attack sequences by Osadar in the *Descartes*. These fabrications Yakov sent as beamed distress signals from several now-silent Guardian Fleet vessels—those warships they were certain were under cyborg control. The recording had helped convince some that the cyborgs had truly arrived.

Yakov changed the holographic image, showing Marten the entire Jovian System.

Counting the Galilean moons, there were sixty-three different bodies orbiting Jupiter. Most were asteroid-sized and contained less combined population than Ganymede, the second most populous moon. Four small moons known as the Inner group orbited Jupiter at less than 200,000 kilometers. In economic terms, they were important, as each was part of the automated, atmospheric system gathering helium-3. None had powerful military forces stationed on or near them, although there was civilian space-traffic there.

The rest of the Jovian bodies were far beyond the Galilean moons. The Himalia group were tightly clustered moons with orbits around eleven to twelve million kilometers from Jupiter.

There were three other groups. In order of distance, they were Ananke, Carme and the Pasiphae group. These asteroid-sized moons were far away from Jupiter and far from Athena Station, some over twenty-five million kilometers.

Marten frowned as he took in the immensity of the system. Jupiter was unlike any of the Inner Planets. There were vastly more moons here that were incredibly distant from each other. If they survived the Zeno, the coming fight would be unlike anything he'd known. Normally in a system, a single planetary body dominated strategic thought. Here, he hardly knew where to begin.

It brought him back to the Zeno. "What are we going to do about the drone?" he asked.

Yakov clicked the unit. It showed the Zeno heading for them. The Force-Leader rubbed his thumb along the control unit. "I'm open to suggestions," he said.

Marten didn't like the sound of that.

## 3

Far from Marten and his troubles was a small spec of a spacecraft. It was in the outer Jovian System and the craft contained one passenger. She presently lay on her bunk, staring at the bulkhead above. Her clothes had worn through in too many places, showing skin. It also showed that her muscles were firm and that she had lost weight. The lost weight heightened the shape of her breasts, and it had caused her butt to return to its shape she'd had at sixteen.

A lifetime ago, Nadia Pravda had slipped out of the Sun-Works Factory in a secret stealth-pod. She'd taken drugs for a time, before spacing them. To combat loneliness, she'd exercised endlessly, often to exhaustion. Despite the exercise, her new thinness had mainly come about because she was sick of the concentrates.

In the other room, a klaxon began to wail. It was at the lowest possible setting, but it caused Nadia to twist her neck as she stared in dumbfounded amazement.

With a frown furrowed across her forehead, Nadia sat up. She didn't—

A bizarre whine occurred as the pod's engine kicked into life. The pod's walls vibrated and the craft's thrust slammed Nadia against the bunk. She wheezed for breath. What was happening?

She blinked again. She had been alone a long time, trapped in these cramped quarters with nobody to talk to. Sometimes, she wondered if life would have been more bearable with Ervil along, even if the man had raped her every day of the voyage.

At least she would have had someone to talk to. The endless loneliness, the weary journey out of the Inner Planets and to the Jovian System—

The klaxon blared as the thrust pinned her to the bunk. Nadia found it hard to lift her chest high enough to draw air. As she did, her ragged shirt pressed against her breasts.

She hated the loneliness. She hated being trapped in a small pod in the vastness of the universe. Why had Marten Kluge left her? She thought about him. She remembered his promises. He had lied. All men lied. All men made promises they never kept. It was their philandering nature to do so.

Then the klaxon and the thrust stopped.

Nadia made a gasping sound as she struggled upright. The frown lines had reappeared, but now she forced herself to sit up and swing her legs over the bunk. She pushed toward the other room, floating in the pod's returned weightlessness.

She made a mouse-like noise upon entering the second compartment. The window shields had opened. Had the command been buried somewhere in the computer's program? She couldn't remember anymore.

What terrified her was the shape outside the polarized window. It was sleek and deadly looking, with military style lettering on the sides and obvious cannons poking from stubby wings. It... the sleek craft had matched velocities with her, seemingly remaining stationary now.

Nadia tried to speak. It had been weeks since she'd uttered anything. She finally croaked the words, "Patrol ship."

The sight and her speech was more than her mind could comprehend. It caused her to forget she was floating weightlessly toward the window. She remembered as her hip bumped against the console and as her face mashed against the cool window. Her nose pressed against the ballistic glass and her tearing eyes stared at the spacecraft.

The throb in her hip combined with the sting of her nose helped engage the neurons in her brain. After endless months and months of journeying, she was near Jupiter. In another three weeks—

156

Nadia blinked her eyeballs. Had she phased out again? It had been happening more these past months. Had those three weeks already passed?

She frowned as a red light began to blink on the console.

With another of her strange yelps, Nadia pushed herself into the pilot's chair and hurriedly strapped in. The red light—

"Oh," she whispered. She remembered what the light meant. This was… was… was….

With another blink and with a trembling hand, Nadia flipped a switch.

"Identify yourself," a female voice said from the com-unit.

More tears welled in Nadia's brown eyes. They were large eyes: ones that Marten Kluge had loved to stare into. The tears helped fire neurons and synapses in her mind.

"This is your final warning," the voice said.

Nadia trembled violently as she opened a channel. She made a croaking sound as she tried to speak. With slow deliberation, she moistened her lips. Then she bent near the console and whispered, "This is Nadia Pravda speaking. Who… who are you?"

"Say again?" asked the woman.

"I'm Nadia Pravda."

"What sort of cyborg name is that?"

"What?" Nadia asked. She knew nothing about the Third Battle for Mars, and she knew even less about cyborgs.

"Are you a cyborg?"

"What's… what's a cyborg?" Nadia whispered.

"Who are you? Identify yourself."

"I'm from Mercury," Nadia said.

"You're Highborn?"

"No!" Nadia said, with the first hint of emotion. Something flared in her eyes then. She moistened her lips again and cleared her throat. She was vaguely aware of hunger. That her stomach had almost shrunken into nothing.

"I escaped from the Highborn," Nadia said. "I want asylum."

"You're a political escapee?" the woman asked.

"Yes. Who are you?"

157

"We're Aquinas Patrol, Boat Seven, of the Guardian Fleet. You're in the outer boundary of the Jovian Sphere. We request an inspection, which means we're going to board you. Will you comply, Nadia?"

Nadia's eyes grew wide. Someone was coming aboard her pod. Why had that made the klaxon wail and the pod's precious hydrogen-particle engine to fire?

She glanced around at her vessel. Several squeezed tubes of concentrates floated in the air.

"If you refuse—" the woman began to say.

"No," Nadia said, terrified that the patrol boat would leave, leaving her all alone again. She was actually talking with someone. It was such a glorious feeling. "I want you to inspect me. I want to go with you."

"Are you well?" the woman asked.

"No," Nadia said. "I think there's something wrong with my thinking. Please—" the tears were streaming down her cheeks. "Please, take me with you."

"Do you have a vacc-suit?"

"I... I don't know. It's hard to think. I've been alone in space for a long time."

"I understand." There was compassion in the woman's voice. "We'll send a rescue team immediately. Patrol Boat—"

"Please," Nadia whispered, "keep talking to me until the others come. I... I haven't had anyone to talk to for a long time."

"Someone will be there soon, Nadia. Tell me about Mercury."

With the back of her hand, Nadia Pravda wiped tears from her cheeks. She had completed the journey. She had made it to the Jupiter System. Finally, everything was going to be all right. As the woman in the patrol boat listened, Nadia began to tell her about the Sun-Works Factory and her harrowing escape from it.

## 4

As Nadia boarded Boat Seven of the Aquinas Patrol over thirty million kilometers from Jupiter, Marten eased into a module in the *Descartes* command center. The command personnel were busy in the nearly silent room. Some tapped at computer screens. Others murmured into their implants. In the middle of the room, Yakov watched the main screen, his face impassive.

An hour had passed, meaning that the Zeno drone was thirty minutes behind them.

Marten switched on his vidscreen. Through the ship's sensors, he watched the Zeno.

"Force-Leader," Rhea said.

Yakov minutely turned his head.

"The Chief Controller wishes to speak with you."

Yakov pursed his lips. "Put her on the main screen."

The image of the Zeno faded away as Chief Controller Su-Shan appeared. There was faint color in her cheeks that hadn't been there earlier, and the serenity that had been in her eyes before had changed. She still wore the sheer robe. Because of the large main screen, Marten noticed her delicate frame and the buds on her breasts. He'd never pictured philosophers looking like this. She appeared to be in a large room. There was a statue to her left of a satyr blowing a reed flute. Occasionally, behind her, an officer in a white robe strode past.

"Force-Leader Yakov, you have made an unwarranted leap in status." Su-Shan hardly moved her lips as she spoke, which highlighted her elfin features.

"Force-Leader," Rhea said. "The drone accelerates."

"Give me a split-screen," Yakov said.

On the main screen was a shot of the drone, its exhaust seemingly doubling the Zeno's length. Beside it was the video image of the Chief Controller.

"Your altered cyborg file shows your duplicity," Su-Shan was saying. "Surely, you did not believe that would fool us."

"We are presently under attack," Yakov said. "So if you could make your point, it would be greatly appreciated."

"I grow weary of your falsified proceedings," she said.

"Send her the sensor readings," Yakov told Rhea.

"Is that wise?" Marten asked.

"Who speaks with such a strange accent aboard a Jovian warship?" Su-Shan asked. "Show him to me."

"I'm in the middle of a battle and must disconnect," Yakov told her.

"Do that and I shall order an immediate bombardment of the Galileo Regio," Su-Shan said.

Marten had glanced at a map of Ganymede earlier. The Chief Controller referred to a dark plain that contained a series of concentric grooves or furrows. It was one of Ganymede's most significant geologic features. Yakov had informed him that it was also critical to the Secessionists, stockpiled with weaponry and with secret planetary defenses soon to go online.

Yakov raised an eyebrow. "You accord my decision far too much weight, Chief Controller."

"Again you prattle falsities."

"Would you clarify your statement?"

"Force-Leader," Rhea said. "The drone continues to accelerate."

"Do not look away from me," Su-Shan said as she accepted a missive from a hand appearing onscreen. She glanced at the message before continuing. "We have discovered your importance in the terrorist plot. As amazing at it sounds, you are either the heart or the intellect of the so-called Secessionist Rebellion. Therefore, you will dialogue with me or the Galileo Regio shall receive several precision bombardments."

"Force-Leader," Rhea said, "you must—"

"Begin the Code Six Defense," Yakov told Rhea.

160

On the main screen, Su-Shan's eyes hardened. She turned her head and seemed to be in the process of giving an order, possibly a most terrible order.

"I am Marten Kluge of the Highborn Shock Troopers," Marten said, who'd been following the conversation closely.

On screen, Su-Shan turned back. It caused her robe to shift, to highlight her smooth skin underneath.

Marten hurried before the main screen. "I've come from Mars," he said. He dug out his credentials. "I am a fully accredited representative of the Mars Planetary Union."

"You expect me to believe such nonsense?" Su-Shan asked. "Firstly, your words are unreasonable, considering your original statement that you are a shock trooper. We have heard about them: Earth troops trained in advanced Highborn space-combat techniques. Secondly, the Martians would have informed us concerning an accredited representative in our system."

"I was a shock trooper who escaped the Highborn. The Martians hired me during their recent struggle and afterward granted me accreditation. They learned that I journeyed to Jupiter and wished to open secret negotiations with you. Unfortunately, they feared Highborn and Social Unity communications-cracking. My proof is this," Marten said, holding up the booklet's cover and then paging through the contents, hoping their video could record it.

As Marten did this, the *Descartes* shuddered. Anti-missile rockets zoomed from the meteor-ship, rocking it with their combined blasts. Usually, Yakov would have detached the rockets before they fired. There was no time now. Point-defense cannons fired for long-range spreads, and the rail-gun shot minefield canisters into the Zeno's likeliest path.

On the split-screen, Su-Shan glanced at something out of sight. "Your credentials appear to be genuine. You should have headed directly to Callisto."

"As a representative of the Mars Planetary Union," Marten said, "I can assure you that cyborgs boarded my ship."

Su-Shan stared at him. "We are aware of the Zeno, Representative. It would have been better for you if you'd headed directly to Callisto. Now your doom is imminent. I

161

suggest you return to your module and trust to Yakov's performance."

Marten hurried into the narrow module. He yanked a strap over his shoulder, buckling it with a click. Through the ship-wide intercom, Yakov was already instructing ship personnel to hurry to their acceleration couches.

Twenty seconds later, the *Descartes* engaged full thrust and began hard maneuvering. A harsh whine sounded and the command room's bulkheads trembled. Marten was pressed into the module as a hardened piece of plastic dug into his side. Then the pressure eased as the ship's thrust minutely changed. Now the side of Marten's head pressed against a cushion.

Meanwhile, outside the warship, the anti-missile rockets sped for the drone. Depleted uranium pellets followed, spreading into predictive paths. Behind them tumbled the rail-gun's barrel-sized canisters.

"Deploy three decoys," Yakov said.

The ship shuddered as electronically powerful missiles left the meteor. ECM pulsed from each as they attempted to imitate the ship's signals. Their task was to lure the enemy onto them instead of on the ship.

"Begin spraying the defensive gels," Yakov ordered.

Rhea initiated the sequence. Outside, tubes sprouted. From them sprayed a thick gel with lead additives. It formed a cloud behind the ship as the engines cut out. In several seconds, the cloud expanded. It was a dull gray with glittering purple motes.

The Zeno gained on them. But now rockets, pellets and canisters zeroed in on it.

Suddenly, the Zeno sprouted targeting rods. Then it ignited its massive thermonuclear warhead. X-rays and gamma rays traveled microseconds faster than the rest of the annihilation. Those rays used the rods to focus and aim at the targeted vessels: two decoys and the meteor-ship itself. The nuclear destruction destroyed the rods and destroyed the targeting computer as the x-rays and gamma rays traveled at light speed toward their destinations.

The two decoys exploded. The other rays hit the gel-field. Some of the energy made it through. One x-ray beam struck the meteor shell and burrowed into it, burning crewmembers on the outer levels. The command room was in the center of the ship. The arbiter's rooms were also deep within the protective core, and the crewmembers there were spared the worst effects.

As Marten stared at the screen, damage reports began to pour in. The ship's motive functions had survived. But the Zeno had struck a blow that affected many personnel and would likely reduce the ship's usefulness for days and perhaps weeks to come.

"Impressive," Su-Shan said from the main screen. "It is a pity we weren't able to give you a dreadnaught to command. Is that why you joined the rebellion? Did we under-appreciate you?"

"I have casualties to contend with," Yakov said. "If you could make this brief, I would be grateful."

Golden-banded Su-Shan studied Yakov. Then she smoothed out her robe. She spoke as before, without inflection. "In the next few hours, the Galileo Regio shall receive precision bombardments. You can thank yourself for it."

"Mass retaliation?" asked Yakov.

"No. This is an eradication of ingrates, a purging of philistines. We have achieved near perfection here, which your rebellion now imperils. I assure you that we shall not watch this occur as bystanders, but ruthlessly act to save our unique civilization."

"It would be good at a time like this if you could speak the truth," Yakov said. "You plan this bombardment in order to save your rank."

"I grieve to hear you utter such a nonsensical comment. In the Confederation, those best suited to rule do so. It is a matter of the Dictates and our rigorous tests."

"If your tests are so accurate," Yakov said, "why are all the governors from Callisto and not from Ganymede, Europa and Io?"

"Ah. Is this the source of your unwarranted arrogance? The answer is easily explained. We at Callisto possess superior genetics because we have striven to improve our bloodlines. Our educational system soars above yours and above those of Europa and elsewhere. If you desire rank, do as we've done. Earn greatness."

163

"We *have* earned it," said Yakov, his gaze boring into hers.

"No. You have acted as philistines and destroyers. We of Callisto serve as watchdogs over Jovian humanity. We use our teeth as it were and our valor to build. You have committed yourselves to the annihilation of things you cannot achieve. Perhaps you do not even understand what you're attempting to destroy."

"That's why you plan to murder thousands of innocents," Yakov said, his sarcasm heavy. "You're proving your philosophic superiority, is that it?"

"You are a clever man, Force-Leader. Who taught you to dialogue as you do?"

Marten pushed himself beside the command chair. This was going entirely the wrong way. These two obviously hated each other. "You Jovians are the oddest people I know," he said.

Su-Shan's left eyebrow twitched, which for her placid mannerisms amounted to wild emotionalism. "You are a barbarian, given to animalistic outbursts. Still, you are an accredited representative and in theory belong to the governing class of Mars. Would you care to clarify your statement?"

"Your system is under massive assault and the two of you bicker over philosophy," said Marten. "Who fired the Zenos at us? Who ordered those ships to attack? No one in the Guardian Fleet did, meaning that cyborgs ordered it. You've seen our data. The *Rousseau* really attacked the *Descartes'* pod and likely stranded an arbiter in space."

"You expect me to believe that obvious fabrication? I am insulted, Representative. The pod's destruction was a clear ploy to murder your arbiter and create a sensation. Yakov achieved both. Now he and his kind will pay the penalty for trying to destroy perfection."

"Have you spoken with Athena Station lately?" asked Marten.

"Of course," said Su-Shan. "The controller there assured me that nothing unwarranted has occurred. And let me add, and this will dismay you: the War Council at Athena Station has decided to act decisively. They will shortly launch needed

164

munitions, sending them to Callisto. Did you hear that, Force-Leader? Your rebellion is doomed."

"What supplies?" Yakov asked.

A faint smile slid onto Su-Shan's face. "Your rebellion has failed before it could truly begin. Disarm, Force-Leader, and save your people in the Galileo Regio."

"Wait!" said Marten. "Athena Station is sending supplies to Callisto? Is that what you said?"

She gave him a level stare, with the faintest hint of a sneer. She looked at him as if he were a buffoon who had committed some buffoonish offense. "I am not in the habit of lying, Representative. Frankly, your insinuations weary me. And it causes me to wonder how you gained your credentials."

"I already told you," Marten said, "the hard way." He was sick of being called a barbarian and fed up with her airy manners. "I gained them by putting my life on the line, by bleeding in combat and by killing armed enemies."

"Gross barbarism," Su-Shan said. "It shows your brute nature and likely your Highborn affinity that you revel in battle. You boast about fighting and killing and thereby show your lack of sensitivity and desire for reasoned dialogue."

"Maybe," Marten said. "But I earned my credentials."

"Your insinuation is that I failed to earn mine. You disappointed me, Representative."

"Have bullets ever whizzed past your ears? Have you ridden a torpedo into a particle shield and stormed your way aboard a warship?"

"I am a governor," said Su-Shan, as she lifted her elfin chin. "I am not a brute guardian. Please, cease these veiled insults."

"You use reason?" Marten asked, stung now. He wanted to break her placid manner, to see if she was human.

Su-Shan gazed at him coldly, as if he emitted a foul odor.

Marten shook his head, berating himself. He was as bad as Yakov and the others. Arguing with the Chief Controller was madness. He cleared his throat, deciding to try a different approach. "The Highborn commander has broadcast his data. He is the former Praetor of the Sun-Works Factory."

"I have heard his proclamation, yes," Su-Shan said. "It is bombastic twaddle. And it confirms my suspicion concerning the so-called Highborn. They are like our myrmidons: genetic aberrations, brutes in love with fighting. The Highborn are bigger than our myrmidons and display greater reasoning abilities, but their days are numbered because they're too emotive. Perhaps you are not aware that emotions are irrational."

"What about the cyborgs?" Marten asked. "You must have watched the files from Mars."

"They are strange," Su-Shan said, "a decided mistake in forced evolution. But that has no bearing on our present situation."

"You're wrong," Marten said. "The cyborgs are here in your system. They've already taken control of many of your warships. I killed three as they tried to board my ship, and I helped destroy a dreadnaught filled with them."

"You have joined the rebels? Is that what you're saying?"

"Your hatred is blinding you to the facts," Marten said.

Su-Shan stiffened. "How dare you accuse me of emotionalism? Reason guides me. Logic governs my actions. That you fail to understand this and insist on showering me with insults proves your brutishness. We are done dialoguing."

"You must alert your orbital defenses," Yakov said.

"They are alerted," Su-Shan said, "never fear."

"You're likely going to need every warship you possess," said Yakov. "I suggest you recall what you can from Ganymede."

Su-Shan laughed softly. "Your ploy is obvious and fruitless, Force-Leader. The warships approach a low-Ganymede orbit. You must tell me quickly, what is your decision?"

"The cyborgs have arrived," Yakov said. "On my oath, it is the truth."

Su-Shan waved a small hand. Golden wires were wrapped around her delicate fingers. "Do you truly expect us to believe that you timed your rebellion with a cyborg assault upon Jupiter? The odds—"

Yakov leaned forward in his chair as he struck an armrest. "Can't you understand?" he asked.

"You have spirit and possess a willingness to fight. None can doubt that. Now, however, you must make a momentous decision. Will you surrender your vessel and save Ganymede from precision strikes?"

Yakov glanced at Marten. It was the nearest to helplessness that Marten had seen from the Force-Leader.

Then it hit Marten, a possible key to turning the Chief Controller. He asked, "What if I show you an actual cyborg?"

"How could you achieve this feat?" she asked.

Marten unclipped a two-way, using his thumb to press a button and open a channel with Osadar. The device crackled more than before, and Marten wondered if the enemy gamma rays had caused that.

"Is there trouble?" Osadar asked.

"Hurry to the command room," Marten said.

"Will you present me with an actor in a suit?" asked Su-Shan.

"You can decide that for yourself," Marten said, as he clipped the two-way back onto his belt.

A minute passed. Then Osadar entered the room, causing command personnel to recoil. Osadar floated to Marten and stood before the main screen. Her melded torso, the branded *OD12* on her forehead, the skeletal arms and legs, and the plasti-flesh cyborg features—Osadar stared at the small Chief Controller.

"It appears compelling," Su-Shan admitted.

"What if Strategist Tan confirmed the cyborg's reality?" Marten asked.

Su-Shan blinked rapidly. "Tan lives?" she whispered.

The strain in Su-Shan's voice startled Marten. He nodded, and said, "Of course."

Su-Shan turned away, and she brushed something out of her left eye. Soon, her small shoulders squared under her sheer robe and her chin lifted. When she regarded them again, she seemed colder than before.

Yakov looked up from his armrest. A small screen was embedded there. He'd been scrolling through something, reading data. "I'd forgotten," he whispered to Marten out of the side of his mouth. "Our Strategist is the Chief Controller's cousin."

"Will that make a difference?" Marten whispered.

Yakov glanced at the main screen, and he rubbed his jaw so his hand partly covered his mouth. "Callisto law is firm, and there are few children among the governors. I doubt Su-Shan has any other relatives in the same generation. Yes. It is important."

"Bring the Strategist into view," Su-Shan was saying. "I would speak with her."

Marten cleared his throat. "I'd gladly do it, but she's presently under Suspend." Suspend slowed all biological functions, putting its recipient into a hibernating state.

Su-Shan's beautiful features turned pasty. "Barbarians," she whispered. "You shall...." With a small finger, she rubbed the inner corner of her left eye as if removing a speck. Then she glared at them, and her eyes glistened. "Revive her at once. Let me speak to her face to face."

"First," said Yakov in his normally calm manner, "you must postpone the bombardment."

"A Chief Controller cannot be blackmailed," Su-Shan said slowly.

Yakov shook his head. "No blackmail is intended. We simply wish to prove our point, to prove the validity of our argument."

"Yes," Su-Shan whispered. "I will grant you an extension. Now hurry, bring me my cousin—I mean, revive Strategist Tan this instant."

## 5

Small Strategist Tan lay nude on a medical slab with a med-officer hovering over her. He removed a tube from her side and sprayed the wound with quickheal. He had drained much of Tan's blood, heating it and pumping it back into her. Then he had shocked her several times. Each shock had caused her to jerk and her thighs to quiver.

Finished spraying, the med-officer draped a thin blanket over Tan's nakedness.

Tan shuddered suddenly and inhaled sharply. The monitor-board clicked, beeped and flashed lights and various numbers. The med-officer observed them as he studied Tan. She eased into a relaxed position and breathed normally. Then her fingers twitched and her eyelids snapped open.

"Lie still," said the med-officer. He wore a yellow smock, with a yellow cap over his round head. He had soft hands and stroked her nearest arm, which lay on the blanket.

Tan blinked at him, and she frowned.

"You can't talk yet," he said. "Your mind is thawing. You'll be fine in several minutes."

It seemed as if she wanted to answer. She stared up at him. Her blinks were earnest and her eyes straining.

Marten watched the proceeding. The entire situation was a mess. The Confederation's philosophical rulers were odd and strangely blind for people who prided themselves on using reason to solve each problem. Instead, it seemed as if they'd cut themselves off from their humanity, or as if they'd failed to consider their emotions. Thinking to become wise, they'd become foolish in bizarre ways. People weren't creatures of cold reason, although people could reason. For instance, why did a man fall in love with a woman? Did that have anything to do with reason? No. It was passion, desire—it was a basic need that erupted with volcanic power.

Marten shook his head. The odds this time were piling against him. Callisto had more warships. The cyborgs had even more. The Secessionists side was the weakest of all. Maybe Osadar had it right. They should flee to Saturn and start over.

"Where am I?" whispered Tan.

"You're aboard the *Descartes*," the med-officer said. "You're in the medical room."

"I can't remember what happened," she whispered.

"It will come back to you."

"Was I sick?"

"No." The med-officer glanced at Marten.

Marten shook his head.

"Then why—" Tan groaned, and she strained to sit up.

The med-officer gently pressed her against the slab. "Wait a few more minutes."

"The barbarians pumped me full of Suspend," Tan whispered. "I have to warn—" Tan stopped talking as she lifted her head and spotted Marten.

"You're helping them," Tan accused the med-officer. "You will be demoted for this, possibly mind-scrubbed and sent to Io."

The med-officer removed his hands from her, stepped back and glanced at Marten.

Marten eased near. "Your cousin is online, wishing to talk with you."

"Su-Shan?" asked Tan.

"There have been a few changes," Marten said. He told her about recent events.

Tan sat up groggily as she wrapped the blanket around her. "If what you say is true, why would Su-Shan order a bombardment of the Galileo Regio?"

"You can ask her," Marten said, trying to forget that she was naked underneath the blanket.

170

Tan rubbed her face. When she lowered her hand and turned to the med-officer, she said, "I need a drink and something to eat."

He gave her a bottle and some wafers. Once finished eating, she slid onto the deckplates and leaned against the med-slab for support.

"I need some clothes," Tan said.

"Yes," said the med-officer. "I'll get them."

*  *  *

"Are you under duress?" Su-Shan asked. She spoke through a wall-screen in Octagon's former chamber.

Marten sat behind the desk. Osadar stood to the side. Strategist Tan faced the wall-screen.

"I am in the Arbiter's room," Tan said. "No one points at gun at me and no one has threatened me. But they did kidnap me from my quarters and hold me hostage under Suspend." She glanced at Marten. "However, I no longer sense hostile intentions."

"How can I be sure of that?" Su-Shan asked.

"Do the bands of Jupiter leak into space?" Tan asked.

A quick grin flashed across Su-Shan's face.

Marten wondered what that signified. Was the phrase a code sequence?

"Where is Force-Leader Yakov?" Su-Shan asked.

"He's indisposed," Marten said.

"Ah," said Su-Shan. "You mean he is busy plotting with the other ingrates. We shall soon break into their signals, never fear. Now, I demand that you escort Tan to Callisto."

"First we must come to an understanding about the cyborgs," Marten said.

Su-Shan hesitated. "What is your analysis concerning these cyborgs?" she asked Tan.

"The one standing in the room with me is real," Tan said.

"Does that mean the others exist?" asked Su-Shan.

"It doesn't have to follow," Tan said. "Still, I think something odd has occurred in our system."

"Yes," said Su-Shan, "the rebellion."

Tan shook her head. "I do not believe that Yakov planned open rebellion."

171

Su-Shan minutely tilted her head as she studied her cousin. "The fact of their successful rebellion means they have planned it for some time. Therefore, Yakov did plan it."

"Agreed," said Tan. "What I meant to say is that Yakov did not plan *to begin* the rebellion this soon."

"How do you know that?"

"Since boarding this vessel, I have monitored his messages. I have also conferred many times with the ship's Arbiter. He was like a living stick-tight and searched for rebellion with unusual zeal. He had his suspicions, naturally, but never the proof."

"Yet the rebellion occurred," said Su-Shan. "Therefore, you failed to—"

"If I may," Tan said, "I disagree with your overall analysis—I am inferring portions of your beliefs, that's true, but I have ingested the thrust of your argument. You and I both know that system-wide oddities have occurred independently of the Secessionist Plot. We have both spoken about the strange events before this. We first suspected the Secessionists, and that is why I boarded the *Descartes*. After seeing one cyborg with my own eyes and witnessing further odd occurrences, I have begun to believe that cyborgs have indeed invaded our system."

"What would be their purpose?" asked Su-Shan.

"Conquest, I should think. Solar System dominion."

"You believe cyborgs have suborned Athena Station?"

"It is a possibility," Tan said, "one worth considering."

"What is your recommendation?"

"I may be the last Strategist of the War Council," Tan said.

"If true, you would be the new Chief Strategist. Your words would have even greater weight, given that you were free to speak your mind."

"While they do not overtly threaten me," Tan said, "obviously, I am a prisoner."

"I demand her immediate release," Su-Shan told Marten.

"Under certain conditions," Marten said, "I believe that Yakov would agree to that."

"I cannot halt the bombardment," Su-Shan said.

"Could you postpone it?" Marten asked.

"Possibly," said Su-Shan, "depending on the timeframe."

"Until the supply vessels from Athena Station reach a low-Callisto orbit," Marten said.

"You believe the 'vessels' will turn into a cyborg strike," Su-Shan said in reproof.

"Why does it matter what I believe?"

"Because it taints your good faith," she said.

"If I'm right," Marten said, "your postponement will have left more of the Jovian System intact. If I'm wrong, you can still send in your warships."

"As the rebels gather reinforcements and send everyone in the Galileo Regio into the deep caverns," Su-Shan said.

"If I'm wrong, you will have an over-powering fleet and easily be able to sweep aside whatever reinforcements the Secessionists have gathered."

"So you're saying it is to be total war?" Su-Shan asked.

Marten thought fast. "No," he said. "Under those conditions, I would urge Force-Leader Yakov to surrender. And as the Mars Planetary Union Representative, I would be forced to recognize the ruling Jovian government."

"You should recognize us immediately," Su-Shan said. "I cannot understand why you don't. As an accredited representative, it is your duty to recognize the lawful government."

"Let us put that aside for the moment," Marten said."

"No," Su-Shan said, "as a representative—"

"Chief Controller!" said Tan, giving her cousin a tiny shake of her head.

"Very well..." Su-Shan said. "I will agree to a temporary truce. You will give Strategist Tan a pod and she can set a course for Callisto."

"I agreed," said Marten. "Now, as to the details of the exchange...."

-6-

As Strategist Tan ejected from the *Descartes* and headed in a pod for a Guardian Fleet dreadnaught, millions of kilometers away Octagon gibbered for mercy.

He lay on a steel table, with his head strapped down and his torso, arms and legs secured by metal bands. He was stark naked, his manhood a shriveled lump that lay like a beaten dog on his hairless scrotum. Whenever he squirmed, punishment *zaps* sizzled across his skin. He quickly learned to lie perfectly still as the two cyborgs in the room continued their experiments.

Hypos, prods, needles and a strange, bulky instrument that looked like an oversized gun were attached to the nearest wall. A medical unit monitored his status, and its occasional sounds sent a shiver of terror through Octagon. He'd always hated doctors and dentists in particular. The taps, massages, drills, the needles and the cold scope on his chest, he had always hated them. Such ministrations had made him feel vulnerable again, as he had as an orphan in his youth.

He'd been reared in a harsh world of Platonic instructors, and Master Gensifer had been the worst of his teachers. Octagon could still feel the slaps against the back of his head, and the evil cheek-pinches by the man's strong fingers. Worst of all, however, had been Master Gensifer's acid tongue. Gensifer had used his tongue like a wire lash, and it had slashed Octagon's young ego with brutal precision. It was strange, but over time, Octagon had come to admire Gensifer. He had seen the old man as a tower of strength. If he could

174

become sharp-witted, if he could slap and pinch others, then he would be safe. He would be strong and secure. Maybe the savagery of his childhood had driven Octagon to excel. Maybe the need to defend himself had forced him to hurt others.

Octagon didn't reason these things out on the steel table. Instead, he felt small again, vulnerable and weak. He loathed these sensations. They shriveled his gut. He was a hurt thing, and he would do anything to stop the hurting, anything to get off the table.

At the moment, Octagon remained rigid—the electrical discharges were too painful to resist. Only his eyes roamed free. A metal band circled his head, keeping his neck from moving. He strained his eyes to the left to see what the nearest cyborg detached from the wall. He peered to the right as the door opened. From the next room came an awful green glow. It implied horrors beyond imagination.

He was still aboard the pod, Octagon was certain of that. Where did they go? What did the cyborgs want with him, other than to convert him into one of them? The idea... is this why he had survived the vacuum of space? It was inconceivable. He had prayed. He had prayed to a myriad of deities.

A horrible thought occurred then. Which of the supernatural entities had heard him? Because he lay on this cold, steel table, the sickening conclusion was that an evil entity must have responded to his prayers. The entity probably laughed at a man's attempt to wrest an ounce of joy from life.

Octagon wanted to whimper, and that made him cringe, fearing more shocks. Maybe whimpering offended cyborgs. However, no electrical discharges were released. Octagon strained to see what the awful beings were doing now.

A cyborg pulled the bulky, gun-like instrument from the wall. The metallic monster turned toward him, raising the barrel of the 'gun'. The weapon showed a large opening, and something seemed to be in it. The cyborg floated nearer, both it and the bulky thing were weightless.

"What are you doing?" Octagon whispered. His voice was badly damaged from prolonged screaming. "I insist that you stop at once."

Octagon writhed then, making horrible croaking sounds as the metal bands activated and *zaps* surged through him.

The second cyborg reached out to the medical board and clicked something. The shocks ceased, bringing blessed relief.

Octagon sagged as he blinked his watery eyes. Had the thing turned off the pain? Before he could think to ask why, the first cyborg pressed the bulky, gun-like thing against his neck.

"Wait," Octagon whispered. "Tell me what you want."

He tried to squirm away from the gun-thing, and this time no shocks tortured him. Octagon failed to rejoice, however. Spider-like claws emerged from the gun-thing and rigidly clasped his neck.

"If you'd just speak to me," Octagon pleaded.

Then he screamed as knifing pain pierced the base of his neck. Hypos hissed against him as drugs entered his bloodstream. His neck numbed, but the cutting feeling horrified him. He tried to thrash away. Tears poured from his eyes and his mouth opened in a silent scream. He could feel the thing digging into him. It seemed the gun-thing deposited metal into his flesh. What was its purpose? Why did the universe hate him?

"Marten Kluge!" he hissed in a dry whisper of hate.

Before Octagon could elaborate on his hatred, his eyelids grew heavy and his bodily functions began to shut down. He did not know it, but the cyborg had inserted a Webbie-jack into him. They had modified him because they desired knowledge that only he possessed among their captives. Through careful tests, the two cyborgs had determined he possessed this knowledge.

As former Arbiter Octagon relaxed and entered sleep mode, the first cyborg removed the jack-gun. The second cyborg began to remove the metal bands. The restraints would no longer be necessary.

\*\*\*

As Webbie Octagon sped toward his fate in the *Hobbes's* pod, Gharlane rode a lift to the surface of Athena Station. He physically wished to observe the missiles launch. Then he would leave Athena Station and head for the *Locke*. The main cyborg fleet was gathering, even as the humans attempted their last-minute ploys.

Gharlane knew a moment of disquiet then, and he realized that once again he'd known better. Through the Web-Mind's wish for one more warship, the biomass brain had possibly lost their advantage of strategic surprise. There were indicators that many of the humans still didn't understand the situation. But Gharlane doubted the data. The chaos-factor humans from Mars had revealed too much, and the chaos-factor Highborn had added to that knowledge.

Gharlane froze with a sudden thought, a new input. He wondered if he should continue to categorize the Highborn as human, or as a subset of Homo sapiens or as new species. Men and chimpanzees were a different species. The relative differences between Homo sapiens and Highborn were stark. Were Highborn as superior to Homo sapiens as men were to chimpanzees? It was an interesting question. The answer might help the campaign to eradicate both. Was it possible for two species to coordinate? Could men and chimpanzees cooperate as allies? It seemed doubtful. The Highborn might be so superior to Homo sapiens that it was impossible for them to achieve a true alliance. The arrangement under which the Homo sapiens fought for the Highborn pointed to a possible master-slave relationship, however.

The lift slowed and the door opened. Gharlane exited into a large lobby of motionless cyborgs, each hooked by cables into a generator. It was a new technique: hot-shotted cyborgs ramped with overloaded energy. The Web-Mind readied a beta unit of overloaded troops. One cyborg with its cable slotted in its chest jittered, causing its metallic feet to rattle against the floor. Gharlane wondered how long that had been occurring. Then the cyborg's eyes snapped open.

Recognizing the danger signs, Gharlane drew a laser carbine from the back-sheath on his vacc-suit. A red beam stabbed through the dim lobby. The fatally damaged cyborg screeched as it tore the cable from its chest-slot. Then its neck-armor melted as the beam stabbed through. Expertly, Gharlane sliced upward. As the screeching cyborg attempted a bounding attack, the beam cut the head in two. Electric sparks and loud

177

whining sounds accompanied the hot-shotted cyborg's clattering death.

Gharlane observed the others. They remained in sleep mode, charging with power. Gharlane was aware of the Web-Mind's observation and assessment of his action. In three seconds, the Web-Mind's presence departed, no doubt realizing that Gharlane had acted correctly.

After exiting the lobby and resealing the chamber, Gharlane floated outside. Several kilometers away the bulk of the Voltaire Missiles waited. They were hidden from view by the curvature of the surface and by intervening buildings.

Gharlane expected no less than annihilating victory from this strike. Cyborgs had modified the giant missiles for weeks, as this day had long been anticipated. Some of the missiles remained as before. Most contained advanced electronics, stolen goods from Onoshi Electronics, once one of the primary Houses of the Ice Hauler Cartel in the Neptune System.

Gharlane had a moment to wonder why the Prime Web-Mind hadn't fully subjugated the Neptune System. It had allowed one massive habitat to survive, a preserve of Homo sapiens. Perhaps it was because of the analysis program that had discovered that the humans of Neptune System produced more technological equipment as free agents than as suborned cyborg units. Gharlane halted as he pondered another input of new thought.

Why didn't the Prime Web-Mind build mini-Web-Minds as technological agents? Was there some creative process lost in the conversion to a mass mind? That was an interesting possibility. Is that why each Web-Mind used a master unit like himself?

That seemed more than probable. It also seemed like something that the Web-Mind would not want him to dwell upon.

Gharlane checked an internal chronometer. Ah, it was ninety-one seconds to liftoff. He waited, with the anticipation building, while his calculations ran through the known data.

Callisto orbited Jupiter approximately every seventeen days. Athena Station orbited every thirty-one days. Considering the position of Athena Station at the time of launch and Callisto's continued orbit, the distance between the two in a straight-line flight would take a little over one hundred hours. The Voltaire Missiles possessed fantastic acceleration and of considerable duration, especially considering the relatively short distances between the two points. But the missiles would not use the fantastic acceleration at first. That would come later, when it was too late for the Jovians to react.

As an added bonus, there would be a second wave assault behind the missiles. The second wave contained a dreadnaught, a meteor-ship, a troop-ship and a squadron of patrol boats. The troop-ship would land on the smoldering surface to complete the destruction.

As Gharlane estimated destructive factors, the first Voltaire Missile blasted off from Athena Station. Missile after missile ignited their fusion core and erupted off the blast-pans. The ground under Gharlane trembled because of the mass exodus of missiles.

The first missile appeared—a space-needle with a bulbous warhead. Behind it followed others. Their hot exhausts blazed like fiery blue tails. There was no sound, as vacuum carried none. The missiles appeared as lazy behemoths, their tails rapidly growing to abnormal lengths. As the tails grew, the missiles accelerated. As each missile zoomed for Callisto, they quickly merged into one continuous blur of motion.

The quake ceased as the last Voltaire Missile lofted into the blackness. In short order, the final missile vanished from sight. Soon, the seemingly fast-moving star cluster vanished—the dots of the missiles' exhaust.

The first strike had been launched. In a little over one hundred hours, the rulers of Callisto and the chief bastion of Jovian power would cease to exist.

Gharlane spun on his heel and headed back for the lift. There was much to coordinate. After his tasks were completed, he would leave Athena Station. He would leave to join his taskforce. A pleasurable sensation filled him, similar to the one he felt in the holographic chamber. He would scour the Jupiter System, ending all resistance. Cyborg victory would be assured.

179

Marten and Yakov sat in the Force-Leader's room, hunched over his desk. On it was displayed the Jovian System, the orbits of the various moons and the known locations of fleet units.

The last few days had built an affinity between the two. Yakov's calm demeanor, his deliberation and his inner intensity appealed to Marten. Most of all, Marten appreciated Yakov's thirst for freedom and his desire to rip the shackles from Ganymede. Yakov reminded him of Secretary-General Chavez of Mars. Both men fought for more than just personal freedom, they also fought to free their world. As Marten mulled over the Jovian map, he wondered about that.

Why was he always running into this sort of man? Was... God trying to tell him something?

Marten shifted in his chair. That was too heavy for him. He was just an ex-shock trooper on the run, trying to stay ahead of an overwhelmingly intrusive political system and crazed genetic freaks with delusions of godhood. He'd fled to Jupiter to escape both. Now he was in the middle of another war, a three-way battle for control and maybe for the soul of humanity.

"If we could combine our fleets," Yakov said, tapping the dot that represented Ganymede.

Marten tried to concentrate on the computer-map. He rubbed his chin and stared at the dots and the various, colored clusters representing warships.

Secretary-General Chavez and Force-Leader Yakov: both men risked their lives to free their worlds. For years, Chavez had struggled against Social Unity. Now the brave man was dead, turned into radioactive dust by the Highborn-launched Hellburner. The struggle had cost Chavez his life. However, Marten doubted the freedom fighter would have wished it any other way.

Yakov had plotted for years, becoming a key mover against the philosophically arrogant Dictates and the rulers of Callisto. The hidden fight had forged Yakov into a steely conspirator and into a ship's captain of abnormal calm.

What did Yakov see in him? Marten wondered. He fought for freedom as hard as anyone did. True, it had always been personal freedom and freedom for the friends around him. His larger goals had always been on the horizon, to flee to a better, safer and easier place. Chavez and Yakov stayed in their bitter situations and fought with others to improve it.

Marten nodded slowly. Chavez and Yakov were superior to him. They had more guts. They stood their ground and they defied their enemies by battling head-on, trying to kick their enemy in the teeth. Maybe it was time to do the same. Maybe it was time to stop running and start advancing. Maybe it was time to realize that there was something more than just personal freedom.

As Yakov adjusted the desk-controls, bringing the outer Jovian System into view, Marten gripped his edge of the desk.

Should he run to Saturn? What if the cyborgs were already there? Would he run to Uranus then, and then run to Neptune? Why stop there? Why not run to Pluto? And then why end his flight at the edge of the Solar System? If his enemies were so powerfully strong, why not board or build a starship and flee to Alpha Centauri?

Marten squeezed the synthiwood edge. The Solar System had become too crowded. Social Unity, the Highborn and the cyborgs... there were too many sides, too many powerful forces all desiring to subjugate free men. He had run out on the Martians. He had been running for a long time, practically since birth if one counted his rat-like existence on the Sun-Works Factory. It was time to stop running. It was time to plant himself on a spot and say as the German Reformer Martin Luther had: *Here I stand.*

Marten looked up. "I'm in all the way," he said.

Yakov gave him a quizzical glance.

Marten placed a palm on the computer-map. "I fled the Sun-Works Factory. I fled Social Unity. I fled from the Highborn and then I fled from Mars. Now I'm done running."

Yakov leaned back as his dark eyes measured Marten. "We could use a soldier with your skills."

"You mean my shock-trooper training?"

"Who else has stormed aboard a warship as you did? By the account, you absorbed more of the Highborn training than anyone else I know."

"It was hell," Marten said. "I never want to do that again."

"No soldier does," Yakov said. "But are you willing to say that you could do more as a slave than as a free agent?"

Marten grinned tightly. "That's why I like you, Force-Leader. You cut through the crap and strike into the heart of a thing. What are you suggesting?"

"At the moment," Yakov said, "nothing. I'm speaking about priorities."

"Yeah," Marten said. "I get it." He squinted at an upper corner of the cramped room. He flexed his hands. Omi and he were the last of the shock troopers. Maybe that's what he should do: train Jovian hard-cases into shock troopers. No one could match Osadar. No one could match the cyborgs, or match the Highborn for that matter. But that didn't mean you should curl up and die. He had killed Highborn before. He'd even killed cyborgs. If free men were going to rise up, if they were going to win, then they needed the best space marines he could train.

He regarded Yakov. The silver-haired Force-Leader watched him. Those dark eyes were too knowing. Marten understood then why Yakov had been the hussade captain.

"If I have to go through Hell to be free," Marten said, "I'll do it."

Yakov remained quiet.

"And if I have to do that so others can be free, yeah, I guess I'll do what every soldier knows is the stupidest thing of all. I'll volunteer for the shitty job because no one else can do it better than I can."

Yakov said, "Being a Force-Leader sometimes means you have to understand that you're the best man for the task, or that you're the best at hand to do a thing."

"Yeah," Marten whispered.

Yakov's lips tightened. He opened a drawer in his desk and took out a bulb and two shot glasses. The *Descartes* was under acceleration, headed for Ganymede. Because of that, there was pseudo-gravity. Yakov squeezed clear liquid into each glass. With a knuckle, he slid a glass to Marten.

Marten waited until Yakov had filled his. They raised their glasses and touched them, causing them to clink.

"To victory," Yakov said.

"Victory," Marten said. He tossed the Jovian whiskey into his mouth and swallowed fast. It hit in his stomach with a blast of warmth. Then his face flushed with the heat of alcohol. This was better than the synthahol he used to drink in Greater Sydney.

Yakov swept up both glasses and the bulb, depositing them back into the bottom drawer. His grin was wider than Marten had ever witnessed. That's how Yakov must have looked on the day Ganymede U won the hussade trophy.

"In a fight," Yakov said, "I've noticed that you're a man that stands. You're one I want on my side."

"I've thought the same about you," Marten said.

"We are guardians," Yakov said. The grin vanished as an inner fire lit his eyes. "The philosophers who wrote the Dictates believe they should rule. They are wrong. The ones who dare should rule."

"Men should rule themselves," Marten said.

Yakov snorted. "You've fought long enough to know that most men cannot rule themselves. They need others to tell them what to do."

Marten didn't want to argue, not now, not with Yakov. Besides, he wasn't going to change Yakov's opinion today. And he was learning that maybe only he among humanity knew that freedom for everyone was the greatest prize. The time to preach that would come later. First, humanity had to survive. The people of the Jupiter System had to live through the cyborg assault.

"I just want you to know that I'm staying until we win or die," Marten said. "If that means going down to Ganymede with a laser carbine, then that's what I'm going to do."

"You're too valuable for ground action," Yakov said.

"Come again?" Marten asked.

"That's part of your skills. You've fought through terrible perils more than once. You know more about Social Unity, the Highborn and possibly the cyborgs than anyone else here does. That knowledge is vital."

"How do you know that?"

"Because knowledge of your enemy is always vital," Yakov said.

"Yeah," Marten nodded, "the HBs have a maxim about that."

"Who are these HBs?" Yakov asked.

"It's what the shock troopers called the Highborn."

Yakov ingested the information before he bent toward the computer desk and began to adjust controls. They had been studying known warship locations.

"The first phase of our strategy is to keep the Guardian warships from attacking Ganymede," Yakov said.

Marten agreed with a snort, meaning, that was obvious.

The two of them had been carefully studying the strategic situation. It wasn't just about who had the most ships. Position was critical too.

Marten pointed at the red cluster of the so-called supply vessels that had launched from Athena Station. "This shows us the cyborgs are frightened."

"An open attack shows that?" asked Yakov.

"Their stealth campaign indicates they would have preferred to strike Callisto with a secret attack. Now, they've launched an open strike."

"Most sensor date indicates they are supply vessels of the *Montesquieu*-class," Yakov said.

"Osadar did some checking. *Montesquieu*-class vessels are similar in tonnage to Voltaire Missiles."

"I am well aware of that."

"Good ECM could be masking some sensor data."

184

"I have radioed Su-Shan again," Yakov said, "arguing the same thing."

"What did she say?"

"That she would relate my words to Callisto High Command," said Yakov.

"I believe the cyborgs are striking openly instead of in secret for a reason," Marten said. "The reason is fear."

"Can cyborgs fear?"

"Maybe not as men fear," Marten admitted. "So call it something else. The point is they're striking now, probably before they were ready to do so."

Yakov adjusted the controls, bringing the fourth Galilean moon into sharper focus. Heavy laser satellites ringed Callisto. On its surface were large missile installations and point-defense cannons.

"If the cyborgs can smash Callisto, they will surely attack Ganymede next," Yakov said. "If they can destroy Callisto… they will have gone more than halfway to achieving victory."

"Would the cyborgs have launched an open strike if they believed it would fail?" Marten asked.

"Are the cyborgs infallible?"

"Their destruction in the Mars System would say no," Marten said. "But I'd hate to bet against them in their first open strike here. They will have studied the matter in depth. If they didn't believe they could smash Callisto, I doubt they would have attacked."

"Did your Osadar cyborg suggest these things to you?"

Marten nodded as he said, "You have to call Su-Shan again. You have to convince her to target the so-called supply vessels."

"You and I know it is the most rational course," Yakov said. "The philosophers will believe otherwise."

Marten bit his lip, wondering how you woke a blind man to his doom. He recalled an ancient quote his father had used. It was from an ancient philosopher named George Orwell. Orwell had said, *'It would take a Ph.D. to believe something so stupid.'* The High Command of Callisto seemed to be hard at work proving the adage.

185

# -8-

As the Jovians and cyborgs readied for the next round of battle, the Highborn ship continued its desperate circuit around Jupiter. Unfortunately for them, things were going badly, and it had forced the Praetor to act directly to save the warship.

In his battleoid armor-suit, the Praetor clanked through the hard decelerating vessel. Deck lighting flashed erratically, creating strobe-light conditions. One light shattered, showering sparks onto the gunmetal-colored battleoid. The suit's servos whined at full power and still the Praetor found it difficult to move through the corridor, as the intense Gs made every step miserable.

The ship's engines had burned at ninety-seven percent capacity for days. One of the dwindling crew had died because of it. Radiation had caused an embolism in his brain. The Highborn had bled to death before anyone discovered the problem.

In the corridor, the Praetor breathed heavily as he slid another armored foot forward. Sweat bathed him even as the suit's conditioner blasted his flesh with cold. In such a battleoid-suit, he could have made one hundred-meter leaps on Earth. With such a suit, he could have taken out a company of SU soldiers or a squad of cybertanks. In the gut-wrenching, decelerating ship, with the murderous Gs pummeling him, the suit could barely move.

The Praetor yearned to halt and rest. His lungs labored for air and his side ached horribly.

"You have three minutes and forty-three seconds to overload," a harsh, Highborn voice said in his ears.

The Praetor snarled, blinking sweat out of his eyes. He wasn't going to have made it to Uranus and back to die as an unsung hero in the Jovian System. Grand Admiral Cassius had thought to trick him, to sweep him from the board like a pawn. He—the Praetor—had won the Third Battle for Mars, launching the missile strike that had opened the way for the Doom Stars. Now he was going to conquer the Jupiter System with a single warship—and a badly crippled ship at that. It was going to be the greatest military exploit in the annals of war. Only Francisco Pizarro of Old Spain would have done something in league with what he planned.

The Praetor wasn't a historical expert like the Grand Admiral, but he recalled his lessens from the crèche-school. Even for a Highborn, he had a phenomenal memory. He'd climbed to Fourth Rank for a reason.

The Praetor laughed madly and wheezed, utterly exhausted. His throbbing limbs threatened to rebel. He would soon be reduced to a quivering lump, unable to move. Then he would die as a loser. Grand Admiral Cassius would have defeated him. Cassius would have won.

"Never," the Praetor whispered, as he forced another foot forward.

The Praetor concentrated until his mind became like a ball of energy. He willed his legs to shuffle forward. He clamped down on the pain, on the exhaustion.

*Will... iron will....*

"I am the Praetor," he whispered. "I will conquer the Jupiter System."

He remembered a lesson from his crèche-school. It had thrilled him with its daring, with its sheer ruthlessness. In his strange state of mind, which was like a feverish dream induced by the constant declaration and his straining effort to cross the ship, the Praetor hallucinated. For a time, he believed he was Francisco Pizarro.

Pizarro had been a Spanish Conquistador, perhaps the greatest of that daring breed. In 1531, Pizarro had set out on the most improbable conquest of history.

Luckily, Pizarro had Hernan Cortez's fabulous conquest of Aztec Mexico before him as a guide. Pizarro knew that Spanish swords, gunpowder-propelled arquebuses and horses combined with Spanish courage could triumph over the hordes of Indian warriors with their stone-edged swords and hatchets. On first sighting horses and their riders, many Aztec and Incas had believed that the horsemen were some odd creature like centaurs. Thus, the horsemen had fiercely intimidated the natives. That didn't mean the Indian nations were primitive in a quantitative sense, at least not compared to the conquistadors. The golden city of Mexico had awed Cortez and his men with its beauty, its teeming population and cleanliness, being bigger and more orderly than any Spanish city of that time. The same held true in the case of the Inca cities and for Pizarro's expedition.

Pizarro had heard wondrous stories about a vast empire in the interior mountains. For years, Pizarro searched for this elusive empire. Then in the fateful year of 1531, he landed at Tumbes, what was now the smoldering ruin of San Miguel. From there, Pizarro marched with a minuscule army into the towering Andes Range. He set off with one hundred and two infantry, sixty-two horsemen, two cannons and a pack of savage mastiffs. He marched toward the Inca Empire, which boasted a standing army of over a hundred thousand veteran warriors.

The Inca Empire was the largest that primitive humanity had ever constructed at such a high elevation. They had gold-laden cities on mountaintop locations, richly cultivated fields on the mountainsides, rope bridges spanning amazing gorges and a powerful veteran host of victorious warriors.

Inca scouts watched the pitifully small Spanish force wind its way through the mountains. The Inca, the Emperor Atahualpa, scoffed at any noble who told him to fear such a weak force of white men. At any time, it was obvious, hardy warriors could ambush the Spaniards and annihilate them.

So Emperor Atahualpa allowed Pizarro to march to Cajamarca, where he waited with an army of over 40,000 warriors. Pizarro and his seemingly frightened men huddled in a walled village, surrounded by the seething mass of highly decorated warriors.

A day passed, and Emperor decided to go see these strange men with white skin and shining armor. He entered the walled compound with five thousand Incas armed only with ceremonial axes. They bore him on a litter into an empty square.

All the Spaniards waited in the buildings, gripping their swords and priming their clumsy arquebuses. Each gun weighed ten to fifteen pounds, the gunner needing to rest the barrel on a hooked stick in order to fire. Finally, a Spanish priest walked alone to face the Inca. With an outstretched Bible in hand, the priest demanded the Inca surrender to them. When the Emperor was given the Bible, he threw it down in disgust. The priest backed away horrified, and with a shout, he gave the signal.

The Spanish erupted from their buildings. On horse and using lances, the cavalry waded into the masses of Inca nobles. The swordsmen hurried after them. The two cannons boomed and the savage mastiffs tore into Indian flesh.

The astounded Incas died as they tried to defend their emperor. The Spanish went berserk, filled with terror at the numbers of their enemies and filled with greed because of promised treasure.

The only Spanish blood spilled that day occurred when Pizarro grabbed a Spanish sword that slashed at the Emperor. It cut Pizarro's palm, but it saved Atahualpa's life. With the emperor's capture and hustling into captivity, Pizarro paralyzed the massive host waiting outside the walled village. As in the Aztec Empire, the Inca or Emperor was considered semi-divine and his person sacrosanct.

The shrewd Spaniards understood this to a nicety. And that spelled the end for the Inca Empire, which had effectively fallen to the gold-crazed, God-besotted and glory-mad conquistadors of Spain.

Francisco Pizarro had conquered an empire of over ten million with sixty-two horsemen, one hundred and two infantry, two cannons, a pack of savage mastiffs and inspired daring.

What a mere preman could do among his fellow subhumans, a Highborn could outdo. The Praetor was absolutely certain of this. First, however, he must survive. Second, he had to end the terrible velocity that had nearly sent him to an inglorious oblivion in the void. The Praetor returned to reality then and realized that he had been standing still in his battleoid-suit for several long seconds.

"One minute and thirty-one seconds," a Highborn said in his ears.

The Praetor hissed a litany of curses as he struck the hatch before him. The battleoid armor supplied him with exoskeleton power. The open palm caused steel to crumple and the hatch to tear from its moorings. It clanged in the conversion chamber as a fierce red glow bathed the Praetor's ten-foot battleoid suit.

Covered in sweat, trembling from exhaustion but driven by a greater will than Francisco Pizarro had ever possessed, the Praetor entered the deadly chamber. Radiation bathed him. He heard the clicks in his suit and knew what it meant, too many rads, far too many. He would have to endure a chemical bath later and ingest many anti-radiation pills. He still might die. But unless someone came in here and fixed the malfunction, they were all doomed.

"I am the Praetor," he whispered.

He shuffled ten more meters and then he un-shouldered the welding unit. Groaning, he sagged to his knees. It was hard to see, and his skin prickled horribly. The warning clicks nearly drove him to despair.

As the missile-ship decelerated, the Praetor began to work on the malfunction, his welder's blue arc the only hope against the glowing red that meant death.

"Twenty-seven seconds until overload," the voice said.

"Sixty-two horsemen," the Praetor whispered, "one hundred and two infantry, two cannons—"

"Lord, are you well?" the voice asked.

"One missile-ship," the Praetor said, "that's all I need to win the Jovian System."

"He's raving," Canus said.

Perhaps Canus was right. The blue arc continued to burn as the seconds reached zero and beyond. Still, the blue arc glowed, and the red glow lessened by agonizing degrees.

Finally, Canus said, "He did it."

The Praetor snapped off his welder and lurched to his feet. He wanted to claw and scratch at his skin. His guts felt awful, but he'd be damned if any of the crew would drag him to sickbay. He would walk there, and he would swallow the pills and take the chemical baths. He had a planetary system to win and enemies to trick. He was the Praetor, and he would endure until the Sun no longer shined on the worlds of men.

## 9

As the Highborn ship circled the mighty gas giant at terrific velocity, and as Jovian and cyborg warships converged toward their various destinations, Strategist Tan found herself involved at the highest level of strategic planning. It was a three-way conference via lightguide laser.

Tan had scoured her pod for listening devices. Stick-tights, insect-crawlers, passive probing, she had studied all of these during her stint as arbiter while aboard the *Kant*, the premier dreadnaught of the Guardian Fleet. The *Kant* was presently at Ganymede, the flagship of the flotilla ready to bombard the wayward Secessionists. After scouring the pod and finding nothing, Tan had concluded that either Yakov was cleverer than she was or her pod was clean.

Yakov could never have achieved his goals without Marten Kluge and his cyborg. They had tricked her regarding Arbiter Octagon.

For hours, Tan had sat in the pod, in a lotus position, practicing her meditations. She'd defeated her grosser emotions of anger and disgust at her naiveté. She was a Strategist. She might even be the Chief Strategist of the Confederation. Therefore, she purged herself of unworthy feelings and filled her mind with syllogisms, logic formulas and pertinent axioms from the Dictates. These soothed her mind. She was honest enough with herself to admit to a stubborn core of... hard feelings against Force-Leader Yakov. Marten Kluge was a barbarian and therefore unworthy of her anger. Yakov on the other hand—

Her musings ended then as she opened a secure channel with her cousin, Chief Controller Su-Shan. It proved the strength of their bloodline that both of them should stand high in military planning. It also proved their educational integrity and fierce drive to excel.

Through the lightguide laser-link, Su-Shan outlined the situation to her. Two days had passed since the supply vessels had launched from Athena Station. Some seemingly insignificant data kept troubling certain quarters on Callisto. Now the Solon of Callisto, the highest wisdom of the Dictates, wished to confer on high strategy with Chief Controller Su-Shan and with Chief Strategist Tan. Finally and decisively, they would decide on the nature of the struggle and act accordingly.

"But I'm only a Strategist," said Tan, "a Strategist of the third class. Surely, there are others higher ranked than me to decide these things."

"I believe that is false," Su-Shan said. "Events have likely propelled you into the highest slot of the War Council. You've also been rigorously trained in strategic matters, you have the required rank and you've witness an actual cyborg."

"Meaning what?" asked Tan.

"That the Solon trusts you. Now clear your mind of clutter. Then fill it with the truths and axioms of the Dictates. We must possibly decide the Jupiter System's fate."

Tan blinked at the vidscreen showing her cousin. She was still far away from her dreadnaught. This—Tan pressed her palms together and sought the inner peace of the Dictates.

"Yes," she said, "I await the three-way."

***

*2351 March 4, the three-way Strategy Conference of Guardian Fleet. The participants: The Solon of Callisto (identifying name submerged in his office), Chief Controller Su-Shan of Callisto Orbital Defense and Strategist Tan of the War Council. Reference symbols: Solon, Su-Shan and Tan. Conference committed via laser lightguide system.*

SOLON: We three have a solemn duty to perform concerning the future of the Dictates and our perfected system of life.

Men, and in this I reference all humans, are born in a chaotic world of seething emotions. It causes endless grief and boundless misery. This we have alleviated by our intellect and rationally reasoned codes. I would like to say we have ended unproductive thought and hence, false actions. By false I mean to say mindless, useless actions, which are ultimately harmful to life. But such thoughts occur even in our idyllic system. This saddens me, a sadness I allow to color my hope but never my overarching reason.

SU-SHAN: You are the Solon of the Confederation. You have achieved rarified rationality.

SOLON: I would be false to the Dictates to dispute your statement. Yes, you speak the truth.

TAN: I am humbled by it.

SOLON: Social mechanisms force us to utter such statements. Perhaps what you say is true. However, rationality does not accept humility, because it hints at false modesty. My reason compels me to say, 'Expunge this humility, Chief Strategist.' Today, you must excel in rationality. I need your logic. I need your intellect. And in saying 'I', I quite naturally mean all the Confederation. I am the supreme mind. In me, I codify all that is best about the Dictates. If I am false, the system we have erected with such care is false. Because the system is true, it means that I must be true and my thoughts filled with penetrating insight.

SU-SHAN: Have you arrived at a conclusion concerning our objective?

SOLON: Your rigor is lacking, Chief Controller. I will not accept that today. A conference of this magnitude means that I have not reached a conclusion. Today, I will add your rational expertise to my incisive thinking to arrive at the needed conclusion. This united effort will achieve greater accuracy than my thoughts alone could do. Even though I am the supreme logician of the Confederation, I will gain by your references and insights unique to your perspectives. Therefore, let us lay out the subject and arrive at the truth through our united reason.

SU-SHAN: Shall I state the problem?

194

SOLON: As the wisest among us, I will state it, and I will state it aptly and precisely. Do I have your full attention?

SU-SHAN: Yes.

TAN: The Dictates guide me.

SOLON: Our society has achieved near-perfection in regards to human potential. In this, naturally, I refer to reason. The wisest among us rule. The most spirited fight and the sensation-gluttons perform the laborious and onerous tasks. Since their minds are already dulled through the indulgence of their basic drives, it harms them little committing these repetitive jobs. Those who love battle, risk their lives fighting. We, who reason, think for the rest, as would benevolent parents. Now, however, a virus attacks paradise, an infestation of hostile organisms that cannot comprehend the damage they do.

SU-SHAN: Pray forgive my interruption. Do you accept the evidence to mean that cyborgs exist in dangerous numbers within our system?

SOLON: Chief Controller, Chief Controller, this hasty rush to assumption is entirely unwarranted. We are the strategic triumvirate. We must deliberate and cogitate with precision. Let barbarians rave and foolishly stumble into decisions. That is not how the Dictates teach us to proceed.

SU-SHAN: You are the Solon.

SOLON: A rational truth spoken with meaning that implies I can guide the three of us into strategic brilliance. I concur, and I know now that my choice in confiding in you two was correct.

TAN: Are we under any time constraints?

SOLON: That is subtle, Chief Strategist. If I have a flaw, it is in waxing prolix. Yes, in war, in battle, time constrains the individual soldier and often the executive agent. I will now turn my intellect onto the first critical subject. Athena Station has launched supply vessels. Incoming data suggests these vessels had jumped to velocities that exceed human endurance levels.

TAN: Our file on the shock troopers indicates that humans can endure tremendous Gs in special suits. The Guardian Fleet does not possess such suits, however.

SOLON: Has the Guardian Fleet possibly built such suits in secret?

SU-SHAN: I am unaware of it.

TAN: No.

SOLON: Can you be absolutely certain, Chief Strategist, that a hidden department in the Guardian Fleet didn't authorize such tests?

TAN: I am certain enough to risk my reputation on it.

SOLON: We are not here for histrionics, Chief Strategist.

TAN: The Dictates prohibit that. And such was not my intent. I feel I must add that in no way does my statement imply histrionics.

SOLON: Hm.... I detect imprecision in your statement. We must study each possibility in turn to arrive at certain knowledge. I will also point out that your reputation does not correlate with possible, secret suit-testing.

TAN: You are the Solon. Yet rationality... compels me to a different methodology.

SOLON: (in a cool tone) Do you wish to instruct me?

SU-SHAN: (hurriedly) Your intellect shines too brightly for either of us to hint at 'instruction'.

TAN: The Chief Controller verbalizes my own belief, sir. Perhaps this is a foolish thought. I will state it in the hope of instruction from the Solon. You, as the guidance of an entire world, of an entire planetary system, have a myriad of responsibilities. Each decision requires time and an iota of nervous energy and firing neurons. As a Strategist and intimately involved in the war—

SOLON: We have not declared a state of war. Therefore, your final statement is false. I must insist that you apply a more rigorous use of the language. Truth is the watchword, our armor against barbarism and its accompanying ignorance.

TAN: Naturally, I agree, sir. But isn't it true that the Secessionists have foisted violent action upon us?

SOLON: 'Secessionist' implies a higher level of sanction to their actions than is warranted. They are terrorists, and as such must be expunged with ruthless vigor as an exterminator sprays for fleas.

TAN: Yes, I see your point. Ah. I wonder if you could clarify a point for me. In an emergency, can an enemy of my enemy act as my temporary ally?

SOLON: Show me this enemy.

TAN: I believe that the growing velocity of the supply vessels lends credence to the cyborg hypotheses.

SOLON: Hm. I have examined this so-called 'cyborg file'. The Mars barbarians or the terrorist Force-Leader staged it. The file shows a single cyborg committing acted sabotage. I find it completely unwarranted to base a strategy on a doctored file and am surprised you suggest it.

TAN: I agree on the doctoring of the file. Still, data from the *Rousseau*, the missile attack on the *Descartes* and the advancing vessels all logically infer a stealth enemy of unique capabilities.

SOLON: Or greater cleverness from the terrorists than we expected. Remember, they have benefited under our philosophical and educational systems. Their ploys could be deeply laid indeed.

TAN: The law of simplicity implies a cyborg stealth-attack as the more probable explanation for these various occurrences.

SU-SHAN: You overstep yourself, Chief Strategist. The Solon can reason all this—

SOLON: There is no need to defend me, Chief Controller. I called for the three-way to add your minds to mine. I concur with the Chief Strategist's analysis.

SU-SHAN: (whispered) You believe that cyborgs are attacking Callisto?

SOLON: Reason would suggest this, yes.

SU-SHAN: I don't understand. You just said—

TAN: The Solon is right!

SU-SHAN: But his preamble implied differently. All those words—

TAN: Don't matter in face of the cyborgs. We must act now to save our system.

SU-SHAN: If the supply vessels are cyborg-controlled— Sir, we must summon the warships from Ganymede to help defend Callisto.

SOLON: It is too late for warships to affect the Battle for Callisto.

*A seven-second period of silence ensues.*

TAN: (quietly) May I query you, sir?

SOLON: I will indulge your curiosity by answering your question before you ask it. The Dictates have failed us versus the cyborgs. It is a galling truth to ingest. For hours, I have struggled internally with this truth. Now we must decide on the future. I have hesitated, and I hesitate still to arrive at the bitter conclusion.

SU-SHAN: Orbital Defense will defeat whatever—

SOLON: There is a high probability that Callisto will never recover from the coming attack. And by Callisto, I mean the paradise created by the Dictates.

TAN: We must not surrender or give in to despair, sir.

SOLON: (monotone) Who do we wish to succeed us? The terrorists have used this opportunity to do us harm. They lack mercy. The cyborgs... do they possess higher reason than we do?

TAN: They're trying to annihilate us. The Dictates show—

SOLON: The cyborgs have reasoned more deeply than we have. Our coming destruction proves their superiority.

TAN: Would such reasoning also imply that the Secessionists are our superiors?

SOLON: (coldly) You are hereby relived of your station, Chief Strategist.

TAN: Article twenty dash A3 states that only a quorum of the War Council can relieve a Strategist from his or her post.

SOLON: You dare to quote articles to me?

TAN: I have begun to wonder if you are well, sir. The strain of office—

SOLON: I am the Solon, the wisest of Callisto. Emotive despair cannot shatter my reason. I am sending immediate orders to the ships at Ganymede to begin their bombardment. If we cannot survive the coming nightmare, neither shall the ingrates of Ganymede. With our death, the cyborgs will have proven our superiors. We can only hope they read the Dictates and see its value in the new order.

TAN: Su-Shan, the Solon is sick. You must send your Orbital Defense arbiters down to the surface and relieve the Solon and his archons from office.

SOLON: I have already relieved you, Chief Strategist.

TAN: (to Su-Shan) I will contact the Ganymede Flotilla and instruct them to coordinate with the Secessionists. We must unite against the cyborgs. We must save our civilization from destruction. Do you hear me, Su-Shan?

SOLON: I am the wisest. You will obey me or face extinction.

SU-SHAN: (softly) I hear you, Chief Strategist.

SOLON: (monotone) We are doomed, but we can decide and should decide on whom is the most worthy to succeed the Dictates. I relieve you both of office. I await the end now that I foresee it with such clarity. Humanity has lost. The New Order of melded-men is at hand.

TAN: Reason implies that you fight until you're dead, sir. We're not dead yet. Therefore, we shall fight to survive and reinstate the Dictates in whatever remains after the war is won.

SOLON: We are doomed. The cyborgs have achieved strategic surprise and superiority. I deem them worthy to replace us—and my voice is decisive. For none can see as well as me, as I am the supreme intellect of Jupiter.

TAN: Send those arbiters at once, Su-Shan, and begin making priority targets. The Solon has said one thing I agree with. Those aren't supply vessels heading for Callisto, but the first wave of the cyborg assault.

*End of the three-way Strategic Conference.*

## 10

From her coasting pod, Chief Strategist Tan spoke urgently to the commandant of the Guardian Fleet flotilla in low-Ganymede orbit.

She sat in the pilot's chair as she wore her Strategist whites. It had taken some doctoring, but now she wore a Chief Strategist's megastar pinned to her chest. A diamond glittered in a five-pointed, golden star.

Tan strove for calm as she stared into the vidscreen. Serenity and authority mixed with assuredness is what she attempted to project.

The flotilla commandant appeared in the screen. He was older, bald, with rejuvenated skin. He had chubby cheeks like a freakish baby. He rode aboard the *Kant*, an *Aristotle*-class dreadnaught.

Static caused his image to waver. Ganymede was in the fierce Jovian magnetosphere, a flattened area or belt that included Io and Europa. Of the Galilean moons, Ganymede was the only one that had its own magnetosphere, which carved a small cavity inside Jupiter's vast magnetic field. Jupiter also acted like a pulsar, a radio-emitting star. Those radio waves often interfered with Jovian communications the closer one approached the gas giant.

As the commandant spoke, his words were drowned out in the static.

Tan adjusted the controls. The chubby-cheeked image wavered worse than before, but finally stabilized. She raised gain, and shouted, "Could you say that again, Commandant?"

"The Solon has instructed us." The commandant had a deep voice. Behind him on the vidscreen, an officer floated past. "We are forbidden on pain of death from having further communications with you."

"If you will check article two of the Warship Code," Tan said, "you'll find that the Solon lacks the authority for such a military order."

The commandant scowled. "We have a war in progress, and—"

"The Solon declared that there is no war."

"What nonsense is this?" the commandant said.

"I have a file of our three-way conference. Prepare to receive it."

"Did you not hear me?" the commandant asked. "I am forbidden from doing so."

Tan gave him a serene stare. "On the possible eve of our destruction, is it rational to follow madness into oblivion?"

"Obviously not," he said. "But your query has no bearing on the situation."

"I suggest you apply common sense to our conversation. What harm can occur from listening to my file?"

"The Solon has declared," the commandant said. "He is the supreme intellect and our guiding light. I dare not disobey him."

"With such a supreme intellect," Tan said, "why did he fail to take into account article two of the Warship Code?"

The commandant received a note from someone off screen. He scanned it and then frowned at Tan.

"I suggest you listen to a selected audio file and compare the voice with the one in your ship's library," Tan said. "You will discover a disconcerting truth."

"I don't have time for this. Quickly, declare your truth. Then I must go. Even now, we are initializing our bombardment sequence."

Tan wanted to scream. Bombarding the Secessionists was madness. Humanity needed to unite against the cyborgs, not gnaw itself to death like a crazed beast. She attempted to calm her anxieties as she let a faint smile touch her lips. She must project rationality.

"I would rather that you confirm this truth yourself," she said. "It will then have a primary validity to your subjective view."

"I am not attempting a dialogue," the commandant said hastily.

"You are wise," Tan said. "Now prepare to receive my audio file."

The commandant glanced off-screen. After a moment, he nodded at her.

Tan moved a toggle, sending the selected portion across the void. The commandant received, listened, ran his file-check to confirm the speaker and then looked at her with raised eyebrows. For him, a governor noted for his imperturbability, it was a gross gesture of surprise.

"The Solon's unraveling is a tragedy," said Tan. "But the proof is undeniable. He has become unhinged."

"So it would appear. The implications... the complications.... What am I supposed to do?"

"I suggest you hold his order in abeyance until you've listened to my logic. Today, you must trust your reason, employing it to its fullest. The survival of our system is at stake, perhaps every human life here. Much now rests upon your choice. Trust the Dictates, your training and your intellect."

The commandant stared at her. He appeared wan, and he chewed his lower lip, before saying, "You are the new Chief Strategist."

"I am the *only* Strategist of the War Council still alive and still human. Thus, I am elevated to the War Council in persona. The chain of command is direct and unequivocal. Particularly in military matters and warship movement, my authority exceeds the Solon's, as his authority is two steps removed through executive channels."

"I'm listening, Chief Strategist."

Tan dipped her head the tiniest bit as she strove for serenity. To persuade, she must achieve apparent disinterest and a seemingly didactic arrogance.

"Callisto faces massive damage," she said. "Pre-battle analysis indicates a world-ending strike. That, of course, presupposes that the cyborgs have added new functions to the existing missiles. Their secret endeavors and the core reality of their existence—the heightened technology that allows their being—indicates cyborgs possess such refinements."

"This world-ending strike," the commandant said, as he continued to chew his lower lip, "it is only for one face of Callisto that we have plotted the course of the projectiles. Therefore, in a worst case scenario, the other side survives."

"Computer analysis indicates massive quake damage on the Jupiter-facing side, and high levels of radiation poisoning."

"Jupiter and Io already send large doses of radiation into—"

"The missile strikes will likely increase the radiation dosage by an entire factor," Tan said. "That is a debilitating amount."

The commandant's cubby cheeks sagged as he whispered, "Continue."

"The cyborgs are obviously attempting a decapitating strike," Tan said. "Logically, the Guardian Fleet should combine with the Secessionists to face the greater threat."

The commandant straightened. "There is no one I know of designated as 'Secessionist'. Now there are terrorists—"

"I am not here to quibble about semantics, Commandant. Extinction threatens. Therefore, put aside your prejudices and let reason guide your actions. At this juncture in time, you are being called to make a monumental decision. Rise to the occasion as a true son of the Dictates."

"Insults are unbecoming in a Chief Strategist," the commandant said. "As a controlling governor in the Guardian Fleet, I have by increasing degrees and training shed all prejudices."

"Come, come, Commandant, speak the truth through reason. Do not quote me governing *ideals*. Remember this as well, that hard and often unpleasant truths are not insults."

The commandant's features stiffened as he leaned toward her vidscreen. "Vocalize your logic."

Tan paused. She could have said that better, yet she had been logical and she'd spoken truth. She now strove for convincing serenity as she said, "The cyborg fleet outnumbers ours by a critical margin. We need the Secessionists to defeat the machine assault."

"I considered your logic earlier, I must confess," the commandant said. "I soon reached a bitter conclusion. Even with the Secessionists, we lack the warships to face the cyborgs. Therefore, the Solon's order—"

"Victory is achieved one step at a time," Tan said. "Logic, reason, selfishness, all point to a united effort in an attempt to thwart our certain destruction."

"…I concur," he said softly.

"Have you read article two of the Warship Code?"

"Earlier, as you may have noted, an officer handed me the section. I read it."

"You understand then that I am correct concerning my military authority," Tan said.

The commandant hesitated, but finally admitted, "I do."

"As the Strategic War Council in persona, I hereby order you to ignore the Solon's order. Further, I order you to ignore any further communications with him concerning military maneuvers."

"You are taking over fleet command?" the commandant asked.

Tan focused on idyllic serenity as she said, "I am."

The commandant bent his smooth face at an angle, seemingly staring at deckplates. He nodded slowly and faced her. "What are your orders?"

"There will be an immediate cessation of hostilities with all Jovians, including those signified as secessionists or terrorists. You will hail the Secessionists and inform them of your new orders. You will also seek to engage their highest authority. Then you will coordinate with me. I will board your dreadnaught in…." Tan checked her computer. "In another few days."

"I acknowledge. Is there anything else?" he asked.

"Yes," said Tan. "Give me a dedicated laser-link and access to your dreadnaught's main computer. I have computations and analysis to run."

"May I ask what it concerns?" he said.

"Victory against the cyborgs," Tan said.

"I have acknowledged your authority and will obey your commands. I feel that I must point out, however, that the cyborgs outnumber us by a too large of a margin to hope for success."

"That is why I must use the main computer," Tan said, "as I search for a way to change the odds. We must go to work, Commandant."

***

As Tan began her computations, Chief Controller Su-Shan began a radical shakeup of command-personnel in the orbital laser stations and down at the anti-missile rocket installations on the surface.

At the same time, the Solon made a Callisto-wide proclamation that left many rulers and philosophers uneasy. A full third raced to the deep shelters on the Jupiter-facing side of the planetary body. A handful sped into space in their private yachts or booked passage on outgoing liners. The rest composed themselves, deciding to reject fate by penning a new treatise, beginning an ode to reason or selecting choice wines to sample on the day of doom.

All the while, the Voltaire Missiles increased velocity, a technological pack of raving machines bent on annihilation. Except for one, each had reached the halfway point. The missile that aborted its progress self-destructed, its crystalline AI following its bitter programming. Its fusion core had failed, and the AI saw it in self-recriminating terms, as a lack of virtue. The thermonuclear explosion appeared on a hundred watching thermal scanners and on as many teleoptic scopes observing the so-called supply vessels. Spectrum-analysis brought a grim conclusion: the incoming projectiles were genocidal weapons.

In the last day of flight, the Voltaire Missiles rapidly closed, traveling the majority of the distance in a burst of acceleration. The velocity gave them several military advantages. They were in the Orbital Defense laser-range for only a short duration. Their velocity would add kinetic energy to any impacts, and the crystalline AIs had less time to dwell on their coming demise. For some, that anticipated demise might debilitate computing power. The crystalline-AI creators hadn't had time to expunge that bug from the system.

In another two hours, several AIs had psychological seizures induced by their fear of imminent death. One AI turned its defensive weaponry on its nearest neighbors. Those hit by the surprise attack retaliated savagely, and soon another Voltaire Missile exploded its massive payload.

As that missile had already dropped behind too far to affect the others, the rest of the titanic missiles bore relentlessly toward the fourth Galilean moon. Behind them and traveling more slowly was the second wave strike: a dreadnaught, a meteor-ship and the troopship packed with cyborg-converted Jovians, plus several patrol boats.

Waiting in her laser satellite in low-Callisto orbit, Chief Controller Su-Shan stood in a governing pit. A blue glow bathed her as monitors ran though their sequence codes. Charging electrons passed through Su-Shan, heightening her awareness and reflexes. Her arms were sheathed in VR-sleeves and gloves and with VR-goggles over her eyes. Her armored laser-satellite was the same as the others orbiting Callisto. It was a torus with asteroid-rock shielding and a large focusing system. The generators were online, with the satellite's fusion core surging at full power.

Twenty-three other satellites ringed Callisto. Many had used the past day to clump closer together, allowing them to beam in concert. Below on the surface were countless blooms: launching anti-missile rockets. In minutes, the rockets zoomed past the satellites as they hurried to do battle with the approaching Voltaires.

Su-Shan watched through her VR-goggles. Her satellite's ECM struggled valiantly against pirated Onoshi Electronics. Even if the Jovians possessed superior philosophies, those of Neptune made better decoys, sensor-buffers and shear-plates.

"Lock-on, I need lock-on," Su-Shan muttered.

There was no one to hear her plea. Su-Shan stood alone in the governing pit, making all command decisions and observations. Technicians waited in the outer shell, ready to affect any needed repairs. Otherwise, they were useless.

Baffled by their failed lock-on attempts, several nearby laser operators beamed their powerful rays at the enemy. Perhaps they'd concluded that would upset the Onoshi equipment, or maybe they'd simply become tired of waiting.

The anti-missile rockets speeding on near-intercept courses concerned the lead AIs more than the lasers did. Nuclear near-explosions and x-ray and gamma ray beams could upset the primary mission. Therefore, the lead AIs opened their point-defense cannons and fired their first flock of anti-missiles.

The launching of the anti-missiles, however, helped the Callisto ECM. At that point, several laser-satellites achieved lock-on.

In her governing pit, Su-Shan grinned with manic delight. She hadn't sleep for thirty-seven hours, and she had ingested too many stimulants with too little food. She was jittery, hated the prospect of death and despised the cyborgs for endangering her. She found it hard to accept that she was going to die, and that made her even jitterier and affected her normally calm demeanor.

With her manic grin came something that might have sounded like a bitter laugh. Her fingers twitched in her twitch-gloves, and she swung her sheathed arms into position.

The laser on her satellite adjusted. The magnitude of power rose. She beamed. The beam sped through space, covering 300,000 kilometers per second. Her laser struck a Voltaire's nosecone.

The sensation caused the missile's AI to engage sub-thrusters. The missile moved to a slightly different heading. The laser beamed harmlessly past it.

In the governing pit, Su-Shan adjusted. Her motions and decisions were aided by a battle-computer that did the molecular-level, precision targeting. She attacked the same missile, heating the shielded nosecone. Again, the AI veered.

The contest took nine point five-three minutes to complete. In that time, the pack of Voltaire Missiles entered into the point-defense cannons' range. Su-Shan's targeted missile exploded a hull section and jinked constantly. At the end of the nine point five-three minutes, however, the AI poked out targeting rods and committed *seppuku*.

Seppuku was ritual suicide predicated on the ancient codes of Bushido, the warrior ethos of the Japanese Samurai. When an ancient samurai lost honor or face, he often went to the one who had offended him, knelt, took out his knife and slit open his belly. Often, a second stood behind him, ready to chop off his head if the pain overwhelmed the proud warrior. In this way and according to Bushido, the warrior regained his honor.

The Voltaire's crystal AI, grown and programmed with a Bushido-like code, ignited its massive payload. As it slit itself through annihilation, it used the nuclear energy to pour x-rays and gamma rays at the offensive laser-station that had caused its life to end approximately eight minutes too soon.

The rays traveled at the speed of light, hitting the shielded torus, chewing through the asteroid-rock and murdering countless systems. In the governing pit, Su-Shan writhed. The x-rays burnt her bones and the gamma rays took away her speech centers.

It was at that point that Chief Strategist Tan broke through the communication system with override command authority. She used the laser lightguide system of the *Kant* and she used the dreadnaught's recognition codes.

Tan's voice was scratchy and distant-seeming, but it was recognizable to her dying cousin. "Listen to me, Su-Shan. You have little time left. Callisto is doomed. There is no saving it. What you must save is the future. Retarget and attack the following dreadnaught—I'm sending you the coordinates. Everyone in the satellites, you must retarget and attack the enemy warships in the second wave. Kill them for us. This is a priority one message from the War Council." The proper emergency sequences followed.

Chief Controller Su-Shan listened to the message. It was the last thing she heard. The gamma rays that had stolen her speech now cooked her brain. She died, having killed a missile. But she failed in her mission to protect Callisto from thermonuclear disaster.

Other armored satellites also went offline, their operators slain, the fusion cores burnt or the focusing system melted into slag. They had taken a bitter toll, however, destroying fifty-seven percent of the Voltaire Missiles. The anti-missile rockets killed or caused to detonate prematurely fifteen percent of the cyborg-controlled missiles. Together, the primary orbital defensive systems took out seventy-two percent of the cyborg surprise attack.

Now, in this short operational window left, the remaining laser satellites retargeted, aiming at the approaching cyborg dreadnaught.

Seven orbital stations lanced their powerful beams at the dreadnaught, what had a short month ago been a Guardian Fleet vessel.

Massive lasers beamed and struck on target, chewing into thick, asteroid-rock protection. The dreadnaught's particle shield absorbed the hellish heat as rock slagged and dust bloomed. Across the hundreds of thousands of kilometers, the lasers relentlessly bore deeper and deeper into the particle shielding.

Over five million kilometers away, Gharlane received data of the retargeting. Since light traveled 300,000 kilometers per second, this information was already seventeen seconds old by the time Gharlane observed it. It also took time for Gharlane and the cyborg dreadnaught Force-Leader to realize the number and intensity of the laser attacks. More time passed as Gharlane ingested the meaning of the attack. Then even more seconds ticked away as Gharlane realized he needed to do something drastic to save his precious warships. Finally, even more seconds faded into the past as he ran through options and then the agonizing decision to use the best means at hand to thwart the lasers. He had not anticipated an attack upon the second wave, but a continuing defense against the Voltaires, as they threatened Callisto with greater harm. This switch in targeting, it went against Homo sapien conditioning.

During those minutes of indecision, another two laser satellites joined the assault. These were heavy, orbital lasers, the strongest in the Jovian System. They lacked Doom Star power, but approached that of a main SU Battleship of the *Zhukov*-class. Such primary lasers chewed through asteroid rock at an incredible rate. As Gharlane transmitted his orders to several selected Voltaire Missiles, more seconds passed as the order sped at 300,000 kilometers per second.

Callisto Orbital Defense lasers now punched through the particle shielding. In four point seven seconds, they punched through the dreadnaught's hull and bored like sonic drills. Lasers smashed through the bulkheads into crew quarters, melting seven cyborgs. The red beams cut into the ship's galley, its gymnasium, the computer core, coils three through nine and directly smashed through the bridge, killing the force-leader, originally a native of Neptune. Then beams burned into the fusion core, and they ignited nuclear-tipped cruise missiles meant to destroy Callisto's Jupiter-facing cities. The combination of hot, slicing lasers and nuclear detonations caused sections of the dreadnaught to slide away in chunks and other sections to explode outwardly. Ninety-seven percent of the cyborg-crew died immediately. There was a three percent probability the others would survive the coming hour.

At this point, the Voltaire Missiles Gharlane had selected exploded. They used x-ray and gamma rays to attack the last laser satellites. Those final satellites had retargeted, aiming now at the second cyborg vessel, a meteor-ship.

It was a deadly contest that demanded perfect decisions. Gharlane had to count the number of remaining missiles, decide on how many he could spare and how important fleet superiority would be in the coming days and battles. Finally, he had to decide how many missiles he needed to destroy Callisto as a military installation. Because Jupiter spewed such heavy radiation, seventy percent of Callisto's population lived on the targeted face. That meant Gharlane possessed a rich field of targets, if he could breach the defenses. He would never face such a powerful concentration of lasers again, as Callisto's orbital defense was the core of Confederation strength.

The cyborg-controlled meteor-ship died. As satellite sensors and interferometers discovered this, the laser stations retargeted, aiming at the cyborg troopship. Then exploding Voltaire Missiles beamed hot radiation and killed the last satellites.

Only the Callisto point-defense cannons on the surface now stood between life and death. Each installation was composed of a massive fero-concrete shell. A magnetic rail-gun poked out of the opening, aiming its tube into space. Targeting satellites normally supplied the needed coordinates. Those were dead. Therefore, surface-based installations provided the data. This resulted in a fifty-three percent decrease in effectiveness.

The rail-guns chugged, lofting nuclear-tipped canisters, which exploded and created a defensive zone of shrapnel and sand. Other canisters sped farther and attempted to kill Voltaires through EMP surges and heat.

The remaining Voltaire Missiles used their last point-defense volleys to obliterate EMP canisters before they ignited.

Then the mighty, Voltaire Missiles smashed through the shrapnel belt, and more of them died. Only eleven percent of the launched strike survived the journey—seven gargantuan missiles. In those fateful nanoseconds as they zoomed at Callisto, seven titanic nosecones opened. Each missile contained five independent payloads of many hundreds of megatons. Thus, thirty-five nuclear bombs exploded within a nine-second window. Missile casings, shells and other assorted mass also struck Callisto at devastating velocities. Together, the united explosions rocked the surface and annihilated millions in the domed cities and down in the deep shelters.

Thirty-five towering mushroom clouds of radioactive dust, dirt and rock rose upward. The columns rose to dizzying heights, expelling matter into low-orbit.

A full third of the population died by the heat and blasts. A fourth perished in the next ten minutes from the vacuum of space, their cities or dwellings ruptured beyond repair. In the coming days, radiation poisoning would slay more. Lack of water, food or sanitation would sweep through the wreckage after that.

Some of Callisto survived, however. The nature of the attack meant that those on the other side had kept their cities, dwelling and point defense installations intact.

As news of the terrible cyborg-strike reached those on the other side—quakes still traveled across the surface like waves—the cyborg-controlled patrol boats and troopship entered far-Callisto orbit.

The agony of Callisto was far from over as the worst horrors were about to descend in the coming hours and days—cyborg drop troops. Gharlane had ordered the genocidal removal of the Jovians of Callisto. Nothing must survive that might jeopardize Jupiter System victory.

# Shock Trooper Kluge

## -1-

Nadia Pravda chewed on a fingernail as the *Occam VII* Patrol Boat decelerated. It was the last of the three vessels making up this Aquinas Wing splinter group.

Nadia sat in the back of the pilot's chamber during a duty-run into possible danger. That was against regulations, but the five-person crew had taken pity on her. They knew she dreaded being alone.

Nadia wore the brown coveralls of a technician and a low-brimmed hat with a sonic screwdriver crest. Black straps crisscrossed her torso, highlighting her breasts. Her magnetic-soled boots were attached to the deckplates. She worried a ragged fingernail, having already chewed it down. Her scrubbed features were clean, if still too pale. Sometimes, she managed a tremulous smile. The others had to call her name occasionally to snap her out of a thousand-meter stare.

Nadia chewed her fingernail, aware that a Highborn warship circled Jupiter. Thinking about that, her stomach had become queasy again. The Highborn were here. Worse, the Praetor commanded the vessel. She knew about him. Everyone in the Sun-Works Factory had traded gossip concerning his evil temper. She'd told the Jovian crew about the Praetor and couldn't understand their shrugs and disinterest. They worried about cyborgs. Nadia couldn't conceive of anything more deadly than the nine-foot supermen from the gene labs.

The patrol-boat's main chamber was larger than her escape pod and longer than it was wide. The pilot and weapons officer sat in front before a small, polarized window. Behind them to the left was the sensor-and-communications operator. She was the woman Nadia had spoken to several weeks ago, Officer Mara. The last two crewmembers were asleep in their quarters. Those living quarters, the boat's galley, gym and engine rooms made up the rest of the patrol vessel. The boat was rakish in appearance, had anti-missile pods and what amounted to point-defense canons. Because of the extreme distances in the Jupiter System, each patrol boat had larger engines than an Inner Planets vessel of this type would possess and a longer-range capacity. Its crews were also conditioned for yearlong stints.

The various Aquinas Wing Patrol Boats had separated some time ago as they investigated the distant moons of the Carme group. Each 'moon' was asteroid-sized, and was mainly comprised of retrograde orbiting bodies. In other words, the moons orbited in the opposite direction as Jupiter spun. The average inclination of these moons was 165 degrees. In this system, an inclination of zero degrees meant that an asteroid or moon orbited Jupiter in its equatorial plane. An inclination of exactly ninety degrees would be a polar orbit, where a moon passed over Jupiter's north and south poles, while an inclination of exactly 270 degrees would be a polar orbit in the opposite direction.

The three patrols boats decelerated as they approached the main moon of this group, the one it was named after: Carme. Carme was the largest of these asteroid-sized moons, 46 kilometers in diameter. It was roughly twenty-three million kilometers from Jupiter. A comparative distance would be a quarter of the way the Doom Stars had journeyed a year ago between Earth and Mars when the two planets had been 100,000,000 kilometers apart.

An observatory at Aquinas Base had noticed strange occurrences here. The base operators had also noticed peculiar activity at several other asteroid-moons of the Carme group. The orders sending the patrol boats had originated months ago.

"Anything?" asked the boat's Force-Leader, who also acted as the weapons officer.

"I'm getting fusion reactor readings," Mara said.

"Do they comply with the outpost's norms?" the Force-Leader asked.

"I'm checking that now."

Nadia watched Mara's thin fingers fly across a monitor-board. According to what the crew had told her, there was a scientific outpost here and a laser-lightguide way-station linked to the Saturn net. Mara read something off the board as she began shaking her head. Mara had a buzz-cut and wore a black quartz hook in her earlobe. Usually, Officer Mara smiled a lot, and often talked with Nadia for hours as they drank coffee. Mara wasn't smiling now.

"This is strange," she said.

"Explain," said the Force-Leader.

"There must be heavy shielding in place. It must be why I failed to detect these readings earlier."

"Explain," repeated the Force-Leader.

Nadia's stomach churned. She didn't like words like 'strange', not when referring to something so close. She removed the finger from her mouth and craned her neck to look.

A dark, irregular blot appeared through the window. There was a single bright mote on the blot, and stars shined on either side of it. Something about that darkness frightened Nadia. She put her finger back near her teeth as she searched her gnawed-down nail for something to nibble. Being here felt wrong—bad. She wanted to beg the others to go elsewhere, but she knew her words wouldn't matter. Besides, the belief that her words had power had died... maybe halfway to Jupiter.

Nadia switched fingers, and she winced as she bit down on a cuticle. She'd become too passive, and she knew it. She had to learn to live again. Was it truly dangerous out here, or had she become a mouse, jumping at shadows?

The weapons officer swiveled back. He had a round Jovian face and a whisper of a mustache. It made him seem too young, even though the mustache was gray. He blinked watery eyes at Mara.

"The outpost's normative energy levels shouldn't have changed," he said.

"I know that," Mara whispered.

"What are the readings?"

Mara shook her head.

"The scientific outpost—" the weapons officer began to say.

"Missile!" the pilot shouted.

The weapons officer swiveled back. Mara yelped as she slapped buttons. Then several things happened at once. A sleek missile burned hotly as it streaked around Carme and sped at the lead patrol boat. What appeared as tracer-rounds shot from that patrol boat's canons. The projectiles smashed into the missile, and the missile exploded silently, an orange ball of energy. Unfortunately for the patrol boat, a second missile had already appeared.

"Brace yourselves!" shouted the pilot, slapping a button that threw them into computer-automated evasive action.

Whimpering, Nadia gripped her restraining straps.

A third missile appeared, zooming around the curvature of Carme. More tracer-like rounds sped at the second missile. The missile jinked as the tracers shot past it. Then the missile hit, and the lead patrol boat exploded.

The *Occam VII* veered wildly.

"Who's firing at us?" the weapons officer shouted. He shoved his left hand into a twitch-glove as he jammed purple-lensed goggles over his eyes.

"By Plato's Bones," Mara whispered.

Nadia's hands hurt as she gripped her restraining straps.

"There!" the weapons officer shouted. His gloved fingers fluttered, and the patrol boat shuttered as ripping sounds came from the front of their vessel, the sound of shells entering the cannons.

"A dreadnaught," Mara whispered. "It was hiding behind Carme."

"What? What?" shouted the weapons officer.

"A dreadnaught is here," Mara said, pointing at her screen, at the vast, spherical shape on it.

The radio crackled with life as the other patrol boat exploded at the corner of the polarized window.

*I'm going to die*, Nadia told herself. *I don't want to die, not now.*

"I don't understand this," Mara said.

"Speak to me," the weapons officer said in a strained voice.

"You have to get us out of here!" Mara shouted. "I have to radio my information to the authorities!"

"What are you talking about?" the weapons officer shouted.

"There's something on the surface!" Mara shouted back. "It's big. The fusion readings—they're coming from there. I don't understand these readings. They're off the scale for what should be here."

"Another missile!" the weapons officer shouted. His fingers fluttered wildly and the ripping sounds of loading shells increased.

Tears flowed from Nadia's eyes. She wanted to live. She knew there was only one way now. She'd fought her way out of doom once before and maybe could do it again. That had been a lifetime ago, however, and with a different Nadia Pravda. Still, the old stubborn Nadia of the past still lived somewhere inside her.

As the patrol-boat veered one way and then another Nadia unhooked her straps. With her magnetized boots at full power, she clanked across the deckplates and for the hatch.

"We have to beam this information to Athena Station," Mara said.

"Not there," the pilot said. "Don't you remember? The cyborgs launched a missile attack from there."

"Right," said Mara. "I'm flashing this… to Ganymede Central." She pressed a transmit button. The patrol boat's readings concerning Carme, the massive fusion core—someone needed to know about this.

As Mara beamed the information, as the pilot jinked and as the weapons officer fired the boat's canons, Nadia made it out of the pilot chamber, through a cramped corridor and into a closest-sized ejection chamber. She was thrown one way and then another by the violent maneuvering. She donned a vacc-suit and crawled into a minuscule pod.

217

Nadia kicked the hatch shut with a clang, clicked her straps into place and yanked the ejection lever. There was a bump and a heavy clanking sound as the pod was loaded into a chamber like a cartridge. Nadia sucked down air. Then acceleration slammed her against the padded couch. Her ejection pod flew out of the patrol boat's side.

The *Occam VII* fled Carme. Missiles no longer launched from the huge dreadnaught. Now point-defense canons fired. They were blisters of light against the mighty warship. Seconds later, the patrol boat died, shredded into metallic parts and smears of bio-matter.

The jet on Nadia's pod burned for several more seconds. It must have registered on the dreadnaught's sensors. A flit-boat launched from a bay, heading toward her.

Nadia knew nothing about that. She hugged herself, moaning in misery. She was alone again, lost. It was a horrible feeling. What she wouldn't give for company—*I need company*, she thought to herself. Anyone would do.

Nadia wasn't aware that fate would grant her the wish, but grant it with a terrible twist.

## -2-

As the information from Patrol Boat *Occam VII* of the Aquinas Wing entered the main computer of Ganymede Central, Chief Strategist Tan boarded the *Kant*.

Outgoing messages from Callisto had ended forty-nine hours ago. Long before that, images of attacking cyborgs had shattered the Confederation. Nothing should move so fast or kill so effortlessly. Cameras caught cyborgs bounding across the surface, shooting anything that moved. The worst shot, played repeatedly on a million screens, showed a young woman with her baby cradled in her arms. The space-suited woman ran for a sealed rover as she hurdled a block of fero-concrete. A chasing cyborg fired a Gyroc pistol. The .75 caliber rocket ignited and blew the head off the young woman, causing her to fling her arms. The baby sailed and thudded against the rover. A microsecond later, another Gyroc shell from the same cyborg obliterated the infant and most of the rover's top.

Videos also caught machine-swift bipeds lunging through bunker corridors, using vibroknives to slaughter the survivors of the Voltaire strike. The herding of naked prisoners was awful to witness. Every news site on the web transmitted the image. The metallic indifference of the cyborgs burned into every heart that watched.

Callisto died, the victim to a thousand calamities. Nuclear-tipped cruise missiles flew nap-of-the-moon onto the Jupiter-facing side, hitting untouched domes. Gigantic mushroom clouds blossomed and radiation spread like a killer blanket.

From low-orbit, cyborg-controlled patrol boats inserted gravity bombs.

The worst scenes were always the individual cyborgs moving too fast, too far and with killer precision. They combed the ruins: hunting, herding and annihilating the former Confederation stronghold.

The rule of the philosopher-kings was just a passing memory now, if still a recent one. The survivors in their space yachts and on the liners were too shocked to insist on their former prerogatives. They fled to Io or began the long journey to the Himalia group moons.

Because of the successful cyborg strike, Ganymede became the premier moon. The highest ranked there had already begun jockeying for power. Only a few terrified people openly considered Gharlane's surrender terms. He came online, presenting the first recorded cyborg transmission in the Jupiter System. It was fitting that he issued an ultimatum. Most people suggested Gharlane's message was a ploy to shock them or to cause greater confusion through divided councils. Some of those jockeying for power radioed the *Descartes* and asked Representative Kluge's opinion concerning Gharlane's terms.

"It's a fight to the death," Marten told them via vidscreen. "Once they've stripped you of your defenses, you'll enter a converter, soon becoming one of the cyborgs yourself."

"The cyborgs are behaving differently here than they did during the Mars Campaign," one Ganymede Secessionist leader pointed out. "Perhaps they realize they need allies."

Marten laughed at the man. "No. It's only to gain time."

"Time to do what?" the stung leader asked.

"Time to subjugate the entire Solar System," Marten said.

Strategist Tan argued along similar lines. She now controlled the warships parked in low-Ganymede orbit. When asked by Secessionist leaders to accept a Ganymede commander, she said:

"I have the ships, the bombs and the missiles to dictate terms, not you."

"With Callisto's passing, your advantage is only momentary," the Ganymede Advisor said.

"Possibly true," said Tan. "Until that time ends, however, I shall direct my ships as I judge proper. Given that reality, I suggest you order your dreadnaught at Europa to join me. We must build up strength faster than the cyborgs build theirs. Then we must engage them and attempt an annihilating victory. We must drive them from our system."

"Ship ratios are still in their favor," the Advisor said.

"That isn't completely accurate," said Tan. "We presently have a superior concentration of warships. And it is a truism in war that such a superiority can bring strategic benefits if properly exploited. Therefore, let us quibble about political power later. Now is the moment to strike if we're to save ourselves."

The debate still raged between Tan and the Ganymede leaders, although the Secessionist dreadnaught had left Europa. It presently burned hard for Ganymede.

The *Descartes* meanwhile had matched velocity with the *Thebes*, a first class liner of the Pythagoras Cruise-Line. It was a huge vessel, bigger than a dreadnaught but without particle shields. It had escaped Callisto's destruction. Now, under Article Seventeen of the Dictates, guardian personnel had commandeered it. The liner carried an abundance of ship-guardians and critical supplies, and it had been ordered to rendezvous with the meteor-ship.

Mechanics in zero-G worksuits and small repair-bots attached docking lines to the *Descartes*. Like some exotic species of space-ant, suited workers exited various bays. Hydrogen spray expelled from their packs as they moved huge crates and circular pods. Other mechanics repaired ship-damage or they took the badly wounded to the *Thebes's* spacious medical chambers. Lastly, technicians replaced torn bulkheads and failing ship's systems. Everyone worked feverishly, including Marten, Osadar and Omi.

Ten hours before detaching, orders arrived via laser lightguide from Strategist Tan. The Secessionist Council confirmed her commands. Equipment worthy of a shock-trooper piled into the cargo bays. Meanwhile, another meteor-ship limped in and matched velocities.

"Something is up," Marten told Omi.

They were in an outer corridor, standing beside tall crates piled to the ceiling. One crate was open, with an armored spacesuit lying on the floor.

The suit was composed of articulated metal and ceramic-plate armor. A rigid, biphase carbide-ceramic corselet protected the torso, while articulated plates of BPC covered the arms and legs. The helmet had a Heads up Display, and a thruster-pack gave motive power. It was reminiscent of the shock trooper armor they'd worn while storming aboard the *Bangladesh*.

"Why are they filling our ship with these?" asked Omi.

"Take one guess," Marten said.

"You and me?" asked Omi. "We're going on the offensive for these people?"

"There's something someone wants taken out by shock troopers."

"What thing?" Omi asked suspiciously.

"I have no idea," Marten said. "But I think we'll find out soon enough."

"I hope there not thinking we're going to tackle cyborgs for them."

"Who else would we tackle, the Praetor?"

"I'm not sure I care for that, either."

Marten kicked the corselet with his armored boot. It had a nice metallic ring, and it proved that the armor-suit was heavy. It was too bad it lacked exoskeleton power. On whatever surface they fought, they'd have to utilize their own muscled power. "These are nothing compared to battleoids," Marten said.

"When did that stop anyone from feeding canon-fodder into the shredder?" Omi asked in a bitter tone.

"Never."

Omi glanced at Marten. "So what are we going to do?"

Marten shrugged moodily.

"We still have Osadar," Omi said.

Marten frowned as he counted crates. There were a lot, and plenty of new ship-guardians had boarded. They reminded him of the guardians who had helped them kill Octagon's two myrmidons. What they needed were more of those genetic killers. But maybe myrmidons were too elemental to fight well in spacesuits.

"Can these Jovians beat the cyborgs?" Omi asked.

"The time for running is over," Marten said quietly.

A hard frown appeared on Omi's normally expressionless face. "I don't think you heard me before. We still have Osadar."

"Yeah, I heard you. But I don't like the idea of killing Yakov's crew just so we can run away again."

"I don't like certain death either," Omi said. "You've watched the videos from Callisto. I don't think even Highborn could face cyborgs one-on-one, let alone us."

Marten took a deep breath. "We don't know that's what the higher-ups are planning."

"Come-on," Omi said. "We know it here." He tapped his heart. "Before, everyone figured they could use us. Why would these Jovians be any different?"

"The Jovians are our friends."

"Balls," said Omi. "They're people in a tight spot who will grab anything they can to stay alive. What I want to know is how come it's always you and me that have to do the dirty fighting?"

"Maybe because we always win," Marten said.

"You think we won on the *Bangladesh*?"

"We didn't lose."

Omi shook his head, and he turned, giving the suit a kick. "This is crap, whatever they have planned for us. We've done our time. Now it's someone else's turn."

"No," Marten said. "Now we're going to teach others how to do it."

"Like we did on Mars?" asked Omi.

"Better than we did there."

Omi studied Marten. "What aren't you telling me?"

Marten took another deep breath. Then, in a quiet voice, he told Omi his thoughts about standing for once and fighting or dying instead of just endlessly running away.

"Dying is easy," Omi said. "Running keeps us alive."

"Dying isn't easy for us two," Marten said. "Let's find Yakov. He'll tell us what's going on."

They found Yakov in his wardroom. The silver-haired Jovian was grim-faced. His elbows were on his computer desk as he massaged his temples. He stared at Marten before looking away.

"Why all the armored spacesuits?" asked Marten.

"Close the door," Yakov said.

Marten and Omi piled into the tiny room. Yakov motioned them nearer. The two of them sat as the Force-Leader straightened. There was a tightness around his mouth, bunched up muscles like little hard balls. He adjusted the desk controls.

"Chief Strategist Tan personally sent me this," Yakov said. "The leaders on Ganymede are still debating what it means."

Marten watched the video-feed from the *Occam VII* of the last Aquinas Wing Patrol. He witnessed the missiles, the destruction of the first two patrol boats and the dreadnaught rising from behind the asteroid-moon.

"This is Carme," Yakov said. "It's at the outer limit of Jovian space. This is what I want you to notice."

A pointer appeared on-screen, showing a large and lighted circular area on the otherwise dark surface.

"What are we looking at?" Marten asked.

"Tan's people have been running an analysis on the readings," Yakov said. "The best estimate is a massive exhaust-port, crater-sized, in fact. The indications are that someone has bored vast tunnels into Carme to massive engines inside."

Marten frowned at the Force-Leader. "That would take years to do."

"It doesn't seem to make sense, I know," Yakov said. "It would indicate the cyborgs slipped into our system long ago and began secret construction there. Maybe they've lived like ants down there, hollowing it out, waiting for this moment. The question is why. Then one of Tan's technicians recalled an intercepted message from the cyborgs."

Omi muttered obscenities.

Yakov raised an eyebrow, but Omi said nothing more. Yakov readjusted the controls. On the vidscreen, the dark surface leaped closer as the picture became grainy. The pointer

224

now showed what looked like low metal domes, but it was difficult to be definite.

"Tan's people are of two minds on these," Yakov said. "Some believe it is the upper part of a vast power-plant. The others think this is where the missiles came from."

"Tell me about the intercepted message," Marten said.

Yakov stared at the images. "It took several days to decode. It spoke about a planet-wrecker."

"Planet, not a moon?" asked Marten.

Yakov looked up as his dark gaze bored into Marten. "That's a shrewd comment. Do you understand what it means?"

Marten and Omi traded glances.

"I'm beginning to think I do," Marten said.

Yakov put his hands on the vidscreen as he studied both ex-shock troopers. "Tan's experts believe the cyborgs plan to move Carme. It would be extremely unwieldy as a warship, but if the experts are right, it will become something much worse."

"Are you going to tell us what that is?" Omi asked.

"The intercepted message said it all," Yakov whispered. "A planet-wrecker."

"Yeah?" asked Omi. "What does that mean?"

The muscles at the corners of Yakov's mouth tightened even more. "If Tan is right, the cyborgs plan to accelerate Carme and drive it into a moon or a planet."

Omi shook his bullet-shaped head. "Why would cyborgs crash Carme into Jupiter? That doesn't make sense."

"I doubt Jupiter is their goal," Yakov said. "Tan thinks this is a clever way to attack Mars, Earth or possibly Ganymede."

"Huh?" asked Omi.

"It would explain why the cyborgs came here," Yakov said. "The Mars Campaign would indicate they're at war with the Highborn and that they turned traitor against Social Unity. I've had trouble understanding why they would dissipate military strength by sending cyborgs to Jupiter. With two such militarily powerful foes, why add to the number of their enemies? The answer may be because they believe this is the perfect way to attack their primary foes."

"You've lost me," Omi said.

"It's basic," Yakov said. "It is also clever. Maybe more than that, it's also based on gargantuan mechanics. That's what makes it difficult to see or conceptualize."

"See what?" asked Omi. "I'm getting tired of your hinting. Just tell us."

"If Tan is right, the cyborgs are taking Carme and attempting to turn it into a weapon of planetary destruction. Jupiter has sixty-three moons, more than any other system. Maybe they'll attach massive engines and power plants to the other moons. If they build up enough velocity circling the gas giant, they could fling the moons at Earth or at Mars perhaps. In time—*bam*," Yakov said as he clapped his hands together. "It's extinction for everyone on that planet."

Omi blinked rapidly. "A planet-wrecker," he whispered.

"You need to send out your warships," Marten said. "Destroy the wrecker before it can begin."

Yakov shook his head. "It's not that easy. The cyborgs have shattered the system, murdering nearly half the Jovian population with their strike on Callisto. The massive fortifications there helped guard the other Galilean moons. Obviously, Callisto doesn't guard them anymore. Athena Station is now the strongest defensive position, and the cyborgs hold it."

Yakov massaged his forehead. "They've slaughtered millions and put us on the brink of extinction, but they've lost four capital ships doing it. That means Tan has a slight edge with the remaining Guardian and Secessionist warships. It also turns out that the Pythagoras Cruise-Line can convert several of their tugs into mine-laying ships."

"That doesn't stop Carme," Marten said.

"No," said Yakov. "But it means that Tan has persuaded the others to send two meteor-ships into the outer system."

"You just showed us the video," Marten said. "A dreadnaught guards Carme. Can two meteor-ships fight past it?"

"Theoretically, we can." Yakov drummed his fingers on the computer-desk. "One has to expect, however, that if the cyborgs have built engines and exhaust-ports large enough to

226

move Carme, that they would have added missiles and laser-bunkers to it."

"I know what to do," Omi said.

Yakov looked at him with hope.

"It's not our problem. Let Earth deal with it."

Yakov shook his head. "It could be targeted on Ganymede. But even if their eventual plan is to target Earth, we can't stand by and let the cyborgs win. If Social Unity goes down and if the Highborn lose, that would likely mean the end of humanity. We have a stake in seeing that doesn't happen."

"Radio Earth," Marten said. "Tell them."

"Tan already has."

"No," Omi said. "Social Unity isn't our friend. Neither are the Highborn."

"You speak truth," Yakov muttered. "Both have done us harm. Yet both are still human."

"That's all beside the point," said Marten. "Two meteor-ships might fail to take out a dreadnaught and an armored Carme."

"The massive exhaust-port shows us that even two meteor-ships might fail to stop the moon," Yakov said.

"I get it," Omi said, with a bitter laugh. "You want to land shock troopers onto Carme, hoping they kill every cyborg there. It's a suicide mission in other words, which means you plan on sending us and other fools to do it."

"Tan has chosen me to go with you," Yakov said quietly.

"We should have killed her when we had the chance," Omi said. "Now she's taking her revenge. Yeah, I know her kind."

"The stakes are too high and her rationality too sound for that," Yakov said.

Omi stared at the Force-Leader. "Don't bet on it."

"You're missing a greater truth," Yakov said, with a faint scowl. "Chief Strategist Tan is sending us because of you two. No one is better at space-marine fighting. You both know it, and you can both lead—"

"Lead other fools to commit suicide?" Omi asked.

"Perhaps we are all fools," Yakov said. "Sometimes, however, fools win."

"Fools luck?" asked Omi. "Marten's and my luck ran out a long time ago."

"So did mine," Yakov said. "Still, in the end, the Secessionists broke free from the Dictates."

Omi stared at the vidscreen, studying Carme and the bright mote on it. He whirled on Marten. "Aren't you going to tell him this is crazy?"

Marten moistened his lips. "It is crazy. The cyborgs are crazy. Breaking a moon out of its orbit, even a small asteroid-moon, and sending it across space to hit a planet—that's lunacy. It tells me this is a war of annihilation, either theirs or ours." Marten flexed his hands. "I told you before, I'm finished running away. It's time to slug it out. Maybe that means you and I are supposed to lead an attack onto that rock. I don't know."

"We'll be facing cyborgs," Omi said.

"Yeah," Marten whispered. Cyborgs—he remembered Olympus Mons. A handful of cyborgs had handled them with ease. If Osadar hadn't shown up, Omi and he would likely be cyborgs now. This *was* a suicide mission. Damn, he hated cyborgs.

Marten scowled. Hadn't he already killed cyborgs here? He'd helped destroy a dreadnaught full of them. It's also likely his action had given the Jovians whatever chance they had of surviving this stealth attack from Neptune. Marten stood very still then. Had he arrived in the Jupiter System for a reason?

A queasy feeling filled Marten's stomach. What did he stand for? Did the cyborgs really plan to make planet-wreckers and send them at Earth? Could he stand by and watch them do it, knowing he could have done something but that fear had caused him to run to Saturn or Uranus for safety? How long could he run in a Solar System ruled by cyborgs?

"Tell Yakov he's full of crap," Omi said.

Marten swallowed a lump in his throat. "Maybe this is crazy," he told Omi. "But we have to do it."

"Why? We've done our time."

"We survived Japan," Marten said. "But Stick and Turbo died there. We survived the *Bangladesh*. Vip, Lance and Kang became sterile motes in space. We survived Mars, but Chavez

228

and the others are radioactive dust. Maybe this is why we lived. We're meant to help stop humanity's extinction."

Omi folded his arms across his chest. After a moment, he said, "Osadar is right. Life is rigged."

"All men die," Marten said. "Maybe it's time to make our existence worth something." He faced Yakov. "I'm in."

Yakov checked a chronometer. "We leave in eleven hours. In that time, I want you to choose which ship-guardians to take along."

"Come again?" asked Omi.

"We had planned to take the *Thebes* with us," Yakov said. "Now we've discovered severe engine damage."

"What?" Omi asked.

"There was sabotage aboard the *Thebes*," Yakov admitted.

Omi laughed bitterly.

"Now we must select the best ship-guardians," Yakov said, ignoring the laugh. "You two must teach them what you can in the time remaining. Then you will lead them to victory once we reach Carme."

It was Marten's turn to laugh. He stared into space as if recalling a grim memory. "We have to choose the best. Yeah, I know what to do. Omi?"

Omi's face had become blank. He gave the barest of nods. Marten clapped him on the back, and that made Omi scowl.

"This is crap," Omi said.

"When isn't it?"

Omi thought about that, and said, "Yeah."

## -3-

"Are you sure you want to do it this way?" Omi whispered.

Marten wore a black uniform with silver stripes and tabs. Omi was similarly dressed. They stood in the spacious promenade deck of the *Thebes*, a first class pleasure liner of the Pythagoras Corporation. It had a rotating torus shell, giving pseudo-gravity to this area of the ship.

"No," Marten whispered. "I'm not sure. If you know of a better way of choosing space marines, let me know now."

Grim-faced ship-guardians standing at attention and in their blue uniforms, complete with medals and battle ribbons, filled the promenade deck. There were too many ship-guardians to take in the two meteor-ships. The guardian-class Jovians stood ready, awaiting inspection.

"I know of a better way," Osadar said.

She stood behind them, the focus of many staring eyes, as the three of them stood before the crowd of ship-guardians.

Marten and Omi turned to her.

"Check their records," she said.

"They're peacetime soldiers," Omi said with distain.

"Do peacetime records lie?" the cyborg asked.

"It isn't that," Marten said. "During war, officers look for fighters. During peace, they look for yes-men, for those who don't make waves. We want fighters. We want soldiers who will stick it out when cyborgs swarm them."

"Sift carefully through their records," Osadar said.

"We don't have time for that," Marten said.

"Is that why you have lined them up?" Osadar asked. "Can shock troopers tell a fighter at a glance?"

"No," Marten said, "not at a glance."

"Then why have you staged this?" she asked.

"You didn't tell her?" Omi asked.

"Tell me what?" asked Osadar.

"The Highborn are bastards," Marten said. "We know that. But they're also better soldiers, better fighters. They had a way to find the tough ones, the battlers."

"What way?" asked Osadar.

Marten cracked his knuckles as he stared at the ranks of ship-guardians. "We know the ones we choose are going to be fodder for the cyborgs. That's the truth of this war. It will be a quick trip to Carme, two or three weeks. There isn't much I can teach them in that time. But I can make sure I take the tough ones along. I can increase our odds a few percentages. Why is it then that I feel like such a bastard doing this?"

"The answer's simple," Omi said. "You're choosing those who are going to die."

"Yeah," said Marten. He set his features. "You tell her what's going on, okay?"

"Sure," Omi said.

"Tell me what?" asked Osadar.

"Okay," said Marten. "Here we go." He left them and strode alone toward the ranks of waiting ship-guardians. Those who had been staring at Osadar now looked at him. It was an animal response to glance at things that moved.

Marten adjusted his collar as he halted before them. He switched on an amplifier there, which would help project his voice.

"So you're the sorry rejects they're giving me to destroy the cyborgs," Marten said, letting contempt fill his voice.

Ship-guardians blinked at him. Many scowled. More than a few stirred.

Marten shook his head. "I fought in the Inner System, both on Earth and in space, capturing an experimental beamship near Mercury. Highborn trained me because they discovered I have an innate ability to kill. I also survive where others die, and I accomplish the missions given me." He pointed at Omi.

"We're shock troopers, which means we're the best soldiers in the Solar System, at least the best among humans. You ship-guardians—" Marten laughed with contempt.

More angry scowls appeared in the ranks.

"Some of you are going to have a chance to prove your worth," Marten said. "You're going to prove if Jovian space training is anything like Highborn training. I doubt it, frankly, but you'll have the chance to show me."

"Yeah!" a blue-uniformed guardian shouted. "And who the heck are you anyway?"

Marten stared at the guardian, a blocky individual. "I'm going to choose who goes and dies and who stays to live under the coming cyborg domination."

"Are all shock troopers arrogant pricks like you?" the guardian asked.

"Ask me an hour from now," Marten said.

"I'm asking you now!" the angry guardian shouted.

Marten drew his needler and fired, making crackling sounds. Guardians shouted in surprise. Many hit the deck. A few screamed as the bulky guardian flopped onto the floor.

"Stay where you are!" shouted Marten.

Pelias from the *Descartes* appeared, the tight-faced woman with black lipstick. She and three other guardians had drawn hammer-guns, aiming them at the crowd.

"I shot him with drugged ice-needles," Marten said. "He's still alive, but his mouth isn't flapping anymore. And that's my first lesson. I know many of you were expecting me to challenge him to a fistfight, to prove how superior my fighting technique was against his. A shock trooper uses overwhelming force when it's at his disposal. You'll do the same, or you'll die to the cyborgs."

Many guardians glared at him. Others stared at the fallen man.

"I will begin the interviews in three minutes," Marten said. "Guardian Pelias will now instruct you."

As Pelias stepped forward and began to shout orders, Marten moved to where Omi and Osadar watched. Omi had been whispering to Osadar.

"Are you ready?" Marten asked her.

"I will interview all of them?" she asked.

"Can you do it?" Marten said.

Osadar raised a reinforced hand and then slowly nodded.

***

The first guardian entered the room. He was a short man with scarred features and a watery left eye. He stopped at seeing Osadar sitting behind a small table. He glanced around at the otherwise empty room.

"Where's the shock trooper?" he asked.

Marten stood in the next room, watching the proceedings with Omi. They watched on a vidscreen.

"It's different this way," Omi muttered.

Marten nodded.

On the screen, Osadar arose without a word. She came around the table, approaching the short guardian.

"What's going on?" he asked.

Osadar slapped him across the face, whipping his head to one side.

Marten winced. "She isn't supposed to maim him."

"I told her," Omi said.

The short guardian clutched his face, backing away from Osadar. "Why did you do that?" he whined.

Osadar stared at him. Cowed, the man looked down. Osadar turned her back on him, returning to her chair. The guardian glanced up slyly.

"If he's going to do anything…" Omi said.

The guardian bit his lip, and he rubbed his cheek. As Osadar regarded him from the table, he looked down once more.

"He's a five," Marten said, writing down the number beside the ship-guardian's name on his computer slate.

Omi pressed a button.

A door opened on the opposite side of the room. Pelias was there, motioning for the slapped man to exit the room.

"I thought I was going to be interviewed," the man objected. "The cyborg just slapped me."

"Hurry," Pelias said. "Come this way."

Avoiding the table and Osadar seated there, the short guardian slunk for the exit.

"I hope some of them show more guts than that," Omi said.

Marten recalled the day he'd entered a room like this. A huge Highborn had slapped his face. He'd attack the HB for it and he'd found his hand stamped with a "2".

The first door opened and another ship-guardian entered the room. Marten readied his computer-stylus. Like Omi, he hoped there were enough Jovians who fought back. They were going to need the tough ones to have any hope of defeating what awaited them on Carme.

## -4-

In a low chamber on Athena Station were countless rows of pallets containing twitching bodies. On the seventh pallet in row two, lay Webbie Octagon. Like the other subjects, a synthi-flesh tube had been inserted into the jack at the base of his neck. It surged every seventeen seconds, expanding as if pumping blood. Pseudo-nerve endings were linked in him, sending the Web-Mind monitored impulses.

Like the other humanoids, Octagon wore a black skin-suit. It showed every gaunt limb and the sunken curvature of his stomach. He had lost weight. The skin was slack under his jaw, giving him jowls for the first time in his life. It also showed the rigid state of his sex organ. Drool spilled from his mouth, and every time the synthi-tube expanded in the neck-jack, Octagon gave an obscene moan of pleasure.

During his stay on the pallet, Octagon had undergone massive brain retraining. The Web-Mind reconditioned him, although there was a stubborn core of hatred in Octagon. The hatred pulsed as two words in mind-numbing repetition. Pain sensations, fear, loneliness and erotic pleasure hit against the hatred like feathers against lead. The words made little sense to the Web-Mind. To Webbie Octagon, they were like a holy creed, a litany of promised revenge.

*Marten Kluge, Marten Kluge, Marten Kluge*—only the highest dosages of pleasure momentarily thwarted the inner chant.

Because of the stubbornness of the memory-clot, the Web-Mind had chosen Webbie Octagon as the next human to head

235

to the cyborg converter. His pallet had originally been slated for conversion five days from now. Instead, a door slid open, and a cyborg pushed a magnetic gurney into the low-ceilinged chamber. The repulsers caused the gurney to hover. The melded biped with highly-controlled brain functions glanced in short, high-speed jerks of his head from right to left. The red-dotted pupils fixated on pallet seven-two. With the whine of knee-servos, the cyborg headed to Webbie Octagon's pallet.

The cyborg waited until the synthi-tube pulsed and Octagon moaned. With a deft twist and a slight sucking noise, the cyborg removed the plug.

Octagon's eyes flashed open. He turned his head, regarding the tall cyborg. Then he cringed as his sex organ began to shrink to normal size. It hurt badly because the organ had been in a rigidly erect state for forty-three hours.

The cyborg slid Octagon's inert form onto the gurney and efficiently strapped him down. Without a word, and with the quiet ever-present whine of servos, the cyborg turned the hovering gurney and pushed Octagon toward the exit. No other cyborgs entered the chamber. No other twitching humanoids left their pallets. From this bin-room, only Octagon was slated for conversion. Only he possessed the stubborn memory-clot, which had reduced his efficiency as a Webbie.

Octagon's awareness returned as the cyborg pushed him deeper into Athena Station. He had no idea that he was heading toward the converter deep in the core of the asteroid-moon.

*** 

Gharlane stood on the bridge of the *Locke*, the single dreadnaught of his battle group. He was a thousand kilometers from Athena Station, near the three meteor-ships and a wing of patrol boats that completed his fleet.

Cyborgs had replaced the former crewmembers. Several on the *Locke* had jacked into the modified controls, while Gharlane used a smaller version of the holographic display deep in Athena Station. He stood among the holo-images, carefully studying data on the Jovians.

Gharlane clicked his hand-component, changing the display. Should he summon the dreadnaught at Carme, enhancing the power of his fleet here?

The superiority of Genus Cyborgus versus Homo sapiens was most apparent on the ground, when individual cyborgs faced humans. Combat in space lessened the differences, although a cyborg taskforce still possessed certain advantages over the humans.

As Gharlane debated strategies, a signal arrived from the Web-Mind. The biomass brain still resided in its original stealth-capsule, parked in a deep hanger on Athena Station.

*I have correlated several new factors,* the Web-Mind told him in lieu of an introduction.

"Yes?" Gharlane asked.

*I have monitored signals and broken several of the Jovian codes. More importantly, I was able to tap into a laser lightguide message.*

Gharlane's head lifted. "Is that possible?"

*Through a third phase induction, yes,* the Web-Mind said.

"Are there new enemy warships?"

*Negative. However, enemy action has led me to reevaluate our strategic concentration.*

Gharlane didn't like the sound of that. It was usually wiser to keep to a single strategic goal instead of switching goals midway through a campaign. "What could be wiser than gathering into a single battle group and annihilating enemy concentrations one at a time? Afterward, nuclear bombardment and cyborg occupation of the major moons will garner us millions of recruits and nearly unlimited raw resources. In time, we can construct a massive strike-force composed of multiple planet-wreckers."

*Time and Saturn-coordination mandates a speed-up of our planetary strike-force.*

Gharlane used his hand-component, changing the holo-images and studying the Jovian moons and the various positions of warships, corporation craft and the largest pleasure liners. The Web-Mind retained control of the lightguide lasers linking them to Saturn and to Neptune. Thus, Gharlane had no way to argue the point or know precisely what occurred outside this system.

*Prepare to receive data,* the Web-Mind told him.

Gharlane stiffened as images and codes flashed into his modified brain. He learned that the conquest of the Saturn System had been swift, brilliant and overwhelming. The Saturn planet-wreckers and accompanying meteor-craft already built up speed, circling the ringed gas giant. The Web-Mind pulsed times, schedules, distances and the orbital positions of Mars, Earth and Venus as compared to the Saturn-launched strike.

*We are behind schedule*, the Web-Mind said.

"At this point in our campaign, is it wise to change our strategic goals? Ultimately, we have the advantage in ship tonnage and now possess the strongest base: Athena Station."

*Our old strategy was based on unlimited time. The Prime Web-Mind of Neptune has decided to accelerate our schedule. We must complete our planet-wrecker and match the target date of the Saturn-launched strike. Even a twenty percent increase of tonnage from us to the Saturn total will ensure annihilating victory. A ten percent tonnage increase from Jupiter will bring an obliterating enemy defeat ninety-three point six-five percent of the time.*

Gharlane changed the holographic sights. An image of Io filled the bridge, as the sulfur volcano-clouds became the center of attention. Strong volcanic eruptions on Io emitted as much as 1000 kilograms of matter into space each second. When holographic Ganymede appeared on the bridge, blue dots indicated the enemy fleet, with the brightest blue indicating the hated dreadnaughts. The Jovians still retained two of them.

Gharlane only half-noticed the images. His mind raced as he absorbed the Web-Mind's data. He could understand the Prime Web-Mind's thinking. Several cyborg stealth campaigns were in operation. Once one proved successful, all effort should be funneled to heighten its success. Strategically, one should concentrate effort to any breakthrough in order to achieve even greater victory rather than worrying about the failed or struggling endeavors. They had not failed here. The Saturn Campaign had simply achieved overwhelming success first. Therefore, the Jovian Campaign now became secondary to them and needed to bolster their attack sequence if possible.

The question was—what was the best way to shift the strategy here to aid the Saturn-strike?

The Web-Mind broke into his thoughts. *I am leaving Athena Station.*

Gharlane stiffened.

*I am headed to Carme.*

"Why there?" asked Gharlane, relieved at this news.

*It is our priority planet-wrecker, soon to begin its acceleration. I have recomputed odds, warship tonnage and strategic goals. The present conquest of the Jovian moons no longer takes precedence. Therefore, you will strike the Galilean moons, using nuclear bombardment to obliterate population concentrations. That will fix Homo sapien attention onto the inner moons. To achieve this goal, you are permitted to accept cyborg fleet annihilation.*

"Wouldn't it be wiser to destroy the enemy fleet first?" Gharlane asked.

*Obliterate population concentrations and industrial capacities of the Galilean moons. All analysis gives high probabilities that the Jovian warships will insert into moon orbits to halt your genocidal tactics. There you may lay tactical ambushes.*

"You are relying on panic factors?"

*I rely on probabilities and known Homo sapien reactions. They foretell a fixation on genocidal tactics, your fleet and Athena Station, in that order. During their fixation cycle, we shall complete the planet-wrecker. Then we shall build up velocity as we coordinate with Saturn on an Earth-strike.*

"You plan to join the planet-wrecker?"

*I will for ninety-eight percent of the journey,* the Web-Mind said. *Eventually, I will abort and return to the Jovian System as the ruling entity.*

"Do your probabilities foresee the cessation of my existence?"

*There is an eighty-three percent chance you shall face obliteration in the coming campaign. Yet you must endure in your task. Your faulty six-percent bio-reactions may take comfort in this knowledge: In time, I shall search Jovian space for lingering pieces of your DNA. With it, I will initiate a clone*

239

*reconstruction of Cyborg Gharlane. You will live again in the eternal process of Web-Mind.*

Gharlane's head twitched. Eighty-three percent chance of obliteration meant a seventeen percent chance of continued existence. He would increase those odds, as he was Gharlane, the prime unit in the cyborg assault of Jupiter.

*I will sweep the station for workers and equipment,* the Web-Mind informed him. *The Jovian planet-wrecker must strike to ensure annihilating victory. Therefore, you must begin to implement your strategic task in the quickest timeframe possible.*

"I hear and obey," Gharlane said, his strange, red pupils fixed on the swiftly changing holo-images around him.

\*\*\*

Webbie Octagon's nostrils twitched as he lay on the magnetic gurney. Harsh chemical odors assault him. The cyborg continued to push him as they entered the main conversion chamber.

Even to Octagon's altered brain, this was a place of horror. A vast machine stood before him. On it were twenty-four naked humanoids. Some bellowed. A few stared in shocked silence. All were strapped down securely and moving headfirst toward a small chute. Beyond that chute chemicals sprayed as skin-choppers began the hideous task of removing the outer layer of epidermis.

Octagon croaked a sound of protest. That caused the hatred to flare within him. Marten Kluge had caused this horror. Marten Kluge must die. Wait! Marten Kluge must *not* die, no, no, not die. Marten Kluge must suffer horribly for the wrongs he'd committed. The barbarian—

Octagon cocked his head and blinked. Barbarian... barbarian... that was a difficult concept. The Web-Mind mandated obedience in the new thinking. There wasn't such a thing as barbarians in Web-Mind terminology. Why then did he concentrate on such a topic?

"Marten Kluge," Webbie Octagon hissed. He began to squirm as the gurney neared the end of the conveyer. Octagon bitterly realized his fate. He would ride the belt into the choppers as he was transformed into a cyborg. He would

240

become strong. He would no longer possess any of himself. He might even lose his hatred of—

"Marten Kluge!" Octagon screeched.

As titanium-reinforced fingers began to unbuckle him, the cyborg stiffened. It stood motionless as the conveyer belt fed the screaming, protesting humans into the machine. The cyborg remained unmoving until the last human entered the chute.

"Marten Kluge," Octagon whispered.

The cyborg reattached the buckle. It turned the magnetic gurney and pushed Webbie Octagon toward the entrance. No fleshy human, Webbie or otherwise, had ever gone in that direction. It was unprecedented.

The pushing cyborg had received an emergency message from the Web-Mind. All the cyborgs on Athena Station had. They were to immediately head for the cargo vessels, the destination Carme. Because of the new command, Webbie Octagon inadvertently avoided conversion. He would join the convoy headed for Carme, to add his feeble muscles to the launching of the Jovian planet-wrecker.

Patrol boats landed on the *Descartes'* shell and on the rock of the second *Thales*-class vessel. The patrol boats lacked the extended acceleration of a meteor-ship, so they would have to ride piggyback. Unfortunately, their added mass would cut into fuel consumption. But it meant the taskforce would have the benefit of maneuverable landing craft.

Marten and Osadar were in the former Arbiter's quarters. Omi was presently running a squad in heavy calisthenics as they sprinted through the outer corridors.

Marten studied the latest advance in Jovian ground ordnance: the Infantry Missile Launcher or IML. It was a tube with sights and a trigger and it held a single Cognitive missile. The Cognitive missile gave Marten hope. The warhead was red and the electronics in it were better than anything he'd used before. Normally, the Cognitive missile gave a foot soldier the ability to destroy tanks or other heavy vehicles. A soldier aimed, fired and ducked like mad. The missile's sensors took over after that, guiding the missile to the target. It used secure neutrino receivers and had the added benefit of a passive designator.

Marten lowered the IML. It weighed nine and half pounds with the missile loaded. Each salvo weighed five and a quarter pounds.

Next Marten picked up something called a PD-10. It was a passive designator. It looked like a heavy Gyroc rifle, but with a large dish antennae on the barrel. The user needed to keep the dish on target. Through secure communications, the PD-10 sent targeting coordinates to any nearby IML-launched Cognitive missiles.

"We need to recode these," Marten said. "Forget about tanks or vehicles, and set them to target cyborgs."

"I'm not a technician," Osadar said.

"I don't mean you have to do it. But what do you think of the idea?"

Osadar glanced at the IML and at the PD-10 before shrugging.

"Technicians will reset the Cognitive missiles," Marten said, "using you as the prospective target. With you, I can also show the troops the capabilities of cyborgs and hopefully find some weak points to exploit."

"They still hate me for slapping their faces."

Marten grunted. He'd chosen his space marines, calling them that now instead of ship-guardians. He'd taken the ones, twos and threes. Most of them were doomed to a quick death. He was probably doomed, too. But he'd chosen them. Now he was trying to figure out ways to keep them alive once they reached Carme. IMLs, patrol boats to land them on the surface, what else could he do? The knowledge that he led these space marines to almost certain death was beginning to weigh on him.

\*\*\*

"How fast does Carme accelerate?" Marten asked Yakov in his wardroom.

"My information says at one-quarter G."

Marten nodded. The *Bangladesh* had accelerated at a much greater rate. He wanted his space marines ready for that possibility. There was only one good way to get them ready.

"I need to take my space marines outside," Marten said.

"We're accelerating," Yakov said. "No one goes outside the ship during acceleration."

"That's why I need to take them out," Marten said.

"You might lose men."

"I might lose space marines on Carme," Marten said. "But I'm still headed there."

Yakov drummed his fingers on the computer-desk. At last, he nodded.

The next day began the high-G training. Marten and Omi went out with each squad. It was grueling work. Everyone checked his or her vacc-suit twice. They lacked the spikes of shock trooper suits. Instead, they had hammer-jacks, pitons and block and tackle gear. Marten led the way.

He shot a piton into the meteor-rock and attached his line to it. Slowly, he crawled forward. Piton by piton he neared the curvature of the ship. The G-forces began to tear at him. It caused his mouth to become dry.

Stars and meteor-rock filled his vision. His harsh breathing was all he heard. Then he opened his com-link and instructed those following him.

Slowly, with Omi at the end, the squad crawled across the backside of the *Descartes*. Terrible G-forces tried to tear them off. More than one space marine shouted curses. Others hissed with fear. Some just silently followed.

It was the fifth time across that the accident occurred. Marten was exhausted. He might have forgotten to give his warnings. There was a scream in his helmet.

"Pelias!" someone roared.

There was a sharp yank on the line. Then there was nothing. Marten's stomach curled tight. While clutching the gear, he twisted his helmeted head. The sight sickened him.

A space marine tumbled away from the meteor-shell. Her arms flailed as she quickly dwindled.

"Pelias," Marten whispered.

"Please," she moaned. "Help me. Send help. I don't want to die."

Her flailing form quickly became too small to see. The *Descartes* and the following meteor-ship burned hard for Carme. They couldn't afford to halt just to pick her up.

"Pelias," Marten said, recalling her black lipstick, the way she'd walked. She would last for hours out there, knowing that she was soon going to run out of air.

As Marten clung to the rock with the others behind him, he recalled the awful image of shock troopers dwindling into the blackness, those that had fallen off the *Bangladesh's* particle shields.

"What are we going to do?" a space marine asked.

Marten squinted into the starry distance.

"Group-Leader Kluge?" someone asked.

Marten gathered his resolve. Why had Pelias been the one? He shook his head. Then he chinned on his line. He was the shock trooper. He was the hard case.

"This isn't a game," he told them. "This is life or death. Pelias forgot that." He didn't know if that was true. But he had to use this to train the others.

He heard someone call him a bastard.

Marten shook his head. He had space marines to toughen. He had to do whatever he could so a few might survive the cyborgs. Probably, they were all doomed to die horribly. Or worse, they would enter a cyborg converter.

"Keep moving, people," Marten heard himself say. "Don't make Pelias's mistake. You have to keep your focus at all times." Then he began to move again, crawling across the surface of the meteor-ship.

*\*\**

Pelias's boyfriend went berserk the next day. He attacked Marten with a blade, trying to stab him in the back in the recreation room where they drilled. A shout from Omi gave Marten enough time to whirl, dodge and chop his stiffened fingers into the attacker's throat. The boyfriend writhed on a mat, clutching his throat.

Afterward, Marten went to his chamber. He broke out a bottle of Yakov's whiskey, sipping once. It burned going down. He shook his head. He hated this. He hated the Highborn and he damn well hated the cyborgs. What had humanity ever done to receive these twin fates?

Marten took another sip before corking the bottle. He had to keep pushing. Destroying the planet-wrecker—he might be saving Earth or Mars. Either way, billions of lives might be resting on what he did. He couldn't go soft now. He had to push.

The door opened and Osadar entered. The cyborg stopped, and she looked at him.

He gave her a tired glance before getting up, going to the desk and turning on the computer. He felt a growing need to do everything he could to make sure some of these cannon fodder space marines would survive the battle. He knew they were going to need every advantage they could find, or they were all going to die uselessly.

## -6-

The debates raged on Ganymede and in the Combined Fleet stationed in mid-orbit there. Chief Strategist Tan held nominal command of the fleet, but that power was slipping.

The warships near Athena Station waited. There was a meteor-ship heading toward them. The assumption was they were cyborg-controlled. They answered radio calls with human officers, citing ridiculous excuses as to why they remained there. But it was obvious they were cyborg ships now. All civilian and commercial spaceships stayed far away from Athena Station. Counting the approaching meteor-ship, the cyborg fleet there contained one dreadnaught, three meteor-ships and many patrol boats.

The terrible meaning of the genocidal destruction of Callisto finally began to seep into the warship-personnel of the Guardian Fleet. Callisto had contained nearly half the Jovian population and well over half the system's manufacturing capacity. Political, intellectual and monetary power had emanated from the fourth Galilean moon. Now it was gone. That left a gaping hole where the heart of the system used to lie. Worse for the warship-personnel, it had stolen their homes, their wives and children and their base, their reason for being. In a myriad of ways, they had been set adrift. They were like souls without bodies, without a political, spiritual or material anchor.

The two Secessionist warships had matched orbits with them, and a few more patrol boats had straggled in. That gave the new Combined Fleet two dreadnaughts, three meteor-ships and three wings worth of patrol boats.

The Force-Leaders, Arbiters and Governors in the Guardian Fleet-warships realized that no base existed for them. Ganymede had declared itself a sovereign state, as had Europa. The corporate mining-executives on Io were already sending delegates to both moons, seeking protection treaties. The Guardian Fleet had formerly existed to protect the Confederation, but that Confederation had vanished into the splintered sovereign states. Smaller, asteroid-sized moons were already talking about defensive alliances with each other.

Astute politicians on Ganymede and on Europa sensed the opportunities. They'd begun sending open and secret delegates to the various warships, trying to win them over to their particular sovereign state.

Chief Strategist Tan recognized the problem. She had daily briefings with the warship commanders. She also sent orders to various outposts, trying to convince them to hold their positions and monitor the cyborgs. The trouble, however, was that everyone wanted to survive the war. Without the might of Callisto threatening them, and with the crumbling of the Confederation, men and women thinking about their future forget their duty. At least, Tan viewed it that way.

She used half her energy trying to hold the fleet together. The other half she saved for deep thought, trying to pierce the cyborg strategy.

Finally, the warships near Athena Station began a burn that would take them to Io. It had every Jovian in an uproar. Many wanted to intercept the cyborgs and protect the mining properties on Io. Ganymede's political leaders had other ideas, namely, that the Combined Fleet remain at the third Galilean moon, protecting them from possible bombardment. Soon, the political leaders on Europa clamored for warships. They wanted to know what would happen if the cyborgs headed for their moon.

A meteor-ship with a Europa-born crew planned on heading for home. It was hard to blame their hearts, even if their strategic insight was faulty.

Tan paced down a long corridor on the *Kant*. Su-Shan was dead. Callisto was a radioactive ruin. Who lived by the Dictates anymore? Could such a philosophically splendid system die that quickly? Was everything she'd learned, everything she'd known, now meaningless? Was mere existence worth all this misery?

Tan slid the silver ring on her right middle finger back and forth. It had a philosopher-king's lion symbol on the signet. Sometimes, it felt as if she was the living embodiment of the Dictates. When she felt this way, it was easier. She knew what to do then. First, she must defeat the cyborgs. Then she must return the Jovian System to the pristine state it had so laboriously achieved through the decades. Something as wonderful as reason, logic and meaning—

Tan groaned as she recalled the horrible images from Callisto. Who had ever created such a horror as cyborgs? What had the creators been thinking? What had been the real purpose behind machine-like men? Perhaps the creators had been mad. That seemed like the easiest explanation, or perhaps their dreams had been infested with mad hopes.

Had scientists in the Neptune System observed the massive, military build-up in Inner Planets? Were the cyborgs a response to the Highborn? What had ever prompted the rulers of Social Unity to gene-warp such fierce super-soldiers? Why construct Doom Stars when they'd possessed the SU battlewagons? Well… that was easier to understand. The allied fleets of Mars and Jupiter had defeated a fleet of SU battleships. It had taken Doom Stars to shatter the allied fleet thirteen years ago. Clearly, the rulers of Social Unity had desired Solar-wide conquest. Then again, with such a sprawling political system there must have been and likely still were vast bureaucracies within the structure of Social Unity that fought at cross-purposes against each other. Perhaps one department had created the Highborn and a different department with different insights and goals had built the Doom Stars.

Tan shook her head as she stared out of a viewing port. Mighty, banded Jupiter slowly rotated, and the Red Spot swirled with activity. That Red Spot was a hurricane in the gas giant's upper atmosphere. It had been blowing and swirling for over five hundred years, changing its deepness of color and speed over the long decades. There was no land inside Jupiter to break apart a hurricane as happened on Earth. There, hurricanes rose from the oceans and they broke apart over the landmasses.

Tan sighed. Social Unity didn't matter now. Highborn, Doom Stars—the cyborg fleet burned for Io. Should she attempt to intercept the fleet? The problem was that compared to the rest of the Jovian moons, the Galilean moons moved in near proximity to each other. What if she accelerated for the cyborg fleet or for Io, and then the enemy made a dash for Europa or even worse, for Ganymede? They could not afford to lose any more Galilean moons or industrial centers. If the cyborgs bombarded Europa or Ganymede—she must defend those two moons at all costs. Io on the other hand....

Tan stared at the great gas giant with its Red Spot. Three Earths could fit into that single ancient storm. Maybe the cyborgs would bypass Io and attempt to destroy the processing centers that floated in Jupiter's upper atmosphere. Did the cyborgs need the helium-3 isotopes? No. She doubted the cyborgs would pin themselves so near the massive gravity-well. Going down to Io or to the processing plants was easy. Climbing back up the gravity-well took hard burns.

She let go of her ring, the one she'd been rotating around her finger. She looked back the way she'd come. The corridor curved slowly. She had already walked the outer-corridor circumference of the dreadnaught. Her heart rate quickened then as she considered a critical problem.

Fleet morale had sunk to abysmal levels. The very idea of the Guardian Fleet was nearly dead. Callisto glowed with radiation and everyone else jockeyed for an unknown future. The rulers of Europa and Ganymede played political games when they needed to concentrate on defeating the cyborgs. She needed to cement her fleet role as supreme commander. This move toward Io by the cyborgs—a cunning mind moved that fleet. A cunning mind had sent the missile strike into the heart of the Jovian System.

Tan whirled around and broke into an unseemly trot. She had to use the move against Io to her advantage. She had to wield these new politicians, using them to create a new Confederation. If she was to win the battle against the cyborgs, they had to give her command authority. As it was, they chipped away at her power.

As she trotted, Tan began to breathe hard. She wasn't used to running and her legs were too short. It was time to speak with the Advisor of Ganymede—the moon's chief politician—and with the Controller of Europa. She had a good idea about what was going to happen next. Io was doomed to nuclear bombardment. That was the horrible truth. The Advisor and the Controller would never agree to let the Combined Fleet head to Io to avert disaster. Therefore, she had to use her foreknowledge and her gift at strategy, both military and political, to break their confidence in themselves. She had to show them that only she could save the Jupiter System. It was time to have another three-way. It was time to join the political games, using her strategic insights to win the power she needed to annihilate the cyborg menace.

\*\*\*

*The three-way conference between Chief Strategist Tan of the Guardian Fleet, the Advisor of Ganymede and the Controller of Europa. Subjective time: twenty days after the cyborg missile strike of Callisto. Held via a dedicated laser lightguide-link.*

TAN: Gentlemen, I'm glad you agreed to meet with me. The situation has become dire. The cyborgs have gathered an appreciable concentration of warships and presently move on a hard intercept course for Io. We cannot afford to lose the mining colonies there.

ADVISOR: I dearly hope this is not another attempt to move the Combined Fleet out of its excellent, defensive position. I've already informed you of Ganymede's total rejection of such thinking.

CONTROLLER: Before we speak about that, let us be clear on one critical certainty. The cyborgs are cunning. We have learned this to our eternal disadvantage. Callisto—it is too difficult to put into words the horrors that occurred there.

251

TAN: We are the leaders of the Jovian System. If you cannot put the situation into words, I suggest the governors of Europa find someone who can.

CONTROLLER: Have a care, Chief Strategist. There are no more arbiters or philosopher-run spy agencies on Europa. We are thus free to think, do and speak as our hearts wish.

TAN: Perhaps that is so. My question for you is. For how much longer will you enjoy these freedoms if you ignore the cyborgs?

CONTROLLER: The Dictates died with Callisto and this isn't a dialogue of the old school. You will not cajole or intimidate me. Know, that I agreed to this meeting for one reason only. I demand that the new, Combined Fleet protect Europa as strongly as it protects Ganymede.

ADVISOR: (sneeringly) How do you suggest this occur?

CONTROLLER: We must split the fleet into equal parts, with one half stationed at Europa and the other at Ganymede.

TAN: That still leaves Io open to bombardment.

CONTROLLER: Such an occurrence would be a terrible tragedy, and I would grieve deeply. All Europa would grieve. However, reality demands that we defend the key, strategic posts. Using population levels and industrial capacity as the rubric, Europa and Ganymede are clearly the critical locations.

ADVISOR: You have a point concerning strategic targets, Controller. Still, your thinking is faulty on two counts. One, Ganymede has four times Europa's population and five times its industrial capacity. That mandates our moon as the primary defensive establishment. Two, splintering our fleet in the face of the enemy is military suicide. I'm sure the Chief Strategist would agree with me on that.

CONTROLLER: (with his voice rising) I demand equal protection.

ADVISOR: To what end do you make these *demands*? Is it in the interest of Jovian Civilization? Or do you make these demands through a selfish desire for personal safety?

CONTROLLER: I make the demand for the same reason you do.

ADVISOR: Surely you jest.

CONTROLLER: Eighty-five percent of the Jovian System's water originates on Europa. Can you survive without water?

ADVISOR: I abhor the thought of the loss of your moon. That is understood, and we obviously need water.

CONTROLLER: Then send us half the fleet. Guard Europa and guard the water supply.

ADVISOR: There is a flaw in your reasoning. In the unfortunate circumstance that the cyborgs bombard Europa and destroy you, tankers will still eventually be able to land there and mine the ice.

CONTROLLER: Irradiated ice? Is that what you wish to drink?

ADVISOR: The water companies will use distillation systems to purify the liquid.

CONTROLLER: I deem your thinking as unreasonable and Ganymede-centric.

ADVISOR: (laughs) There are no philosopher-boards to hear your complaints. Ganymede is the supreme moon, and we control the fleet. You would do better to adjust yourself to the new realities. Instead of berating me, you should try to cajole me. What can you offer Ganymede? Come, Controller, what is your continued existence worth? If Europa decided to become our largest fiefdom—

CONTROLLER: Are you mad? We have just won our freedom from Callisto.

ADVISOR: You have won nothing. This freedom was *granted* you through the cyborg missile strike.

CONTROLLER: The same holds true for Ganymede.

ADVISOR: That is completely false. Ganymede citizen-guardians within the fleet boldly took charge of their vessels and—

CONTROLLER: (shouting) We won't crawl on our knees to you! Send us warships! Without Europa and with irradiated water you will all die!

ADVISOR: Calm yourself, sir. Your tirade is unseemly, and it suggests to me that you're unhinged.

TAN: Gentlemen, please—

CONTROLLER: I warn you both. Europa controls a meteor-ship, and—

ADVISOR: (scoffing) One meteor-ship—you are the weak sister.

CONTROLLER: We wondered if this day would occur. We had hoped we were wrong, but we've long distrusted you.

ADVISOR: Insults are unadvisable, and in your situation, highly dangerous.

CONTROLLER: (laughs harshly) Do you believe so? Then let me inform you both that patriots of Europa have planted secret bombs in the warships.

ADVISOR: This is madness you spout, the fantasies of a deranged mind. You cannot be serious.

CONTROLLER: Doubt me at your peril, Advisor. We long suspected your trustworthiness. Therefore, we decided to create insurance, giving you good reason to treat us in a civilized manner.

ADVISOR: How do I know that your statement is true?

CONTROLLER: Twice you have impugned my good name. I am the Controller of Europa, a governor of tested integrity. You know this to be true because I have spoken and I am an honest man. More insults will result in—

ADVISOR: No, no, this is a dire thing, you say. A cunning man could make your claims, acting the part of an honest broker. In this, you must confirm your statement.

CONTROLLER: You mocked me earlier. Now I begin to question your reason. What you ask, I cannot verify it for a simple reason. By its nature, a confirmation invalidates the threat of a secretly-placed explosive. You will have to accept this on faith or face the destruction of your fleet.

*Three seconds of silence ensues.*

CONTROLLER: I repeat my demand. Send half the fleet to Europa.

ADVISOR: I can understand your desire. You are a true guardian, a valiant servant of your state. However, I would beg you to reconsider. From a purely strategic standpoint, Jovian Civilization can afford to lose Europa. Naturally, we would all deeply regret it. And I hope you did not take my small joke earlier to heart.

254

CONTROLLER: That Europa became Ganymede's prized fiefdom?

ADVISOR: Hearing you repeat the joke causes me to wince. My humor was definitely ill-advised. Now that I've admitted that, I ask you to reconsider your 'demand'. We must examine strategy in light of future Jovian Civilization. Our system cannot afford to lose Ganymede, to lose its highly-trained population and nearly sole heavy industrial basin. Therefore, to protect the system, we must ensure Ganymede's survival. Then we must carefully husband our strength to defeat the cyborgs when and where they attempt another decapitating strike. That means, naturally, that the fleet will do everything in its power to protect Europa.

CONTROLLER: Yes, by parking warships in mid-Europa orbit.

TAN: Gentlemen, if I could intervene in your argument.

ADVISOR: I'm not sure your interruption is warranted, Chief Strategist. The Controller and I are politically chosen representatives of our sovereign moons. You are a cipher in the antiquated Guardian Fleet. You must obey the new political authorities. While it is true the Controller and I have disagreed on some minor points just now, we do so in a legal and ethical manner. Your intrusion into grand strategy—no, it is unwarranted.

TAN: Speak to the cyborgs about ethics.

ADVISOR: Is that a threat?

TAN: The cyborgs will soon attack Io. Knowing this, the strategically sound move that protects both Europa and Ganymede is clear. We must send the entire fleet on an intercept course and live or die by that battle.

ADVISOR: That is sheer hysteria.

CONTROLLER: I don't agree. Her proposal interests me.

ADVISOR: My dear sir, surely you see her trickery. She cares nothing about Ganymede or Europa, but wishes to cement her place at the head of the fleet. Then she will blackmail us both into a subservient position.

TAN: Perhaps I wish to defeat the enemy.

ADVISOR: Do you take us for fools? Do you think we lack the understanding of basic deception?

TAN: If you would listen—

ADVISOR: It is clear that the cyborgs are ruthlessly cunning. They use their fleet to lunge at Io, attempting to lure our fleet out of position. Once that occurs, they shall burn at a harder acceleration than any human could endure. Oh, I've studied their last attack in detail. I know beyond doubt that they desire a nuclear bombardment of Ganymede. They hope to finish the war with one more strike.

CONTROLLER: I have a counter-proposal.

ADVISOR: My dear sir, we must unite on strategy so the Chief Strategist doesn't divide and then exploit us through Dictate-derived guile.

CONTROLLER: First, let me remind each of you that secret obliteration devices reside in the warships.

ADVISOR: I feel driven to point out that activating the devices will leave Europa at the mercy of the cyborgs.

CONTROLLER: I understand. But I refuse to passively stand by and watch Europa's destruction. If the second Galilean moon dies, the fleet perishes.

ADVISOR: Forgive me for saying this, but that strikes me as a selfish attitude.

CONTROLLER: Nevertheless, it is my attitude. However, I no more desire death than you do. Therefore, if you refuse to split the Combined Fleet into equal parts, then I demand that you move the fleet into a position halfway between Europa and Ganymede. In this way, if the cyborgs lunge at either moon, the Combined Fleet will rush in to protect that target.

ADVISOR: In no way do I wish to disparage your intelligence. Yet a simple understanding of space mechanics will show you the folly of such a proposal. A fleet needs a gravity-well to help it accelerate and slingshot at its targeted destination. Since the Combined Fleet already rests at the—at *a* primary defensive post, it should logically remain here. If the fleet were already at Europa, I would suggest the same thing.

CONTROLLER: Your statement is questionable.

ADVISOR: I am unused to anyone calling me a liar, even someone as noble as you are, sir.

TAN: Gentlemen, please, this bickering is useless. The cyborgs are on the verge of destroying us, of bombarding Europa and Ganymede.

ADVISOR: Our fleet stands in their path.

TAN: Gentlemen, let me outline the cyborg strategy.

ADVISOR: (scoffing) You claim to understand them?

TAN: I understand how I would act given their situation.

ADVISOR: If your highly vaunted insight reigns so supreme, why didn't you foresee the strike against Callisto?

TAN: The cyborgs are trying to annihilate important, strategic targets in turn, hoping to paralyze us into inactivity. If we let them bombard Io, we are that much closer to the abyss of extinction. We must meet their fleet, risking life or death. Otherwise, we give them the strategic initiative.

CONTROLLER: Could you explain that, please?

ADVISOR: She speaks Dictate-style gibberish in an attempt to confuse us. I advise against listening to her.

CONTROLLER: No. I would hear her insight. After all, she was a Chief Strategist under the old rule.

ADVISOR: Don't let her deceive you. She was a junior strategist elevated to the highest rank through the simplest expedient of being the sole survivor of the War Council.

CONTROLLER: Nevertheless, she was trained in war theory and execution.

ADVISOR: That means she is highly cunning and deceitful.

CONTROLLER: Then let us use her deceitful practices to deceive the cyborgs.

ADVISOR: That is mere sophistry, sir, which I had thought died with Callisto's passing.

CONTROLLER: (his voice hardening) I insist on hearing her insights, *sir*.

ADVISOR: Bah! It is a waste of our precious time. However, to show you that I am capable of bending over backward to please an ally, I will submit to her diatribe.

TAN: (serenely) This is no diatribe, gentlemen, but an assessment of the strategic situation. The cyborgs threaten us with the horns of a dilemma, thereby hoping to pin our mobile elements into static non-movement.

ADVISOR: You're speaking strategic gibberish to blind us to your political goals.

TAN: In my first days at the Academy, we read an ancient book called *Strategy*. B.H. Liddell Hart wrote it.

ADVISOR: I am unaware of the author and suspect you are deviating from the true topic of our three-way.

TAN: *Strategy* is a treasure trove of military insights. What I find interesting is that the cyborgs seem to be applying the strategy of an ancient soldier named General Sherman. He termed the phase, 'on the horns of a dilemma,' which I just elucidated. In his 'March to the Sea' through a place called Georgia, General Sherman always took a line of advance that left his enemies in doubt of his destination. Would he march on Macon or Augusta next, or later on Augusta or Savannah? He forced his enemies to defend multiple places. The place left open, he destroyed. In this way, he annihilated the productive areas in a land called 'The South.'

Now, the question for us is this. Do we park our fleet in a single place, waiting? Do we allow the cyborgs to burn through the Jovian System as General Sherman burned his way through Georgia? If we answer in the negative, if we hope to thwart our fate, we must strike boldly. We must use everything we possess to smash the enemy and regain the initiative.

CONTROLLER: The risks are great, and perhaps you are wrong. Do the cyborgs truly wish to destroy Io? If they attempt it, it will put their warships deep in Jupiter's gravity-well.

ADVISOR: I believe the cyborgs hope to lure our fleet out of position. I find that I agree with the Controller. We must wait.

TAN: Haven't you been listening? Io isn't the target, but a possibility. The cyborgs have put us on the horns of a dilemma. We cannot possibly defend everything. Therefore, we must risk the fleet and our moons to attack instead of waiting to die piece by piece.

ADVISOR: Controller, your words have convinced me. We must wait. We must hold and defend. Unfortunately, I lack complete authority regarding the Combined Fleet. My vote, however, is to place the fleet in far-Ganymede orbit, thereby putting it closer to Europa, ready to dash to your moon in its savage defense.

CONTROLLER: A mid-point between our moons would be better.

ADVISOR: I believe if you confer with your space tacticians, you will find that an inadvisable proposal.

CONTROLLER: ...I will confer with them.

TAN: Gentlemen, the cyborgs will destroy Io if we do nothing. Then they might well send patrol boats into Jupiter's upper atmosphere and bombard the floaters. They might also strike the inner group, the processing moons, blowing up the storage facilities there. Several year's-worth of helium-3 and deuterium are at risk.

ADVISOR: You cannot know these things with such certainty. They are illusions built to suit your political aspirations.

TAN: My words are recorded, gentlemen. I will stand by them. Then all will see that I could have saved Io and whatever else we shall lose, while you two dithered, too filled with fear to make the bold move.

CONTROLLER: Your insults leave me cold, Chief Strategist. Advisor, I must confer with my tacticians concerning these space mechanics you mentioned.

ADVISOR: Yes, excellent. I must also depart and relate this meeting to our Quorum. Chief Strategist, if you will excuse me, and Controller, if I have your leave.

CONTROLLER: You do, for now. But I will expect an elevation of Europan fleet personnel into command positions. This must have occurred by our next meeting. If you find that unacceptable, then a substantial number of warships must be en route to our moon. Otherwise, the destruct codes will be activated. I suggest you both think carefully on that.

ADVISOR: You are a bold man, Controller. I welcome you as my ally in these harrowing days.

TAN: Unless you gentlemen agree to my strategy, our extinction is a real probability.

ADVISOR: Your days are numbered, Chief Strategist.

TAN: No more than yours, Advisor.

CONTROLLER: (a static line).

*The end of the three-way.*

## 7

On Carme, Nadia Pravda crawled through a claustrophobically tight tunnel. She wore a rebreather with tank and a pressurized slick-suit. A headlamp washed over asteroid-rock with sharp points and dust on the uneven floor.

Nadia stapled a thick power cable into place. Her arms ached from lugging the stapler and her body throbbed with fatigue and desperate lack of sleep.

Out of an original bin of sixty unmodified humans, Nadia was one out of few to have survived this long. Haulers brought in more captured humans, along with needed equipment. The humans withered like leaves. They withered from overwork, undernourishment and despair.

Nadia's breathing was harsh. Through the rebreather's ballistic glass mask, there were dark circles around her eyes and a strange, haunted quality. A cyborg had shaved her head and sprayed her with burning chemicals. She had survived this long because she practiced several vile expedients.

She crawled on her elbows, carefully searching the floor and then the tight walls around her. She'd found dead workers before, their slick-suits torn by rock. The slightest cut could kill, allowing vacuum to finish her.

Nadia pressed the stapler against the cable and pulled the trigger. The unit trembled, and it pushed sharply against her hands as it drove a staple over the power-cable and into the rock. She dragged herself another few feet and repeated the process. She'd been in this tunnel for over sixteen hours. She had another eight to go. The cyborgs worked people in twenty-four hour cycles, with a four-hour sleep and eating period.

Nadia had survived because she stole nutrients from the dazed, the dispirited and the dying. When she found a dead worker, she slept for twenty or thirty minute periods. Then she claimed whatever work the dead had accomplished as her own. She did this because the cyborgs killed anyone who failed to reach their work-quota.

Nadia had been here since the *Occam* patrol boats died. She refused to quit. She'd beaten Hansen, the Highborn and Ervil and now she was going to beat the cyborgs. It was an act of futility. She understood that. She wondered if Marten Kluge had influenced her with something of his essential nature.

As she pressed the stapler against the cable and pulled the trigger—her hands lifted upward—she frowned. That pained her eyes. They burned all the time, and it hurt to blink. The sound of her breathing—she scraped her armored elbows across the gritty rock floor. She dragged herself over the cable and as she brushed up against the rock walls.

Nadia froze then, and slowly backed up. With blurring eyes, she stared at a sharp, rocky protrusion. Her stomach tightened as she checked her slick-suit. There was a line where the rock had pressed against it. But the suit hadn't torn—she almost wept in relief.

She realized in a foggy way that she'd almost killed herself. Slowly, she lowered herself onto the floor. She needed to think. She had to collect herself. The cable made it impossible to relax, but she needed a few seconds of peace.

A new thought… it seemed profound as it welled into life. In the escape-pod traveling to Jupiter, she'd given up. Listlessness had been her constant companion. Here, on this hellish surface and with nightmarish overlords, she struggled to live. That didn't make sense. It was a hundred times more painful here. She ached to sleep. She was hungry all the time. Instant death, it plagued her every move in these horrible tunnels.

This tunnel snaked endlessly into the darkness. She was alone down here, and she could possibly wedge herself at any turn. Here she fought on through mind-numbing horrors. Why hadn't she fought on with similar courage against the loneliness of the escape-pod?

Her mind was too blurred to understand. With a groan, she forced herself up. She had to keep working or she might fail quota. If that occurred, a cyborg would simply rip off her mask and pitch her quivering body aside. She'd seen cyborgs do it over a hundred times to other unmodified humans.

Why—?

Nadia wondered then if she had the answer to her question. The escape-pod had been bitter loneliness and emptiness. There had not been anything to latch onto. There had been nothing to fight but for nothingness. Here, she saw her demons. She felt the tortures. It was something to endure. Maybe it was easier to endure hateful torture than to endure silence, stillness and aching loneliness and nothingness. That seemed strange.

Nadia listened to her harsh breathing and she squeezed her burning eyes. She wanted to sleep, but she'd have to wait another eight hours for that. Carefully, she slid past the sharp rock. Then she pressed the stapler against the black cable—it also disappeared into the tunnel that seemed to go on forever.

Nadia pressed the trigger. Her hands lifted, and another staple appeared around the power cable. She helped the cyborgs build their planet-wrecker, but Nadia didn't know that. She endured for endurance sake, a human rat struggling in an alien sewer. If there was one thing life had taught her, it was that things changed. Nothing remained the same forever. On that small truth, she placed every hope, every drive to survive this endless ordeal.

## 8

After a year of desperate travel and weeks of hard deceleration, the *Thutmosis III* was docked beside a built-up asteroid-moon. The tiny moon was part of the Carme group and known as Demeter. Heavy docking girders were locked onto the big vessel, with lamprey-like tubes attached to the ship's airlocks.

Demeter was a Guardian Fleet outpost, a munitions depot housing several patrol boats. Silvery domes and towers dotted the seven-kilometer moon. Large bots were attached to the *Thutmosis III*. They glowed with bright, arcing light, effecting repairs. Another multi-armed bot presently left a hanger, its jet a stab of flame. It headed for the docked warship, for one of the weapons pods.

After the missile strike on Callisto, the base personnel had fled Demeter, taking most of the patrol boats. The Praetor had captured one boat. Its sole occupant had been the base's former Force-Leader. Her interrogation had revealed Demeter, the base's proximity and function.

At the moment, the Praetor marched through a munitions chamber deep in Demeter. He wore his battleoid-armor, with its heavy hand-cannon mounts. Around him, huge missiles lay in storage. Within his armor-suit, the Praetor grinned as he viewed the lettering on a missile's nosecone: *Voltaire Missile, AE 1133, Article Seven-Twelve*.

Since saving his ship, the Praetor had lost weight, and the glow to his pink eyes had grown even stranger. Radiation poisoning had done the damage, but he was functional again, regaining strength by the hour and sustained by stimulants. With an exoskeleton-powered gauntlet, he gripped a metallic leash. It glittered whenever his headlamps washed over the former commander of Demeter Outpost. The woman's left eye had puffed shut. She was missing teeth, and by the wincing way she spoke, it was obvious it hurt her to talk.

The Praetor mentally shrugged. The Force-Leader could have saved herself the permanent scarring and the brutalization. But she was a preman, a subhuman. It meant she could only learn through her own mistakes. That was the problem with possessing limited humanity. A Highborn learned through other people's mistakes, not just his own. A preman was too stupid to use such elementary logic.

The Praetor tugged the leash, making her stumble after him. The empty base now belonged to the Highborn. Soldiers effected repairs and restocked the missile-ship with inferior Zeno drones.

The Praetor jerked the leash. The small Force-Leader bumped up against his armor. Servos whined as he peered down at her. In order to heighten her fear, the Praetor lifted one of his battleoid arms. He put his gauntleted fingers around the top of her head.

"With the twitch of my fingers," he boomed through the suit's speakers, "I can crush your skull."

She whimpered. She was a broken reed, her entire body fleshed with purple and yellow bruises. There hadn't been time for refinement as speed was critical.

"Show me the secret locations," he boomed.

He allowed her to look up. She was such a child compared to him. Ah, this was living. This was why he'd been born— born into the world, not hatched from a test-tube as the hateful Social Unity propagandists claimed.

He shook her head. "Show me."

"I've shown you everything," she whispered.

"I've studied the outpost's specs," he told her.

She frowned.

He laughed. "My mental acuity is ten times yours. What takes you days to read, I can scan in an hour. Either you erased sections of your outpost's logs before you left, or your

265

overlords possessed a smattering of cunning and failed to add them to the specs. Now show me the secret locations or I shall squeeze your skull until blood runs out your nostrils."

She stared up at him. Her eyes—

The Praetor stiffened at what he read in her, and he nodded. So… she attempted deceit.

"I will show you," she whispered, with a quaver in her voice. "If you will follow me…."

He gave her play with the leash. She shuffled ahead of him, past the nosecone of a giant Voltaire Missile. With his chin, he lowered the helmet's receivers. He didn't want to burst his eardrums with what he was about to do.

His helmet and chest lamps washed over various control mechanisms. Yes, he understood now. It made him grin ferociously.

The woman said something. He couldn't hear the precise words, because his gain was way down. He recognized her pointing into the darkness, however. Then she lurched toward a hatch.

"Is that the secret way?" he boomed.

The Force-Leader hunched her battered shoulders before nodding.

"Show me," the Praetor said.

She shuffled toward the hatch. With a shaking finger, she reached for a control board. He let her hand get to within an inch of it. Then, with savage strength, he yanked the leash. She lifted off her feet, yelping in animal surprise and pain, and then possibly screaming with terror. He didn't give her time to attempt anything else. Gripping her head, he twisted with exoskeleton strength.

He twisted her head, ripping the flesh and breaking the neck-bones, tearing the head from the torso. Blood jetted everywhere, spraying in gouts. Disgusted, the Praetor pitched her torso aside. It hadn't been fear that made him use his battleoid-suit at full power, but a desire to protect the Voltaire Missiles from even the slightest harm.

The former Force-Leader had just tried to explode a hidden bomb. Perhaps this control-board contained the base destruction switch. He had seen the subtle change in her. He had been so certain, too, that she'd been broken.

"Praetor!" Canus said over the suit's radio-link.

"I am here."

"We have established a laser-link with Earth. Do you wish to speak with the Grand Admiral?"

"Soon," the Praetor said. They had lost radio contact with Highborn High Command many long months ago. Had the Grand Admiral believed him dead? Was news of the missile-ship's survival a rude shock to that cunning old soldier? The Praetor concentrated on the here and now, and told Canus, "Before I speak to Cassius, we must first make contact with the Confederation ruler."

"The chief representative of the Confederation has been asking to talk with you for some time."

The Praetor studied the headless Force-Leader. Blood oozed from the torn neck and pooled on the floor. Could he have underestimated these premen? No. That seemed unlikely. A wild impulse must have reignited the woman's training. Perhaps he should have—

"No," he said.

"Praetor?" asked Canus.

"I'm coming back up," he said. "Then I shall speak with their leader. What was his name again?"

"Not a man, lord, but a woman."

The Praetor grunted with contempt. "That seems fitting, a woman to rule them. What was her name again? It's hard remembering these subhuman names."

"Chief Strategist Tan, lord."

"A grandiose title for a preman, don't you think?"

"They love to give themselves gaudy titles," Canus said.

"It is a flaw in their makeup," the Praetor said. Then he began giving Canus instructions regarding the dead Force-Leader and the deadliness of this underground chamber.

*\*\**

The Praetor sat in his command chair on the *Thutmosis III*. It had been a long time since he'd worn his dress uniform. It was black, with a stiff white collar and a blue Nova Sunburst on the right pectoral. He wore his black beret with a red skull

267

pinned to the front, indicating that he belonged to the Death's Head Battalion. The unit had originated in the Youth Barracks. It had contained the toughest among them, only joined by those who had either killed on the practice mats or so badly injured another that the instructors had ordered medics to drag the wounded to the infirmary.

Even as a boy, he had been dangerous, a lion among his fellows. In turn among subhumans, he was a T-Rex, a legendry creature that all must fear.

The Praetor smiled and his pink eyes shined. "Open the channel," he said.

"Opening... now," Canus said.

Before him appeared a holographic image of Chief Strategist Tan. There was more than twenty million kilometers separating them. It meant there was a seven-second time delay between each transmission.

The holographic image showed him a soft woman, a small preman with a peculiar cant to her head and a bizarre... manner. He wondered if she were a cretin, if this was an arrogant, preman joke, played on him by someone who loved using proxies. She almost smiled like an idiot without a thought.

The Praetor's eyes narrowed. Canus offered a comment then. Perhaps the soldier had been watching him, maybe a little too closely.

"I've just a found a file on her," Canus said. "She follows the Dictates, which is a heightened, philosophical code."

The Praetor grunted with annoyance.

"According to their philosophical beliefs," Canus said, "each attempts to practice serenity."

"What?"

Canus pointed at a holographic image.

The Praetor saw the image of a bald, bearded man who wore a toga.

"This is their base image," Canus said. "It is their model, the one they attempt to pattern themselves after. He is their Socrates."

"Ah," the Praetor said. The Socrates shown here had the same buffoonish smile as the woman portrayed. It was an affected idiocy, a philosopher's trick. She attempted to mock him in an effort to anger him into revealing something critical.

The Praetor settled back into his command chair. Instead of a predator's smile, he would show her solid indifference, playing the part of a soldier's soldier. If it were possible, he would attempt to appear simple. He would have to throttle back on the speed of his analytic abilities, lest he give away his surpassing superiority. He recalled reading or hearing somewhere that philosophers were the blindest of people, observing reality through the prism of their foolish creed.

The holographic image of this puny woman opened its mouth. It began to speak. "I welcome you to our system, Commander. It is unfortunate that we have this communication under such dire stress. The cyborgs have arrived at Jupiter just as they arrived in the Mars System a year ago. We know they fought together at Mars with the fanatics of Social Unity. Together with the usurping Social Unitarians, the cyborgs inflicted unheard of damage against your Grand Admiral. Yes, they destroyed a Doom Star and nearly annihilated a second. Therefore, I do not need to underscore the deadliness of these mechanically-created aliens."

She paused then, no doubt deciding to let him utter a greeting. The seven-second delay made a conversation odd— for those who weren't used to long-distance talk. As a ship commander, he was more than used to it.

The Praetor clamped down on his irritation. To liken the Highborn Fleet with Jovian foolishness, surprised by the cyborgs and losing ships to stealth attacks—He breathed deeply. What he needed now was information.

The Praetor inclined his head. "The days are dark as the cyborgs advance with their customary ruthlessness. Highborn High Command has pledged itself to their destruction. Even though these are evil times, I am pleased to have arrived at this critical juncture. I am formally placing my ship at the disposal of the Jovian Confederation. The implication of your greeting leads me to believe that we can work in tandem."

The words came hard, but the Praetor maintained his pose. It was ludicrous to think that Highborn could harness themselves with subhumans. Could even a philosopher believe such an absurdity? Well, she was a preman. Therefore, he could easily lead the conversation. He needed her to request his ship to travel deeper into the gravity-well to join the Jovian forces. Then he could maneuver onto a Galilean moon. Once his Highborn reached a planetary body—then he could implement his Pizarro strategy to its fullest scope.

After a short delay, she began to speak again. "Your words give me hope, Commander. We are in dire need of alliance. That you've reached Demeter at this time—could it be Dictate-derived intervention?"

Did she believe in divine beings? Ha! That made her even simpler, practically a stooge in intelligence. Conquering the Jovian System might actually prove easier than he'd expected. The cyborgs would prove the challenge. He would have to gain leadership of these Jovians fast. Could this preman understand the hope he brought with his vessel? Sometimes, these subhumans were inordinately proud. If she desired victory, logically, she should immediately offer him supreme command. Should he hint to that effect? It was probably too soon. No. He would mask himself for a little while longer. He needed to gain the Jovian levers of power before he revealed his true nature.

"Let me repeat my offer, Chief Strategist. The *Thutmosis III* has been restocked with armaments. Likely, it is the most powerful warship in the system. By its addition, the Confederation will gain immensely. We are soon ready to depart and could reach Ganymede in one hundred hours."

Time passed. Then she said, "Your offer is generous, Commander. I accept. I wonder... could you place me in communication with the base personnel of Demeter. There seems to have been a com failure, as we haven't been able to speak with guardian personnel there for some time."

According to the former Force-Leader, the Jovians had fled Demeter in secret. The Praetor pondered that. He smiled inwardly. Then he began to speak.

"Our nearness activated a secret stealth attack. We landed as cyborg-converted Jovians finished the butchery of their former comrades. The bloodshed was hideous. We avenged your follow soldiers and obliterated the cyborgs, never fear on

270

that score. Unfortunately, we must have inadvertently activated secret destruct codes. Perhaps you could send us the deactivation sequences so we could keep the base from further damage."

The transmission took seven seconds one way, seven seconds the other, in addition to the time needed for the Chief Strategist to digest the words and form her reply. The Praetor almost frowned. What was taking her so long? Could she suspect duplicity on his part? That seemed inconceivable. He had woven the perfect cover story, and he understood how those under siege grasped at straws. Her need should smooth over any suspicions she might have. Perhaps he'd stumbled onto one of those paranoid preman. The best way to deal with those was with a bullet through the brain.

"Another tragedy has occurred," Tan finally said. "Since you have uncovered another of their stealth attacks, you can more readily understand how deadly their secrecy is."

*No*, the Praetor wished to tell her. *I now understood how gullible you are.* Instead, he replied, "The cyborgs are a virus, one we must ruthlessly purge. Having witnessed their savagery, I now pledge myself to their eradication from the Jovian System."

"Your words give me relief," said Tan.

The Praetor shifted in his command chair, holding back braying laughter. How pitifully easy it was to lull premen! Only their vast, teeming numbers and large industrial base gave the subhumans a lingering ability to resist the Highborn.

"I suspect that my relief will also be your relief," Tan said, "for we have uncovered a diabolical plan." She went on to describe the Carme planet-wrecker, the desperate Jovian taskforce heading toward it and the likely cyborg targets of Mars, Earth or Venus.

A cold feeling entered the Praetor's stomach. His baleful features stiffened and his weird eyes gained a crazed look. As he sat in his command chair, the cyborg strategy seemed to unfold before him. Seemly attempting to conquer the planets of the Jovian System, rather they were here to create planet-wreckers from the many stray asteroids. These errant rocks and moons would orbit around Jupiter, building up velocity. Then they would hurl the planet-wreckers at the Inner Planets. It was brilliant, vast in scope and a scheme of genocidal ruthlessness. It awed him, and despite his growing hatred of the cyborgs, the Praetor found himself admiring them.

"Commander," Tan said, "fate seems to have given you the prime task of halting the planet-wrecker. Our main fleet must remain among the Galilean moons or we shall face extinction. We have sent a taskforce, but now you have arrived. I ask you, Commander, what could be more important than your ship heading to Carme and obliterating the grave threat?"

The Praetor tapped the arm of his chair. The cyborgs surely would heavily defend this planet-wrecker. The *Thutmosis III* was a raid ship, best employed with long-range stealth tactics. To race toward the planet-wrecker like a Doom Star was folly. The preman wanted him to do their dirty work. The idea was enraging.

"I will speak to Highborn High Command and relay your critical information," he said. "We are presently repairing ship damage. Could you transmit to me all pertinent information regarding this planet-wrecker and the strategic situation between the Confederation and the cyborgs?"

"You are wise, Commander," Tan said. "If you are prepared, I will transmit the information now. I urge you to make a speedy decision, however. Whatever we do, we must do quickly."

The Praetor seethed. How dare she urge a Highborn to move with speed? None could act more decisively or more boldly than Highborn. Despite his anger, he nodded and ended the conversation with a salutation of seeming equality and a promise to act soon.

Afterward, he realized that he would have to speak with the Grand Admiral and relay the terrible news. The Inner Planets war had just broadened to include Jupiter.

## 9

Gharlane stood in a viewing port of the *Locke*. He stared down at Io with its strange land patterns. Io looked like a rotten orange, with a dozen intermixing colors.

The planetoid was the most geologically active body in the Solar System, possessing over four hundred active volcanoes. Many spewed sulfur dioxide. Some of the sulfur blew more than five hundred kilometers high, drifting into space. The sulfur added to Jupiter's magnetosphere and it created the Io plasma torus. The torus was a belt of intense radiation. It was a doughnut-shaped ring of ionized sulfur, oxygen, sodium, and chlorine, created when the neutral atoms in the 'cloud' surrounding Io were ionized and carried along by the Jovian magnetosphere.

Io's largest volcanoes were over ten kilometers high. The spewed sulfur created huge umbrella-shaped, yellow plumes in the atmosphere. Pele, one of the biggest volcanoes, was named after an ancient Hawaiian goddess.

As he stood in the viewing port, Gharlane shifted his stance. He saw white streaks, meaning that patrol boats entered the slight atmosphere.

Today, the boats had two critical tasks to perform. The first was unloading cyborgs troops. Io was a harsh moon, rich in ores but deadly to life. Most of the habitats were near the hot sulfur lakes created by the constant volcanism. Company workers mined the lakes. They endured while working in heavy radiation-suits and they lived under lead shielding. Many roved over the lakes on crystal platforms, specially treated to withstand the lava-like sulfur.

The cyborgs in the descending patrol boats planned to swarm each habitat, killing any who resisted. Gharlane allowed himself the stimulation of a pleasure center, the cyborg equivalent of a smile. He would also kill those who surrendered. The Web-Mind had ordered him to eradicate all life on Io. Since the Web-Mind hadn't told him the exact method of death, Gharlane used his initiative. He would kill using cyborg troops. In this way, he would save missiles and bombs. He would need those later against Europa and Ganymede. Athena Station was too far away to re-supply now.

Each patrol boat had a second task, and it was related to Athena Station's distant location. The landing cyborgs had been ordered to collect radioactive material and fuel.

Gharlane shifted his head, scanning the moon. He'd taken a risk coming to Io. But it was a calculated risk. To reach the inner Galilean moon, the fleet had traveled deep into Jupiter's gravity-well. Now the warships would have to burn hard to escape up it. The enemy position in the well could give the Jovians possible advantages. Against all reason, however, the main Jovian Fleet remained at Ganymede.

Soothing chemicals kept Gharlane's thinking level, eliminating the need to emote. He wanted Ionian radioactive material for a tactical reason. The humans reacted badly to terror attacks. If their fleet continued to sit at a single location, then it was time to teach the Jovians another lesson elsewhere.

Gharlane's head swiveled sharply as his eyes locked onto another white streak. The streak was minuscule compared to the moon's surface. It showed Gharlane that another squadron of patrol boats entered the atmosphere.

Using patrol boats like this would damage some. Io's atmosphere was weak, but it was still an atmosphere. The patrol boats were space vehicles, with a limited ability to maneuver anywhere but in vacuum.

Gharlane's servos whined as he shrugged.

He saved his missiles for the battle with the main Jovian fleet. This would cost him the use of some patrol boats. However, he had a surprise for the Jovians that should negate the negatives here. If the main Jovian fleet remained static for another week—

Gharlane lurched closer toward the viewing port. His plasti-flesh eyebrows contorted as a flash appeared on the moon's surface.

Gharlane turned to a scope and clicked his hand-unit. A second passed as the scope caused an image to leap into view. It showed a mushroom cloud rising from Io's surface.

Gharlane stepped to the scope's board and typed fast, keying information. The nuclear explosion came from Pele Platform Three. The company habitat had a Callisto Corporation number. Ah, it was the Diana-Bacchus Company, and it was first on the cyborg itinerary. Two patrol boats should have landed there.

Gharlane's eyebrow-contortion smoothed out. It would appear the humans had used a nuclear device. Perhaps one of them had gone insane. That would mean—

Another explosion occurred elsewhere. Probability factors shifted Gharlane's thinking. One nuclear device indicated a crazed individual. Two explosions indicated a prearranged plan.

Gharlane raised his hand-unit and chattered in high-speed binary.

In a second, he told his communications Web-team: "Abort the landings and order all patrol boats to accelerate for space. I repeat, abort all platform landings. The Ionians are defending with suicidal desperation. Probability factors indicate that they are waiting until the boats disgorge troops. Then they are igniting nuclear devices to annihilate cyborg personnel. Emergency sequencing is ordered. I repeat, abort all landings and return to low orbit."

As Gharlane chattered at high-speed, another explosion occurred on the moon's surface. He would have to expend missiles and gravity bombs after all. He would rain destruction from space and obliterate the humans. Then he would reorder select patrol boats down to the surface, there to hunt for survivors. The enemy had finally entered the tertiary mode of the campaign, practicing kamikaze tactics. He should have foreseen the possibility.

More chemicals entered his brainpan, soothing his unease. Without the radioactive materials....

Gharlane turned from the viewing port. He would have to adjust his strategy. On all counts, he must continue to fix the enemy's attention on the Galilean moons. He must give the Web-Mind time to complete the planet-wrecker and gain the needed velocity. The Web-Mind needed to launch for the Inner Planets in tandem with the Saturn-strike. Nothing must be allowed to delay the master plan.

-10-

Io's nuclear ambushes stimulated the Web-Mind to a feverish state. Orders went out and on Carme, the activity increased. Time passed as the accelerated teams worked around the cycles. The endless labor worked to death the hardiest Jovians as they stapled power cables, lugged coils and welded lines to the blast-pans.

Then the Web-Mind's Athena Station convoy landed. Its large, black-matted stealth-capsule entered a tunnel. Carefully, the Web-Mind maneuvered the capsule into an armored chamber specially constructed for survival. Cyborgs had built these tunnels and chambers long ago, as they'd worked in secret for years. At the beginning of the stealth assault, the cyborgs had boiled onto the surface, capturing the Jovians here and attempting to complete the massive task.

The rest of the convoy vessels spilled their cargoes of cyborgs, Webbies, equipment and missiles.

Octagon found himself panting as sweat soaked the inside of his vacc-suit. In a domed chamber seething with motion, he heaved coils into place. Later, he inserted screws with a sonic drill and afterward, he loaded lifters with boxes of point-defense ammunition.

Ten hours after the convoy's landing, the fateful hour arrived. Every patrol boat entered a hanger as everyone hurried to his or her position.

With other Webbies, Octagon strapped himself onto a long couch. The clicks of their buckles filled the room. The insertion

277

of Web-jacks was a softer sound. It caused many to slump and twitch as they entered a pleasure state.

Elsewhere, with a dozen other labor-survivors, Nadia Pravda lay on a slat. She waited in a metal shed that had been built on a protrusion of rock. It was exposed to any stray meteor or high-speed dust-mote that happened along.

Silver-dome clusters abounded on the uneven surface with its rocks, craters and low hills. Towers arose among them, some with antennas and others with dishes and even more with waiting anti-missiles. Point-defense guns ringed the small planetoid. The massive exhaust-ports dwarfed everything else.

As Carme continued its monotonous orbit, a pulse of plasma blew out of an exhaust-port. Another pulse flowed out of a different port. In a nanosecond, hell erupted, changing everything. The generators poured power through the fusion engines deep in the moon. Blue plasma now spewed from the multiple exhaust-ports. The generators increased output as other engines came online. For several minutes, Carme shivered as if hit with the longest quake in history. Then the generators revved up the scale to maximum output. Massive amounts of power surged through hundreds of cables. A blue brilliant glow of plasma stretched thirty kilometers behind Carme. Slowly, the Jovian moon increased orbital speed as it increased velocity.

The first Jovian planet-wrecker had begun its acceleration. There were no cheers, however, no backslapping cyborgs. The melded bipeds lay on their couches, emotionless and expressionless. They awaited orders from the Web-Mind. The few that possessed minuscule anomalies processed their stray thoughts. Those thoughts did not prevent their full functioning, however.

Among the jacked-in Webbies lying on the long couches, a few frowned. Two laughed and one seethed. Octagon was one of the latter.

Pressed against his couch, Octagon remembered the time in the pod as he'd headed to the *Rousseau*. Marten Kluge had done that to him. Marten Kluge—Webbie Octagon grinded his molars together. It was a vile sound. Despite his new way of examining reality and his plugging into the Web-Mind, he yearned for revenge. He yearned to hurt Marten Kluge. If only he could cut Marten's flesh. If only he could reach in and pull out the kidneys and then the liver and finally the heart as it pumped hot blood all over his hands.

For the first time in ages, Octagon smiled. It was a twisted thing, perverse and perverted. Marten Kluge's blood, he would bathe in it as the barbarian died. Nothing could feel as good. Marten Kluge, Marten Kluge… Marten Kluge must die a hideous and painful death.

Elsewhere, in a shed on a low hill, Nadia groaned. The massive engines caused Carme to accelerate. Her spine ached as it pressed against the metal sheet and her heart beat faster.

*Am I having a heart attack?*

Breathing hurt and she arched as a spasm made her scream. Then her beating heart slowed to its normal rhythm. Nadia panted as sweat poured from her heated skin. After a time the sensation passed. She slumped on her sheet. Within a minute, she slept.

Nadia dreamed of suffocation, which was horrible. But for the first time in weeks, she slept for more than a four-hour stint.

Nadia woke once in the darkness, feeling Carme tremble with its new life. Maybe the worst horrors were over. She smiled at the thought and fell back asleep.

-11-

Marten stood beside Yakov in an otherwise empty patrol boat. The Force-Leader sat at the controls as the craft lifted off the *Descartes'* meteor-shell.

Marten swayed as the patrol boat lurched, able to shift his weight as needed.

Yakov gave him a sidelong glance, but otherwise made no comment on his standing.

Lines of strain showed on Marten's angular face. This morning, he'd found his first gray hair. He'd plucked it, staring at the offensive sight. Then he'd thrown the hair into the chemical sink before shaving.

Yakov's small hands played across the controls. The patrol boat lurched again, changing heading.

Marten shifted his weight without being aware of it. He glanced out of the polarized window. From here, Jupiter appeared as the brightest star by several magnitudes. The *Descartes* was already out of sight as the patrol boat headed toward the taskforce's second meteor-ship. Yakov wanted to inspect it before they began the hard deceleration for Carme.

"I asked you to join me for a reason," Yakov said.

Something in the Force-Leader's voice warned Marten. "Should I sit down first?" he asked.

Instead of answering, Yakov turned on a vidscreen. He pressed another key, and the wide face of the Praetor appeared.

Marten lifted an eyebrow.

"The Highborn in our system have been in communication with Tan," Yakov said.

280

"I'd expected that."

"Tan believes the Highborn stormed onto the Demeter Depot, killing everyone there, allowing them to restock their missile-ship."

"That sounds like the Highborn," Marten said.

Yakov gave him another sidelong glance. "Tan's tactical team thinks the missile-ship was badly damaged during the Battle for Mars. It must have headed out of the Solar System and barely turned around to reach Jupiter."

"If the ship was so badly damaged, how did it fight its way onto Demeter?"

"I asked the same thing. Tan believes the Demeter Force-Leader foolishly attempted to lure the Highborn there in an attempt to capture the vessel."

Marten laughed harshly. "The Praetor is a bastard's bastard."

"Maybe. He has agreed to help us storm Carme."

Marten's gut hardened.

"We definitely need the help," Yakov said, as he pressed another computer key.

A grainy shot of an asteroid appeared with the name *Carme* written underneath it. It had a long, blue plasma tail. Yakov used a unit, clicking it. A white arrowhead appeared on the screen. The arrow moved to a dot a little above the asteroid's horizon.

"This was taken several hours ago," Yakov said, "by interferometers on Pasachoff."

"Where?"

"Pasachoff is another moon of the Carme group."

Marten nodded.

Yakov pointed at it. "Tan thought the cyborgs might move the dreadnaught toward the Galilean moons. As you can see, it still guards Carme."

"We'll take care of it," Marten said.

Yakov took his time responding. "Two meteor-ships will have a difficult time defeating a dreadnaught with such a defensive position."

"Difficult or not, you must do it so we can land."

"Can space marines defeat cyborg troops?"

281

"If we can't," Marten asked, "why are we out here?"

"Highborn battleoids will assist us."

Marten's features tightened. "I'm surprised the Praetor is willing to risk it."

"Tan believes the Praetor spoke with their Grand Admiral on Earth. The Grand Admiral likely instructed the Praetor to destroy the planet-wrecker. What makes that interesting is that Tan is sure the Praetor would rather head in-system."

"What does any of that have to do with our attack on Carme?"

Yakov sat back in the pilot's chair. "Thirteen years ago in the Mars System, many in the guardian class lost family to the Highborn."

"Okay," Marten said, waiting.

"For his help, the Praetor demanded command of the Carme assault."

Marten blinked, digesting that. "So what did Tan tell him?"

"She agreed," Yakov said. "She agreed because we need his ship and battleoids."

"We're really going to take orders from the Praetor?" Marten asked, starting to become angry.

"We are, for at least long enough to fight our way onto Carme."

"What about afterward?"

Yakov gave him a level gaze. "If we defeat the cyborgs, a doubtful possibility, then we must escape Demeter's fate."

Marten pressed a key, bringing back the Praetor's image. The Highborn were in the Jovian System, and now the bastard who'd wanted to castrate him led the assault. He was actually going to take orders from a Highborn again. They had excellent memories. He had no doubt the Praetor would remember his face.

Marten tapped his fingers on the console.

"What are your thoughts?" Yakov asked.

"I need something to pull my space marines together, to help them forget about getting slapped, and to forget about Pelias and her boyfriend."

"You mean to use the Praetor for that?" Yakov asked.

Marten tapped a finger on the Praetor's forehead. "This bastard is finally going to do me his first good deed. If we beat the cyborgs, the trick will be staying alive long enough to appreciate our victory."

# -12-

The Praetor seethed as he rechecked his battleoid-armor. Time conspired against him. The Grand Admiral, this puny Chief Strategist and the hateful cyborgs—

The Praetor roared an oath as he slammed his fist against a bulkhead, denting metal. He began to pace like a caged beast.

The missile-ship was under one-G acceleration. The *Thutmosis III* left Demeter behind. The tactical game against the planet-wrecker and its shepherding dreadnaught had begun. Soon, he would give the critical orders.

The Praetor whirled around, and he stalked back to the ten-foot battleoid-suit. It was a marvel of engineering, a thing of deadly beauty with a titanium shell of exoskeleton strength. On Earth, battleoid-armored Highborn leaped one hundred meters, sometimes assisted by Dinlon jetpacks. Hi-powered slugthrowers, lasers, plasma rifles and tiny tactical nukes gave the battleoids massive firepower.

The Praetor found it difficult to believe that battleoid-Highborn had failed to stop attacking cyborgs on the *Hannibal Barca*. He'd learned that the Grand Admiral had lost a Doom Star at Mars. Another had taken critical damage.

The Highborn Fleet was weaker today than at any other time. Three Doom Stars held Earth, Venus and Mercury. Social Unity regrouped at Mars, gathering its last warships. On Earth, Social Unity fought like crazed beasts, successfully resisting in South America. Now the cyborgs attempted to launch a planet-wrecker from Jupiter.

The Praetor pressed his palms together in front of his face. He breathed deeply as he lowered his pressed palms to his stomach. He practiced a calming technique, taught him in the Youth Barracks.

Time conspired against him. If he'd reached the Jovian System even two months earlier, he could have already reached Jupiter's inner system. Then he would be among the Galilean moons, able to lead the overawed Jovians against the cyborgs.

The Praetor picked up an electro-analyzer and carefully began checking his armor. It beeped by the right elbow-joint. He adjusted, frowning at the tiny screen. It flashed red and showed the words: *photonic coupling*.

The Praetor set aside the analyzer and opened his battleoid-kit. Like all Highborn, he could take apart and rebuild any weapon. The same held true for a battleoid-suit. He set to work, immersing himself in the task, momentarily forgetting his rage.

Later, he clicked each tool back into its foamed indention. Then he took up the electro-analyzer and continued to sweep it over the armor.

Short by two months—time conspired against him. Worse, Grand Admiral Cassius continued his sly tricks.

The Praetor showed his horse-sized teeth in a feral grin. It lacked all humor and lacked any warmth. He—the Praetor—had won the Battle for Mars with his missiles. He had risked his life later to bring the High Fleet critical intelligence concerning the enemy. Because of his courage, the *Thutmosis III* had almost left the Solar System forever. Only through cunning, relentless fervor and an indomitable will had he saved his ship and crew.

Now the Grand Admiral dashed his dream of Jovian conquest. He must throw away the *Thutmosis III* on a mad attack against a heavily fortified moon. Meanwhile, in the inner system, the cyborgs outmaneuvered the foolish Jovians. The premen had already lost Callisto and Io. Now the cyborgs lunged at Europa as the Jovian fleet vainly waited at Ganymede.

The Praetor shook his head. Social Unity possessed several clever tacticians. It appeared the Jovians didn't even have those.

285

He cracked his knuckles and flexed his big fingers. He was tempted to disregard the Grand Admiral's orders. The old man was cunning, however. During the lightguide transmission, the Grand Admiral had sat among the High Command, and their accompanying vote had been unanimous. To disregard the order would now mean acting against the unified will of the High Command.

The Praetor squinted at his battleoid-suit. He must use what he had. He must twist fate and time into his service. If the cyborgs won here because the premen lacked even basic tactical skills, it still meant he could fight gloriously.

An insightful preman, General George S. Patton, had once said: *As a man thinketh, so is he. The fixed determination to acquire the warrior soul and, having acquired it, to conquer or perish with honor is the secret of success in war.*

The Praetor made a fist. He'd been born with a warrior's soul. Since then, his determination had become legendary.

The cyborgs accelerated Carme. But an asteroid-moon, even a small one, had immense mass, much more than the combined Doom Stars and the Highborn orbital stations of Venus and Earth. It would take the cyborgs time to build-up velocity, giving him time enough to configure his attack.

The Jovian's original plan to storm Carme had been suicidal folly. With his ship and genius, victory became a possibility.

"Conquer or perish," the Praetor rumbled. His chest swelled. "I will conquer, and I will set my foot on the Jovians and on the cyborgs. Then—"

The Praetor smote his chest. "Then I will return to Earth and deal with you, Cassius. On that, I vow the essence of my warrior soul."

## -13-

Marten paced in the *Descartes'* rec-room. Mechanics had dragged out the exercise mats and set up rows of folding chairs.

Osadar waited by the main door. She wore combat-armor, hiding her cyborg body and limbs. With her greater height, her plasti-flesh head almost reached the ceiling.

Omi opened the door. He wore a Gauss needler and a stern expression. Behind him were the squad-leaders. They filed into the room, filling up the back rows first.

The meteor-ship was under half-a-G of deceleration. After the meeting, Yakov would increase the Gs, slowing the ship even more. The taskforce already followed the Praetor's instructions. The decisive moment was fast drawing near.

Earlier, Marten had stood to the side, out of camera range, as the Praetor had given Yakov his orders. The voice had sent a chill of loathing down Marten's spine. The Praetor was the same arrogant prick from the Sun-Works Factory. Nothing had changed about the lordly Highborn. Hearing the Praetor's voice had confirmed Marten's decision that he'd remained hidden.

In the rec-room, the last space marine sat down. Most stared blankly. A few scowled. A few gave him a deathly stare. Their muscles showed as they shifted in their seats, tightening the fabric of their tunics.

With his hands behind his back, Marten stared at the assembled squad-leaders. It caused him to recall Training Master Lycon, the day of the briefing of the *Bangladesh* assault. That seemed like a lifetime ago. He'd been in the Mercury System then, now he was in the Jupiter System. Now he was a free man, a commander of shock troopers. Well, they weren't shock troopers, but they were space marines. They were about to engage in the greatest assault of the war, stopping a planet-wrecker. It was too bad most of them were going to die. Maybe they were all going to die. Who could defeat cyborgs on the ground?

Marten stood at attention and he snapped off the crispest salute of his life.

Squad-leaders stirred, and there was a murmur of whispering among them.

He backed beside the screen on the wall and touched a button. A grainy shot of Carme appeared with its long plasma tail.

"Gentlemen and ladies," he began, "this is our objective. As you know, the cyborgs accelerate one of your Jovian moons. They call it a planet-wrecker. If Carme builds up enough velocity, it will be able to break Jupiter's gravitational grip and leave its orbit. The name suggests the cyborg tactic: to ram Carme into a large moon or a terrestrial planet. The outcome of such a collision is obvious: total extinction for the humans and animals on the target world."

Many eyes narrowed.

"Imagine for a moment what it means if a planet-wrecker smashes into Earth," Marten said. "Imagine what it means if everything on Earth dies. No event in human history will have ever wiped out more people. It would be an unparalleled catastrophe.

"It may be that we're the only hope for billions of humans. Our task isn't to defeat the guarding dreadnaught, but to slip past it in the patrol boats. We'll land on the surface and we'll fight our way into Carme's engine rooms. Once there, we'll destroy everything."

"What about the cyborgs?" a man in back asked sharply. "Everyone knows that one cyborg is worth ten men? How are we supposed to defeat them?"

"Stand up!" Marten said.

The man hesitated. Then he shot to his feet. He was shorter than average and had larger ears that stuck outward.

"Squad-Leader Tass," Marten said. "Do you care to expand on that?"

"How can we win?" Tass asked belligerently.

"It's true that cyborgs normally butcher men," Marten said slowly. "I knew that truth and still accepted the responsibility of taking out the planet-wrecker. I accepted for a critical reason. Omi and I stormed onto the Beamship *Bangladesh*. You've studied our tactics. You know we're shock troopers and that we know more about infantry space-combat than anyone else in the Jovian System does. I also had Osadar slap each of you across the face. I closely studied your reactions, looking for the fighters among you."

More than a few space marines scowled.

"I needed first class soldiers," Marten said. "During our trip, I've tried to teach you critical skills. Space walking under hard Gs led to Pelias's death. That death might have seemed pointless, but it wasn't. You know more today than you did at the start of the journey. Does that mean you can defeat cyborgs?" Marten shrugged. "I doubt the shock troopers fired at the *Bangladesh* could take out cyborgs."

"Then why are we doing this?" Tass shouted.

"If we don't try," Marten said, "the cyborgs win. If we do try, there's always possibility that a miracle occurs."

"By Plato's Bones!" swore Tass. "Miracles are myths. Everyone knows Brand's Axiom proving that."

"Maybe," Marten said. He had no idea who this Brand was or his axiom. He didn't care.

"So you're saying that this entire attack is hopeless?" Tass asked.

Marten touched the wall-switch. The grainy shot disappeared, replaced by the Praetor's face.

"Is that a Highborn?"

"His name is the Praetor," Marten said. "He also happens to be our new commander."

"What?" several squad-leaders asked at once.

"Chief Strategist Tan has bargained with him," Marten said. "To gain the aid of his ship and his battleoids, she agreed to give him tactical command. We're following his plan, and he's using us ruthlessly."

"You mean he plans to kill us?" Tass asked, outraged.

"He's Highborn," Marten said. "He believes we're subhumans. Of course, he plans to kill us. He wants the prize for himself."

"And we're just going to lie down and die for him?" Tass asked.

"Those bastards killed my father and uncles at Mars thirteen years ago," a squad-leader hissed.

"I'll never fight for a Highborn," another squad-leader yelled.

"Attention!" Marten shouted.

Reflexively, the squad-leaders shot to their feet.

"Sit down," Marten said coldly, using his training voice.

The squad-leaders sat. A few looked confused. Some seemed abashed. Tass was still angry.

"This is war," Marten said. He clicked the grainy Carme shot back onto the screen. "That is a planet-wrecker. We must destroy it. If that means we all die doing it, then we die."

"Just like our fathers died in the Mars System?" Tass growled.

"First we destroy the planet-wrecker," Marten said. "Then we stay alive, and maybe, just maybe, we kill some Highborn."

The squad-leaders stared at him.

Marten clicked the Praetor back onto the screen. "This Highborn wanted to castrate all the shock troopers under his command in order to turn us into Neutraloids. The only thing that stopped him was the surprise attack by the *Bangladesh*. Perhaps you can understand then that there is no love in my heart for him."

A few squad-leaders grinned.

"The Praetor and his battleoids are killers," Marten said. "His cunning might help us win the fight. Then again, it might not. Remember, cyborgs are even deadlier than Highborn."

"What chance do we have then?" a squad-leader asked.

This was the point Marten had been waiting for. He took three steps toward them as he hunched his shoulders. In detail, he told them the story of the *Bangladesh*. He told them how he'd escaped off the beamship with Omi and how Lycon had picked them up in the shuttle. Then he told them how he'd

290

spaced the three Highborn and gained control of the *Mayflower*.

"Bluntly stated," Marten said, "your chance is me. I've outsmarted Highborn before and killed them. I've trained you, and you know my ways. Your one chance, my one chance, is that you now learn to obey me because you want to, not just because of duty."

Slowly, short Tass stood up.

"Yes," Marten said.

Tass glanced at his fellow squad-leaders. "Marten Kluge is a...." Tass licked his lips. "He's a killer, and so are the Highborn. So are the cyborgs. But Marten Kluge is our killer. He's a man just like us. I'm going to follow him onto Carme, and I'm going to obey his orders so we can win, so we can survive."

Another squad-leader stood up. "I agree with Tass. I didn't like getting my face slapped. But I can see now why he ordered it."

Marten glanced at his chronometer. "Carme is rushing near and A-hour is almost here. Good luck, and Godspeed. We're all going to need it."

As the *Thutmosis III* decelerated hard, the Battle for Carme began with a barrage from Demeter. Four Voltaire Missiles left the lifeless rock, igniting and quickly accelerating for the asteroid-moon.

The Praetor had planned the attack, using lessons learned from the Third Battle of Mars and from lessons learned by studying Hernan Cortez, the greatest conquistador of them all.

He was the Praetor, Fourth-ranked in the ultra-competitive world of the Highborn. He would risk everything to win everlasting glory. Besides, his ship lacked particle shielding. The *Thutmosis III* had been designed for a precise mission in the greatest battle of the war. Given time, he could have employed the ship using its stealth-sheathing. First, he'd first burned hard to catch up with Carme, and now he decelerated hard so he could land on the surface. The cyborgs had detected their approach. The Praetor knew because Canus reported sensor lock-on.

Wearing battleoid-armor, the Praetor sat in his command chair. The other Highborn on the bridge were also encased in their battleoid-suits.

"Why haven't you told me about our lock-on?" the Praetor boomed.

"We see them with teleoptics," Canus said. "But their ECM is still too good for us."

"It's better than Highborn tech?" the Praetor asked.

"Yes," Canus admitted.

The Praetor leaned forward. *Damn the cyborgs.* The *Thutmosis III* decelerated hard enough that the ship likely appeared as a nova star on enemy screens.

"The dreadnaught is slipping behind Carme," Canus said.

The Praetor nodded. It was the obvious move.

"I'm detecting—missiles are lifting off from Carme," Canus said.

"Fire everything," the Praetor whispered.

Canus and com-officer turned toward him.

"It's too soon," Canus dared say.

"No one challenges me on my bridge!" the Praetor roared. "Fire everything and then heat up the laser."

"Yes, lord," said Canus. "But it is still too soon."

"We'll hit them with a mass barrage," the Praetor said coldly. "We'll inundate them as we attempt to land on the moon. Everything is timed with the Jovians."

"Carme can obviously absorb our drones and lasers," Canus said.

The Praetor rose to his feet. Amplified, exoskeleton strength gave him the ability in the high Gs. He began clanking toward Canus.

The Highborn officer concentrated on his weapons board as he began launching the Zenos they'd stolen from Demeter.

Soon, the Praetor loomed behind Canus's armored back.

Canus activated the ship's lone laser. Without turning around, he said, "As per your orders, I'm saving the rail-guns as a last surprise, lord."

While docked at Demeter, they'd welded weapons pods to the ship.

The Praetor studied Canus's board. One after another, Zenos left the tubes.

"Shut down the engines," the Praetor whispered. "Begin deploying the defensive fields."

Canus's armored fingers roved fast, his reactions startling quick. Outside the ship, masses of prismatic crystals chugged out of various pods. Shielding gels sprayed out in turn.

The mighty engines stopped, bringing weightlessness to the ship.

"Enemy lasers—" Canus shouted.

The Praetor grinned tightly. He'd studied the cyborgs. They were melded creatures, governed by computer-like logic parameters. It had seemed obvious to him when they would begin firing at his ship. What he hadn't counted on was the laser's strength. The Praetor had expected stolen Jovian technology, not the laser long ago built inside the hollowed tunnels.

Carme's main laser now stabbed at the triple-hulled missile-ship. It burned through the gel cloud and the prismatic crystal field. In seconds, the laser burst through the hull, chewing through the ablative foam sandwiched between hulls. It hit the second hull, heating the alloy, stabbing through the foam behind it. Seconds ticked away as more crystals and gels sprayed from the ship. Before they drifted into place, the laser burned through the last hull. Then the heavy laser burned coils, sliced through inter-ship bulkheads, burst through empty wardrooms, empty rec-rooms and hit the number three fusion-shield.

"Lord!" Canus shouted. "We have an emergency."

The Praetor had been reading a damage control board, and his decision was instantaneous. "Foam the number three engine room."

Canus moved fast.

Deep in the *Thutmosis III*, ablative foam poured from wide-gage nozzles, filling the number three fusion engine. Before an explosion could destroy the ship, the ablative foam first absorbed the laser fire that burned through the fusion-shield. Secondly, the ablative foam damped the fusion reaction. By that time, Carme's laser no longer cut through the ship. The prismatic crystals floating in space protected them. The heavy laser burned crystals, slagging many and causing others to melt and vaporize. As that occurred, the sparkling, mirror-like crystals redirected laser light and thereby weakened the beam's power.

All the while, more crystals and gels sprayed from the *Thutmosis III's* tanks, building a thicker protection. It was a battle between the amount of crystals the ship held against the laser's energy requirements and possible overheating. Eventually, however, the contest always went to the laser,

294

given that the laser continued to beam. There were only so many prismatic crystals that any ship could hold.

"Estimate time of the second burn-through?" the Praetor said.

"Eighteen minutes," Canus said.

The Praetor turned away. With the crystals and gels in place and pumping to replace losses, their own laser was useless. The cyborgs had emplaced at least one heavy laser on the moon. That was going to make things difficult. Missiles launched from Carme sped toward them in the meantime. They would arrive in less than an hour.

"We're going to need the rail-guns sooner than expected," the Praetor said.

"Lord?" asked Canus.

"In seventeen minutes, the rail-guns, the lasers and the activated Zenos will attack in conjunction," the Praetor said.

"We can't storm our way onto the moon," Canus said. "They've clearly decided that we're the primary threat. Now if we had a SU battlewagon with heavy particle shielding—"

"If we had a Doom Star, we would be the lords of Jupiter," the Praetor said in a scathing tone. "Instead, we have the *Thutmosis III*. It's still a crippled ship." He grinned like a wounded tiger. "And we have eighteen Highborn. It's a pitiful number compared to the likely masses of cyborgs. But we have more than enough pods and a dozen patrol boats to get us onto the moon's surface."

"Where we shall die," Canus said.

The Praetor disliked Canus's pessimism. He would have enjoyed throttling him, but he needed every officer he had.

"Did we survive this past year and finally decelerate here to die as a useless gesture?" Canus asked, scowling. It caused his burn-scar to turn even redder than normal. "Highborn should always fight to win."

"We will win," the Praetor said.

"After another—" Canus checked his board— "sixteen more minutes, the *Thutmosis III* will die to the heavy laser."

"Have you rerouted the ship's controls to the shuttle?"

"If it matters, I have."

295

The Praetor clunked a gauntleted hand on Canus's armored shoulder. "We defeated our despair at the edge of the Solar System. Let us defeat our despair once more and win through to victory."

Still scowling, Canus glanced up. "Lord, your self-confidence borders on insanity."

"That's what others must have told Pizarro."

"Lord?" asked Canus.

"We have fifteen minutes left," the Praetor said. "So make sure you do everything right the first time, because we won't have a second chance."

-15-

As the *Thutmosis III* made its death-ride to glory or hapless oblivion, the *Descartes* and its fellow meteor-ship closed in on Carme as they decelerated. Compared to the missile-ship, the Jovian taskforce came from a ninety-degree angle, bearing down on the rogue moon. The *Descartes* led the assault, with the second ship following, using the *Descartes* as a shield.

Carme continued to accelerate, with the cyborg dreadnaught still hiding behind the moon. The main laser still attempted a burn-through on the *Thutmosis III's* prismatic crystal field.

The *Descartes* looked much as it had the first day Marten saw it. The meteor-shell still looked like a junkyard with hosts of pods, girders, dishes, missiles, cubes and patrol boats seemingly magnetized to it. Today there was a singular difference. Marten viewed the meteor-ship from its surface.

He sat in the front of a patrol boat, beside Osadar. She was in the pilot's chair, making last minute checks on her control board.

Marten wore his combat armor, presently minus his helmet. An IML was beside him and a Gyroc rifle. He had grenades, a vibroblade and an upset stomach.

Marten twisted back. Omi inspected the two squads piled into the patrol boat with them. There was heavy breathing, the clatter of equipment and the noisy sound of someone vomiting. The smell of sweat and fear was strong. Many of the space marines had thousand meter stares. Others glared. A few looked terrified. More than one trembled.

Marten found that his spit had vanished, making it hard to swallow. He hated pre-battle jitters. He hated the tingle in his arms and the roiling in his gut. He supposed it must have been like this thousands of years ago when David had tested his sling before racing out to challenge Goliath. That had been his favorite Bible story, his mother reading it to him as she sat on the edge of his bed. It was strange that he should think of her. Did that mean he was going to die?

Under his breath, Marten cursed softly. Then he shook his head, and he stared out of the polarized window. The surface of the meteor-shell was filled with junk and with other waiting patrol boats. Each of them contained its two-squad complement of space marines.

Marten dug in a pocket, producing a stick of gum. He opened it and popped the gum into his mouth, beginning to chew, beginning to produce spit so he could swallow.

Why did this feel like entering the torpedoes he'd ridden onto the *Bangladesh*?

"I'm ready," Osadar said.

Marten blinked several times before her words made sense. Then he stared out of the window again, searching for signs of Carme. He'd see its long, comet-like tail first as Yakov had shown him the runaway planetoid via teleoptics.

The radio crackled and Yakov's calm features appeared on the screen. For some reason, that reminded Marten of the *Rousseau*, how the screen had stayed blank that day.

"The cyborg laser has achieved a burn-through," Yakov said.

Marten scowled. Why couldn't he focus on what was going on? What was wrong with him?

"Now the cyborgs are hitting the Highborn ship," Yakov said.

"Right," Marten said. In way, he was relieved. He'd never liked the idea of fighting with Highborn, certainly not with the Praetor.

Yakov laughed savagely. The laugh unnerved Marten. He'd come to appreciate the Jovian's calmness, to appreciate the Force-Leader's deadly seriousness.

"Shuttles are launching from the missile-ship," Yakov said. "They're maneuvering behind it, or behind what will soon be the ship's wreckage. Wait, Rhea is telling me—oh, this is good."

"What?" Marten asked.

"The Highborn ship accelerates onto a collision course with Carme. The Praetor seems to be using his ship as a shield. I wonder how many Highborn he's sacrificing. The entire crew can't fit into those few shuttles, can they?"

"I'm picking up Voltaire Missile signals," Rhea said in Yakov's background.

"This is it," Yakov said. The Force-Leader stared out of the screen at Marten. "We're in range of Carme, Representative Kluge."

"Good luck, Yakov."

The silver-haired Force-Leader nodded brusquely. "It's time to pull the ring," he said in a dead-calm tone.

'Pull the ring', was a hussade term. Marten knew that much.

"Enemy sensors have locked onto us," Yakov said. "It's time for you to lift-off."

Marten tried to say a last word, but Osadar snapped off the link. Then she ignited the patrol boat's engine, causing the craft to vibrate.

"Hang on!" Marten shouted to the men.

As the last syllable left his mouth, Osadar blasted off the meteor-shell, heading for Carme.

## 16

Carme trembled from its violent acceleration. The gargantuan ports spewed blue plasma. The generators hummed as power surged through coils. Deeper in the rock, mighty fusion engines separated atoms, creating nuclear energy. The combination meant that Carme's rocky hills shook. Ancient stardust stirred on the cratered floors. The gleaming towers quivered as dishes rotated, as antennae collected thermal, mass and neutrino data on the approaching enemies. Missiles poked upward, ready to launch. The main laser spewed a torrent of focused light, cutting, slicing and separating the black-matted, Highborn ship. From low barracks, stubby point-defense cannons swiveled back and forth, ready to chug their depleted uranium shells at incoming enemy. Tac-lasers warmed up and several magnetic-guns shined with inner flashes of blue light.

There were five clusters of towers, buildings, barracks and underground entrances on Carme. Each had a separate defense grid, each powered by one of the mighty engines. Many tens of kilometers separated them, and there were more than enough suited cyborgs at each cluster to repeal any foolish space-drops.

The Web-Mind computed all this in a matter of seconds, as a paranoia program insisted on a quick probability check. It had seemed senseless then, and the numbers indicated the Web-Mind had been correct. However, there were some trifling possibilities that caused the Web-Mind a moment of unease.

The future master of the Jupiter System waited like a mechanical spider deep in its armored bunker. The greatest technological marvel of the 24th Century was built into its stealth-capsule. That capsule was parked in the dark, with hundreds of radio-links and communication and power cables attached to it.

The Web-Mind processed all the incoming information that its sensory stations on the moon's surface collected. In seconds, it ran through hundreds of military scenarios. It had cyborgs on the ground, guns, missiles and laser stations and a roving dreadnaught ready to rise into view and attack the enemy ships and missiles. It could not lose. No, that wasn't completely accurate. A five percent probability existed that the Highborn or Jovians possessed a secret weapon that could grant them victory.

Billions of neurons fired in the hundreds of kilos of brain-mass that composed the core of the Web-Mind.

A five percent probability of defeat was minuscule. That gave it a ninety-five percent probability of total victory. If Gharlane and the fleet had accelerated here instead of heading in-system to Io—

No, the probability of harm increased under those conditions. Whether Gharlane won or lost among the Galilean moons, the critical factor was the launching of the planet-wrecker. There were several smaller wreckers under construction in the outermost Jovian System. Carme-wrecker, however, was the only one able to launch in the window of the coming Saturn System attack.

A powerful confidence-boosting program now surged forward. The Web-Mind shrugged off the five percent probability, as it was too small to deflect the confidence program. With renewed zeal, the Web-Mind inspected near, mid and far space relative to Carme.

The wreckage of the Highborn ship burst through its weakened crystal-gel fields. There were twenty-three clumps spread over a kilometer. Those clumps contained thousands of smaller pieces.

A warning surged though the Web-Mind. Like a meteor shower, the wreckage was an intercept course for Carme. A quick calculation showed that none of the pieces would hit building clusters one through five. Even so, the kinetic energy of the multiple strikes could cause quake damage. That might harm the coil linkages, always the weakest connection between fusion cores and lasers.

A subordinate function of the Web-Mind continued to fire the heavy laser. After the missile-ship's destruction, it used priority targeting. Zenos first, rail-gun canisters second, cannon shells third and—

Warning beacons fired through the Web-Mind's biomass brain. What the Web-Mind had believed to be more missiles traveling behind the *Thutmosis III's* wreckage was now—the Web-Mind rechecked the readings to be sure. There were life-support systems hard at work on what it had conceived as missiles. The Web-Mind ran configuration checks. Those were Highborn shuttles!

Had Highborn survived their ship's destruction? Why would the military creatures continue to head here then? Why didn't they accept defeat and attempt flight and continued existence?

The Web-Mind yearned to run a re-analysis on Highborn psychology. This wasn't the time, however. With the approaching shuttles—the Web-Mind ran through a fast executing probability script.

An annoyance factor seethed through the Web-Mind. As incredible as it seemed, the shuttles added a percentage point to the odds of enemy success. There was now a six percent chance of defeat.

Angered, the Web-Mind launched more missiles, and it sent a flash-message to the dreadnaught's commander. If Highborn landed on Carme's surface, the chance of defeat rose to an amazing eight percent.

In Carme's deepest bunker, behind the stealth coating of its capsule, the Web-Mind computed, rechecked data and widened its sensory checks. Then it sent a pulse to other bunkers, bringing many cyborgs to active status. If the Highborn landed on Carme, they would die.

The Web-Mind contemplated a new possibility. If Highborn landed, the cyborgs could capture several. Then it could use the captives as test subjects, running thousands of experiments and learning everything there was to know about the highly aggressive subspecies. That would also give it something to do during the long journey in-system. The Web-Mind almost purred with delight. Fresh data for thousands of hours, it would enjoy that.

The experiments could also determine the provocative question concerning Highborn. Were they an entirely new genus? Or were the Highborn merely a larger subspecies of Homo sapiens?

The inquisitive aspect of the Web-Mind, the curiosity, actually hoped that a shuttle-full of Highborn made it onto the surface. It might almost be worth the negative percentage points to let them land. No, the landing would give the enemy that eight percent chance of victory. Those were unacceptable odds.

The approaching Highborn must die, just as the attacking Jovians were about to face obliteration.

## 17

Force-Leader Yakov was thrown hard to the left by his maneuvering ship. Only the restraining straps of his chair held him in place. The main screen was a blizzard of images as Carme hove into sight.

The rogue planetoid still accelerated, the spewing gases from its exhaust-ports attempting to propel millions of metric tons of rock and trace metals. Bright dots of light appeared on Carme's surface. Those could be launched missiles or batteries of point-defense cannons. Both possibilities filled Yakov with dread. The laser-beam stabbed elsewhere for the moment. If that beam swerved to focus on the *Descartes*....

Yakov blinked. There was hoarse shouting. The ship's fusion-engine whined. Then came the sound of sharp whistling, indicating a breach somewhere.

"Incoming shells!" Rhea shouted.

"Attempting sensor shear!" the ECM officer screamed.

"Decks five and six are off-line, Force-Leader! I think they've been breached. I'm initiating emergency bulkheads."

Seconds later, loud booms sounded from within the ship.

The pilot was pale with fear as he held up his hands. "I'm putting the ship on emergency auto-sequencing!"

"No," Yakov ordered.

Because of the strain of G-forces, Yakov had to use a motorized control as he spun toward the pilot's module. Now that the back of his chair was no longer resisting the Gs, Yakov was thrown laterally against his restraining straps.

"Maintain heading," Yakov said. Although he didn't shout or scream, his voice cut through the bedlam. The pilot stared at him, wide-eyed.

"Force-Leader—" the man began objecting.

"Take us in," Yakov said.

"It's death to—"

"You took an oath," Yakov said, his voice harsh. "You swore to defend the Jovian System. Today, we earn our berths."

Before the pilot could argue, Yakov's chair purred and once again, he faced the main screen. Years of training, of endless drill, study and late nights perfecting his art allowed him to read the bewildering screen. There were dots, triangles, cones of probability, dotted lines indicating flight paths—it was a plethora of information. The increasingly tightening space between Carme and the attacking vessels was dense with multiple forms of death.

EMP surges washed over armor-sheathed electronics. Nuclear explosions added x-rays and gamma rays as well as deadly heat radiation. Shredding pellets, shards of metal and even particles of sand slashed through the vacuum at hi-speeds.

Both meteor-ships had launched every Zeno drone they carried. The point-defense cannons barked endlessly. Rail-guns projected canisters that exploded killing shrapnel ahead of it. Ninety degrees from them the hurdling pieces of the former *Thutmosis III* headed for the surface. Carme's laser had melted many of the largest pieces and deflected others. What was left of the prismatic and gel shields drifted at a constant velocity toward Carme. Following behind the fields were the missile-ship's Zenos, the shuttles and farther behind, but coming on fast, were the four deadly Voltaire Missiles.

The tactic was simple and obvious. Zeno drones led the way. The ships followed. Behind came the shuttles and patrol boats, using everything before them as shields. With the countless explosions, shells, missiles and sand zones it seemed that nothing should survive unscathed. But even here, the volume of space was vast, the individual masses tiny in comparison.

Now Zenos began to ignite their thermonuclear warheads, using x-rays and gamma rays to attack the sensor installations and bunkers of point-defense cannons on Carme.

In return, the *Descartes* shuddered as an enemy Zeno blasted seven hundreds meters to starboard. X-rays traveled at light speed, flooding the starboard side of the ship, killing personnel and destroying delicate equipment. Behind it followed depleted uranium shrapnel. The impact caused the shuddering, and it created three massive cracks that splintered around the meteor-shell.

As that occurred, the dreadnaught rose from behind Carme. Its particle shielding protected it except for five-meter slits. From those slits poured point-defense shells, anti-missiles and laser-beams.

The cyborg-controlled warship was like an SU battlewagon. It was meant for long-range fights, using lasers as its primary weapon. The meteor-ships were even more unsuited for this intense barrage, built as raid vessels. The dreadnaught possessed the particle shielding, and that was a critical advantage. It would turn the battle decisively for the cyborgs.

"Force-Leader!" Rhea screamed.

Somehow, among the clangs, the sounds of more bulkheads slamming into place, the shouts from other officers, Yakov heard her.

"There's a message from the Praetor!" Rhea screamed. "I'm patching it through to your chair."

Yakov moved a toggle. On the armrest's tiny screen and through heavy static appeared the Praetor's wide features. The Highborn looked strained, his skin taut. His eyes were like burning pits of madness.

"They've destroyed half the Voltaire Missiles," the Praetor said in his deep voice. "I'm not sure the others will make it through to the dreadnaught."

Mute, Yakov nodded.

Maybe because of EMP blasts or enemy ECM, the static increased. It was now impossible to hear the Praetor's next words.

Yakov raised his head. "Rhea—"

Rhea worked feverishly on her board. She stabbed buttons and twisted a dial. "Try it now!" she shouted.

Yakov clicked a toggle and the static appeared to lessen. He could barely make out the Praetor. He leaned closer to the chair's speakers.

"You have to take out the dreadnaught," the Praetor said. The static became too much again. But it didn't matter now. Yakov understood. If the dreadnaught survived, they had lost the battle.

The Force-Leader calmly flipped an emergency cover on his armrest. He pressed the red button there. It gave him override authority over the ship's functions. Yakov savagely wiped his eyes. They were dry, but they burned with fatigue. He didn't want to die. Ganymede had finally gained its independence from Callisto. Everything had begun for him long ago at Ganymede U when he'd won the hussade trophy. Now he was here, fighting a losing battle against the impossible cyborgs. How could men defeat such evil creations?

Yakov shook his head. He didn't know how. He knew, however, that he had to try. He had to ram this attack down the cyborgs' throat. He had to give the Praetor and his Highborn a chance for victory. He had to help stubborn Marten Kluge. Yes. The Earthman showed the way. Kluge fought even when the odds were impossible. He went in and tried, hoping a miracle would occur.

"Force-Leader!" Rhea shouted. "We've lost ship functions. We're headed on an intercept course for the dreadnaught."

Yakov ignored her. He controlled the *Descartes* now.

"They have sensor lock-on!"

"All hail Ganymede U," Yakov whispered.

Lasers from the dreadnaught struck the meteor-ship, slagging rock. Point-defense shells followed and missiles attempted to race the gauntlet between the fast-closing vessels.

The shouting in the command room lessened.

"He's taking us into the dreadnaught," Rhea said, as she clutched her choker. "We're the missile now."

That brought silence as officers in their modules stared at Yakov.

The silver-haired Force-Leader snapped a crisp salute. Then he watched the main screen as the firing dreadnaught began to fill his world.

## -18-

"Yakov, you fool," Marten whispered.

On her screen, Osadar pointed at the crippled *Descartes*. Then she switched cameras as the patrol boat continued its wild, jinking, twisting ride toward Carme.

Marten was lurched this way and that. Behind him, space marines shouted as their armor clattered and clanked. Outside through the polarized window, weird colors flashed everywhere. Zipping, and often glowing shapes, burned past like planetary meteors.

During the hell-ride, Carme constantly became bigger. Now surface features were visible. There were silver domes and tall towers. They were clustered together in what seemed like a mechanized village at the end of a valley.

Marten leaned toward the window, peering upward, straining. He saw the dreadnaught, its lasers stabbing, burning into the *Descartes*. Yakov piloted it now. Weeks ago, Yakov had rescued him from the sealed pod and had saved him from Arbiter Octagon.

"No," Marten whispered. He'd lost too many friends these past few years. Marten banged a fist against the window. Social Unity, Highborn, cyborgs and now pontificating philosophers—

Was there no end to it?

The meteor-ship *Descartes*, the splintering vessel, smashed head-on against the larger cyborg-controlled dreadnaught. Particle shielding and meteor-shell burst apart, sending rock and pulverized dust in an expanding ball of debris. The massive destruction unleashed tons of kinetic energy. Dreadnaught lasers quit firing, and like an interstellar billiard ball, the dreadnaught caromed leftward, away from Carme.

"Here we go," Osadar said.

The patrol boat sank with sickening speed. Marten lost sight of the dreadnaught. Yakov, the mad fool, the insanely brave Force-Leader of Ganymede, he was dead. The calm guardian was likely a jellied mass. It hurt to know that. It brought—

It brought sadness, but then Marten had new troubles to occupy his thoughts. Osadar madly maneuvered the patrol boat as the vessel's computer fired the boat's cannons. The ripping sounds occasionally timed together with a white blossom to their left, their right and then directly in front of them.

"Seal your helmets!" Marten roared. He checked his, and he heard radios click online in his receivers.

The patrol boat violently shuddered. There was howling, and Marten felt a fierce tug on his straps as if he might fly upward. He craned his head. A large, jagged rip in the ceiling let him view the stars. Patrol-boat debris shot out of it. Something had torn off the vessel's sheeting, releasing the precious atmosphere.

A Jovian screamed in Marten's headphones.

"The moon!" another Jovian roared. It sounded like Tass.

Marten felt faint as Carme's surface rushed toward them. Carme was huge. Craggy-spiked mountains loomed. A crater skimmed below them.

"Now!" said Osadar.

Marten was slammed forward as the final retros fired. Gleaming silver towers rapidly drew near. A sensor dish—it vanished as something from the heavens crashed against it. Beams washed over the towers, over the domes. The beams quit almost as soon as they began firing.

The hardest, most violent jolt of all caused Marten's armored chin to smash against his chestplate. There was ringing in his ears and it seemed as if he were a thousand light-years from this place. Vaguely he was aware of terrific jolts and repeatedly slamming against his straps. Then it ended, and there was peace.

"Marten! Marten Kluge!"

Groggily, Marten moved his eyes. That hurt and caused an explosion of pain in his head.

"Marten Kluge?"

"Don't shake him." That sounded like Omi.

*Omi…. That meant….*

"Marten?"

Marten focused and saw Osadar's worried face before him.

"We've landed," Osadar said through the radio-link. "We've landed on the front part."

Marten raised a feeble hand, trying to release a buckle. It was the front part in relation to the hot plasma expelled from the back at the crater-sized exhaust-ports, giving Carme its one-quarter G.

"Let me do that," Omi said.

"What happened?" Marten slurred.

"Do you wish to avenge your dead friend?" Osadar asked.

*What did that mean?* Oh. Yes. Yakov had died to give him, to give the space marines, cover so they could land on Carme. The entire complement of the *Descartes'* crew had died, including beautiful Rhea. It was a shame he'd never made friends with her, had never kissed her. He'd seen the crashing meteor-ship. He'd never forget that awful slight.

With a grunt, Marten heaved himself to his feet. Here, Carme's acceleration gave the surface pseudo-gravity. It was nothing like the *Bangladesh*, however. Marten turned his head, glancing back. Jovian space marines waited for him.

"It's time to move," Osadar said.

Marten nodded. Oh, that hurt his head. With a slap of his hand, he struck a precise spot on his chest. That activated his medkit. He heard a hiss as his suit-hypo shot him with a stim. He chinned his radio to wide-beam.

"Listen up," Marten said, "and maybe you can help me do some damage to these mother-loving cyborgs."

He didn't have time to wait for the stims. Time had run out for all of them. He began barking orders, leading the first wave of space marines onto Carme.

"Watch your footing," Marten said over his crackling radio. The static was insane, a constant in his headphones.

Carme's surface was rocky, with sharp protrusions and plenty of stardust. Every step left a print. Sometimes dust puffed upward.

The stars shined above as nearer, flashing objects glowed and disappeared, some smashing into the moon. Otherwise, it was dark and eerie. Jupiter was the brightest 'star' by many magnitudes, brighter even than the Sun.

Marten yearned to reach the towers and domes, to get his men under cover. If an EMP blast went off nearby or a missile exploded, it could kill the lot of them. He also wanted to gather a large number of space marines in one place in order to defeat the enemy in detail, hitting small cyborg parties with as many men as possible. Unfortunately, it was impossible to call down other patrol boats, as the interference was too strong.

"There!" crackled Omi's voice.

Marten swiveled his head to look back, to see what Omi pointed at. Something flashed at the corner of his eye. He turned forward again and saw an impossibly fast humanoid running toward them. The humanoid had a laser carbine, with a bulky pack on his back. He shot from the hip with flashes of light that stabbed at them, hitting his soldiers.

"Down!" shouted Marten. "Get onto your stomachs!"

"Pericles is hit!" a space marine shouted.

"Kallias—I need help! Kallias has lost his helmet!"

Marten threw himself onto his stomach, hitting rocky ground, making dust puff around him.

The charging cyborg was killing his space marines fast. It was extremely efficient when compared to mere humans.

Marten clawed the IML from his back. He targeted the cyborg even as the beam slashed into more of his space marines. In his HUD, Marten saw a green flash, meaning: *target acquired*. He jerked the IMLs trigger. It shuddered as the Cognitive missile ignited and zoomed at the cyborg.

The thing was incredible. It threw itself down even as it aimed and fired at the incoming missile. The beam slashed a scant milli-fraction from the warhead because the Cognitive missile swerved then. It poured a final burst of thrust and slammed into the cyborg. There was an explosion and then showering shards of metal and hot plasti-flesh.

A ragged cheer battled the static in Marten's ears.

"We'll advance by over-watch teams!" Marten shouted. He wanted to stay calm. Yakov had known how to stay calm in a fight, but the silver-haired Force-Leader was dead. He hated this war. He hated cyborgs.

Marten reloaded the IML. The Cognitive missile tactic had worked. He'd killed a cyborg.

"Six men are dead," Omi said on the command channel.

The headache that had begun with the crash-landing blossomed with renewed pain. Then something flashed overhead at the edge of Marten's visor.

"Look," someone said, "a patrol boat."

*Reinforcements*, Marten thought. *Good. We need more—*

An explosion of bright light ended the thought. Marten had no idea if depleted uranium shells, canisters, wide-area sand-shots or a tac-laser had killed the patrol boat. In the end, it didn't matter what had killed it. All those reinforcements were dead.

"Here come more cyborgs," Omi said. "I count seven of them."

"Spread out!" Marten shouted. Then he remembered an old Highborn maxim: *A commander must give concrete, tangible commands*. "A-team," Marten said, "head left. B-team...."

313

The cyborgs carried lasers. Marten and his space marines used IMLs and Cognitive missiles, with Osadar firing a Gyroc rifle. In the end, they killed the deadly things with saturation fire, but lost half their number doing it.

Armored bodies lay everywhere, with neat little holes burnt through ceramic-metal plates.

"We'll never win like this," Tass said over the radio.

Panting, Marten lifted a loaded IML off a corpse. The space marine's faceplate was slagged ballistic glass, the head inside a horrible glob of protoplasm.

"Wait here," wheezed Marten. His conditioner-unit hummed, washing his sweaty skin with cool air.

"Sir?" a space marine asked.

"I'm going to scout ahead," Marten said. "We need to group our forces, hit the cyborgs as one. Omi, Osadar...Tass, follow me."

"What's up?" Omi asked on the command channel.

"This looks like a safe spot to leave the others," Marten said. "We'll take the risks right now."

Omi gave a noncommittal grunt.

The four of them advanced across rocky terrain, with someone always crouching behind a boulder, with an aimed missile ready to fly. The cluster of domes and towers slowly grew larger.

"Look," Osadar said.

Marten glanced back where she pointed. Cyborgs climbed over rocks, heading toward the others.

"Damn," Marten said. "Let's go." Then he tried to warn the others, but the static was too heavy.

The cyborgs moved with twitching, inhuman speed and fired with uncanny laser-accuracy—they were cyclones of death. Marten and others used their Cognitive missiles, hitting the enemy from behind. It killed the last cyborgs, but no space marine left behind survived the firefight.

Gasping for air, with sweat dripping down his chin, Marten knelt, and he shook his head.

That's when the first piece of good luck occurred. Another boatload of space marines joined them. Well, half the patrol boat's complement joined them, a squad's worth. They marched from behind a low hill, waving IMLs to identify themselves. Once they were close, they were able to talk over the worsening static.

Together, they humped over the terrain, soon sliding down a hill as a tower rose before them. A broken dish rotated at the top. The nearest dome was cracked as something visible sheeted out of it.

"Look," Osadar said.

She was the tallest among them and had stolen a bulky laser pack and carbine from a dead cyborg. Osadar pointed with the tip of her carbine.

Two shuttles glided low over a hill. They could have been twins to the *Mayflower*. The shuttles floated toward the cluster of towers and domes.

"Idiots," Omi said.

Stubby barrels poked out of two low barracks. Marten wished he could radio the shuttles. The barrels were point-defense cannons. It surprised him the Highborn were so foolish as to try to land directly among the buildings. He could have used the reinforcements.

Then a huge missile flashed overhead, speeding ahead of Carme. The missile rotated. A beam lanced from the nosecone. The beam hit the first barracks. The point-defense cannons of the second barracks shot depleted uranium shells. Those shredded the lead shuttle. Metal rained onto the surface. Some chunks splattered against the hills like meteors. Then the missile's beam hit again, and the second barracks was destroyed.

"The Highborn are using a Voltaire Missile," Osadar said.

In his cooling helmet, Marten raised his eyebrows. The giant missile hung out there like some guardian angel, rotating, firing its engine to pull ahead and then rotating back to fire. No doubt, the Praetor or one of his Highborn lieutenants controlled the Voltaire. Marten recalled how he'd once controlled the *Mayflower* via his handscanner's keypad.

From where he stood on a hill's slope, Marten watched the landing shuttle. He also saw the Voltaire's beam slag cyborgs spilling out of a low dome.

That did something to Marten's chest. It took him a moment to understand what. Then he did understand. He had hope again. Battleoid-armored Highborn had arrived, and they had an altered drone to provide covering fire. Maybe there was a way to win, or at least to disable this blasted planet-wrecker. Yakov's sacrifice had achieved something.

Marten nodded, vowing that his friend's death would count, even if he had to take some Highborn's orders for the next hour, even the Praetor's orders, to achieve it.

"All right," he said. "We're going to try to link up with them. But keep a close watch on your sensors. We don't need any more nasty surprises."

## -20-

The Praetor seethed with pent-up rage, fear, adrenalin and a singular Highborn passion: an exalted need to dominate, to win.

He stood in his battleoid-armor, with a heavy plasma cannon similar to the weapon Marten had used on the cyborgs that had invaded the *Mayflower* many weeks ago. The shuttle had landed, had made the awful journey through Carme's killing zone. His single remaining Voltaire was dedicated for his use.

"Kill major weapon systems first and cyborgs second," the Praetor ordered through his battleoid's radio.

A lone Highborn would remain aboard the shuttle. He presently sat at a board, controlling the Voltaire.

The Praetor grinned as his pink eyes gleamed with dominating passion. If he died, nothing else mattered. He had predicated his strategy and tactics on that. The first shuttle had been a drone, meant to absorb enemy attacks. The second shuttle held sixteen Highborn. The remaining two of the *Thutmosis III's* eighteen Highborn had been badly hurt. Therefore, they'd piloted different shuttles, meant to act as decoys. All fourteen healthy Highborn would join him in the ground assault.

Could fifteen, battleoid-armored Highborn conquer Carme? They had Jovians for fodder and the melded humanoids as enemies. The Praetor laughed. It was a harsh sound. The two greatest conquistadors, Hernan Cortes and Francisco Pizarro, had both won through capturing emperors. Both the Aztecs and

317

the Incas had raised theocratic empires, where the emperor was considered a god or the son of the ruling gods.

These last few days, the Praetor had studied everything learned about the cyborgs and all the known data concerning a technological marvel called Web-Mind. Highborn Intelligence on Earth had uncovered interesting aspects from Social Unity sources, while the Mars Planetary Union had supplied some critical facts they'd learned during the Third Battle for Mars.

To the Praetor's thinking, these Web-Minds seemed like Aztec or Inca emperors. Before the *Thutmosis III's* destruction, he had picked up telling signals. Those signals had matched others from the Third Battle for Mars. Those signals had indicated a broadcasting Web-Mind on Carme.

In his time, Hernan Cortes had fought many battles against masses of Aztec warriors. At times, the odds had been one hundred Indians versus one Spaniard. The *Mexica* warriors as the Aztecs called themselves had ranged each of their bands under a gaudy leader decked out in flower-ornamented, cotton armor. In those battles, Cortez had ordered his handful of iron-armored knights to charge into the Aztec hosts. Those knights had one goal: to wade through the masses and spear the gaudily-clad chieftain. When the chieftain died, his band fled the battlefield. After the horsed knights slaughtered enough chieftains, and after enough Indians had fled, then the knights charged a last time, killing the Aztec Host Commander. Afterward, thousands of cotton-armored Mexicas had littered the gory battlefield.

Today, the strategy was simple. The best strategies always were. Find the Web-Mind, kill it and hope that paralyzed the remaining cyborgs. Including himself, the Praetor had fifteen battleoid-armored Highborn to do it, fifteen horsed knights, as it were.

The Praetor pressed a switch. The main hatch blew outward, throwing the doors thirty meters in either direction. The doors landed hard, sending up a geyser of moon-dust.

Then the Praetor's exoskeleton-powered suit moved out of the shuttle and onto Carme. The hour of decision had arrived.

## 21

Deep in the cavern of its armored chamber, the Web-Mind collected data. Eighty percent of the Highborn shuttles were destroyed. A Voltaire presently stayed ahead of Carme. The drone used its defensive armaments as weapons platforms to provide covering fire for ground troops.

The Web-Mind ran a configuration program and then ran an analysis on munitions and laser-fire expenditures. It concluded that the thermonuclear warheads had been removed to provide greater munitions-carrying capacity for the Voltaire.

The Web-Mind pulsed retargeting data to select point-defense bunkers and laser stations. It was time to take out the last Voltaire.

Nanoseconds later, the Web-Mind counted the number of patrol boats, those destroyed and those that had landed. Cluster Three had been breached. Cluster Four faced a concentrated attack, while Cluster Five was untouched and Clusters One and Two had received minimal damage and faced a minuscule number of suited Jovians.

Cluster Three was the danger point.

The Web-Mind sent myriad orders, recalling many cyborgs and ordering them to converge on Cluster Three. Then it ran a probability scenario for Cluster Three. A stubborn five percent probability continued to exist of possible danger.

Few Cluster Three cyborgs remained. Others were on the way, however. This was interesting. There was a complement of Webbies in a holding cell on Cluster Three.

Suiting need to action, the Web-Mind pulsed an order to them. Webbies were inefficient battle units, but they could shave off half a percentage point of threat, possibly even a full percentage point. Even better, they might help the reinforcement cyborgs on their way to Cluster Three. They could help the cyborgs capture several Highborn.

A surge of greed boiled in the Web-Mind. It wanted captive Highborn. Yes, it dearly wanted them in order to practice experiments during the long journey to the Inner Planets.

*** 

Webbie Octagon was the first on his padded couch to sit up and yank out the plasti-flesh insert in his neck-jack.

Jovian space marines and Highborn battleoids were on Carme, were nearby in the towers and domes. They were to dress, arm and kill the invaders.

Gaunt Octagon slid off the long couch. He was in a large, oval chamber, with various control readings on the nearest wall. More lights flickered on, brightening the chamber. A panel slid open, revealing brown vacc-suits.

Hunger twisted Octagon's stomach. He felt weak from lack of nutrients and from lack of exercise. His arms were thin and his legs trembled. He staggered toward the vacc-suits, his shoes making clicking noises. Behind him, other Webbies stirred. Some coughed, while a few had the temerity to urinate on the metallic floor. Those were the most emaciated, they had worn their neck-jacks the longest.

The kill-order beat in Octagon's mind. But it was a pale imitation to the need to find and slay Marten Kluge. The logic was direct. Space marines were on Carme. With a desperate loathing, Octagon hated Marten Kluge. Therefore, he would find Marten among the space marines because the need had become gargantuan.

With shaking fingers, Octagon tore a vacc-suit off the rack and began to unseal it. Others staggered toward him. Octagon sneered at a tall woman with long hair and circles around her eyes. Once, he would have found her naked hips appealing. Now all he wanted was to kill Marten Kluge.

Hurrying, Octagon thrust his arms into the suit, flexed his gloved fingers and began to close the seals. Soon, he jammed a helmet over his head and turned on the air. It was stale. Without waiting, Octagon staggered for a hatch.

The kill-order beat like a pulse, put there by the Web-Mind. He would find weapons in a nearby locker. The combination sequence throbbed in his forebrain.

Octagon hissed, and he rubbed his gloved hands together. Marten Kluge, Marten Kluge, Marten Kluge—he was finally going to gain vengeance on the hateful barbarian. He was going to hurt the man. He was going to hurt him repeatedly and listen to him scream in agony.

The desire brought small groans of pleasure and moisture to Octagon's eyes. He forgot about his hunger and forgot about his weakness. To hold a stunner and blast the barbarian, it's all that mattered.

Octagon panted, forcing himself to hurry.

## 22

Marten's gut tightened with fear. He led the way, entering a new lane between a cracked dome and a broken tower. The tower cast a deeper shadow, the light shining from Jupiter.

Marten gripped a Gyroc rifle, ready to fire rocket-propelled shells. He had a clip of APEX rounds, Armor-Piercing EXplosive. Each shell had a super-hardened penetrator packet. The loaded IML hung by a strap from his shoulder, clunking against his armor as he slunk a step at a time.

Osadar followed, with Tass behind her, leading the spread-out space marines. Omi brought up the rear.

It was eerie, with the radio static constantly washing over Marten's headphones. The occasional clicking of his suit's air-conditioners made him flinch.

Marten tried to scan everywhere. His helmet used short sensor-bursts to find and warn him about hiding cyborgs. Wherever he aimed the dedicated weapon—the Gyroc now—crosshairs appeared on the targeting portion of his visor.

Dust, rocks, a stray piece of cable, a staple-gun and other manmade junk littered the area. This near, the silver structures showed pitting, and there were various entrances or cracks running down them.

Marten's head throbbed, and he felt himself getting distracted. He gave himself another stim.

"The Highborn entered this place three hundred meters to our left," Osadar said.

"We should broadcast our position," Omi said. "We don't want to surprise each other."

Each time someone spoke, Marten bent his head, trying to decipher their half-garbled words through the static.

"You do remember Japan," Omi said over the command channel. "A battleoid was worth more than one of our platoons. Sometimes they were more deadly than a company of men."

"Do you think we killed all the cyborgs?" Tass asked nervously.

"No," said Osadar.

Marten flinched again as his suit's air-conditioner clicked and began to hum with greater power. He was too shaky. Seeing cyborgs slaughter his space marines earlier, this was a hell-world, a rogue moon meant to bring about humanity's extinction. He hated this place, but they had to destroy the engines, to wreck the wrecker.

"Cyborg!" a space marine screamed.

A red-tipped carbine poked out of a shadowed entrance. A beam slashed. A visor melted as another space marine died.

A half-second later, Gyroc shells burned in flight. Instead of retreating, the cyborg bounded out of the dome and toward them. The APEX shells blew apart the entrance, sending chunks flying.

The laser carbine spat again. Two more space marines died, their visors drilled with deadly little holes.

From where he lay, Marten tracked the cyborg. It moved with uncanny speed and it swiveled its carbine with evil precision. The HUD's crosshairs centered on it. Marten pulled the trigger three times. The cyborg hit the ground, rolled fast and killed another space marine. Marten's shells missed the cyborg and pitted the hard surfaces at his feet instead. Pieces of rock sprayed up into the cyborg's midsection. Then two APEX shells slammed into it. One blew apart an arm, another tore off a leg. One-armed, the cyborg burned another space marine. Three shells struck the torso in rapid succession then, and it died.

Marten swore harshly, surprised that he still lived. The things were impossible to kill, and they spewed murder until the last circuit flickered out.

He ordered Tass to take a headcount.

"To our right," Omi said. "That's where the Highborn beam slaughtered cyborgs before. We'd better be careful. Some of those things might have lost legs, but many will still continue killing."

Marten raised himself up onto an armored knee as he lifted the Gyroc. His arms trembled, but the stim was steadying him, and his headache receded. He felt that something was out there. Someone watched. He moved the Gyroc to the left.

"Lower your weapon or you die, preman."

Through his headphones, Marten recognized the commanding voice of a Highborn. It sent a chill of remembrance through him. Then a ten-foot tall battleoid stepped from behind the dome. Another Highborn rose into view on the dome's cracked surface. Both battleoids aimed plasma rifles, heavy weapons by anyone's standard.

Marten lowered his Gyroc. It would likely take two or three APEX shells in one spot to penetrate battleoid-armor.

"We hunted that cyborg," a Highborn said. "It is the last one here."

"No," the other Highborn said. "Look. Another cyborg. It must have captured these premen, using them to lure us."

"Wait!" Marten shouted. "The cyborg is with us. She's broken her programming."

Anything might have happened as the battleoids aimed their rifles and as Osadar raised her laser.

"What does 'broken her programming' mean?" a Highborn asked.

"We sent the Praetor information about her," Marten said. "Didn't he pass it onto you?"

"You're no Jovian," the nearest Highborn said. "Your voice patterns are wrong." The battleoid approached, its plasma rifle minutely switching from target to target. The Highborn on the dome remained where he was.

Highborn were quick to pick up nuances. Marten knew he should have remembered that and tried to mask his Earth accent. "I was at Mars during the battle," he told them.

"The Third Battle of Mars?" asked the towering Highborn. The battleoid bristled with weaponry, with an auto-cannon on the left arm, a missile launcher on the back and a large vibroblade sheathed on its armored hip. An antenna sprouted from a shoulder. Here on Carme, the suited Highborn was like a legendary giant.

"Sure," Marten said, trying not to feel intimidated.

"He is truculent," the second Highborn said. His tone implied that such a one should be punished.

"Where are the rest of your space marines?" the nearest Highborn asked.

"We're it," Marten said. He had eight men left. "We've run into several parties of cyborgs."

"You premen killed them?"

"We're still standing," Marten said, hating the smugness of the question, hating to have to explain anything again to a Highborn. He'd had his fill of them on the Sun-Works Factory. Being in the presence of the so-called Master Race intensified the old feelings about them.

"They are fodder," the Highborn on the dome said.

"Yes," said the nearer one. "You will follow me." Without waiting for confirmation, the intimidating battleoid turned around and began trudging in the direction it had first appeared.

As Marten hurried to keep pace and then to catch up, he had to tell himself that cyborgs were worse than Highborn. Cyborgs were inhuman, a death-plague. Highborn were insufferably arrogant, scary-strong and capable, but still human after a fashion. In the best of worlds, the two would murder each other and leave the Solar System to mere humanity. It was a nice wish, but would likely take years of heartache and fierce combat to achieve—if it was even possible.

\*\*\*

The Highborn led Marten and his space marines into another cracked dome. Smashed machinery and broken panels littered the floors. One mirror-like shard glittered as Marten kicked it and it skittered across the tile-plates.

There was a large airlock ahead. Everyone entered, with the battleoid dwarfing them. It reminded Marten of exiting the Deep Core Mine in Greater Sydney. It was the day he'd first met Highborn.

Air pressure pushed against his armor. The airlock's other end opened and they entered another large room, this one with a low ceiling. The chamber held over a dozen battleoids. That wasn't what tightened Marten's gut, however.

He saw the Praetor, who was in the act of removing his helmet. He stood before a processing machine with various lights and readings running on it. The huge Highborn stood with his gauntleted hands on his battleoid hips. The Highborn had the same strange, fur-like pelt of hair that Marten remembered. The Praetor turned then, and the intensely weird eyes chilled Marten. Here was a psychotic killer, a mass-murderer.

The Praetor indicated that Marten should remove his helmet.

Marten complied. What choice did he have? He had eight men against almost twice that number of Highborn. He opened the seals, twisted and lifted the heavy thing. The chamber's cold air washed against him. A strange taint stung his nostrils. But the air was breathable, if filled with alien odors. Was it wise taking off your helmet in a battle zone?

The Praetor scowled down at him. "You are familiar to me. Tell me how that is possible."

Part of Marten wanted to spit. He wanted to lift his Gyroc and blow the smug bastard away. He would die in turn, however. Every man here would die. Another part of him wanted to sneer and tell the Praetor what he thought about gelding men. That part wanted to boast to the Praetor about what he'd done to Lycon. There was a third part, fortunately, a saner portion of his mind. It had seen Yakov die heroically for a noble cause. That helped Marten remember how to play the role of the subservient preman. He did it for a higher cause: the continuation of the human race.

"I am uncertain, lord," Marten said, as he lowered his eyes before one of the supreme race.

A harsh laugh was his reward. "Yes. I know you, preman. You are Shock-Trooper Marten Kluge. I recall your voice as well as your face. I am unique among Highborn in that I can recall various features among the lower races. To most Highborn, premen look the same, or nearly the same. There are some obvious variations in skin pigmentation, but that is inconsequential."

Marten looked up into those intense eyes. Despite his resolve, Marten grinned insolently.

The Praetor's already taut features tightened, making it seem that his skin might tear. "During your flight to the *Bangladesh*, I heard your traitorous words. You had sworn an oath to us. That oath you broke, making you foresworn."

"You were going to castrate us."

"A trifling matter," the Praetor said.

"Not to me," Marten said.

"What happened to Lycon? He went to rescue shock troopers. How is it that you are here in the Jovian System?"

The old rage returned as hard words spilled out of Marten. "I killed Lycon."

The Praetor's eyebrows rose. "You, a preman?"

"I spaced three Highborn, took their shuttle and headed here."

The Praetor's terrible eyes seemed to shine, and an even weirder smile stretched his lips. "The Training Master and his crew were inferior Lot Sixers. And it seems you are a throwback."

Marten shook his head, not understanding the reference.

"During prehistoric days, bestial premen must have been savage hunters. How otherwise could they have survived those times? You are like them, a natural killer. I despised the weak Training Master. Thus, I grant you life in ridding me of him. But for daring to spill Highborn blood—a terrible crime for a preman—I will personally geld you after I destroy the Web-Mind. Then I shall keep you as an example to show Grand Admiral Cassius."

Behind Marten, seals snapped open. He heard metal sliding in grooves, and there was a faint *popping* sound. Before him, the Praetor's head swayed back as the Highborn's lips twisted in loathing.

Marten looked back. Osadar had taken off her helmet.

"Cyborg," the Praetor whispered.

"She's broken her programming," Marten said.

The Praetor's head twitched, which might have indicated curiosity or perhaps it was another manifestation of loathing.

"So," the Praetor whispered, "this is the infamous Osadar Di. I've read her specs, and I'd hoped she had survived."

"Why threaten Marten with gelding?" Osadar asked. "It is unreasonable."

The Praetor stared at Osadar, glanced once at Marten and then continued to study her.

"Lord," one of the Highborn said, using the battleoid's speakers, "Marcus has detected cyborgs. They're racing here from another cluster, and should arrive in... approximately eleven minutes."

The Praetor's nostrils expanded. He pointed at Osadar. "I've detected a Web-Mind, and I mean to destroy it. I believe that its destruction will render Carme inoperable." The Praetor put a huge, armored gauntlet on the humming machine. "Can you use this broadcasting unit to pinpoint the Web-Mind's location?"

Osadar stepped toward the Praetor and toward the large machine. He was bigger, bulkier and radiated intensity. She was cold, moved in a frighteningly quick manner and despite her humanoid shape and features, seemed alien.

Osadar pulled off a glove and twisted her forefinger's tip, unscrewing it. She plugged the forefinger into a jack. Osadar froze then as her eyes closed. In seconds, her head jerked, her eyes flickered open and she yanked her finger free.

"You know where it is," the Praetor whispered.

Osadar regarded him. Then she turned to Marten. "Should I tell him?"

"You will speak," the Praetor said, with menace.

"First rescind your gelding threat," Osadar said.

Battleoids stirred, everyone one of them lifting their weapons.

"I am in command here," the Praetor said. "I will rescind nothing."

"You might as well tell him," Marten said.

"You once told me—" Osadar began to say.

"Let's kill this Web-Mind," Marten said, "and stop the planet-wrecker. Everything else is secondary."

"You are wise, preman," the Praetor.

For once, Marten held his tongue, but it was hard to do.

"Give me the Web-Mind's coordinates," the Praetor said.

Osadar did so.

## 23

Marten resealed his helmet as the Praetor gave terse orders.

The entrance to the Web-Mind's underground chamber was in a different dome, but within this cluster of buildings.

They reentered the large airlock and exited the cracked dome. Outside, the stars and Jupiter shined as eerily as ever. The silver buildings cast shadows. Carme's low hills surrounded them, a sterile wasteland of asteroid rock and ancient dust. Dead space marines littered the area, as did shredded cyborgs. The majority of the melded creatures had perished to Voltaire laser-fire.

The last drone no longer hung in the sky, however. Likely, the cyborgs had destroyed it.

The Praetor had allowed Marten access to the Highborn battle-net. He thus heard the Praetor order eight Highborn along with Tass and the remaining space marines to intercept the approaching cyborgs. The others were to stop the melded humanoids in order to give the Praetor, Marten and the rest time to destroy the Web-Mind underground.

Two cyborgs ambushed them as they approached the dome. Lasers speared out of jagged cracks. The two beams focused on one battleoid.

From behind a rock, Marten snapped off Gyroc rounds, pitting the metallic wall, but failing to enter the jagged cracks, which were at an oblique angle to him. Orange plasma hit, and globs of molten metal dripped off the wall or drifted into the vacuum. Then a cyborg dashed out. Heated plasma killed it, melting its helmet and head. A Gyroc round entered the crack, along with a red beam.

The last cyborg stopped firing.

"Is it dead?" Omi asked.

Marten counted the fallen Highborn. Three battleoids lay prone, with laser holes burnt through the heavy armor. The suits could absorb more punishment than space marine armor, but eventually broke under concentrated laser-fire.

"Shock Troopers Marten and Omi," the Praetor said, "scout the dome. See if the cyborg still lives."

"Screw him," Omi said.

Marten heaved himself from behind his rock and began running. He snapped off three shots. Then a red light flashed on his HUD. *Rifle empty.* He tore out the clip and slammed in another. By that time, he reached the jagged crack. It was barely wide enough to squeeze through. Breathing hard, his body taut with fear, he poked the barrel in and slid against metal. The cyborg was sprawled inside, a hole in its chest sparking. As he stared, the cyborg's right hand twitched.

Horror and hatred washed through Marten. He yanked the trigger. Each slamming APEX round made the thing jerk and twist.

"It's dead!" Omi shouted.

A red, empty light was flashing in Marten's HUD, and he was still pulling the trigger. He stopped as Omi touched his shoulder.

Wordlessly, Marten switched clips.

"Everything is clear," Marten heard someone say. Then he realized it was his voice. He had to get a grip. He shot himself with another stim. Too many, and he'd go paranoid. He laughed. It wasn't a good sound. This was another firefight he had no business being in. Digging out a Web-Mind, they were all mad.

The wall behind them shuddered. Big pieces of metal and masonry flew off. Then a battleoid foot smashed through. A moment later, big gauntlets gripped an edge of wall and created an even bigger opening. Soon, the others joined Marten and Omi in the dome.

"Continue to scout," the Praetor said.

Omi's helmet turned toward him. Marten saw Omi's features, the hollow eyes and the terrible strain etched across his friend's face.

"Yeah," Marten said, hefting his Gyroc. He chinned infrared, scanning the place, observing the cracks above, the broken equipment everywhere and the littered floor. Then he started across it.

It might have been smarter switching to his IML, but he was going to save the Cognitive missile for the Praetor. Let the Highborn think him a dog to sniff out trouble. In the end, this dog would bite and finish what he'd started with Sigmir and continued with Lycon.

\*\*\*

As Marten scouted through the dome, the Web-Mind awoke to its danger. It had been running a prognostication program. Through it, it divined the Praetor's plan.

With quick calculation, the Web-Mind assessed its immediate military assets. The Webbies waited with their pathetic stunners. Yes, it must radio the leader. They must scour the deleted cyborgs and confiscate laser carbines. That would give the Webbies enough firepower to kill Highborn. The Web-Mind then began to activate its cyborg protection team. They'd waited in storage, having been interned there in the Neptune System. Unfortunately, thawing them would take time. Lastly, the Web-Mind radioed a distress call. All cyborgs were to converge here to annihilate Jovians and kill or capture Highborn.

The Web-Mind regretted leaving Gharlane with the in-system fleet. Worse, perhaps, with deletion as a possibility, the Web-Mind knew a growing and bitter jealousy. It was wrong that any cyborg should survive his demise. It was an even greater wrong that the troublesome and annoying Gharlane should survive his master.

Before the Web-Mind could dwell on that, however, a pre-inserted optimism program began to run. This would be the last opportunity for the inferior species to harm it. As Web-Mind, it was going to destroy Jovians and capture Highborn. First, it must send the correct pulse to the Webbie commander.

* * *

Webbie Octagon's hatred for Marten Kluge had undergone a transformation in the last ten minutes. He staggered under the heavy load of a laser-pack. He hunched like an old man. It would have been worse if Carme were under greater acceleration. But it was already bad enough.

Octagon cradled the carbine as sweat bathed his body. His brown vacc-suit's air-conditioner was broken. He wheezed, as he tasted the sour odor. He followed another Webbie as they descended at an angle toward the Web-Mind's armored chamber. They were supposed to intercept invaders. They were supposed to *kill, kill, kill.*

Octagon now possessed cunning thoughts. His hatred of Marten Kluge had damaged his Web-conditioning. It had left him with some of his former personality. That personality wanted Marten Kluge to suffer. Now that he—Octagon— suffered miserably, an old emotion surfaced. It was self-preservation, which allowed him to practice the cunning.

That crafty self-preservation had caused Octagon to drag his feet. He had pretended to be weaker than he was. He'd pretended almost without being aware he did so. It meant that he was the last Webbie to enter the slanting tunnel. It also meant that the distance between him and the next Webbie grew with each passing second. Certainly, Octagon still yearned for Marten Kluge to suffer a thousand agonies, but first he'd have to stay alive. He could not rush this.

As Octagon debated plans, the screams began over his headphones. The screams were filled with mortal pain and they caused Octagon to freeze. The killing impulse tried to make him run toward the firefight. He resisted such madness, although he wasn't completely able to overcome it. Therefore, Webbie Octagon took one slow step at a time toward the fighting.

* * *

Marten's heart raced as he leaned against a tunnel wall. The Praetor and his Highborn had taken point. They pushed deeper and farther into the long tunnel, moving fast. According to

333

Osadar's data, there were several entrances to the armored chamber.

The Praetor had made a loud sound when Osadar had brought that to his attention. He'd ordered his small force to advance faster.

Marten and Omi were the rearguard now. It was pitch-black down here. Marten could only see a green and red world using his infrared HUD.

Tiny droplets oozed onto his face. No amount of cool air could stop the sweating. It was being underground that made his pores ooze. He knew it shouldn't matter. He'd fought in worse places. But the fear of being buried alive had begun to claw at him. Maybe it was an atavistic dread, something he couldn't help. Maybe the Japan Campaign had affected him more than he'd realized.

"I hear more Webbies coming," Omi said.

The Korean's voice was clearer than before because the static had almost vanished. It must have been because of the shielding rock.

Marten shifted his grip as he scanned the dead. The HUD read them as humans, which meant half-converted Jovians, Webbies. They wore simple vacc-suits but lugged cyborg laser-packs and carbines. They had been slow, unarmored and suicidal.

"They remind me of the Kamikaze squads in Japan," Omi said.

"Yeah," Marten whispered, licking salt off his lips.

Then more Webbies advanced around the corner. The HUD showed them as red, vaguely humanoid objects. Some sprayed laser-fire like a hose, beaming into the ceiling and high on the walls.

With careful, deliberate fire, Marten cut down one Webbie after another. After each shot, he changed positions. The igniting Gyroc shells were like flares, giving him away. Then something clattered in front of him. It showed up hot on his HUD. It must be tunnel-rock, burned off by a laser.

Then, as suddenly as the firefight had stared, it ended.

Marten squeezed his eyes shut. Would the tunnel collapse if enough laser beams hit? *No, no*, he told himself. That was irrational. *Think about the Praetor cutting off your balls. Stay angry.*

"Do you think that's it?" Omi asked.

"I'm turning up gain," Marten said. He chinned a control and he listened for tunnel sounds. Somewhere far away… there was something slight. Maybe he imagined it. After twenty seconds of listening, he said, "I think we got them all. We'll head back to the surface, covering each other along the way."

"You don't want to run after the Praetor?"

Marten was sick of these tunnels. "No. We'll stay near the surface, making sure no one comes down after the Praetor." Marten picked up his IML with its Cognitive missile. There were likely more cyborgs on the way. He wanted to shoot them on the surface, not face the impossible creatures down here in the tunnels.

Omi studied him, shrugged after a moment, and said, "Sure."

## 24

Like Marten, the Praetor hated the tunnel, but for different reasons. This was too direct, letting the enemy know his exact route of attack. Therefore, he believed speed was critical. Thus, four battleoids and a deprogrammed cyborg charged deeper, covering several kilometers in a matter of minutes.

They blew open huge hatches with their plasma rifles and jumped through red-glowing holes. Finally, they reached what had to be the main chamber, a great oval area sheathed with masses of processing units.

"Lamps," the Praetor said.

Powerful headlamps snapped on. It showed a parked stealth-capsule. The vessel was over one hundred meters long. It sat on a huge tripod, with a hundred lines attached to it like some vast, mechanical spider.

At its sight, the Praetor knew a moment of supreme exaltation. What other Highborn could have achieved such a spectacular feat and with such paltry numbers? Surely, he was the greatest fighting Highborn alive. He was also proving the combat superiority of living flesh versus the melded horrors. Nothing compared to the ultimate super-soldier.

"A hatch opens!" Canus shouted.

Cyborgs leaped out, firing lasers with uncanny accuracy. They centered on the first battleoid, the beams cutting through reinforced titanium with brutal speed.

Four plasma rifles lifted, together with Osadar's laser. Orange globules roiled through the underground chamber. The hot plasma struck cyborgs and the capsule's hatch. Two cyborgs went down in a shower of sparks. Three survived after a fashion as they continued to beam, killing one battleoid and then a second. Another plasma volley hit the crippled cyborgs and the one bounding at them. It clattered to the floor, a heap of smoldering flesh and fused machine parts.

"They're down!" roared the Praetor, as he kicked a smoking cyborg head, watching it bounce across the floor. His entire being was filled with the unique, Highborn battle-madness. It was like a human going berserk, but with a critical difference. There was a cold, soldierly mind in charge of the seething passions. It made the Highborn berserker a frightening killer, wanting to taste blood and pulp flesh, but guided with cunning ruthlessness.

At that moment, the capsule's exhausts began to flicker.

"No!" shouted the Praetor. He mustn't let the prize escape. "Follow me!" He marched for the hatch. Canus and the others hesitated. The Praetor whirled around. "Come! We must enter and destroy the Web-Mind."

Canus lifted his plasma rifle. "Let us destroy the vessel."

"Cowards!" shouted the Praetor. He faced the vessel, and with practiced precision, he used exoskeleton power. In three terrific bounds, he reached the glowing hatch. "Let the greatest among us achieve the ultimate victory." Then the Praetor grabbed the frame and hauled himself into the huge stealth-capsule.

Osadar hung back from the others. Perhaps her innate pessimism suspected a fatal trick, some last-minute screw-job. Her helmeted head twitched toward the capsule's exhaust as more propellant exited. As Canus and the others aimed their plasma rifles, cables began to pop off the capsule's outer-skin. With extreme haste, Osadar retreated into the tunnel.

***

Canus raised his heavy plasma rifle. At that moment, the vessel's glowing hatch clanged onto the floor. What must have been an emergency seal slammed down in its place.

"The Praetor is trapped," a Highborn snarled.

"Aim there!" shouted Canus, pointing with his plasma rifle. Before he could pull the trigger, an EMP blast blew outward from the giant stealth-capsule. It washed over the battleoid-suits and the heavy rifles. Each of the battleoids froze, the circuits destroyed and the Highborn in them trapped.

If he could have moved his armored finger and pulled the trigger, Canus would have found his plasma rifle useless. He roared curses inside his suit, struggling.

As he did, the huge stealth-vessel swiveled on its tripod base. Then hot propellant gushed from the exhaust-port. The vessel lifted and began to move. It was the last sight Canus had. The hot propellant cooked him in his frozen armor-suit, killing him and the other helpless Highborn.

# -25-

The over-watch technique was a laborious way to retreat or advance. At its most basic, one soldier watched, with a ready weapon aimed at the most dangerous area. The other soldier moved into a new position. Then he stopped and watched while his partner now moved. They leapfrogged back or leapfrogged forward. It could be done by man, by squad and sometimes even by platoon.

Marten and Omi used the over-watch maneuver heading up the tunnel and back toward the surface. They halted and waited as the tunnel shook and as hot gasses rushed past like a hurricane.

When it stopped, Omi asked, "What was that?"

Marten shrugged.

"What should we do now?" Omi asked.

"Keep moving," Marten said.

They did, covering one another as they advanced. Then Marten saw a Webbie with a heavy laser-pack stagger around a tunnel corner.

"Wait," Marten whispered.

Omi froze.

Through infrared, Marten watched the suited Webbie stagger and shuffle. By his actions, the Webbie seemed delirious. The HUD's specs showed that the Webbie was like the others they had slaughtered earlier.

"Kill him," Omi said.

"He's no cyborg," Marten said.

"He's a Webbie, and they're almost as bad."

"Has anyone ever captured one of those?"

"Who cares?" asked Omi. "Kill him."

"Maybe we should—"

Omi's Gyroc kicked. The rocket-packet ignited. The APEX shell moved fast.

\*\*\*

Webbie Octagon was exhausted. He'd shuffled under the heavy load for a long time. His shoulders ached and a point in his back knifed him every time his right leg moved. He yearned to throw off the laser-pack, but the kill-order prevented him from doing so.

He longed to glimpse Marten Kluge again. He would burn off a leg first, then an arm and then maybe a foot. He would enjoy the spectacle. Yes, it would be glorious to hurt and maim Marten Kluge. It was his greatest wish to see that barbarian—

It might have been a premonition, but Octagon looked up then. He saw a spark in the darkness. It rushed toward him. He switched on the vacc-suit's helmet lamp. The beam washed over a kneeling, armored figure. The soldier's helmet was aimed at him. The visor was clear. In it, he spied Marten Kluge.

Octagon hissed as he raised the laser carbine. Finally, his greatest life's joy was about to be—

Omi's APEX shell struck Octagon in the chest. The round pierced his body. Then the shell exploded, raining bits of rib-bone, heart-muscle, fat and brown vacc-suit. With its gaping, smoking hole, the corpse thudded onto the floor.

\*\*\*

"You're getting slow," Omi told Marten.

"Did he look familiar to you?" Marten asked.

"Don't be crazy. Who do we know that could have become a Webbie?"

It was then Osadar reached them via radio and told them what had happened in the armored chamber.

"The Web-Mind trapped the Praetor," Omi said. "It escaped."

Marten scowled. Then he picked up his IML. "If it's over, we have to get out of here."

"And do what?" Omi asked.

"Find a patrol boat and escape," Marten said.

Omi shook his head. "It's probably already too late for that."

"When we're on the cyborg converter, then it's too late. Until then, we keep trying." Marten shouldered his IML and started back for the dome.

## -26-

Inside the large stealth-capsule, the Praetor struggled mightily. Because of the EMP blast, his battleoid-armor had frozen. With continuing grueling effort, he unlatched his suit's seals. Sweat poured from his flesh and his muscles quivered at the effort. Rage gave him the power as his indomitable will drove him.

The Web-Mind had tricked him. It had trapped him.

*Never!*

With a roar, the Praetor tore off the last seal and heaved the battleoid open. Slippery with sweat, he slithered free of the encasing armor. He thus became the first enemy to see a Web-Mind.

It was a living nightmare. There were rows of clear bio-tanks. In them, were sheets of brain mass, many hundreds of kilos of brain cells from as many unwilling donors in the Neptune System. Green computing gel surrounded the pink-white mass. Cables, bio-tubes and tight-beam links connected the tanks to backup computers and life-support systems. The combination made a seething, pulsating whole, with the brain-mass sheets squirming slightly. The bio-tubes gurgled as warm liquids pulsed through them. Backup computers made whirring sounds as lights indicated a thousand things.

As the Praetor glared, a panel opened. Out of it rolled a robotic device with multi-jointed arms. At the ends were laser welders, melders and calibrating clippers. The various arms moved as the robotic device charged across the floor at him.

***

The Web-Mind's gloating at capturing a Highborn and burning the others changed to panic. Against all probability, the Highborn had struggled free of his frozen armor-suit. Now the giant humanoid was inside the chamber.

That meant the Highborn must die. It would have been enjoyable to test the Highborn's psychology during the long trip to Earth. Instead, it ordered repair units to dismember the shouting creature.

At the same time, the Web-Mind piloted its stealth-capsule through the tunnels. It headed for the surface and safety. The attacking vessels and missiles were gone. It was time to re-link with Gharlane and it was time to relay information through the laser lightguide with the Prime Web-Mind in the Neptune System.

***

The fight was short and vicious against the two repair units. It left the Praetor bleeding from six deep wounds as his right arm dangled uselessly. Gore oozed from the hole where his left eye used to be.

"You freakish bastard," he mumbled. Then he stumbled at the bio-tanks. With a metal strut broken off a repair unit, the Praetor shattered ballistic glass. He thrust the metal strut through his belt, and with his hand, he began to tear out clots of pink-white brain mass. Gel spilled onto the floor as a klaxon began to wail.

"That's right!" the Praetor snarled. "Scream while I kill you. Scream for me, my pretty. Scream."

***

The Web-Mind sent out a distress call to the remaining cyborgs on Carme. Even as the Highborn destroyed computing power, it maneuvered the stealth-capsule.

The black vessel exited a tunnel and flew to an approaching party of cyborgs.

Then something akin to horrified panic erupted. The bleeding, dying humanoid smashed another globule of brain-mass. The destruction initiated a deep and hidden program.

343

Web-Minds were the ultimate creation, sublime beings beyond the capacities of inferior creatures to understand. Each Web-Mind was akin to what lesser creatures conceived of as gods. It was unthinkable that lower order creatures capture gods. It was vile to consider creatures tearing down a god or rendering them half-operable and imprisoning them. Destruction was preferable to creature-slavery.

As the harsh and unyielding program ran through its logic parameters, the shouting Highborn dug his large fingers into brain-mass. He yanked out the section that held the primary deletion program, meaning that sub-systems took over, trying to reconfigure the exact sequencing.

In its growing terror, the Web-Mind opened all channels, calling for all cyborgs to converge immediately on its coordinates. Then it began to search for a place to land.

\*\*\*

The Praetor coughed up blood. Pain racked him. He hurt everywhere. It stank horribly in this awful place. Despite that, he forced his legs to move, and he hammered more ballistic glass. Then he continued to pluck out fistfuls of pink-white mass. It was brain tissue. He knew that much. He was killing his hated enemy.

Then he heard binary chatter. It came from speakers all around him. Was the Web-Mind trying to speak with him? Was it asking for mercy?

"Never!" he hissed. He squeezed his hand as mass squished between his fingers. Then he began to rip out more.

\*\*\*

Marten and Omi exited the dome as binary chatter came over their headphones.

"What is that?" Omi asked.

"Cyborg speech," Marten said.

"Who is that?" asked a harsh voice.

"What did you say?" Marten asked.

"I didn't say anything," Omi said.

"This is the Praetor speaking. I am in the Web-Mind."

Marten and Omi glanced at each other.

"Where are you?" Marten asked.

"In the Web-Mind's ship," the Praetor said with a wheeze. "I'm dying, yet I am killing it."

"Osadar said—"

"Never mind about your tame cyborg," the Praetor snarled. "If you see a ship, shoot at it. Destroy the Web-Mind and we might still achieve victory."

"Look!" Omi shouted. "There! I see a ship."

Marten looked where Omi pointed. A dark blot of a vessel slid overhead. Marten lifted his IML, and he switched settings. He'd been saving this for the Praetor. Now the arrogant bastard—Marten pulled the trigger before he could finish the thought.

The Cognitive missile exited the tube. Its fuel burned and it shot up at the giant stealth-capsule, heading straight for it.

\*\*\*

As the Web-Mind opened all channels and called for cyborg reinforcements, it heard the Highborn and the unmodified humans talk to each other over its communications system.

During that time, more of its brainpower vanished. The destruction was ongoing, and it confused the subsystem deletion program.

*Delete, delete, delete—*

The core of the Web-Mind sent delete pulses to the surface. It must delete. It must ensure that no creature capture valuable cyborg technology. Every unit must self-destruct and destroy-destroy-destroy.

The Highborn creature bashed at bio-tanks and life-support equipment.

*Delete—*

A missile struck and exploded, opening the stealth-vessel to the vacuum of space. As the Highborn swung his metal strut for the last time, the core of Web-Mind began to die from depressurization.

Then the vessel headed for the accelerating moon, soon smashing against it.

## 27

Carme continued to accelerate. The mighty fusion cores, eighty-seven percent of the coils, the generators and the gargantuan exhaust-ports were untouched by the battle.

Marten, Omi and Osadar reentered a dome. The EMP blasts, enemy ECM, explosive shells, zooming missiles, they had vanished with the Web-Mind's death. Marten radioed other space marine survivors, all seventeen of them. No Highborn remained, not even the wounded one at the shuttle's board.

The *Descartes* had vanished, while the second meteor-ship floated as wreckage many thousands of kilometers away.

A cautious several hours revealed the location of three working patrol boats, several control centers for various Carme-engines and two metal sheds full of unmodified Jovians.

"We should kill them," Osadar said.

Marten stood with her in the same dome and chamber where the Praetor had first interrogated them. The control unit worked, and Osadar had spent most of her time attempting to master it. Through it, she'd discovered the two sheds and the Jovians.

Marten scowled. "What possible reason could you have for such a barbaric action?"

"Our attack here succeeded," Osadar said. "Even more amazing, we are still alive and free agents. The universe cannot tolerate that, and therefore it will attempt to screw us. These so-called unmodified Jovians must have latent psychological commands. Given a chance, they will harm us or harm our mission."

"The screw job is that we're alive," Marten said.

Osadar turned around from where she worked on the control unit. She cocked her head.

Marten laughed grimly. "We stopped a planet-wrecker. But there's still a cyborg fleet in the system. Logically, there are still cyborgs in Neptune and probably more elsewhere. Social Unity remains. The Highborn still possess Doom Stars. Our continued existence means more endless conflict."

"That is the nature of life, as the universe despises happiness. As long as one breathes, one must fight. Do not expect joy from life, Marten Kluge, or you will be endlessly disappointed."

Despite the victory, Marten's chest felt heavy. Maybe Osadar had a point, at least about endless disappointment. Everywhere he went, people died, usually in great numbers. All the space marines he'd picked—all but seventeen of them were dead. Yakov was dead. Every person from the *Descartes* was dead, including Rhea. He should have gotten to know her.

He knew he should rejoice at their marvelous victory. Instead, he felt soiled, a killer who brought death and destruction wherever he went.

The large airlock hissed and rotated open. Omi stepped through, together with a person in a brown vacc-suit. Maybe it was one of the unmodified Jovians. Omi helped the Jovian, keeping a hand on his or her elbow.

Marten lifted a com-unit. "Is there trouble?"

Omi shook his helmeted head as he brought the Jovian closer.

The Jovian froze then. Omi released the elbow.

"Here is the screw-job," Osadar said. "I can feel it."

For some reason, that troubled Marten. He blinked, wondering what this feeling meant, if anything.

The brown-suited person unsealed the locks and then threw off the helmet. It banged on the floor and rolled. She had brown hair and pretty, familiar features. The brown-suited person staggered toward him.

"Marten," she whispered.

Marten blinked again, and the terrible weight in his chest vanished as he recognized Nadia Pravda. Marten groaned as moisture welled in his eyes. This couldn't be real.

"Nadia?" he whispered.

She reached him, staggering into his arms, bumping him so he took two steps back. They clutched each other. They hugged fiercely.

"Marten Kluge," she said, as tears flowed from her eyes.

Marten held her face, and he stared into her eyes. "Is it really you?"

She nodded, and she was laughing and crying all at once.

Marten hugged her again, and then, as gently as he could, he pressed his lips against hers. Nadia Pravda was in his arms. She was his Nadia, and she tasted sweet.

She responded, and together, they kissed in the cyborg-built dome on Carme, the rogue moon, the ex-planet-wrecker.

Marten whispered, "You'll never leave me again."

She tightened her grip, nodding.

"Nadia," he said, and there was joy in his heart that was impossible to describe. He had found his Nadia. In an evil and harsh universe, he'd finally found an oasis of bliss.

## 28

Like a wave in a pond created by a dropped pebble, the Web-Mind's radioed deletion-codes trickled outward from its last position. Many millions of kilometers away on Athena Station, a special receiving unit from Neptune intercepted the faint radio signal.

An emergency computer there ran probability scenarios, trying to decipher the need for the deletion codes. After three minutes, it sent a questing radio call for the Web-Mind. It continued to do this for seventy-one hours.

Seventy-one hours of silence indicated the Web-Mind's deletion. The odds of this were beyond the ninety-ninth percentile. Another special program activated in response to the Web-Mind's deletion, seeking out the chief cyborg unit in the Jovian System. Shortly, the emergency program caused a short-burst information packet to speed to Gharlane. It sent him the lightguide laser code to Neptune. It also activated an accounting program in him.

Thus, Gharlane soon found himself hooked to his warship's primary com-station, sending pulse-packets to the lightguide laser. That tight-beam laser in turn sent a grim accounting to the Prime Web-Mind in the Neptune System.

\*\*\*

*CHIEF CYBORG UNIT: JUPITER ASSAULT*
*GHARLANE PRIME, BATTLE COMMANDER*
*LIGHTGUIDE LINK: JUPITER-NEPTUNE*
*STEALTH CAMPAIGN SUMMARY*

*Tenth Cycle, Rotation 24*

*Concluding battle report No. 7*
*The Ganymede-Europa Lunge*

The clever enemy meteor-tactic absorbed approximately thirty-one percent of our laser strikes and twenty-seven percent of our missile launches. Given their local warship-tonnage superiority, I broke off the penetration raid on Ganymede, leaving a screen of damaged patrol boats. They had been preloaded with Onoshi decoy equipment and they drew fifty-eight percent of enemy fire before their destruction.

The meteor-tactic proved decisive and indicated a primary enemy commander of level two or three ability. The analyzers confirm the reunification of Jovian political and military authorities.

The Ganymede-Europa Lunge caused a sixty-seven percent loss of warship-tonnage that originated from the Athena Station start-point. Enemy losses were computed at thirty-one percent.

The battle maneuver and combat resulted in the destruction of Io, eighty percent of the processing stations on the inner moons and critical Jovian loss on Europa. Monitoring the enemy news sites has revealed five critical hits on the water moon and a seventeen percent surface covering of Io-spawned radioactives.

Current warship ratios mandate a defensive cyborg strategy based on Athena Station. Enemy manufacturing presently runs at twenty-two percent of pre-stealth campaign levels. The probability battle-computer estimates a two-year struggle before the Jovians can eradicate our presence here.

I await instructions and reinforcements, Gharlane Prime, reporting.

# The End

Made in the USA
Middletown, DE
05 December 2016